Praise for *The Burning Air*

'*The Burning Air* is a classic of the genre and puts Kelly firmly into the same league as Ruth Rendell writing under her Barbara Vine pseudonym; both women showing a great gift for characterisation and a mastery of understanding human nature's twisted desires . . . an involving read.'
Sunday Express

'An author in total command of the tensions within dysfunctional families . . . Gripping all the way.' *The Times*

'Creepy and claustrophobic.' *Sunday Mirror*

'A tense family drama that demands to be read in one sitting.'
Daily Record

'A masterfully plotted dark tale of how a small injustice can have devastating consequences. I devoured it in one sitting.' *Irish Independent*

'Written with empathy, psychological insight and a real feel for the menace and conflict at the heart of families, it's a superior example of its genre.' *Big Issue*

'Very cleverly written and full of unexpected twists as the tension keeps being ratcheted up another notch before the big reveal at the end . . . Deeply enjoyable but deeply unsettling: the perfect mixture for a psychological thriller!' *Fabulous*

'An absorbing thriller.' *Choice*

'Family politics mixed with revenge make for a super-spooky read.'
Look

'Erin Kelly is brilliant at showing the relentlessness of obsession and the evil that can be done in the name of love.'
Elizabeth Haynes, author of *Into The Darkest Corner*

'Kelly excels at thrillers set in middle-England idylls, that sidestep the clichéd and the cosy to go for the jugular. [*The Burning Air*] sees her reach another level.' *Independent on Sunday*

'It's not often I read a book where the twist is so surprising, I have to go back and work out how I missed it . . . Brilliant and heart-stopping.'
Woman

ERIN KELLY

The Burning Air

HODDER

First published in Great Britain in 2013 by Hodder & Stoughton
An Hachette UK company

7

This paperback edition first published in 2018

A CIP catalogue record for this title is available from the British Library

Paperback ISBN 978 1 444 72834 7
eBook ISBN 978 1 444 72833 0

Printed and bound by Clays Ltd, St Ives plc

Hodder & Stoughton policy is to use papers that are natural, renewable
and recyclable products and made from wood grown in sustainable
forests. The logging and manufacturing processes are expected to
conform to the environmental regulations of the country of origin.

Hodder & Stoughton Ltd
Carmelite House
50 Victoria Embankment
London EC4Y 0DZ

www.hodder.co.uk

For – but not about – my mother

Mrs Birling: But Inspector, he's just a boy!
Inspector Goole: We are *all* boys to our mothers.

J.B. Priestley, *An Inspector Calls*

LYDIA

I

I mean this to be my confession, and my apology. I write it in secret, when Rowan is at work. 'The last first day of a spring term,' he said at breakfast. 'I'm halfway through my year of lasts.' He's talking about the academic year, of course. For him, the year begins not when the calendar changes but in September, when the school fills again. He is proudly institutionalised after fifty years here. I won't be here to see him retire in July. These are days of lasts for me, too. I have eaten my last Christmas goose, sung my last Auld Lang Syne, and paid my last visit to Devon.

'Enjoy your day, darling,' he said as he shrugged on his gown and straightened the only tie he has ever owned.

I waited until the door of our apartment had closed behind him and I heard his footsteps across the quad. Then I dragged myself to bed where I dozed for three hours, dreaming about my single remaining first, my unborn granddaughter. I woke up invigorated by the promise of her. I <u>will</u> see her. I will <u>hold</u> her.

At noon I rose to force down some soup and return to my writing. I struggle to grip the pen these days. My script has become that shaky old-lady writing, rickety letters that suggest an age their author will never attain.

This diary is identical to the dozens of volumes that preceded it, in which I have recorded everything from my marriage to my magistracy. I have written about everything that ever mattered to me. Everything but <u>the</u> thing. It is such a beautiful book, and such a pity that I will have to destroy it after writing.

I am compelled to write, despite the risk of discovery. I can't say why, only that the compulsion has been with me since my diagnosis, and gathers strength daily (comparisons with the tumour are grimly inevitable). Until I have written, I can't know whether I will give the words time to breathe on the page or tear the paper from its binding before the ink has dried. What I do know is that it can never be read by eyes other than mine. This I will make sure of.

It's strange, but in a way I would rather the confession were made public than read by my family. Our reputations would suffer: my career on the bench would be retrospectively undermined, as would Rowan's relationship with the school. But beyond that, nothing; what I mean is, no conviction. The law I broke was relatively minor and in any case it comes down to that slippery fish, intent. Until officers of the law learn to read minds, I will remain unpunished.

Public judgement is as nothing compared to what Rowan and the children would think of me if they read my account. Reputation is one thing; family is quite another. Family <u>matters</u>. It would destroy each of them for different reasons. It is not vanity but love for them that calls me to preserve their image of me as decent and truthful.

Of course it was love for my children, love for my son, that caused me to act as I did. It was a lapse of judgement. If I could have foreseen the rippling aftershocks that followed I would have acted differently, but by the time I realised the extent of the consequences, it was too late.

In my years on the bench, I heard all the excuses. None of them applied to me. I wasn't young, I wasn't impoverished, I wasn't uneducated. Motherhood was my only excuse. I was trying to do right by my son and it made me momentarily blind to the interior laws I have always tried to live by. We all want the best for our children, but I crossed the line between protection and offence.

The Cathedral clock has just chimed twice. I have no more time to write today if I am to keep my appointment. I am ashamed of *the relief I feel. My confession will have to wait for another of my borrowed tomorrows. For now, I will lock my diary and call a taxi to take me to the hospital. I should be back before Rowan knows I was ever gone.*

My doctor disapproves of my decision to keep my illness from my family. But why put them through months of pre-emptive grief? I don't believe that sharing my diagnosis would prepare them for life without me, and in a sense I have been doing that, for my children at least, every day of their lives. A good mother loves fiercely but ultimately brings up her children to thrive without her. They must be the most important thing in her life, but if she is the most important thing in theirs, she has failed.

SOPHIE

SOPHIE

2

They say that you forget the pain, that the survival of the species depends on it.

In the morning, Sophie was still telling herself that it was not a pain but a *sensation*. Perception was all. Reframe it as an intense sensation, a necessary part of the process, and it wouldn't hurt. She paused on the threshold of the hospital, inhaled, exhaled and allowed herself to experience the *sensation*, which was in any case only a false alarm, practice contractions until the real thing started, and completely normal. Inhale, exhale, straighten up, keep going.

Saxby Wellhouse hospital was built in the Victorian high gothic style: little natural light made it through the pointed-arch windows into the atrium, which was as vast as a cathedral, its tiled floor scuffed by shuffling feet whose owners, both patients and their relatives, moved their lips as if in silent prayer. A young nurse in scrubs laid a hand on her forearm and said, 'Are you all right, love? Do you want the maternity ward?'

Sophie looked towards the gleaming white corridor that led to the modern extension of the birthing unit.

'No, thank you.'

With a leaden heart she persevered into the dark architecture that housed birth's opposite. There was a queue for the lift, and anyway she did not think she could bear to be still and enclosed, even for the short journey to the second floor. The stairs were shallow, and her midwife had encouraged her to keep active. She was glad of the excuse to pace, to fidget, to maintain the perpetual kinesis that she sometimes felt was the only thing stopping her from screaming. Sophie used her left hand to pull herself up, her right hand on her belly. The banister was old, worn smooth, although every now and then her fingers would jolt against a brass stud that some nineteenth-century killjoy had put into the wood to stop people sliding down. She paused halfway up to catch her breath, reassured to feel the baby kick sharply in protest. When you were in real labour they slowed down. In the blink between her collapse and her slide into this living death, Lydia had vowed that she would live to see the baby born, which Sophie had taken to mean that the child's arrival would give her permission to die. She would happily stay nine months pregnant forever if that was what it took to keep her mother alive.

She bypassed the polished terracotta length of the public oncology ward, heading straight for the little private room at the end of the corridor. Rowan and the others were already there. The dimensions of the family were all wrong, grotesque. Lydia had shrunk further in the night, her body a bony Z under the kind of cellular blanket you'd use to cover a baby in a cot. There was something diminished too about Rowan, his head too big for the body that was folded into an armchair. Tara seemed even more substantial than usual and looked like Felix's mother rather than his elder by one year. The prospect of motherlessness had affected them conversely. It had aged her by a decade, drawing the fault lines of middle age around her eyes and mouth, while Felix had regressed to the wide-eyed nailbiting of his teens. Sophie, round as an egg, fit to burst with life, eased herself onto the hard empty chair at her mother's side. She strained to brush her lips against Lydia's cheek. The violet splash of bruise where the drip entered Lydia's hand seemed to have spread since yesterday.

'How is she, Dad?' asked Sophie. 'Have you been here all night?'

Rowan nodded.

'Does she know we're here?' said Sophie, panic like heartburn in her chest. What if Lydia was no longer able to communicate properly? Did that mean they had already said goodbye?

'We don't know,' said Tara. 'She's only staying awake for five minutes at a time and when she does she's not coherent. Some of the things she's come out with are hilarious.'

'It's not funny,' snapped Felix. 'She was really distressed. And she's in so much pain. I almost wish—'

'Don't say it, Fee,' said Sophie. She held her mother's hand as she had done as a child, on her wedding day, at the births of her sons, and squeezed gently, not expecting an answering grip yet disappointed when none came.

The four of them stayed there all day, taking it in turns to sprint to the cafe on the other side of the building for coffee and sandwiches that Rowan ignored, Felix picked apart, Sophie forced down and Tara finished off. The others would not allow Sophie to go, insisting that she conserve her energy, not listening when she tried to tell them that she had *excess* energy, that she couldn't seem to use it up. On her frequent toilet breaks she made forbidden calls to Will, the sound of his voice a balm. He too was poised for devastation but his connection with Lydia was not a blood one, and, unlike the rest of Sophie's immediate family, he had room in his breaking heart to support her. After ringing off she vented her grief in concise, measured sobs, each unit of anguish just enough to last her until the next.

Back at the bedside, Sophie rearranged the sunset-coloured tulips on the bedside table, hoping that the bright blobs of colour would pull her mother's eyes into focus next time she stirred. When it was time to fetch the boys, Lydia still hadn't woken up properly, but her breathing had changed, growing faster and shallower. Sophie longed to lie on the pitifully roomy bed, to press her belly into Lydia's back, but was terrified that she would dislodge some vital tube or shunt. She settled instead for her head on the pillow and a whispered 'I love you'. There was the strength of a lifetime's feeling behind the words but still they seemed impotent.

In the corridor, she passed a nurse.

'Will it be today, do you think?' Sophie asked her. 'She's panting, like she's climbing a hill. Is that a sign?'

'You know I can't say,' said the nurse, kindly. 'It can seem touch and go and then they pull through. But something seems to have upset her today, and they often get like that just before they pass away. It's as though they know. And then, in the last hours, a kind of peace often comes. It sounds strange, but it can be very beautiful in its own way.' She tilted her head to one side. 'But how are *you*?'

'Are you talking to me or the baby?'

'Both,' she smiled. 'Do you know what you're having?'

'A little girl,' said Sophie.

'Oh, how lovely, a daughter,' said the nurse. Daughter. The word sounded like something she was, not something she had. 'Seriously, are you looking after yourself?'

'Oh, don't worry about me,' said Sophie. 'I can cope.' She was glad that none of her family was around to correct her.

In the car, another cramp fanned across her lower back and belly. Ten minutes later, an echo of the same stole her breath, but she fetched Toby and Leo from the prep school and then Charlie from the adjacent nursery as though nothing was happening. At home, the post was scattered across the hallway. With an unsteady plié she bent to pick it up. She put the bills and bank statements on the sideboard and paused to consider the final letter. It had the thick envelope and stiffness of a greetings card. Who would have sent that? It was too early for either congratulations or condolences. The sound of three little boys hitting each other drowned out the television and her thoughts. She put the envelope to one side and rolled up her sleeves, ready to referee.

Boys, tea, bed. Husband, supper, sofa. After ten o'clock, Sophie could no longer pretend that this was a dummy run. She was in labour, and a labour that seemed to be progressing much faster than the others had. She said nothing to Will, who was slumped in front of *Newsnight*, brandy in his hand and long legs, still in pinstripes, outstretched before him. He looked tired; he had shaved that morning but a blue-black shadow already dusted his jaw. He was in for a long night, too, and she knew that he was easier to manage when the prospect of imminent fatherhood had not yet adrenalised him. While he watched television, she pottered about the house, turning off all but the smallest, softest lights, feeling protected by the half-dark. Inhale, exhale. Not a pain but a *sensation*.

Sophie tidied the already orderly desk that had been hers as a teenager and now served as a telephone table, sifting through letters about sports days, parents' evenings, school hats, crumpling those that were out of date and smoothing those that were still relevant. She ran her fingers over the letter D, a recent graffito, engraver unknown, and straightened the line of books that hemmed one edge of the desk, books she had worked on in the short life between leaving one family and creating another. For a second she wished herself back in London, childless, successful, parents immortal.

The shrill of the telephone jerked her back into the present.

'She's still the same,' Tara said. 'Still talking nonsense . . . OK. I'm going home to get a couple of hours' sleep, check on Jake and then go back in the morning. Dad's sleeping there tonight so she won't be on her own.'

'Any news?' Will called, using the established euphemism for 'Is she dead yet?'

'No change.' He held out his arms to her and patted the space beside him on the sofa. She craved his embrace but was reluctant to join him: up close, he would know the baby was coming and the door would close on denial.

Her attention returned to the unopened envelope. She fumbled in the desk drawer for her letter opener, a little dagger that had once belonged to her grandmother. The vellum was sliced to reveal not a greetings card but a few glossy black-and-white photographs. The first couple of images were fuzzy; she could make out human figures framed by a window, but not much more. She flicked the overhead light on. Each image in the series was clearer than the last, as though the photographer had taken a step towards his subject with each shot, or pulled a long lens a little closer each time. By the time Sophie got to the fifth and final image one of the figures at least was no longer blurry but in sharp, incriminating focus, his features as clear as they were familiar. No. No. No, no, *no*. She stared, hoping that the photograph would somehow transform itself into something beautiful, a seascape, a family snapshot, a blossoming tree, and only then did she take in the date, digitised figures at the bottom right-hand corner of the print. A twinge that might or might not have been another contraction made her drop to her knees, the photographs falling from her hand, dull grey slates against the blues and rusts of the Persian rug.

Will was on his feet, then kneeling beside her, his face blank with alarm.

'Soph? Has it started?' He reached for the car keys, picked up the hospital bag, put it down again, picked up his phone. 'Shall I call Ruth?'

He did not know that he had been found out and ironically this lent him a kind of innocence. This strange thought rode the crest of a wave of the strongest *sensation* yet. With a clawed hand she reached for the worst of the pictures.

'What's . . . what *is* this?'

Will took it between thumb and forefinger. Sophie saw horror, incomprehension, horror again. He actually staggered back, until he was almost in the sitting room.

'Oh, Jesus hell,' he said. 'I can explain . . .'

Sophie eased herself onto her hands and knees. Will stepped towards her, arms outstretched. She waved him away.

'Look, we can talk about this later, but I'm taking you to the hospital,' he said.

'No!' said Sophie with a force that juddered her whole body. 'No! I don't want . . . I'm going to get Ruth to drive me. If you come, I'll say you're violent, I'll say you're drunk, I won't let them let you in. I'll get them to call the police if I have to, I mean it, Will.'

He went quiet. She could tell that had wounded him. Good. She could see too that he was deciding whether to use her past against her. Bad. He opened his mouth and in the second's hesitation before he spoke she snarled, 'Don't you *dare*.'

From his expression she knew that he would not challenge her. Ignorant she might be of his past actions, but she could still predict his responses. Kneeling, she gathered the photographs together and put them in the side pocket of her bag.

There was another wave of pain. Not sensation but *pain*, pure, insuperable pain, shaking her limbs and blurring her vision. The world was reduced to pain, attacking her from all directions. She surrendered to it. She could no more control this than she could anything else.

3

They had reached the point in the journey to Devon where the battle to make the children go to sleep was replaced by the game of trying to keep them awake until they reached their destination. It was half-term and their excitement had peaked too soon. Will opened all the windows. Here and there, the scent of bonfires was borne on the cold evening air. After gentle coaxing of the radio, Sophie managed to find a station that played dance music and turned it up loud to drown out the insistent minor key of Charlie's whingeing.

The familiar road to Far Barn was this time paved with doubt and fear. Coming together this weekend to scatter Lydia's ashes had seemed like a good idea at the time of arrangement. The nearer it drew, the clearer it was that time and history, place and purpose were individually weighted with their own significances, the sum of which would likely be intolerable. The family had always observed Bonfire Night as seriously as Christmas, visiting the Ottery St Mary Carnival which was held on the first Sunday of November every year. As well as a huge bonfire and a funfair there would be the rolling of the tar barrels: a health-and-safety-defying custom, its origins obscured by the smoke of centuries, where locals careered through the narrow Georgian streets carrying blazing barrels on their shoulders. Sophie closed her eyes and envisaged the town, the shop fronts that had barely changed since her own childhood, the same old friendly faces, the pubs. She could almost smell the woody scent of the fire and the gunpowder trace of the fireworks. The tradition had seemed comforting when she had arranged this long weekend but now she wished she had chosen a villa somewhere abroad, somewhere light and neutral. Far Barn had of course the advantage of familiarity. It also had the disadvantage of familiarity. There would be plenty of shadows but nowhere to hide.

'You OK?' asked Will. In the passenger mirror, she checked the back seat. Toby was listening.

'I'm fine!'

Will's hand brushed against hers as he changed gear. Instinctively she flinched, giving lie to her words. This weekend was to be the first real test of the fragile truce that existed in their marriage. Tonight and for the rest of the break she would have to sleep in the same bed as him. This made her edgy around him, in a grotesque parody of first-date nerves. Wrapping her arms around herself, she toyed with the idea of asking Felix, who was always the last up to bed, to give up his room and crash on the sofa, but that would mean explaining.

The road thinned to a one-track lane as they began the descent into the valley and dipped so steeply the children's ears popped. As they came within a mile of the barn, the hedgerows themselves seemed to squeeze their oversized car along the road like a clot through a vein. Branches jabbed witchy fingers through the windows, making the boys scream with something between terror and laughter, and Edie echoed their sounds. The signpost for Far Barn, white paint on a black wooden plaque, had faded into illegibility but new visitors were rare. Will made the right turn into the rutted track that connected their land to the rest of the world.

The barn was a black mass on a cloud-blind night, the only sign of light or life the reflection of their own headlights in the blank windows and against the gloss of the ebony slats. There was no sign of another car. It was normal for them all to make their journeys from Saxby to Devon separately, but unusual for the Woodfords to be the first to arrive. Sophie mouthed to Will, 'He's supposed to be here. He should've got here this morning.'

'Maybe he got held up by something,' suggested Will.

By what? Since Rowan's retirement in July from the school he had attended as a boy then taught at as a man, his life had revolved entirely around his remaining family. The dutiful devotion he had shown to hundreds of pupils was now distilled, concentrated on his four grandsons – all of whom were pupils at the Cath, so the severance with the school had not been total – and Edie, whose birth often felt like the only reason they were all still standing. It was not an exaggeration to say that he lived for them, that their needs and routines shaped his own. It was unsettling for him not to be at the door, arms open, smile wide.

Toby and Leo undid their seatbelts as Will slowed to a halt, and were out of the car and swinging on the handle of the huge front door.

'Don't, it's locked,' called Sophie, but Toby had opened it and was swallowed by the dark, Leo hot on his heels. Sophie extricated a dozing Edie from her seat, held her close, leaving Will to deal with Charlie, and followed the boys into the barn. Despite the darkness, it was warm inside, stifling even. The radiators threw out the burning dust smell they always did when switched on for the first time in a season. One of the boys let out a ghost-train howl.

Sophie took three small steps, stroking the bare walls until her fingertips located the light switch. She blinked as her eyes accustomed not only to the light but to the proportions of the place, relishing as she always had the short minutes after arrival in which it still assumed a degree of novelty. The interior, from floor to high ceiling, was ribbed with beams and rafters and the rich reds of the sofas, rugs and tapestries gave one the impression of standing in the belly of a great beast. Sophie's eye was drawn to a framed family snapshot, taken one summer when she was around seven and the others were babies: it was a thrown stone in the still pond of her grief, and she forced her gaze elsewhere.

She scanned the sitting room again, this time looking for shoes, coats, books or mugs, anything to signal recent occupation.

Another stable door to the back of the sitting room gave onto the extension that housed the kitchen. It too was in darkness. At the right-hand side of the room was a steep staircase which led to the old hayloft, now subdivided into bed and bathrooms. The sleeping quarters were as cramped as the living space was cavernous, the exposed struts and joists and high ceiling of the main interior preserved at the bedrooms' expense. A corridor linked a series of interconnected bedrooms and bathrooms tucked awkwardly into eaves and booby-trapped with uneven floors, low ceilings and tiny doorways. Sophie switched on the landing light: nothing. Where *was* he?

With great solemnity, Toby began to wind up the ancient grandfather clock that stood against the wall facing the fire, a ritual of arrival that he had made his own. Job done, Toby became a child again, joining his brothers as they vaulted sofas and slalomed around teetering standard lamps.

The barn, Sophie now remembered, was a new parent's nightmare. They had been so sure that Charlie was their last, but now they would have to baby-proof the place all over again, probably before going to bed that night. Where did they keep all the socket covers and fire guards? I'll ask Mum, she thought reflexively. A single acid tear stung the corner of her eye. Edie sighed and gently Sophie placed her on the seat of the big easy chair, grateful for her daughter's ability to remain asleep through multiple transitions from cot to bed to car seat to embrace.

A thud from above told her that Leo and Charlie had found their way upstairs. The sound had seemed to come from directly overhead, suggesting that they were in Rowan's room, but this didn't necessarily mean that was where they were. The barn had a way of throwing its voice, some rooms entirely soundproofed yet other spaces virtual whispering galleries where hushed conversations elsewhere were perfectly audible. This ventriloquy had once been part of its charm, but these days Sophie liked to know exactly where all of her children were, and – almost more importantly – liked everyone else to know that she knew.

The door to the mudroom was ajar but it was impossible to tell from here whether it had been disturbed. Three generations of wellingtons and waxed jackets were stuffed into racks and hung on pegs, spilling onto the floor and piled high on the hulking washer-dryer (which was the only modern, expensive, energy-efficient technology in the house. The knackered old range cooker had its charms, as did the whistling kettle and even the rumbling fridge, but this machine needed to be able to wash and dry the kids' clothes as fast as they could dirty them). When dressing for outdoors everyone tended to grab the nearest thing, so Sophie never knew whether she'd come up with her late grandfather's ancient, mildewed Barbour or a modern Gore-Tex.

In the kitchen, the smell of burning dust was replaced by something stronger, as though a fire had recently been set, but Sophie put a hand to the stove and touched cold iron. The uncurtained kitchen window reflected back at them their own images, the double glazing making a ghost of Sophie's own face, so that everything appeared twice, including the purple pools of her eye sockets and brackets around her mouth. A small, white face pushed itself out of her ribcage like something from a horror film. It wasn't until a few seconds after Sophie had screamed that she realised it was Toby, and that he was on the other side of the glass, in the garden. Toby screamed back.

Will took the key from the back door and let Toby in.

'I've found Grandpa.'

Outside, the source of the burning smell was clear: the dying embers of a bonfire glowed in the middle of the garden. The kitchen window cast a rhombus of light onto the ground. Rowan sat in one corner of it, slumped on a sun lounger with its cushion missing. He held a port glass, clotted with the dark red liquid. His glasses were askew.

'Dad, what are you hiding out here for? Where's your car?'

'Round the back.' The words were tossed on a current of ether, Rowan's voice thick and his teeth purple. He was profoundly, spectacularly drunk. Sophie was astonished. Of course she had seen him merry before, after dinner or at weddings, but she had never seen anything like this level of intoxication, this loss of control. He had known the children were coming: what had he been *thinking*? She felt an unwelcome stirring of contempt.

His words were slurred but his half-sentences were clipped.

'Your mother. Not what I thought. Made a mistake. I can't do this without. Nothing's right.'

'Oh, *Dad*,' said Sophie, knowing she was wasting her breath, that reason had been drowned. 'Look, we all miss Mum, but we had to get together sooner or later, didn't we?' Rowan stood up, ash falling from his clothes, and staggered forward. The glass slipped from his fingers and smashed on the flagstones. He trod the shards like they were sand.

'Want to see my grandchildren. Only decent thing left. The only point. The only *reason*.'

'Bloody hell, Dad, watch where you're—'

'TOBY!' shouted Rowan. The silvering blond hair that was usually swept back from his temples fell into his eyes.

'Dad, *no*.'

'You can't stop me,' he snarled and for a second he was unrecognisable. 'Toby? Come here, son. Leo? Charlie? Edie, darling? Where's the baby? Where's my girl?' He lurched sideways and crashed into the wall. Sophie had never seen anything like this; Rowan was the man she trusted and admired most in the world, was the sole custodian of her bruised values, and now she was as unsure of his next move as she would have been with a drunk in the street, with a stranger.

Before she could call for Will, he was at her side.

'Swap places?' he asked her, and then said to Rowan, 'What are you doing, setting fire to the garden? We can get it ready tomorrow, there's no need for you to prep the ground now. Let's get a pot of coffee on the go, shall we? Sophie's going to put the kids to bed now. Better to see them in the morning.' Rowan sagged as though his strings had been cut, and let out a small grunt of obedience. Sophie was stung that Will had succeeded where she had not, but grudgingly grateful for his help.

She marshalled the boys up the stairs, a stirring Edie on her shoulder.

Toby brought up the rear with deliberate slowness, which meant he was about to ask for some arbitrary eldest-child privilege. 'Can I stay up until Jake gets here, *please*?' he begged.

'No, darling. It could be midnight by the time they arrive. You've got all weekend to be with your cousin.'

Toby demurred but conceded and Sophie was gratified that in this domain at least her authority was still recognised. As usual, the boys were to occupy the sloping room above the garage extension, known as the bunker. It had always seemed so depressing to her, with its single slit of a skylight and severe sloping walls, and there was something mean and military about the thin metal bunk beds, but that was what the boys seemed to love about it. Thanks to some over-zealous insulation by the local builders, it was the snuggest room in the house by far and was almost completely soundproofed, even with the door ajar. Once the door was closed, the soundproofing was so efficient that she had to use Edie's baby monitor in case Charlie called for her in the night. The grandfather clock chimed the quarter-hour while she was up there but the sound barely penetrated, and she saw no signs on her sons' faces that they had registered the shuffling and belching in the corridor outside as Will guided Rowan to his room.

She unclasped her bra, began to breastfeed Edie and sat in silence as her children's breathing slowed and regulated. As each child crossed the border into sleep, she felt a corresponding relaxation in her own body. Her boys were as distinct in sleep as they were awake. Leo's was the motionless coma of the bodily exhausted. Toby slept fist to forehead with his brow furrowed, a philosopher dreaming. Charlie, as usual, was the last to drop off. Even then he was edgy, unstill. He was making little clutching gestures with his hands, as though milking a cow, and his mouth formed silent words.

Sophie closed the bunker door behind her, placed Edie in the middle of her own bed and zipped her into the sleeping bag that she wore at night instead of bedclothes. She was hot and a little damp where she'd been wedged into the crook of Sophie's elbow; a single platinum curl kissed her flushed cheek goodnight.

The corridor led Sophie back past the bedroom her parents had always shared. A deep snore resonated from within. Will had removed Rowan's shoes and socks and covered him with the eiderdown, but it had been flung off again. His sweater had ridden up to expose his soft hairy belly and the pillow was damp with pale lilac spittle. The sight of her strong, capable father helpless as an infant bewildered as well as repulsed her. She wondered if this binge really was as unusual as it seemed. Had he started drinking heavily, and had she been too wrapped up in what was happening at home to notice?

The room itself looked unsettling, unfamiliar, as though it had been ransacked, but in fact there was no mess and it took Sophie a few seconds to realise that that was precisely the problem, that all the clutter and character of Lydia's occupancy had been removed. There in the corner were all her photographs and paintings, stacked face down, topped with the little velvet box that held her MBE.

Rowan may have been her father but it was a mother's impulse that made her pull the eiderdown back over his shoulders to tuck him in. There was something shiny on the pillow next to him, the size and shape of a jar of instant coffee; she leaned closer then recoiled as she recognised the small silver urn containing her mother's ashes. It was the first time she had seen it since the funeral. She touched it with a forefinger and was, ridiculously, surprised to find it cold. It was ash, not flesh. Nevertheless, she arranged the urn in the middle of the pillow then smoothed the bedclothes over it.

Rowan's present condition and his earlier distress now made sense. Perhaps it was still too soon. Perhaps it would always be too soon. What did the ritual of scattering the ashes achieve, anyway? It wouldn't bring Lydia back. Let him sleep with his wife one last night in the place they had always been happiest. Let him cling to her dust for the rest of this life if the prospect of parting with it reduced him to this.

4

If Far Barn made few technological concessions to the twenty-first century, it barely acknowledged many of the breakthroughs of the late twentieth. There was no television. There was a telephone for emergencies, an old-fashioned kind with a curly wire and grubby push-buttons. Mobile phones were useless here. The barn was deep in a valley, and thanks to Lydia's extensive campaigning not to have a mobile telephone mast erected at the top of a nearby hill, signal reception was a five-minute drive or a fifteen-minute walk across open country in any direction. There was also an old record player with a single tape deck and unreliable FM receiver. Its casing had room below for LPs, a collection of vinyl that came to an abrupt end in the early 1980s. Sophie blew dust off an old Fleetwood Mac album and inexpertly dropped the stylus halfway through the opening track.

'I can't bear to see him like that.'

'I think you're getting it all a bit out of perspective,' said Will. 'He's had a bit too much to drink, that's all. It happens all the time.'

But it *didn't*, not to Rowan, and although Will had not spoken unkindly his words immediately put her on the defensive. She was angry at Will for failing to sympathise, angrier still at herself for expecting him to.

She simply shrugged, took the proffered glass of wine with a low murmur of thanks. 'God, you're covered in ash. What was he *doing* out there?' Had the little urn on the pillow been empty? 'Oh no, he wasn't . . . Mum's . . . ?'

'That's what I thought too, but don't worry, no. Apparently he was setting tomorrow's bonfire. I couldn't get much sense out of him, but – hang on, where's Edie? The travel cot's still in the boot.'

'She's in our bed. We can put the cot up in the morning.'

It was as though a bad wind had blown through the building. 'How long are you going to keep this up?' he said, but his voice had dripped dry of the recrimination that would have soaked the question months ago. What Sophie feared was not so much his touch as her reaction to it. In sleep she might drop the guard she fought to maintain by day. He folded his arms and locked his eyes on hers. The impasse broke only when twin shafts of white light swept down the lane and in through the windows.

Sophie felt relief chase the wine through her veins. 'Tara or Felix?' she wondered aloud.

There was the slam of car doors, then a bunch of keys was dropped onto the doorstep and a female voice said, 'Oh, for fuck's *sake.*'

'Tara,' they said in unison, and the crack was papered over, for now.

'It's open,' called Sophie. She embraced Tara, then held her at arm's length.

Tara had dropped a few pounds, although it was hard to tell how much weight she had lost under all those layers: she always dressed as though for a yoga class, in loose clothes made in increasingly bizarre, ecologically superior fabrics like recycled cotton, hemp and even bamboo. Sophie's jeans and gilet, which had oozed weekend chic in Saxby, suddenly made her feel prim. 'You look *great,*' she said.

'I know!' said Tara, dropping her bags to tick off a list on newly slender fingers. 'We've all given up wheat, dairy, caffeine and refined sugar!' Behind her, Matt and Jake exchanged the briefest of looks that spoke of secret pizza and Coke binges.

'Why didn't you tell me?' said Sophie. 'Everything's all pasta this and bread that. You won't be able to eat anything.'

'I think we can relax it for three days,' said Matt. 'Hi, Soph, good to see you.' She kissed his cheek, then Jake's, astonished to see how her nephew had grown in just the last few weeks. Was he ever going to stop? At nearly fourteen, he was as tall as Matt, and was that *stubble* on his upper lip?

'All right, Sophie?' He had dropped the 'Auntie' years ago. He rubbed his legs. 'My knees are literally going to snap off. That's not a back seat, it's a shelf.'

Sophie looked out of the window. Next to their tank, Matt's sports car was a silver bullet. Will and Matt greeted each other in the usual way, a loose uneasy sequence of handshake, hug and punch. Both men were dark-haired, but Matt was stocky like a boxer while Will was as wiry as a marathon runner. Side-by-side, they looked like doctored photographs of a notional average man, one slightly stretched horizontally and the other vertically.

'Can I interest you in a beer, old boy?' said Will.

'I wouldn't say no, old boy.'

'Can *I* have one?' said Jake. Sophie turned to Tara, who shrugged a loose approval, or gestured that this battle was long lost, it was hard to tell.

'Sure,' said Sophie. 'Just outside the back door.'

'I might have some wine after all,' said Tara. She combed her scalp with her fingers, trying to make her hair look tousled, part of her lifelong campaign against a tidy fall of straight fair hair that never needed colour or styling. Sophie smiled to find herself smoothing down her own hair. Having achieved the desired degree of dishevelment, Tara flopped onto the long maroon chesterfield. Matt joined her, lying parallel. Sophie and Will occupied separate armchairs. The contrast between the two couples was obvious to Sophie. Would Tara pick up on it? She and Matt seemed more of a couple than they did although – no, *because* – they weren't shackled together by four children. They didn't even live together, although Tara, when discussing it, had begun to append a 'yet' to that statement.

There was some idle catch-up about the kids, the shape the weekend was to take, the forecast fog and what time Felix was going to arrive. Matt and Will, who had established a jovial rivalry in the kitchen, revealed to each other the recipes they were going to cook for supper on Saturday night. Matt had brought his own chef's knives down from London as he couldn't work with the ones here in the barn. Will went one better, producing something that looked like a little chrome fire extinguisher.

'What the fuck's *that*?' said Matt, leaping back as a jet of blue and orange flame shot several feet across the kitchen.

'Blowtorch,' said Will. 'Crème brûlée. You can't get the right finish under the grill. It's a professional one. I go straight to the wholesaler now, it's the only way to get the quality.'

'You could power a rocket with that,' said Matt, examining the torch and releasing another jet.

'Makes you feel like Zeus, doesn't it?' said Will. Matt set the blowtorch down on the worktop and looked forlornly at the pestle and mortar he had brought down.

'I think this is the metrosexual version of mud-wrestling,' said Tara, rolling her eyes. 'Can you see Dad and Uncle Richard discussing the perils of making cheese soufflé in a range?'

'Ha! Hardly,' said Sophie, and then to Will, 'I want that somewhere the boys can't reach it. Or even see it.'

Matt started describing the process of preparing langoustines in garlic and tomatoes to Will in mouthwatering detail.

'Every time he makes one of his Masterchef creations, he spends an entire week's food budget on the ingredients,' murmured Tara.

'I don't even want to *know* how much he spent on that flame thing. And whenever they create one of these five-course banquets, I end up cooking a parallel supper that the children actually want to eat,' said Sophie.

Overhead, there was a sudden creaking of beams followed by a few heavy footfalls, and the sound of Rowan throwing up, repeatedly. Sophie hoped he was in his own bathroom – hoped he had made it to a bathroom at all.

'Is that one of the kids?' asked Tara.

'Dad's drunk.'

'*Dad*?' Sophie was vindicated that Tara's level of consternation matched her own, and shot Will a triumphant look that missed its target. 'I didn't even know he was here. His car's not outside. Are you sure he's drunk?'

'Yes. He's had a whole bottle of port and started a bonfire.'

'What's he burned?'

'Newspapers. He says he's preparing the ground for tomorrow's fire.'

The vomiting ended with a series of billious retches.

'Jesus,' said Matt, his voice straddling disgust and awe. 'He's really going for it, isn't he?'

The conversation drifted away from food. Another bottle was uncorked. An ancient box of Trivial Pursuit was pulled out of a drawer but not opened. The grandfather clock doled out portions of the night.

'I wonder where they've got to,' said Tara.

'They?' said Sophie.

'Felix said he was bringing a girl.'

'*Did* he?' said Will, at the same time that Sophie said,

'Felix has got a girlfriend? First I've heard of it. Does Dad know?'

'I don't know if Dad knows. I didn't know *you* didn't know. Still, he must be quite taken with her if he's bringing her down here.'

'First girlfriend, at the tender age of twenty-nine,' said Will. Sophie and Tara glared at him.

'Below the belt, Will,' said Tara. 'You know he's funny about his scar.'

Will held up his palms in conciliation, and rolled his eyes at Matt in the vain hope of finding an ally. Matt studied the small print on his beer bottle: he still regarded MacBride familial bickering as a spectator sport rather than one he could participate in.

'I wonder if she's like the rest of his friends,' said Tara.

Sophie hoped not. Since his mid-teens, Felix had lived entirely ironically, hanging out with a group who dressed anachronistically in smoking jackets or old heavy metal tour T-shirts, held ironic Royal Wedding street parties, ate ironic meals, served fish finger sandwiches at dinner parties, and even went on ironic holidays to Butlins and Benidorm. The weekend would hold enough tension without some self-styled retro princess sneering at their beloved traditions and stonewalling their jokes.

'What *do* we know about her?' pressed Sophie. 'What's her name, for a start?'

'Literally, I don't know anything more than I've told you,' said Tara. 'I wonder what she'll make of the old place.'

It was a MacBride theory that a person's first reaction to the barn told you all you needed to know of their character. Will, the only boyfriend Sophie had brought to the barn, had explored the whole place in silent wonder before giving the verdict, 'This would make an architect cry. I *love* it. But then I knew I would: it's such a big part of you.' Tara often said that one of the reasons she and Matt had lasted was that on crossing the threshold for the first time he hadn't admired it, criticised it or analysed it, but had dropped his bags and let out a long cheer just to test the acoustics.

Soon after midnight, Felix's ancient orange Skoda (ironic) came to a noisy halt in front of the barn. Then the stable door opened and Felix was there, in a coat with mittens hanging from strings at the wrists, and a deerstalker hat.

The first thing Sophie noticed about the girl was her hair: long, matte, dark and thick. It hung in a curtain over most of her face but could not disguise exquisite features, all eyes and cheekbones, the one-in-a-million perfect proportions of the cover girl or movie star. She dressed that part too, in slim trousers, heels, a thin white vest under a tailored, dove-grey leather jacket. Was Sophie being over-sensitive to imagine that the girl's beauty ridiculed Felix's own disfigurement? He was trying to look casual, as though he had stunningly beautiful girlfriends to stay in Devon all the time.

'Kerry, these are my sisters, Sophie and Tara, and this is Will, and this is Matt, and this is Jake. Everyone, this is Kerry.'

For a second or two Felix let slip his mask of irony; when he looked at Kerry it was with the pride and adoration of a bridegroom at the altar. It was the first genuine emotion Sophie had seen cross his face since Lydia's funeral.

Kerry flicked the briefest of glances at each of them, then lowered her lids again and went back to staring at the floor. She did not speak, and nor did she look around her new surroundings. Sophie locked eyes with Tara for a second. *No* reaction to the barn was unheard of. There was already much to discuss.

Felix closed the door behind him, bent down to as if to kiss Sophie, but instead plucked the wine glass from her hand and drained it. 'Good bouquet, strong nose, lovely vintage,' he said, back to his usual self. 'Sit down, Kerry, I'll get you a drink. Bloody *hell*, it's hot in here.'

He shrugged off his jacket and Kerry removed her own. She wore no bra under her camisole, and Sophie felt herself blush on her behalf. Opposite her, Tara cringed while Matt and Will, both old enough to affect ignorance, began an earnest discussion about the best way to peel a king prawn, while poor Jake shifted and pulled a cushion over his lap.

Erin Kelly

Kerry said nothing for the rest of the evening. She answered any questions directed her way with nothing more than a smile. She seemed genuine enough, but let Felix talk for her. Was it true, then, that cliché about beautiful people not bothering to develop a personality because their looks did all the work for them? When Felix went to the fridge, Sophie followed him on the pretext of recycling a wine bottle and pulled the door closed behind them.

'Well?' she said.

Felix was too drunk, or tired, or delighted, to bother hiding his smirk. 'What do you reckon? I'm punching above my weight, I know, but . . . she's *amazing*, isn't she?'

'She seems very . . .' Sophie groped for the right word. Beautiful was too obvious and wasn't there an implicit insult there? Strange? Naïve? Shy? *Rude*? 'She seems . . . *sweet*. But does she speak?'

'I'm sure you wouldn't exactly be at your most loquacious if you had to meet an entire family all at once.'

'Maybe,' she conceded. Will had been a little overawed at first, but then he had been very young. She couldn't remember the first time Matt had met the family en masse, but she did recall that some of his predecessors had been dumb in the face of the MacBrides' energy and solidarity.

'So, where did you meet her, what does she do, how long have you been together, what kind of background is she from? I want to know everything.'

'Christ, you're *so* like Mum,' said Felix. 'OK. In no particular order. She came into the shop about two months ago and we've been together since the night after that. She isn't working at the moment. As for background, you vile snob, I don't think she's got much in the way of family. Not that I mind that, you lot are more than enough for one man to deal with.' Sophie smiled to herself; he'd paraphrased another theory she and Tara had come up with, an idea that they were drawn to people with sparse backgrounds because they were so easy to assimilate into the MacBrides. A competing clan might have proved an unstoppable force to the immovable object of their own unit. 'She's a riddle, wrapped inside an enigma, hidden inside a mystery . . . all lurking behind a fantastic pair of tits.'

'Felix!'

'I promise you, you've never seen anything like them,' said Felix. 'They're—'

'Strangely, I'm not particularly keen to imagine your girlfriend's breasts,' said Sophie, folding her arms across her own chest, very aware that milk had only temporarily restored to her the full breasts of her twenties. Not that Will saw them in that context any more, not since long before Edie was born. She breathed through the surge of anger until she felt calm, then surprised herself by throwing the empty wine bottle into the recycling bin so hard that it smashed.

Back in the sitting room, Felix tossed a beer each to Jake and Matt, then stretched out next to Kerry. Her jacket was back on, and her appearance less provocative, but the shift in the atmosphere had not been so easily remedied. Tara was staring through a fine veil of hair. The men were ignoring her now, Matt and Jake in conversation. Will was ostentatiously ignoring Kerry, as he did all attractive young women. The tension a stranger can introduce is different to the kind that can exist between people who know each other well. It is less elastic, more likely to shatter than stretch.

Felix curled an arm around his mute, beautiful girlfriend. Unusually it was the eager expression on his face rather than the features of it that showed his vulnerability. Kerry made no reciprocal gesture and Sophie was struck again by the conviction that such an uneven match could only end in Felix getting terribly hurt. For the first time since Lydia's death Sophie was glad that her mother was not around to see what might unfold.

5

Edie had served her purpose as a human bolster in the night: now she functioned as a human alarm clock, seizing a fistful of her mother's hair and hooking a fat little finger up her nose. Sophie gathered her up, still in her sleeping bag, and got out of bed. The open bathroom door and the synthetic citrus scent of disinfectant told her that Rowan was already up and last night's mess dealt with.

Tara was in the sitting room, doing half-hearted sun salutations on the Indian rug. Rowan was at the kitchen table, a pot of tea on the go, looking fresher than he deserved to.

'Edie!' he said brightly. 'Come and say good morning to Grandpa!' He bounced the baby on his lap.

'Dad, are you OK?'

'Why wouldn't I be?'

He was using his headmaster's voice, which meant that this conversation would go the way he wanted it to – in this case, no further. Fine. It was with relief that she let the subject go. There were enough difficult conversations to be had as it was.

Rowan stroked Edie's cheek. 'She's so like you were at her age, Sophie. It's like having you back again.'

'I'm right here,' she said, but she knew exactly what he meant.

Outside, dawn was tentatively uncloaking the grey garden, the naked orchard of knuckle-dragging fruit trees, the piles of leaves, the lawn turned to mud. Although Sophie had spent all her childhood summers here, when she thought about the garden it was always in this state, stripped for winter, brown and bare. It was as wild and sprawling as their courtyard garden at home was cultivated. It sloped gently upwards and a foot-high dry stone wall separated it from a scattering of crumbling outbuildings that were all that remained from the estate's days as a working farm. A hundred yards over the prow of the hill stood a derelict labourer's cottage. Only its shell survived, each strong wind robbing the roof of a few more of its remaining tiles. Ugly steel at the door and windows kept the children out.

The farmhouse itself – a tiny, two-roomed shack – had been three centuries old when it was pulled down by Lydia's grandfather. This had been in the 1950s and before the conservation movement had reached their part of Devon. The old foundations had finally been dug out just five years ago, with the intention of levelling the land and building a cabin on the site to create an overspill barn for the growing family. Planning permission had never been granted and the right-hand side of the garden remained a maze of deep dykes and ditches which the boys had commandeered for a mysterious, noisy war game known as Death in the Trenches. Next door Tara's exhalations developed an air of conclusion, prompting Sophie to consider that this might be the last time all weekend she had her father to herself. It seemed important that they discuss Lydia's ashes alone, a legacy of the childhood in which she had frequently been old enough to be party to information that her siblings were deemed too young to understand. She turned her back to the window.

'Dad, about Mum's ashes,' she said. 'We don't have to scatter them this weekend if you don't want to.'

The usual grief that arced across Rowan's face upon hearing Lydia mentioned was this time corrupted with something else that Sophie could not identify.

'I'm sorry,' she said quickly. 'Forget it, I shouldn't have mentioned it.'

'No, it's time,' he said.

'OK.' She gestured to the garden. 'The obvious place is out here, I suppose. We could plant a tree, maybe? Or even another orchard. Or we don't have to plant anything, we could just say a few words and . . . *when* should we do it? I don't know, Dad, what do you think?'

'Mooorniiiing!' Tara bounded into the kitchen. 'I'm starving. Shall we get breakfast on?' Her exuberance closed the possibility of serious discussion.

Sophie knew that the smell of a full English breakfast beckoning its way up the stairs would rouse the sleepers. She threw some rashers in a pan, melted a knob of butter for eggs. The grease worked its way into her skin and hair but that smell would soon be overpowered by woodsmoke.

Rowan watched Tara run a breadknife through a loaf of unsliced white and said, 'I can't believe that, in women of your generation and of your education, it's still you who do all the cooking and the men who come downstairs and eat it.'

'Not true,' said Tara. 'Will and Matt are doing some big supper thing later. And anyway, not *all* the women are downstairs cooking.'

Rowan looked blank.

'Felix has brought a girl with him,' said Sophie.

Shock stole the colour from Rowan's cheeks so that the full force of his hangover showed on his face. 'But I thought . . . I thought it would all be *family*,' he said.

'Matt's not technically family,' said Tara.

'That's different. I *know* Matt. And I knew he was coming. This weekend is – I just didn't bank on having to deal with a stranger.' He peered into his mug as though the answer lay in the tea-leaves. 'What's she like, then, this . . . ?'

'Kerry,' said Sophie, cracking an egg into the pan. 'She's . . . quiet. Pretty.'

'She's not *pretty*,' said Tara. 'You're pretty. She's *stunning*. It's like the Phantom of the Opera has pulled Helen of Troy.'

Rowan raised his eyebrows, whether at the news that Felix had a beautiful girlfriend or at Tara's uncharacteristic breaking of the *omertà* surrounding her brother's looks, it was impossible to tell.

The cooking smells had worked their magic and suddenly the kitchen was full of pyjamaed kids and hastily dressed adults fighting for a place at the table. Toby was engrossed in a tattered book about maritime disasters, open on a page about the *Mary Rose*.

'Did you know that one theory about how the Tar Barrels began is that they're connected with the beacons that warned the Spanish Armada was coming?' said Rowan.

'The *Mary Rose* wasn't in the Armada,' said Toby. 'She sank in 1545.'

'I knew that,' laughed Rowan. 'I was testing you.'

'Well, I passed.'

'Tobes, it's bad enough that Grandpa wants to be a teacher on holiday,' said Jake. 'But it's all kinds of wrong that you want to be at school.'

Rowan sat at the head, with Will opposite, everyone else cramming onto the long refectory benches so like the ones at school.

'All these children, it's enough to instill misanthropy into the most open of hearts,' said Felix cheerfully, hoisting Charlie onto a bench. 'Will, you're a walking advertisement for the benefits of vasectomy.'

'I haven't had a vasectomy.'

'Exactly.'

Will and Sophie's children had, by chance, arranged themselves in age order. The colour of their hair ran the spectrum from Edie's white blonde to the dark sand of Toby's mop, the fading blond a chronometer of childhood. It was as though the older her children got, the more they came to resemble Will. When she was pregnant for the first time, Will had told Sophie that it was a good job he was dark, that if any of the MacBrides were to reproduce with another blond their children might be invisible. Tara had already taken this pursuit of melanin to its logical extreme: Jake's curls had been a rich dark gold when he was a child, and these days he wore his hair so short it was a shadow on his oak-coloured skin. He sat next to Edie's high chair, helping her guide her food into her mouth.

'He's turning out so well,' said Sophie to Tara, so that Jake couldn't hear. 'Aren't you glad now that Dad and Will bullied you into sending him to the Cath?'

Sophie immediately wished she'd phrased it better. 'Bullying' was absolutely the wrong word for the intervention Rowan and Will had staged, rescuing Jake from drowning in the huge inner-city comprehensive where the children wore what they liked and drug pushers at the gates outnumbered the mothers. Tara, who had never quite outgrown a teenage socialist phase, had interpreted the arrangement and funding of a place for Jake at the Cath as a criticism of her parenting style. Of course the real shame was not that they had the privilege, but that that privilege was not standard in state education. Lydia had often said that if all children could attend the Cath, the world's problems would be solved in a generation. Sophie could see Tara's point, but what were you supposed to do? Sacrifice your children's education to prove a point?

Trying to persuade Tara, Rowan had made a throwaway comment about boys of Jake's colour needing the best education they could get to arm them against a prejudiced world. Accusations of racism had been flung, and Sophie and Lydia had to step in and work hard to convince Tara that they were acting not out of snobbery but love. Tara had remained defensive about the subject, so now Sophie was amazed to see her sister smile. 'You know he's made the first eleven?' Tara could not keep the pride from her voice.

'Under sixteens, surely?' Sophie corrected her.

'No, they think he's going to play for the school next summer.'

'Tara, that's unheard of, that's *fantastic*!' Sophie whispered. 'Especially when you think how angry he was a couple of years ago. You must be so proud.' They both glanced at Jake; if he was listening, he was hiding it well. His concentration was all on Edie, spooning food into her mouth and, frequently, her hair.

'I am, I am. I mean, I'm not deluding myself that that was his *entire* teenage rebellion and I'm sure there's more to come, but obviously the Cath's knocked some of the feral off him. I'm sure one of the reasons he went a bit wobbly at the comp was that they only had games, like, once a week, and you can't do that with boys, can you, they need to run off their energy or they start looking around for other ways to use it up.' She lowered her voice further. 'And actually I think Matt's done him the world of good, too. Not just because he's stuck around but because he isn't trying to be Jake's dad. There's none of that jealousy stuff surrounding Louis.'

Jake gave up on Edie and produced his mobile from under the table. He might not have been able to receive a signal but he could still play *Plants vs. Zombies* until his thumbs seized up.

Will cleared his throat but Matt beat him to it. 'Come on, Jake, you know the rules,' he chided. 'Not at the table.'

'Sorry,' said Jake, in a voice that went from batsqueak to basso profondo in a single word. Without pausing his game, he tucked in his knees and twisted around on his bottom to get off the bench.

'The idea was that you left the phone, not the table,' said Matt.

'It's not my fault I've got no concentration span. My neural pathways have been rerouted by short-term stimuli. It's a generational thing.' He went and sat down in the sitting-room and continued to play.

'They teach you too much at that school,' said Matt, but he winked at Tara to soften the admonishment. Will craned to see Jake bent over his phone on the sofa. For a moment Sophie thought he was going to march in and confiscate the thing; Will was used to giving Jake the kind of telling off that only came from *real* love, the kind that makes you cruel to be kind. She looked at her husband and saw not anger but hurt and knew it was because Matt had usurped Will as Jake's father figure. Sophie could not help but love Will for loving Jake. She watched his shoulders drop as he let it go, and she loved him for doing that, too.

Kerry – who had yet to say a word – sidled into Jake's space, directly opposite Sophie. She took the baby spoon and used its soft plastic edge to scrape the purée from Edie's cheeks, leaving a little orange goatee that made Charlie laugh, before wiping Edie clean with a muslin cloth. Edie spat out the proffered mouthful and batted Kerry's hand away. This was the point at which most people gave up, turned to Sophie and said, 'I think she wants her mum,' but Kerry bent to Edie's level and whispered something in baby talk that made Edie burst into delighted life. Kerry didn't break eye contact as she continued to feed the baby and was rewarded with a particular giggle that Sophie had thought was reserved for her. Sophie had seen these women before, innate mothers, nurturing since they were given their first doll and with no ambition other than reproduction. She had never quite understood them, and they made her uneasy. At least she had *tasted* professional success, at least she had *tried*.

'She's a good feeder, isn't she?' said Kerry. 'And she's got such a lovely laugh.' The shock of Kerry's voice temporarily robbed Sophie of her own. It was feminine in pitch but scraped and gruff like that of a heavy smoker. Sophie had expected an accent but there were only the neutral vowels of somebody reasonably – if not privately – educated. She spoke slowly, as if each word had been selected and examined carefully before it was uttered.

'She's a good girl all round,' said Sophie.

'You've got a babysitter for life, there, I reckon,' said Felix. He buttered Kerry a slice of toast. She nibbled at the crust as the rest of them began to clear their plates and shift in their seats. Before they all dispersed for the morning, someone had to bring up the subject of Lydia's ashes. Sophie felt that the responsibility rested with her, even though it made her feel intensely uncomfortable, as though she were officially assuming the role of the new matriarch.

'I thought today we could . . .' She caught her father's eye and lost her nerve. 'Who's up for building a bonfire? If we get started after breakfast we can get a really good blaze going by the time it gets dark.'

'Good plan,' said Felix. 'I'm all for a bit of child labour. What about you, Edie? Are you going to muck in and earn your keep, or just lounge around in your nappy all day?'

Edie smiled through a new beard of butter and crumbs. She scanned the empty plates for leftovers and, with admirable subtlety for a child of nine months, crawled her fingers towards Kerry's toast. Smiling, Kerry tore the slice into little pieces and gave them to the baby, leaning in close to feed her. Edie put up her hand to Kerry's face, grabbed a dangling lock of hair and tugged. I should have warned her about that, thought Sophie, who was used to seeing bunches of her own hair suddenly appear in her daughter's hands, but she smiled to see that Edie was actually trying to tuck Kerry's hair behind her ears, the way Sophie wore hers.

For the briefest of seconds Kerry's neck and ears were exposed. Both her earlobes were mutilated, the flesh appearing to drip like soft wax either side of a vertical scar. The image of someone pulling out a pair of earrings with sufficient speed and force to tear the flesh was inescapable. Automatically Sophie put her hands up to her own earlobes as if to protect them. Kerry saw her doing it, darkened and wrapped her hair around her neck like a scarf. Although she had seen by accident, Sophie felt guilty of a terrible intrusion. She glanced up and down the table: no one was looking at either of them. She tried to smile at Kerry, to communicate that she would not betray the secret, but Kerry's eyes were firmly on her empty plate. You poor girl, thought Sophie. Perhaps you have more in common with Felix than we guessed.

6

The flaming Tar Barrels carnival was a public custom that the MacBrides had taken to their hearts, but the day of woodgathering was a tradition of their own making. After breakfast the woodshed would be emptied and the bonfire in the back garden laid. Then, the family would set out with their baskets to gather enough fallen wood from the surrounding land to put in the shed for the next year. At dusk, the guys would be perched on the top of the pyre and the whole thing lit. It was rather a naive, childish tradition, begun when Sophie was herself small and never abandoned, maybe because there had never really been a gap between the MacBride siblings being children and having children of their own. The routine was only deviated from in years when the weather made setting a bonfire impossible, but this weekend had so far been fine and dry.

In years gone by, Lydia had made the guys, one for each child, from clothes so worn that even the MacBrides baulked at using them as hand-me-downs. Nobody contested Sophie for this task, and she was happy to stay behind while Edie had her nap. From the upstairs window, she watched them traipse up the sloping garden and then over the stile to the woodland beyond, each with his own basket, even the little ones.

At the far end of her parents' – her *father*'s – bedroom, was a mismatched pair of pine wardrobes. One housed Rowan and Lydia's things, the other looked like the back room of a charity shop the week after Christmas. It was stuffed with clothes outgrown or forgotten, spares of various sizes left by guests and saved for visitors who didn't know how to dress for the country. The tops of the wardrobes brushed the eaves: the triangular space behind them was also crammed with suitcases and carrier bags of clothes. She rummaged at leisure, each tiny odd sock, each holey pair of jeans evoking memories of little boys with white-blond hair.

Sophie heard a noise on the landing and tiptoed down the hall to her bedroom, where Edie was sleeping in the travel cot that Will had set up that morning. The curtains were drawn; the room was dim rather than dark but still it took a few seconds for Sophie to identify the grey hazy figure standing by the cot as Kerry. What was she doing? As Sophie's eyes adjusted and the room came into focus, she saw Kerry bend down to retrieve Cloth Rabbit from just outside the cot. She placed the toy next to the sleeping baby and stayed for a few seconds with an expression of such tenderness on her face that Sophie felt like a voyeur. If only I could catch her looking at Felix like that, thought Sophie, this strange uneasy feeling I have about her might go away.

She announced her presence by swaying slightly to the right, knowing the loose floorboard beneath her feet would squeak softly under the pressure. Kerry did not start but turned slowly towards her, placed her finger over her lips to show that she understood and tiptoed away from the cot.

When they were both safely in the corridor, Sophie noticed that Kerry was barefoot.

'They sent me back to find some boots. My shoes were all wrong.' The suede pumps Sophie remembered from breakfast would not have carried her more than a few paces in the boggy autumn countryside.

'Did you have a look in the mudroom?' Now Kerry only nodded. It was as though, thought Sophie, she was only permitted a certain number of words per hour, and had used up her quota until the clock struck one.

'OK, let's see what we can find for you,' said Sophie, leading the way to Rowan's room. 'What size shoe do you take?'

Kerry splayed the fingers of her left hand and held up her right thumb to make six. Inches from Sophie's nose there was a single Hunter boot in racing green, the number six stamped into its sole, but its partner was nowhere to be found.

'They said if there weren't any I could stay and help you make the guys for the boys.'

'I'll be quicker by myself,' said Sophie, and then, realising how harsh that sounded, 'I mean, why don't you just keep me company instead? I won't be long.' She continued to sift through the jumble and then let out a gasp as her fingertips brushed against something soft and scratchy and shockingly familiar. The next moment she was holding up a sweater of Lydia's that she hadn't seen since she was a teenager. Instinctively she put it to her nose and inhaled. To the objective eye it was a horrible home-knitted eighties creation in marbling pastel wool, ice white and lilac with tiny flecks of silver in it. The rush back through time, to their house in Cathedral Terrace, was so swift that Sophie half expected to feel her hair flying. 'This is older than you are,' she told Kerry. 'My mother knitted this when she was pregnant with Felix. Oh . . . it's like hugging her. Or being hugged by her. Strange how something so ugly could have such sentimental value.'

'It's not ugly,' said Kerry. 'I tried on something like that in Topshop last week.'

'Really?' said Sophie, folding it and placing it in the 'keepers' pile. 'That makes me feel ancient . . . Things I think are horrible are so old they've come back into fashion again. Anyway. I'll hold onto it forever.' She slid the pile of clothes into a drawer at the bottom of one of the wardrobes. 'There. They should be pretty safe in there.'

Kerry watched so closely that Sophie felt self-conscious.

'I haven't got anything that belonged to my mother,' she

said. This is more like it, Sophie thought, seizing on the potential for intimacy. She thought hard about how to broach the subject of Kerry's ears in a way that would establish her as a sympathetic listener rather than an interfering big sister.

Her concentration was shattered when something hit the dormer window with a gunshot crack then ricocheted away again. Sophie's scream was a reflex action, so loud that the silence it left was somehow purer than the one that had preceded it. Kerry had her hand on her breastbone as if to still a hammering heart.

'I'm so sorry, it was only a firework,' said Sophie, nodding at the telltale carbon smut on the pane. Embarrassed by her loss of control, ashamed at how near to the surface her tension was, she started to gabble. 'Kids get overexcited and throw them – they can travel for miles. Where is everyone? If I'd screamed like that in the city we'd have sirens, lights, the lot. Look. Listen.' She spread her hands out wide to indicate the lack of response, laughed to show that she was joking. 'Nothing. You can do anything when fireworks are kicking off. Scream, fire a gun . . . Mind you, out here you can do anything you like anyway. There isn't a soul for miles around.'

Kerry was looking at Sophie's hands which were, she now saw, shaking furiously. A few doors away, Edie started to cry.

'Let me get her up for you,' said Kerry, almost falling over her feet in her haste to leave.

If the women had reverted to type by cooking, then the men had done the same by taking seriously the task of building the fire over the ashy remnants of the one Rowan had made the day before. The boys had made firesticks by rolling up year-old newspapers and they carefully laid these, along with twigs and other tinder, at the bottom while Matt and Will hefted the large, slow-burning logs to the top. Four little guys sat atop the woodpile, their clothes and features indistinguishable in the dusk.

Exertion had forced the men to strip to their shirtsleeves but the female spectators were swaddled in jackets, scarves and boots. Jake, presumably devastated by Kerry's absence from the woodgathering expedition, had gone to great lengths to locate the other size six Hunter. Rowan, Will and Matt helped the MacBride boys light the fire, men young and old sharing the same serious, primal concentration on the task. Edie watched, strapped into her buggy and at a safe remove from the flames, not frightened but mesmerised. The guys took the flames more readily than the wood; now every detail was illuminated. A vile green nylon coat, a present for one of the boys, melted rather than burned and shrivelled away in an initial burst before the rest of them caught light slowly and steadily. Jake cheered on his own effigy as a curve of flame caught its stuffed head and caused it to roll off. Why did boys always love such gruesome, sinister things? Would Edie, in years to come, be the same? Sophie shivered in the heat. The thought of harm coming to any likeness of Edie's, no matter how crude, was chilling.

One of the guys seemed to be burning brighter than the others, almost shooting out sparks. Sophie watched it, first with curiosity and then with horror as she realised that the pyrotechnic display was the burning of the tiny silver threads in her mother's sweater. For a few seconds it was impossible to tell if the roaring noise was coming from inside her head or from the fire. She could not hear herself think and was unable to blink or move as the garment was consumed the same way it was created, stitch by stitch, row by row, until the urgency of the situation pulled her out of her trance. Only Kerry would have known it was there. Why would she have done something so cruel? She remembered the jealous note in Kerry's voice when she had talked about her mother. Could that be it?

There wasn't time to understand why.

'Who put that there?' said Sophie, raising her voice above the roar of the fire.

'Who put what where?' said Felix.

'Who put that . . . what is that *doing* there?' No one spoke, so Sophie grabbed Kerry by the arm and shouted into her face, 'What were you thinking? Get that back. I *told* you what it meant to me. Get it back. *Get it back!*'

Felix put himself between Sophie and Kerry. 'What are you doing, Sophie? Stop it. Get off her!'

Felix's casual grip was stronger than Sophie's most powerful effort could ever be, and she let Kerry go. In the seconds that followed, Sophie was only vaguely sensible of her family screaming and of more dark figures running up behind her. She might not be strong, but she was quick, and she scaled the loose smoking lattice of twigs at the base of the fire and found herself face to face with the blaze itself, her hands forming claws ready to clutch at the sparkling, sparking sweater, to save what she could. She was about to plunge her hand into the flames when she felt Will grab her left arm and another man – Matt, Jake, Felix, she couldn't tell – seize the right. She persisted until the pain in the sockets of her arms and her shoulders won. She relaxed as quickly as she had sprung into action, so that all of them fell backwards and landed in a heap on the ground. She closed her eyes and listened to her sons' sobs, her own eyes smarting.

'Jesus,' said Tara. 'Someone get the first aid box.'

Seconds later Tara was applying some kind of balm to her hands. Sophie assessed the damage in a detached sort of way. A single knuckle had swelled into a big pink blister that seemed itself to contain a miniature inferno, but this was the only pain. Kerry was telling Felix that she would never do something like that, that she didn't understand how it had got there, that it was a mix-up, a mistake.

Will was crouching beside her, half his left eyebrow missing.

'Soph,' he said. 'Sophie, what happened?'

'It must have been Kerry,' she said. 'She was the only one who knew it was in the bottom of the wardrobe. She's jealous of my mum.'

'Sweetheart, what are you talking about?'

'I couldn't bear to see Mum's stuff burned,' she said. 'I had to stop it.'

It sounded as absurd as it had seemed reasonable moments before. Will said nothing more, but she could see what he was thinking. Lying on the grass, lungs scorched, knuckle singing out in pain, she was for the first time terrified that he might be right. She looked up at Will, Kerry standing behind him, the pair of them shadows through the smoke, and for a second she was forcibly, painfully reminded of the grainy photographs, a sheet of hair behind him, and she allowed herself to wonder if— *No.* Last time it had started like this, a slow loss of confidence in her own judgement, wild conclusions jumped to. She was sure she had put her mother's sweater aside, but then Kerry had come in with Edie, Sophie's concentration had been broken. Just because she couldn't remember having done it did not necessarily mean it hadn't happened.

Someone threw a switch and the glare of the outdoor light dulled the bonfire's glow. She squeezed her stinging eyes closed. When she opened them, Will was still there, but Kerry had gone. This was how it had begun before, different realities presenting themselves to her between blinks.

7

Outside Felix's room she raised her hand to knock, trusting that the right words of apology would come to her as soon as she saw Kerry's face. But from within came sounds that barred her like a locked door: a slap, a giggle (Felix?), a groan (definitely Felix, *eugh*) and the sudden thud of a headboard. Hastily she backed away, creeping along the corridor and tiptoeing down the stairs.

The sitting room was empty. High-pitched battle cries from outside told her that the boys were playing Death in the Trenches by the security light. At the kitchen table were Edie and the adults, who were talking in hushed, not-in-front-of-the-children tones. Sophie smiled; they flattered Edie if they thought she was old enough to understand, let alone repeat, their conversation. But as she drew closer and she could make out the odd word, her smile was knocked off its perch. She heard her own name and Kerry's and the words 'bonfire' and 'lost it'.

Heart kicking at her ribcage, she pressed herself against the wall and approached the kitchen so that she could hear without being seen. If I stay here, she thought, perhaps they will tell me something about myself that I cannot grasp.

'I thought she was better?' said Tara to Will. 'She seemed fine until just now. She's been her old self since before Edie was born. Hasn't she? None of us want a repetition of the Charlie thing . . . You'd tell us if it got that bad again, wouldn't you?'

Matt said, 'The Charlie thing?'

'Didn't I tell you?' said Tara, in a tone that suggested she had deliberately kept it from him; Sophie felt a warm rush of gratitude at this unexpected loyalty that immediately began to ebb. 'She had acute postnatal depression after Charlie was born, but nobody picked up on it. We all just thought she was knackered, as you would be with two boys and a baby, and it all came to a head one day when she just dumped him in a supermarket, left the buggy in the middle of the cereals aisle.'

Tara was wrong there. It had been the rice and pasta aisle. Sophie would never forget the way all the labels on the food had seemed too vivid, all the colours turned up to neon and glowing as if lit from within, with Charlie's face the brightest, hottest light of them all.

'*Shit*,' said Matt.

'I know. I know. It was awful. The people at Waitrose called the police in but it was quite a while before they could identify him. Because he was supposed to be with Sophie all day, no one reported him missing and he was officially in care for about five hours, until Sophie didn't pick the other boys up from school and the school rang Will. It took three days for them to find her. We were all out looking for her.'

It was strange to hear them recount it like this, in calm, dispassionate voices, as though there hadn't been screaming and tears at the time.

'And where had she gone?' said Matt.

'She'd taken herself off to an hotel and locked herself in the room,' said Rowan. 'They had to break the door down. We all thought she'd done the worst.'

'By then we were so relieved she was safe that we didn't have the heart to be angry with her,' said Will.

'Not that anger was the appropriate response,' said Rowan. 'She was *ill*. The police were very sympathetic, in the end, after Lydia had spoken to them.'

'Will, mate,' said Matt. 'What a nightmare.'

'It was, yeah,' said Will. 'I blame myself for a lot of it. I should have noticed sooner, shouldn't I? And then later on, I didn't handle it well either, I . . .' Sophie drew a serrated in-breath. *He's going to tell them about how he 'handled' my breakdown, and because of what they have just seen, they won't even blame him. For her family to know about his infidelity would make the humiliation complete.* This, then, was to be her punishment for eavesdropping. She felt her lungs begin to strain and heard Will's own deep inhalation before he said, 'It's just . . . it's just grief, isn't it?' Sophie finally let out her breath; she had been holding it for so long she was panting. 'You're all going through it. *We're* all going through it.'

There was no response, just the noise of mugs being picked up and set down, the ting of teaspoons on crockery, the scraping of chair feet, the gentle constant of Edie's high-pitched babble.

'But she seems so on top of things,' said Tara, eventually. 'I mean, she organised this whole weekend, for a start.'

And Will said, 'Well, that's Sophie, isn't it? The more ill she gets, the more highly she functions, until one day she just . . . *doesn't* any more.'

'Will, I know she's my daughter but you can always talk to me, man to man,' said Rowan.

Will made no reply. Someone drummed their fingers. Now the house itself seemed to hold its breath.

Matt cleared his throat and steered the conversation towards the familiar and unthreatening. 'Well, supper isn't going to cook itself, is it? Come on, Will, let's see what you're made of.'

'Let battle commence!' said Will, in the voice he used when he wanted to make light of something dark. Sophie wondered if he had any of the rest of them fooled.

8

Morning made a million-dollar necklace of the spider web that spanned the kitchen window. A heavy white mist had settled in the valley overnight, and the cold sun struggled to cast a milky opaque light. Only the nearest parts of the garden were visible: the sooty patch of land where the bonfire had been and the gouged earth of the trenches.

Leo and Charlie had an uneven wrestling match under the coffee table. Toby had reached the chapter about the twentieth century in his book of maritime disasters. 'Ask me *anything* about the *Titanic*,' he said to anyone whose glance crossed his.

Tara was in the sitting room, wearing a Slanket and nursing a mild hangover. By the kettle, Jake heaped a cup of tea with sugar. Sophie caught his eye and he flushed, caught redhanded in the shameful act of caring for his mum.

'Just as well we had the bonfire yesterday,' observed Rowan. 'We'd have had the devil to fight to get the wood to burn on a day like today.' He went around closing the windows as he always did when the air was thick.

Sophie privately thought that the strange atmosphere within the house was far more threatening than any conditions outside it. She could no longer blame the unsettled mood on the stranger in their midst. After last night's outburst, she had to admit that some (all?) of the responsibility lay with her. Sleep had dispersed the ambiguities and confusions that had led to her flare-up, leaving her only with a sense of shame that was compounded by the fact that the children had witnessed it. It must then be up to her to salvage what was left of the weekend, to remind all of them that they could still unite in pleasure as well as grief.

She had changed her mind about scattering Lydia's ashes. She was fairly confident that if she did not mention the subject again no one would press the matter. With Edie on her hip, Sophie went to Rowan's room to check that the urn was still safe. She placed Edie on his pillow and ran her fingers over the bedclothes and then through them, feeling uneasy first at this intimate trespass and then because she found nothing. Panic had begun to brew in her belly when she noticed the urn standing alone at one end of the shelf that had been cleared of all Lydia's things. This time she did not recoil but picked it up. It was surprisingly light. The ashes shifted like the sand in Edie's toy maracas as she tilted it first to the left and then to the right. How could someone so determined, so full of life as her mother, diminish to this?

'I think it might be starting again, Mum,' she said to the urn, almost laughing because if talking to a pot of carbon dust didn't signify that all was not well, what did? 'What should I do? What would you do?' The answer was as clear as if Lydia had spoken: she would have turned to her husband, as she always did. Sophie saw with piercing clarity that if she was going to survive this, if it was happening again and she was not to be consumed by it, she needed Will on her side. They might not have the unassailable marriage of her parents, but neither was it irretrievably broken down, not yet. The children were already aware of the frost between their parents, and Toby and Leo were old enough to remember what she had been like last time. She could not do this to them again. Perhaps the real purpose of this weekend was not to heal the family that had made her but to save the one she had created.

* * *

Felix suggested giving Kerry a guided tour of the valley. Everyone went, even though they all knew the land well enough to walk it blindfold – which was just as well, as the mist thickened in pockets, so that visibility was sometimes reduced to a few feet. Even Jake didn't demand to be left alone in the barn with his phone, although the way he remained a steady five paces behind Kerry, who was wearing tight black leggings and a short jacket, suggested he might be motivated by something other than familial solidarity.

'Jake's got a stiffy!' Leo told Toby in a stage whisper, at which Will stuck his second son under his arm, carried him like a surfboard, and gave him a sotto-voce dressing down underneath a tree.

Sophie made several attempts to fall into step with Kerry and make the apology she still owed her, but it was something she wanted to do in private, and there was always someone demanding something of her, a small hand to be held as they crossed uneven ground, or an adult wanting to finalise plans for the evening.

They took it in turns to carry Edie. At nine months Charlie had refused to be held by anyone other than his mother. Sophie's back was grateful that her daughter would ride happily in other arms, even if her heart sometimes struggled to see it that way.

The only landmarks – a neighbouring farmhouse and the road beyond it – were miles away in the haze. They trudged up to the scattering of shacks and huts in various stages of decay that had witnessed many a childhood game of hide-and-seek and sardines. The only structure whose purpose was recognisable was the old cottage.

'We used to play here when we were little,' Felix explained to Kerry, who had been carrying Edie for the last half-mile or so. 'We'd take camp beds out there sometimes in summer. It's a complete death trap, obviously.' He stood on tiptoe and pulled gently at a slate. It slid to the ground, bringing several of its neighbours thudding down with it. 'Didn't seem to bother Mum and Dad when we were little but now it's all sealed up in case the precious grandchildren break a fingernail or stub a toe in there.'

Kerry nodded gravely, shifting Edie a little higher on her hip. Sophie suppressed a stab of jealousy at the baby's ease with this relative stranger.

She was walking in silence with Tara, when Toby shouldered his way between them and slipped his hands into theirs. Over his head, the sisters exchanged looks that said, He hasn't done this for a while, and then, I wonder what he wants.

'What time are we all going to the Tar Barrels tonight?' said Toby.

'I think you'll be going with Daddy and Grandpa and everyone,' said Sophie. 'But I've got to stay in and look after Edie. She's much too little to take.' She turned to Tara. 'I'm not even sure whether I should be bringing Charlie, to be honest.'

'Oh, Mum,' said Toby. 'You *always* stay with Edie. You never do anything with us any more. Girls are crap.'

'Don't say crap. It's not because she's a girl, it's because she's *little*. And she won't be this young forever.'

'Yeah, well,' said Toby. 'I'll be a grown-up by then, and you won't even care. You don't care about anyone else since she was born.'

'Toby, that's not true!'

'It is. Whatever. No one gives a *crap* if you're there or not.'

He stomped off and was swallowed by the mist.

'I could always stay here and look after Edie,' said Kerry, suddenly materialising at Sophie's right shoulder. 'I don't like the sound of all this fire and crowds and stuff.'

The thought of leaving Edie alone with anyone but family made Sophie panic. Instead of the planned apology to Kerry she found herself on the offensive. 'I don't think that's such a good idea. Here, let me take her.' She hadn't meant to snatch, or for her tone to be so abrupt, but she left Kerry standing with empty arms, whispering a bewildered apology. Sophie walked on and stared fixedly ahead, but could feel Tara's eyes on her.

'What?' she said.

'Give that poor girl a break. Why shouldn't she look after Edie? Why are you always too proud to take help when it's offered?'

Sophie was stunned. 'What's *that* supposed to mean?'

'Me and Matt were just saying how it would be good if you came out tonight. I mean, that it would do *you* good.'

'Oh, I'm glad my private life provides material for your pillow talk.'

Tara clicked her tongue. 'Soph, don't be so bloody defensive. We're all trying to help you, if only you'd let us.' Now she looked down at her feet. 'And anyway, Toby's right. The boys aren't blind.'

'Tara, that's bullshit!' How *dare* Tara judge her? How could someone with only one child know what it was like to love four?

'I'm sorry if I've got the wrong end of the stick,' said Tara, in a flat voice that implied neither regret nor misinterpretation.

What light had struggled through the fog was fading but the boys, led by Jake, were playing MacBride cricket, a game of their own devising with some balding tennis balls, Rowan's old school cricket bat and, incongruously, a basketball hoop instead of a wicket. Sophie sat in the mudroom and kicked off her jacket, wrestling Edie out of her all-in-one. Will came and crouched at their feet, pulling off Edie's wellingtons. Edie slid off Sophie's lap and slithered into the kitchen.

'Tara says that Kerry offered to babysit Edie, but you said no,' said Will, addressing Sophie's knees. '*I'd* really like it if you came out tonight. Have a drink, get some fresh air. It'd do you good. I don't mind driving.'

'It's just – I don't think Edie's old enough to be left on her own.'

She knew what he was thinking: Edie was older than Charlie had been when she abandoned him in the supermarket. It would have been an easy weapon for him to wield, and Sophie respected him for mastering the impulse.

'I haven't got any formula with me, let alone bottles or anything like that.'

'Soph, she's nine months old. She ate a plate of baby pasta bigger than her head at lunchtime. She's hardly going to starve.'

'We don't know Kerry that well.'

'I gather Felix is quite familiar with her. And more to the point, Edie *loves* her. You've seen what they're like together. What's going to happen out here, anyway?' Will swallowed, hard. 'Please, Sophie, do it for me, for the boys, for *us* . . . for you. Put someone other than Edie first. It's just one evening. How often do we get free babysitting? Edie loves Kerry, you can see that. *Please*, Sophie. We *miss* you.' His expression so reminded her of Toby's that even if she had not made a pact with herself to fully return to her marriage she would have been powerless to resist. She felt a bittersweet relief as she surrendered, the flood plain sacrificing itself for the greater good of the city.

'OK, fine,' said Sophie. 'Edie can stay here with Kerry. I'll come with you.'

'Really?' he said. He was still kneeling before her, in a strange echo of the position he had adopted when he asked her to marry him. Then he had taken her hands in his but this time he held out his arms. After only a second's hesitation she slid to the floor, fell into them and held on tight to him for the first time since Edie's birth. His familiar body had changed completely. How had she not noticed how much weight he had lost? Where once had been solid lean muscle she could now feel ribs, a collarbone, vertebrae. His grip on her tightened.

'You know that if it starts . . . if you get ill again, if you can't cope, you know I'm here, don't you? You know you can trust me, that I'll never hurt you again? You know how much I regret it, don't you? Do you know that?'

Sophie wanted to shake her head but found herself nodding. Her shoulder grew wet with his tears.

Sophie fed Edie, changed her into pyjamas and her sleeping bag, placed Cloth Rabbit in the corner of the cot, laid out baby wipes and nappy cream and the change mat across the floor so that everything Kerry might need was easily and instantly accessible. She wrote her mobile number and Will's in large print, as though Kerry were visually impaired, and blue-tacked the piece of paper to the wall above the telephone, telling her to call if she was in any doubt at all about anything. She was still issuing instructions as the others sat outside in the cars, Tara and Matt in the sports car, everyone else in the people-carrier. Jake, thrilled at the prospect of leg-room, called shotgun.

'She shouldn't need changing again now unless she's dirty. If she does, there's a new packet of nappies by her cot. All you need to do is keep her awake for the next half-hour, so you could read to her.' There was a tooth-marked copy of *The Very Hungry Caterpillar* on the coffee table: Sophie thrust it into Kerry's hands. 'She likes this one.'

Outside, Will sounded the horn.

'Come on, Mum, you big snail,' shouted Leo.

'Do say if you don't want to do this,' said Sophie.

'We'll be fine,' said Kerry. With reassuring gentleness she took Edie's wrist and guided the baby's fat little hand into a goodbye wave. Sophie left her daughter with a blown kiss.

As they drove slowly into the thickening night, she was astonished to find herself relaxing. She had expected to feel as though she had left a part of herself behind, but she was eager, impatient, as if on the way to reclaim something much missed.

9

By the time their two-car convoy reached the steep roads around Ottery, the festival was well under way and the streets had long been closed to traffic. Stewards in orange tabards directed them into a makeshift car park in a bumpy field. Jake had a parallel social circle in the town, boys and girls whose parents also had second homes in the area. They were in year-round touch on Facebook and he had been in constant contact with them since coming within range of a mobile phone signal. By the time they parked the car, he had a gang of mates waiting for him at the edge of the field. Sophie gave an internal stutter at the realisation that the last time she had seen these teenagers, who all seemed to have cans in their hands, they had been children not much older than Toby was now.

'Don't forget, we're all meeting back here at *eleven*,' said Tara, tapping the bonnet of the car. 'If you're late, I'll get them to put out a lost child announcement.'

'You wouldn't,' scowled Jake.

'*El-ev-en.*'

They watched his back until he and his friends were blobs in the crowd.

The streets leading down into the town were steep. Smoke rose up to mingle with the mist, so that the acrid, mineral vapour smelled damp. The first time Sophie had inhaled that smell had been over thirty years ago, her hand in Lydia's. Then, they would have to stop every few paces to catch up with someone Lydia knew from her own childhood. Tonight, many of those old faces, and those of their children and grandchildren, would still be present. Then, the crowd would have been a tenth of this size. Tonight, the place was overrun with people from all over the county, students from Exeter and foreign tourists. Then, you were lucky to see more than one police officer all night. Tonight, they lined the route in groups of two and three, and she wondered what percentage of the county's constabulary were deployed here.

Matt and Tara walked ahead with Felix, who had thrown on the hood he always wore in crowds. Toby and Leo were circling each other with excitement and Sophie was relieved to see that Charlie took his cue from his brothers, smiling and clapping when they did. As the streets narrowed and the crowd thickened, she made sure that each of her sons was attached to an adult. Matt kept his promise to carry Charlie on his shoulders, while Will took Leo's hand and Rowan took Toby's.

In the square, a woman wearing huge mittens made of sacking hefted a barrel of burning tar onto her shoulders to the whoops and catcalls of the crowd. When Sophie was a girl the festival had been menfolk-only and the women were there to dress their wounds afterwards. Felix shrugged off his hood. A voice from somewhere in the throng said, 'Hallowe'en was last week, mate,' to a ripple of laughter, but it was impossible to tell who the culprits were. Felix's exposed face fell, and Sophie experienced the same surge of protective anger she felt when one of her sons came home from school with tales of a big boy picking on him.

'Fuck this shit, I'm going to the pub,' said Felix.

'Oh, *Fee* . . .' said Tara, but he had gone, shouldering his way towards the Lamb and Flag. The queue to the entrance was six deep but Felix parted it like Moses.

'I'll go and make sure he's all right,' said Matt, hoisting Charlie off his shoulders and placing him in Will's arms.

With the ratio of adults to children in their party diminished but still over the crucial one-to-one, the remainder of the family made their way to the funfair where it was easier to see: the heat, the lights and even the sounds conspired to clear the mist. They bought the boys hot dogs and candy floss then gave them money to go on enough rides to make them throw the lot up again. Toby and Leo came to blows over a pound coin.

'It's mine, you asshole!' said Leo.

'*Leo*!' said Sophie. 'You are not American. The term you're looking for is *arsehole*.'

The boys exploded into shocked, delighted laughter. Wasn't that the first thing that had gone last time, her sense of humour? And hadn't its return marked the beginning of her recovery?

'Want to come on the carousel with me?' said Tara, taking Charlie by the hand and waving a fiver at the warring older brothers. She threw a stage wink over her shoulder at Sophie and Will. Rowan caught sight of someone he knew and wandered over to bellow a conversation over the furious dance music pumping from every ride. She could tell from the dip of Rowan's head and the answering hand on his forearm that he was breaking the news about Lydia.

Someone was trying to hold her hand. Automatically she looked down, then up again, to find the hand attached to Will.

'May I have this dance?' he said.

'What?' laughed Sophie. 'It's hardly The Blue Danube, is it?'

'Dance with me.'

He dragged her over the bumpy ground in a clumsy waltz, both of them laughing. For the second time that weekend Sophie felt the butterflies of a teenager on a first date, but now with anticipation rather than dread. They trod on each other's toes as they covered the ground between the dodgems and the ghost train. Frenetically remixed songs by Katy Perry and Lady Gaga battled for supremacy, but when he kissed her, it was as though someone had turned the volume down on the world.

'You're laughing,' said Will, pulling away.

'I'm *smiling*. I feel about fifteen.'

'You look it,' said Will, tucking a loose strand of hair behind her ear. 'It's all going to be all right, isn't it?'

She answered him with a kiss. How incredible it was that a single night out with her husband – and, she could now admit to herself, away from Edie, who she willingly let consume her – had done more to restore her sanity than any talking cure, any medication, ever could. It was so simple. Why hadn't she done this months ago? It didn't feel like an exaggeration to say that this evening had saved her life. She felt little eyes on her.

'That. Is. Disgusting,' said Toby with a pantomime retch.

'So gross,' confirmed Leo. 'Can we have some more money?'

When the pocket money had twice been replenished and depleted, and Tara had prised Charlie from the carousel, the family made their way to the bonfire at the foot of the bridge. It was a twenty-foot conflagration of wood and crates, broken-up MDF wardrobes and old bedframes. As they watched, someone threw a three-legged stool onto the teetering pyre. They were well back from the source of the heat but something had tipped Charlie from nervous wonder into terror. As the sound of the crowd competed with the roar of the flames, he buried his face in Will's shoulder. Then, like a man climbing between window ledges on a skyscraper, he edged his way from his father to his mother until he was clamped onto Sophie, his fists in his eyes. He was rigid with fear, more like a toddler than a four-year-old.

'Ow, Charlie,' she said, feeling the pinch of his fingers through her coat. 'No need for that.'

'Please don't do it, Mummy,' he said.

'Charlie, stop it.' He tightened his grip. 'Don't do what?'

'Don't climb on the fire, *please*,' he said. Guilt rinsed through her.

'Oh, that was just me being silly, yesterday. I promise I won't do it again. Look, this bonfire's big, and there are men standing around it to make it nice and safe.'

'No!' screamed Charlie. 'I don't like it! I want to go home! I hate it here!' He began to thrash. Will tried to pull Charlie's little hands out of his eye sockets but his fingertips became wet with his son's tears.

'Come to Grandpa, Charlie,' said Rowan. 'No blubbing, there's a big boy.'

Charlie screamed, shriller than a firework.

'I want to go home. I want to go *home!*'

Sophie and Will exchanged desperate looks, both recognising a tantrum that had gone beyond the point of no return.

'What can we do?' said Sophie. 'He's terrified, and he's exhausted. Maybe we should go back early.'

'Oh, *Charlie*,' said Will, ruffling the blond head as he thought. 'Look, it's only just gone half nine, it's not fair to cut the other boys' night short. I'll be the quicker driver; if I drop him home now, Kerry can put him to bed and I can be back in time to get the rest of you at eleven. Hey, little man,' he said to Charlie. 'Want to come home with Daddy? Go home and play with Kerry?'

'*No!*' screamed Charlie, a small fist finding its way into Will's face. 'I don't want you, and I don't want Kerry, I want Mummy to take me back and I want Mummy to put me to bed.'

'It's not worth it,' said Sophie, stroking Charlie's hair, drawing on reserves of tenderness and patience deepened to the point of infinity by self-reproach. She was glad now that she hadn't had a second glass of cider. 'I'll do it, give me the car keys.'

Will got them out of his pocket but dangled them over her palm and, with a feeling like a pebble dropping through a well, Sophie understood why he was so keen that he be the one to drive Charlie back to the barn.

'You still don't think he's safe with me, do you?' she said. She had shouted to make herself heard over the noise and chaos and, although Tara didn't acknowledge that she'd heard it, she gave an involuntary twitch.

'Soph, don't be daft,' he said. 'After everything I said this afternoon? I was actually thinking that if you took Matt's car, there would be enough space in ours to bring everyone home, and you wouldn't have to do that drive twice in the mist and the dark.' He half-turned to Tara. 'You keep a spare key, don't you?'

'Oh,' said Sophie. Of course he was right. By the time she had driven all the way back, and settled Charlie, which might take hours. 'Right. Tara, could I . . . ?'

The keys were in her palm before she finished the question.

Will kissed her, this time on the top of her head. 'Wait up for me?' he said.

She fought her way through the throng with Charlie in her arms, whispering soothing nonsense in his ear until they reached the relative calm of the country lane and she felt his body submit into floppiness. He refused to get down and walk, though, and by the time she got to Matt's car, she was exhausted, her legs ached, her back and shoulders were screaming in agony, and she was pouring with sweat. The relief when she set Charlie down on the ground was inexpressible. She took off her jacket, grateful for the cold shock of air on her hot damp body, and folded it in half twice to make a makeshift booster seat for Charlie in the passenger seat.

Before she put the key in the ignition she checked her phone, to see if Kerry had sent her an emergency voicemail.

The screensaver, a picture of Edie asleep with Cloth Rabbit, was clear of messages.

Sophie could not remember having driven with such extreme caution before. The mist was now a solid wall of white, a bizarre inversion of darkness. Had visibility been so poor when they left the house they would not have risked driving in these conditions, festival or not. Headlights did little to disperse it, just spotlit the whirlpools of vapour that spun in mid-air. She had not felt so nervous behind the wheel since her driving test: Will had been right, he was the more confident driver, he would have made a better fist of this. The few cars she passed were all driving with the same tentative care. The fog was dense in patches, strange flashes of clarity before the cloud began to descend again, so that just when her eyes had adjusted, the situation would change and she was temporarily blind again. Fireworks would occasionally illuminate it, tinting the white mint or flamingo or iceberg. Her only consolation was that she was driving the zippy little automatic sports car through these lanes rather than her own lumbering people-carrier.

Charlie's head hit his chest. Good; one less job for her to do when she got back to the barn. She would march him directly up to the bunker, wrestle him out of his boots and let him sleep in the clothes he had on, she decided. Then she would check on Edie, kiss her or maybe just watch her for a few minutes, and after that talk to Kerry, maybe open some wine, see if she could coax some conversation from the girl.

She turned the car into the drive. Down here in the valley the mist was at its most solid and for a second she didn't trust that the barn would still be there. She felt ridiculously relieved at the warm welcome of its lit windows.

Charlie was easy to scoop up out of the passenger seat and Sophie made straight for the stairs. On first sweeping glance she did not see Kerry in the sitting room. Perhaps she was upstairs with Edie. Had she woken to find Sophie not there? The thought was a knife. But there was no sound; if Edie *had* woken, Kerry was doing a good job of settling her again. On tiptoes Sophie mounted the stairs, reassured by the soft light that spilled out of her own bedroom. She laid Charlie down on his bunk, pulled off his boots, socks and coat, tucked him under his duvet and closed the door firmly but silently behind her. With as light a tread as she could manage – although the house still made itself heard – she promised herself that she wouldn't go in and distract Edie or wake her up, but that she'd just look in, check Kerry was coping all right without undermining her.

The room was exactly as Sophie had left it a few hours before, from the sealed packet of nappies to the counterpane hanging over the side of the empty cot, perfectly parallel to its base. Cloth Rabbit remained in pride of place at the head of the mattress. The sheet was smooth, the pillow plump. It had not been slept in at all.

10

Sophie's instinct was to scream, but she managed to tell herself there was no point in losing her cool. Edie and Kerry were somewhere else in the house, that was all. She forced herself to breathe deeply and slowly, concentrated on putting one foot in front of the other. She checked the other bedrooms one by one, starting with Felix's chaotic room, with its unmade bed and its mess of clothes and bags. Inhale, exhale. Left foot, right foot. She progressed to Tara's room, then Rowan's. Inhale, exhale. Left foot, right foot. She checked both bathrooms, pulling back the shower curtains. In each room she entered, she turned on the main light expecting, hoping, to floodlight a blinking, apologetic Kerry. She left all the lights on behind her. This wasn't funny. Inhale, exhale. Left foot, right foot. With each tread on the stairs, she told herself she would find them downstairs.

But when she called Edie's name, and then Kerry's, into the silent cavity of the sitting room, only the tiniest of echoes bounced back. The kitchen was in darkness and so was the mudroom. A few coats and kicked-off boots remained in there, but none was a size six. Were they *outside*? What reason could Kerry have to take Edie out into this fog? Sophie flipped the switch on the kitchen wall that would illuminate the outside light, but the garden remained in darkness. God, of all the nights for the bulb to blow. There was a large torch in the mudroom but its beam faltered a few yards into the swirling garden. At the side of the house she picked out the dull black and orange bodies of Rowan's and Felix's cars.

The country silence was broken only by the odd whistle and bang of a faraway firework. Inhale, exhale. Sophie whispered Edie's name, repeating it until it was a shriek, running back into the house, no longer caring if she woke Charlie as long as his voice was echoed by Edie's. She searched the bright empty bedrooms for anything that would contradict the fact of Edie's disappearance. Inhale, exhale. Inhale, exhale.

Perhaps there had been an accident, perhaps Kerry had had to call an ambulance. Sophie looked wildly around for signs of some kind of tussle, or a fall. There was none, but broken bones and blocked airways would not necessarily leave blood. If something had happened, wouldn't Kerry have left a message on her mobile? Sophie seized on the possibility that a message had been left while she was driving in one of those dead zones that the mobile phone masts couldn't reach. Perhaps she had missed the ambulance by minutes. She waved her mobile phone around in the air, as though sheer force of will could create a signal, then suddenly remembered that she could access her voicemail from a landline, Edie's birthday the code that would grant her access, and walked over to the telephone table. She picked up the receiver. These old phones felt unfamiliar to her, so used was she to speed dialling everything. Something about it felt foreign, wrong. She punched her number in, then waited for it to connect and ring. No sound came. Sophie swore under her breath: now was not the time for her to misdial her own telephone number. She hung up and when she picked up again realised what had really been wrong the first time. There was no dialling tone. The phone was dead.

An animal whimpering escaped her lips and solidified into a swearword. Had Rowan let the line rental lapse? It was out of character but then so was much of his behaviour these days. She took a deep breath. More likely there was a problem with the line that none of them were aware of because the telephone was so rarely used. Had any of them made a call this weekend? Or was it simply a loose cable, pulled from the wall by little fingers? She dropped to her knees, examined the cable for signs of wear, tear or deliberate damage, but it looked perfect. Perhaps then it was loose in its socket. She yanked it out, but it took forever to reinsert into the tricky little hole with its trapdoor. Why didn't they make this easier? When finally she managed to click it back in, she picked the receiver up again. There was still no tone, no lifeline. She bashed the receiver on the wall, carving a chunk from the plaster, and then, incongruously, replaced it very carefully as though she could trick the phone into coming back to life, but there was nothing. She actually relaxed at this. *This* was why Kerry hadn't left a message, the barn phone wasn't working. Why hadn't she left a note instead? Perhaps there had not been time. Sophie and Will's numbers remained stuck to the wall. Perhaps Kerry had been in such a hurry that she had forgotten to take them, and was currently kicking herself for the oversight, or perhaps she had stored them in her own phone and was even now trying to get through. Sophie held her useless mobile phone in one hand, the useless landline receiver in the other, and stared stupidly for a few seconds before some subconscious impetus propelled her into action.

Mobile in hand, she got behind the wheel of Matt's car, turned the key, put the automatic gearbox into drive. She could feel her heartbeat in the soles of her feet and in the palms of her hands as she drove back down the lane, one eye on the road in front of her, the other checking the screen so she would know the second she was in range of a signal. The vehicle that had seemed so easy to drive on the way here suddenly redoubled its unfamiliarity at a time when what she needed most was to go on autopilot and not have to think about driving, and although her left hand was free, it sought the reassurance of the gearstick for something to do. Her attention briefly snagged on the folded jacket on the passenger seat. What was that doing there? She squinted into the mist and tried to calculate—

Charlie. She had forgotten Charlie.

Sophie put her foot on the brake and kept it there. He was asleep, and unlikely to wake up. But what if it had not been an accident but some brewing domestic emergency that had forced Kerry out of the house? It could have been a gas leak; the whole place could be about to blow. The part of her that still believed that there was a reasonable explanation for this, that the answer to the horrible riddle of the vacant barn lay stored electronically in her voicemail, told her that Edie was fine. That belief, along with a sudden vision of a darkening carbon monoxide circle – why hadn't she checked? – and the thought of what would happen if the others came back and found him alone again, sent her back to the barn.

The accelerator on this car was more powerful than she was used to and on the forward motion she shot forward into a hedge. Trying to reverse, she got confused without the clutch to root her feet and depressed the accelerator instead of the brake. Her insides flipped and her body received a powerful dull impact and suddenly Sophie found herself on her back, staring not at hedgerow and track but up through the windscreen into the swirling sky. The car bonnet rose up before her like a great steel wall. It took her precious seconds to understand that the back half of the car was in the ditch. She opened the door, and managed to haul her body out. She landed ankle-deep in the stinking brook. Clods of mud stuck to her legs as she scrambled up the shallow bank.

Turning around, she saw Matt's car at a 45 degree angle. The headlights slashed a lucid diagonal through the haze; not impossible to retrieve but impossible for her to do it alone.

She ran as she had not run since she was at school, cross country. Inhale, exhale, inhale, exhale; her breath ripped open her lungs. She was dimly aware of a creeping cold wetness in one of her boots, saturating her sock. With each stride she felt every fibre of her leg muscles flex and contract.

As she neared the barn, hope began to rise that the whole thing had been a mistake. She wished herself insane, prayed that this was some kind of late-onset postnatal psychosis, would happily sign herself back onto the psych ward for a year if it meant that Edie was near and warm and well and the only terrible power at work here was her own imagination.

The light spilling through the open door promised warmth, welcome, reunion, but the interior remained empty, dead, hostile. There was still no sign of anyone having been there and certainly not of anyone having returned. Inhale, exhale. There was not the faintest trace of gas and the carbon monoxide monitor gleamed innocent and white. She ran up the stairs, leaving a trail of muddy footprints on the runner, picked Charlie up and, bundled him downstairs. Her shoulders were still tender from the effort of carrying him to the car park. How would she get him down the lane? Edie's pushchair, folded in the corner, was meant for someone half Charlie's size but it would have to do. She laid her stirring son on the sofa and tried to use her foot to undo the catch, a one-step move that she had perfected by now, that she had done with a baby on her hip and another child in reins in pouring rain in a supermarket car park, but now, with both hands free, the mechanism defeated her. Careful depression of the correct lever gave way to frantic rattling. Inhale. Inhale. Inhale. Inhale. Inhale.

And then the sound of tyres on the gravel outside, doors slamming, footsteps, angry shouts and frightened cries carrying from darkness into light.

Will was first through the door, his eyes as black as his hair. He gripped her arms.

'Jesus, Sophie, thank *Christ*. I thought something terrible had happened. You're OK? Charlie's OK?' Her insides dropped as she understood that he was reacting not to the mystery of Edie's whereabouts but the discovery of the car in the ditch.

'What's happened, Mum?' asked Toby. Leo stood behind him, his bottom lip trembling.

Sophie's protective instinct swam to the surface of her panic. Snapping on a smile, she mustered enough outward calm to say, 'Tara, could you get the boys into bed, please?' Her voice was controlled but her eyes must have successfully telegraphed the emergency, as Tara went straight into mother mode too, scooping Charlie into her arms and giving orders in a brisk voice Sophie had never heard before.

'Come on, Toby, Leo, up to bed. No ifs, no buts. Jakey, give me a hand?'

'But what's—'

'*Jake*.' Also grasping the gravity of the situation, Jake followed his mother's lead, walking behind Toby and holding Leo by the hand. Sophie waited until the landing door had clicked shut behind the last of them.

'They've gone,' she said simply.

'Who?' replied Will. Sophie let out a noise somewhere between a scream and a growl. Wasn't the lack of them palpable in the house, more powerful than a presence? How could he not have divined the situation from the empty sitting room, from her face?

'Edie! Kerry! I don't know what's happened. Edie's – missing.' The word was a barbed hook being ripped up through her throat. 'They weren't here when I got back. Edie's sleeping bag is gone but Cloth Rabbit's here and the phone isn't working and I can't find out if she's left me a message here and anyway I don't even know which hospital she would have taken her to. That's where I was going in the car, to try to get a signal, in case there's a voicemail. I've been everywhere, all the lights are on, I was screaming in the garden but no one came. She hasn't got any nappies with her, and the boots are gone.'

Will shot a look at Rowan that Sophie couldn't decipher. He seemed confused rather than afraid: his voice was slower than usual, exaggeratedly deliberate.

'Edie doesn't wear boots.'

For fuck's sake. 'The boots Kerry was wearing, you idiot!' said Sophie.

She could almost see him counting to ten to stop himself losing his temper. They didn't have ten seconds.

'OK, let's get to the bottom of this.' Will took both of her hands in both of his, fixed his gaze to hers. 'Tell me what you think you know.'

She broke away from him and threw her arms wide.

'What I *think* I know? Look around you! Look in the bedroom!' Matt took this as an instruction and bounded up the stairs two at a time. 'Edie's gone, Kerry's gone, what more do you need to see? I don't *think* Edie's missing. I *know* she is! *Where are they*?'

'Oh, Christ, oh no,' said Will. His face blanched further as his understanding caught up with hers. Rowan and Felix were a second behind him and for a moment fear rearranged their features so they seemed to resemble each other.

'What do you mean, *missing*?' said Felix. 'There's got to be some sort of reasonable explanation. I don't know, maybe Edie was ill and Kerry took her out for some fresh air.'

'What, all night long? No. Something's happened, they've had to go somewhere. I don't know how, though. Dad's car's still there, your car's still there. I've looked all around outside, I've screamed for them, I've been in every room of the house. She hasn't taken any nappies. What if Edie's hungry? What if she needs changing? What could be so urgent that they had to go somewhere without even having time to pack a *nappy*? What if they're all in the hospital now, and her nappy needs changing?'

'I've had my phone on me all the time,' said Will, slowly. 'There hasn't been a message. Sophie, I don't think it's that . . .'

'*Daddy*?' said Sophie, but it was clear that her father was in no position to provide solutions. His brow was damp with sweat and his eyes bulged.

'I'm calling the police,' said Rowan. He picked up the telephone, dropped the receiver, then began the same futile series of taps and tests that Sophie had conducted. He stared at the mouthpiece. 'It isn't working,' he said, aghast.

'I *told you* that!' Why wouldn't anyone take her word for anything?

'It must be,' said Will, taking the receiver from Rowan and stabbing the number nine three times.

The landing door clicked open and Matt's figure momentarily blocked the light from the landing. Sophie held a second's silly hope that somehow his relative unfamiliarity with the layout and rooms of the barn would enable him to see something she had missed, a trapdoor or secret passage of childhood fantasy. 'It just looks normal, like we left it before we went,' he said. 'Windows all closed, no one's there, there's no, like . . . it's not like there's been a struggle or a break-in or an accident or anything.' Every scenario he dismissed was a door slamming in Sophie's face. 'I'm going to check the back door.'

'It'll be open,' said Sophie. 'I told you, I've been out the back. *They're not here.* I've checked the garden.'

'I'll check it again, then,' said Matt, helplessly, making for the kitchen. 'I can't just sit around here, not doing anything.'

'Right, I'll go and use my mobile,' said Will. 'Sophie, how long have they been missing?'

That *word* again. They needed another word.

'I don't know. I don't know. They were gone when I got back.'

'Hang on a sec, Matt,' said Will. Matt shot back in from the kitchen. 'I'll go and call for help and then I'll go out in the car and look for them. If I give you a lift to the top of the lane, do you think we can get your car out of the ditch and you can take it around and do a separate scout?'

'Of course. Anything, whatever.'

'Stay here. The police won't be long,' Will told her. On foot it would take ten minutes to get to the top of the valley but in the car it would take three or four. Sophie drew comfort from the fact that before the clock next chimed, help would be on its way.

She turned back to her brother. He appeared to have lost control of his hands: they fluttered like winged creatures around his face.

'Felix, is there anything you want to tell me?' she said.

'*What?*'

'Do you know any reason why Kerry might want to take Edie?'

'No!' Felix was violently indignant. 'No, I don't. None of this makes sense to me. None of it *rings true.* Why are you all assuming Kerry's taken Edie? Isn't it just as possible, isn't it actually *more likely*, that someone came and took both of them?'

Sophie pressed her fingertips to her temples to still her spinning mind and allow this new idea to board. It was true that a woman alone with a baby in an isolated house was vulnerable, but only if someone knew they were there. Far Barn was a pinprick on the map, impossible to find unless you were looking for it, and anyway nobody outside the family even knew they were there. Until Kerry offered to babysit earlier that afternoon, it would have been she, *Sophie*, alone with Edie.

'Felix, if that's the case, where are the signs of struggle?' said Rowan. 'You heard Matt, there's nothing upstairs. You can pick up a little baby and carry her without permission,' he looked at Sophie, 'I'm *sorry*, darling – but you can't do the same to a grown woman. It really doesn't look as if anyone else has been here.'

'It doesn't make any sense,' repeated Felix. 'I'm as confused as you are, I just . . . I *know* Kerry.'

Their earlier conversation echoed in Sophie's head, innocent words given terrible new meaning in the terrible new circumstances. 'You don't, though, do you? You don't know the first thing about her background, you admitted it yourself.'

'I know her in the ways that *count*.'

The legs that minutes earlier had carried Sophie at speed through the dark now began to shake. She sank onto the sofa and began to cry.

'Jesus, Felix, just because she's a good shag doesn't mean she can be trusted to . . . It's my fault. It's my fault. What was I *thinking*? What the *hell* was I thinking allowing her to look after my baby? She could be a monster. She could be anyone. Felix, can you think of anything that might explain this, anything about Kerry, anything she's said?'

'Don't you think I'd have told you if I did? I swear on my life, *no*,' said Felix in a broken voice. 'I swear on Mum's memory.

I'm going to search the valley. Dad, I'll go up in the direction of the orchard, if you do the bit past the trenches?'

'Right behind you,' said Rowan, who was on his knees and examining the telephone cord. 'I'm going to give this one last try.'

Blind with tears and swallowing snot, Sophie dashed back up the stairs. Matt had left the landing in darkness. Sophie prayed that the bunker's legendary soundproofing would hold as she scrambled from room to room, flicking the switches on again as though Edie and Kerry were shadows that could be flushed out with light.

She turned to the room that Kerry had been sharing with Felix. Without knowing what she was looking for, she began to search. She turned Kerry's pink holdall upside down and picked through the resulting heap of clothes, dirty knickers, a condom in a tissue, a slippery tube of hair serum that shot from between her fingers and across the room. No purse, no keys, no phone. Sophie didn't know what she was hoping to find. A signed confession? An X-marks-the-spot map describing their whereabouts? When she had emptied the pink bag of clothes and toiletries she turned it upside down and shook it. A single sheet of paper, folded into quarters, slid out of an inside pocket. Before she uncreased it, Sophie knew that it was an official document of some kind, nothing personal, nothing that would shed any light on the state of Kerry's mind or her intentions or what the hell had happened to her baby. At a glance, she recognised it as the paper counterpart to a driving licence photocard, and dismissed it, searching again for something that would lead her to understand where they might be.

It was another minute or two of frantic shaking and searching before the part of Sophie's brain that had scanned the document made contact with her conscious mind. When it happened, her body jerked, like a dog exceeding the bounds of its lead. She stopped tearing at the lining of a jacket, retrieved the discarded licence and this time reread the first line. What she saw made her insides drop.

The printed name was one from her family's past that she had hoped never to see again. She could not guess what it meant in this context, but it could not be a coincidence. The name Kellaway barred the possibilities of accident and spontaneity and threw open the doors to premeditation and violence.

There was only one other person in the family, now that Lydia was dead, to whom it meant something. Clutching the terrible clue in sweating hands, she walked down the stairs to show it to her father.

DARCY

12

My mother had few possessions: the books, a sparse wardrobe of clothes we shared, and a set of Russian matryoshka dolls, the only leftovers from her own childhood, from her half-life before me. The dolls lived on our mantelpiece in place of the family photographs that ordinary people keep in this spot. I doubt that they were worth anything much but with their painted jewel-box colours they seemed as valuable to me as any silver-framed heirloom. I loved the richness of detail, the tiny brushstrokes of brocade on their shawls, the individual eyelashes, the little swirling flowers of their headscarves.

They were for looking at, not for playing with. I never saw my mother touch them but she must have because their arrangement would occasionally change. Usually they would be lined up in descending order of height, with the big-hipped mother doll on the left and the tiny skittle of the baby on the right. The dolls' eyes were slightly cast to one side so that in this arrangement every matryoshka seemed obliquely to smile at her smaller self.

I remember them not in a row but stacked one within the other, seven separate but same selves. I picture them this way not because that is how I last saw them but because something about this formation speaks to me of myself. The outer shell contains everyone I have ever been, a series of identities formed at those points in time when, through no fault of my own, life has become intolerable and I have had to shut down, start again, assume the next in my progression of identities.

Inside the polished exterior I present to the world now is the shell of myself at twenty-two, at seventeen, at fourteen, and of course at twelve, the year I applied to the Saxby Cathedral School and first encountered the MacBride family.

The school was, and is, known locally as the Cath. It is a strange mix of traditional and progressive, fee-paying but with widely advertised scholarships, uniform-wearing but co-educational, and its four-centuries-old walls house science and computer laboratories equivalent to any university. It had always loomed large in our lives, much as its buildings and land and the Cathedral that gave it its name dominated the town. Saxby has city status but it is one of the smallest in England, smaller than many towns, cinched by a ring road that it then had yet to breach, a modern version of the ancient city walls that still remain here and there, chunks of mediaeval masonry between the Carphone Warehouse and Starbucks.

My mother loved the Cathedral Quarter. Its vast sloping greens, the uniform honeycomb stone of its buildings and its ancient, academic architecture of secret quadrangles and cloisters reminded her of the place she had been first at her happiest, and later at her unhappiest. The Cathedral bells were my lullaby and my morning alarm. I remember walking with her around the boundary of the school, my hand in hers, the discrepancy between our strides and the fact that we were out of doors suggesting that I was very young indeed. This school, she promised, would be my salvation as I had been hers, my attendance there the only thing that could justify my leaving her for such a large part of every day. A child as unique and special as I was deserved, needed, a unique and special environment. The Cath had a prep school that accepted children from nursery age, but the upper school's intake began at thirteen, and a single annual scholarship was awarded to one child of this age whose family could not afford to pay for their education. I was eleven when the first official approaches began.

At that time our rooms were on the top floor of a house on the end of the Old Saxby Road that was ripe for gentrification. The houses on our street were let to students, immigrants and those whose rent was paid by social security. The people in the rooms below ours came and went. Whatever their ages and ethnicities, they were always uneducated and incurious like Orwell's Proles; she called them the 'nothing people' and I was forbidden to talk to them. My mother vacuumed the common areas of the building every day, paying as much attention to the patches of carpet that were black with overuse as she did to the corners where the wool was still a soft royal blue. On alternate weeks she washed the walls and the skirting boards. Few people ever climbed the top two flights of stairs to admire our spotless landing. Those callers we did receive tended not to be social. Health visitors, education inspectors, doctors and the occasional bobby, new to his beat, who found me in the city centre during school hours and picked me up for truanting.

School for me was a small room with a narrow frosted window, a single bed and a desk at which I read and wrote and recited and criticised and compared and translated and conjugated and memorised. Theoretically this room was also my bedroom but usually I shared Mother's bed, as she believed that it was not good for me to sleep where I studied. She believed that if both were done in the same space then the opposing necessities of sleep and work would bleed into each other until both were compromised.

It was one of many principles that shaped my childhood. She was as strict with my nutritional diet as she was with my intellectual one, believing that too much food slowed the system down and led to living through the body, instead of the mind.

'We're above all that flesh and blood nonsense,' she often said. 'Our aim is to live entirely in the mind. Only weak and stupid people live through their bodies. We are superior to all

that. We are *cerebral* people. The body is sex and shit and birth
and mucus. What good can ever come of all that?'

She was intolerant of vanity. We had no mirror. Clothes
came from the charity shop and once every six weeks or so
she would hack my hair off at the chin in the same crude
pageboy style that she wore, although mine was an even dull
black while hers was threaded with silver. I knew enough from
my excursions into Saxby city centre to realise that I looked
different to other children my age, and while the subtleties
of fashion were lost on me, it was clear that one aspect of my
appearance had to change.

'*Please* can I have a brace on my teeth?' I'd plead, after I'd
glanced into a shop window and seen a buck-toothed urchin
in an Oxfam jumper blinking back at me.

'Your teeth are perfectly healthy.'

'Other kids my age have braces.'

'Other children your age are also walking around dressed as
gangsters or prostitutes. They don't see any conflict between
being walking hoardings for sportswear and eating junk food
until their blubber hangs out of their denims. It's so important
that you don't define yourself by your appearance now, not
before your character is formed. Anyone who judges you on
the arrangement of your teeth is not someone whose approval
you need. It is your intellect, the words you leave behind you,
that make you who you are.'

The tears would always come then. '*You* had a brace when
you were a teenager!'

She stroked my cheek. 'Yes, I did. I was a beautiful young
woman, and look where it got me.' And then she would fix
me with a stare that brooked no debate and an inhospitable
silence. My mother had a repertoire of silences that put most
people's entire vocabulary to shame. The subtle differences
between the companionable calm in which we spent most of
our days, and the punishing frost that came when I was lazy

or slow, were perceptible only to me. I could hardly blame her for these taciturn rages. Other mothers, lesser women, might have turned the circumstances of my birth against me, but not her. I never felt anything but love and gratitude, and she never put me to bed without breaking her silence.

'You saved me,' she would say, stroking my hair as I fell asleep in the pillows that smelled of us. 'As soon as I knew about you, you were a tiny candle in the darkness, only your flame never gutters, does it, but burns brighter all the time. You will be *brilliant*, Darcy. When my life was . . . stolen, like that, I thought that was the end of it, that I would never be brilliant, that I would never make my mark. And then, when I saw you, I understood at once. We can achieve it all through you, Darcy. I don't want you to be my equal, but my *better*.'

I was twelve when we made it through the initial selection process to the interview stage of the scholarship award. My place at the Cath was presented to me as a fait accompli, and the culmination of her life's work. But in pushing me towards that school, and the family who were as much a part of it as the keystones of its Great Hall, my mother was matchmaking me with her own murderer.

13

December 1996

On the day of the interview Kenneth came to collect me. I was
supposed to call him Uncle Kenneth but he wasn't actually my
uncle or even my mother's, just some kind of distant cousin
on her side, also estranged from the family. Somewhere in
England were an ex-wife and two grown-up children. He had
placed one bet too many and a home had been lost, children
removed from their school in a perfect storm of bitterness
and shame. He frequently pledged never to lose us, his second
family. He could not see that we were never really his to lose.
We belonged only to each other.

Kenneth oversaw those aspects of my education that Mother
could not. His science was decent and he was an inspirational
tutor of mathematics. His entire life was about practical
application of the driest of theories, using complex algebraic
formulae to calculate the true odds behind the bookmakers'
figures. Even his home, a basement flat in the city centre, was
determined by geometry, it being equidistant from the town's
three betting shops with Saxby itself a centrepoint between
the racecourses of Cheltenham, Goodwood and Taunton.

Kenneth was wearing the tweedy green blazer he called
a sports jacket and a dark red tie. I was suddenly conscious
of my charity shop slacks and boxy shirt that were the most
formal clothes I owned.

'Do I look all right?' I said.

' "Dress is at all times a frivolous distinction, and excessive solicitude about it often destroys its own aim",' said my mother (I don't know what other mothers did when they were nervous: mine quoted Jane Austen). 'It's not a fashion show and anyway, there's a chance it could work to our advantage. Apparently they often give it to children from materially poor backgrounds. A child who'd grown up in *care* got it a few years ago. And soon you'll be in uniform, just think! You'll wear that uniform with twice the pride of the other children. To the people of the town, it will speak of privilege and birthright and wealth. And to the other pupils and the teachers you will be a *gifted child*, one who walks the corridors on merit rather than simply through inherited wealth. And *we* will know' – she looped her hand around to include all three of us – 'that you will be restored to the kind of people you come from, an intellectual elite.'

My mother was clever, telling me the story of my birth before I was old enough to understand it. By the time the subtext filtered through to me, my subconscious had been assimilating it for years, and I was less distressed than if it had been broken as news. I vowed never to raise the matter with her directly, and forced myself not to think about it either, sure that if I locked it down securely enough, no password would release it.

Within the laurelled railings the place was familiar yet the perspective was not. I felt as though I had stepped into a famous painting. Inside, the entrance hall was dominated by two staircases which curved like the wings of a giant angel preparing to fly or embrace. The wooden panels of its walls were gilded with the names of boys (and, since the mid-1980s, girls) who had captained sports teams or been heads of their house. I stood for a moment and saw myself climbing those stairs, book under my arm, my clothes replaced by the smart, bottle-green livery of the Cath. I let myself imagine my name painted onto the walls. Games Captain? Head of House? Head Prefect? Unfamiliar with the hierarchies of achievement, I did not know which was the greatest honour. Beside me, I felt Kenneth fidget.

A long corridor was broken up by full-length windows of dimpled glass that cast boxes of light onto the parquet floor. The walls were lined with pews and seated maybe fifteen other candidates. Were they the sum of my competition? For all I knew they interviewed this many children every day for a week. I was the only one not in pristine school uniform, and most of them had both parents there. Many carried musical instruments and immediately I felt my disadvantage; it was the one thing that my mother and Kenneth could not teach me.

The parents swapped rumours about the various scholarships, referring to the 'circuit', and from the conversations that took place above my head I gleaned that most were entering their children for multiple scholarships, up and down the country. They talked about Winchester, Roedean, Marlborough, Wellington, Benenden, schools that I knew encompassed the breadth of England. I was astonished, not by the parents' drive (that expression was as familiar as, and indivisible from, affection) but by the idea that they were prepared to send their children far away in pursuit of their education. My mother had told me time and again that it was Saxby or nowhere, that she could not bear to lose me at term-times. It was already out of the question that she should move house: she could not even leave it to buy food.

A sixth-former, herself a winner of the scholarship, gave us a guided tour before the selection process began.

'This is where we do the exams,' she said with a theatrical shiver, when we were inside the sweeping Great Hall with its portraits and busts.

I was one of the first to be called to interview and was led through double doors to a room with more panelling, deep red carpets and a wide desk behind which sat two men in long black gowns, and an elderly woman wearing a navy pillbox hat.

'Welcome to our school, Darcy,' said the fair-haired man in the middle. 'I'm Rowan MacBride, the admissions tutor.' Even with hindsight I can't honestly claim that I felt any sense of foreboding. 'This is Dr Bedford, our deputy headmaster, and this is Mrs Mawson-Luxmore, widow of the late Judge Mawson-Luxmore, our benefactor. Now, Darcy, I think the first thing to do is to congratulate you on making it this far along the application process. We've had a particularly high standard of applicants this year.' He glanced down at his notes. 'I'm all the more intrigued by your application as it tells me that your achievements come from being home-schooled. The local authority inspectors have been very impressed with the standard of your education, as are we if these essays are anything to go by. We'll test your academic mettle after lunch, of course, but for now I'm interested in things you like to do in your spare time.'

'Oh,' I said. I was thrown; my mother did not believe in spare time. Perhaps by that they meant time away from my mother? In that case . . . I thought of the looping explorations I made of the city when Kenneth was in the bookie's. 'Well. I like to run.'

'Ah, track and field,' said Mr MacBride. 'I ran for the school myself at your age. What's your preferred distance?'

'The longer the better.'

'Ah, cross country. And what's your best time?'

'I don't know,' I admitted. 'We haven't . . . I don't really count it. Perhaps I could do a lap of the Great Hall for you?'

I hadn't meant to make them laugh, but I don't think they knew that, and afterwards the interview went very well.

'Nearly done,' MacBride said. 'We've established what you can offer the school. But why do *you* want *us*?'

All I told was the truth.

'It's very important to my mother, she wants me to be a real success, academically. I've got a lot to live up to; she wants me to do better than her – she never got to finish . . .' Spent adrenalin, or relief that the day was drawing to a close, had loosened my tongue. My throat grew suddenly parched, my tongue seemed twice its size and instead of words, only a freakish noise, somewhere between a click and a cough, came out.

'Are you quite . . . ?' began Dr Bedford, before reaching forward to offer me a glass of water from the carafe on the desk. While I downed it, the adults' eyes locked together, loaded with meaning I couldn't understand. The lady in the pillbox hat made a note and showed it to the men. I croaked my way through a few questions about my favourite periods in history, my voice and composure returning slowly to normal. They thanked me for my time and wished me good luck in the examination.

Back in the corridor, Kenneth obsessively checked his watch like the White Rabbit.

'You're driving me mad,' I said. 'If there's a race on, why don't you just meet me back here at three, when it's all finished?'

'I couldn't possibly leave you here,' he said, but in his mind he was already placing his bets and I was relieved when he went.

They gave us all lunch in the long chilly refectory. The other applicants and their parents exchanged rumours about the scholarship. A Chinese boy with a violin said that if you got in, they sent a big, stiff envelope full of forms while a small thin letter meant you hadn't made the cut. Afterwards we were ushered into the Great Hall where sixteen chairs and tables laid with papers waited. I turned the page with a soaring sense of glee: practical criticism was Wilfred Owen and Rupert Brooke, history was the Russian Revolution and the mathematics and science were so easy that I chewed my pencil not through concentration but to stop myself laughing out loud.

Kenneth was late meeting me, as I had thought he might be. I used the spare time to go into the Cathedral and pray for acceptance into the school. We did not go to church (although of course we kept the King James Bible as a literary text) and I was unaccustomed to the ritual, but I knelt as I saw others doing. When I closed my eyes it was not the face of Christ or the Virgin I saw but that of my mother, and she was smiling.

14

The letter did not come until the other side of a Christmas during which my confidence remained robust. Whenever I reran the exam and the interview in my head I could find no fault in either. It had not otherwise been a good holiday; on the 22nd of December the doctor had been to visit, wasting his peppermint breath on advice about fresh air and exercise and telling my mother that it would be a good idea if she could visit him at the surgery next time. She pressed the prescription he gave her with the others, in the gap between *Emma* and *Persuasion*, and did not speak again until Christmas lunchtime, when Kenneth arrived with a John Lewis hamper that made her recoil.

The letterbox finally broke its silence after noon on the 10th of January. The envelope was small and flimsy. What did that boy know, I told myself as I dragged my feet up the stairs. I couldn't have failed. I'd done my best. I couldn't have let her down. It was unthinkable. But as my mother read, her lips thinned to razors.

'I don't understand,' she said, handing the letter to me. I scanned it, took in something about the high standard of applicants before the letters began to swim. 'You said it went well.'

'I thought it did!' I said. At first I mistook her silence for anger at me, but it was more of a contemplative hush. In the street outside, someone threw a series of bottles into the banks. Further away, the Cathedral clock chimed the quarter-hour.

'Well then, there's been some kind of mistake,' she said eventually. 'Of *course* you got in. You were *destined* to. This, "Rowan MacBride, admissions tutor",' – she spat quotation marks around his name and title – 'he's obviously got you muddled up with someone else. I'll have to . . .' She looked at the telephone, reached out, snatched her hand back as though it were hot. I remain unsure whether that was the point at which her agoraphobia expanded to include outgoing telephone calls, or if it was just the first time it happened in front of me. Then she was at her desk, writing a letter of her own. When she had finished she handed it to me and said, 'This is asking for an investigation to see how the mistake was made, and asking them to put it right. Remember it might just be that this Rowan MacBride's secretary put the wrong name on the letter. Be gracious about it, show them how well brought up you are. It's going to be terrible for the other boy or girl who thinks they've got a place, but what else can we do?'

I made the miserable, pointless walk into town last as long as I could. By the time I approached the Cathedral Quarter it was half past four and Rowan MacBride was leaving school, wrapped in a thick grey coat and a school scarf. I watched him turn right into Cathedral Passage, the narrow, covered alleyway that ran between the high school walls and the back of Cathedral Terrace, a long row of four-storey townhouses in the same faded gold stone as the school and the Cathedral. The terrace broke halfway along the alley, and he disappeared through the back gate of one of the corner houses.

I could hardly follow him, so I walked through the gap in the alleyway and viewed Cathedral Terrace face on. The pavements were worn flagstones and the lampposts the original Edwardian fixtures, and a grassy bank lined with mature plane trees set the houses back from the pavement and the Cathedral Green beyond. Each small front garden had been tastefully converted into a short driveway.

He had entered number 34. I climbed the steps and pressed the bell, a little white ceramic button set in concentric circles of polished brass. The door was opened by a girl in her late teens who had the kind of looks that made a mockery of my mother's attempts to make me invulnerable to beauty. She had smooth blonde hair, English Rose skin, a straight arrowhead nose and full lips that parted to reveal a flash of complex orthodontistry.

'Hello,' she said.

I tried to talk without showing my own teeth, but it was impossible. 'Is Mr MacBride in?'

'Dad!' she shouted over her shoulder. 'He's got selective hearing when the cricket's on. *Daaaad*! Visitor!'

I turned my attention to the interior of the house. The doors were inset with stained glass harlequin windows that threw diamond lights on the mosaic floor. When Rowan MacBride opened one, the hall became a kaleidoscope. His daughter finally tore her gaze from my mouth and flitted through the door before it closed.

'It's me,' I said, but his face was blank. Anger bubbled inside me. Only days ago he had written the letter that had ruined my life and my face was already dismissed from his memory. I gave my full name, one he had read out and written down. He had signed the letter addressed to it. Still nothing.

'I'm sorry,' he said. 'Can I help you?'

I held out the letter. This time recognition did dawn.

'*Ah.*'

'I've come to ask for another chance. Another interview, another exam. Can I make some kind of appeal?'

'I'm sorry, Darcy. As the letter says, there was a very high standard of applicants this year, and I'm afraid that one boy had the edge over the other children, a prodigiously gifted musician.'

Two more children, a boy and a girl, also blond – what was this place, some kind of Aryan breeding experiment? – emerged in the hallway. This time they were about my age. She wore the uniform of the Cath, a pleated skirt and V-neck sweater. He was dressed for its prep school in shorts and tasselled knee socks. The boy in particular looked anachronistic, like an evacuee from the Second World War. They must have been as aware of the chasm between their privilege and my disadvantage as I was. I felt my heart harden against the whole family.

'If I don't get into this school, my life is over,' I said in that strange new parched voice.

'Well, that's rather dramatic, and it's certainly not true,' he said. 'The comprehensives round here are *excellent*.'

Now his hypocrisy fired my resentment.

'If the comprehensives are so good then why don't *they* go there?' I asked.

'Felix, Tara, back inside now,' he said without looking at them. This time his tone was slow and deliberate. '*Excuse me.* How I educate my children has nothing to do with you. The place has been allocated this year, to a deserving child, and there really isn't anything I can do to help you. I'm sorry. Good evening.'

The door was as solid as a wall.

I looked up to see the boy and the girl, Felix and Tara, in an upstairs window. I had already begun to return her smile when I realised that she was forcing her top teeth over her lower lip and raising her hands up beneath her chin to impersonate a rodent. Through the plate glass I heard her brother squeak. They laughed so hard they had to wipe their eyes.

I kept it together on the walk home but the minute I was back in our rooms I cried. 'I'm so sorry. I did my best. I only wanted to make you proud of me!' I told her everything: the lovely house so close to the school. How Rowan MacBride hadn't even known who I was. How his beautiful daughter had stared at me as if I was a freak (even as I told the tale through tears, there was a tiny part of me that was hoping this might sway her on the braces front. I was only twelve, after all). The casual way he had told me that my scholarship had gone to a musical prodigy. How his children had laughed at me. By the time I had finished, Mother was rigid with fury; her hands were all knuckles.

'To reject, then bully, a *child*,' she hissed. 'What kind of people are these MacBrides? All the power and the privilege they have and they abuse it like that. I can't bear to hear it. I am in *unimaginable* pain. The way to hurt any parent is through their children. What happens to you happens to me.'

'Oh, I wish I hadn't told you!' I said. 'I didn't want them to hurt you, too!' I lost control again, hating myself even more in the light of what she'd just said, every tear I let slide a fresh strike on the raw welts of her own pain.

'Oh *darling*, no, I don't blame you. You know how special you are. You *know* that. I blame them. Not only stupid for not recognising what you are but rude and cruel, too. This is typical of academia, I'm afraid: those that deserve aren't always those who receive. Well. We'll get to the bottom of this. I'm sure there's more to this rejection than meets the eye. We won't let that school – that family – get away with this.'

Suddenly she leapt up from the bed, and her grief-mask was replaced by a bright smile.

'Well! We mustn't let this little setback slow down your studies! We've got to coach you into *Oxbridge*, darling. We've got even more to prove now. Maybe if we really cram, you can go a year or so early . . . Do you know, I think you're probably old enough to start some Spenser.'

She stood on tiptoe, retrieved a brick-like anthology from

her highest bookshelf, sat down and patted the bed next to her. This lively, mad optimism was almost more intolerable than her pain, but still I nestled into the curved steel of her embrace and began to read aloud from *The Faerie Queen*.

The hour for supper came and went. When hunger got the better of me and I asked if we had anything in, she gestured to the sugar-free sweets in a bowl on the windowsill. I ate some of those while I made a cup of tea for both of us. She had stopped taking milk in hers and all we had was the powdered sort. I ate crumbling lumps of that, forcing them down like the bulge in the throat that heralds tears.

15

On the first day of the autumn term I watched the new intake of Cath pupils pour through the school gates. The youngest MacBride, Felix, was among them. He was accompanied by his older sisters, their father – who looked smaller without his gown – and a mother who waved them off, blew kisses through the railings before returning, shadowed by me, to 34 Cathedral Terrace. She seemed in many ways the inverse of my own mother – fair, plump, happy and confident, diluted between three children and a husband instead of poured, concentrated, into one child. The family was everything we were not, and had everything we did not.

I spent a great deal of time that autumn walking the streets of Saxby, from the market place to the ring road to the little ancient warrens that threaded the Cathedral Quarter. I always contrived to pass Cathedral Terrace, and would pause before number 34, leaning against one of the plane trees to watch the family. Dark can see into light, but not vice versa. They did not hang net curtains in their huge plate windows, so after dusk the house became a little toy theatre, the MacBrides playing out their domestic dramas against the deep red walls of their sitting room. I say dramas; there was little conflict in that self-reflecting, self-satisfied household. They seemed to be entirely ignorant of the world outside and the pain they might have caused to those with whom they shared their city.

I would stand for hours, watching them come and go, a warming envy in my veins, before returning to our rooms on the Old Saxby Road, where the litter was piling up and the stairs had not been vacuumed for months. Since the rejection, Mother had lost what little weight she had ever carried. She spent hours with her head in her hands, as though it was heavy with the weight of her task, working out where things had gone wrong and looking for a way to redress the balance. Sometimes she wouldn't even notice me come in.

It was not uncommon for me to find her going over my entrance letter, or the mock examinations she had set me before my entry, convincing herself that the standard of my work was enough to scrape an A Level pass, wondering again what had happened to intervene between me and my birthright. She laid the blame entirely at Rowan MacBride's feet, spoke endlessly of his poor judgement and bad manners. I wondered if she protested so violently against him because it cost her too much to think that the one at fault might be me.

One afternoon in late October, I was making the day's final circuit of the Cathedral Quarter when I saw Felix MacBride in conversation with a red-haired girl. Their uniforms were a jealous green. She carried a flute while his little black case contained what I guessed to be a clarinet; the timbre of their voices corresponded with their instruments. The wind was behind them so that their words were thrown over their shoulders, and I could hear them from a distance of ten paces.

'My mum doesn't do paid work,' honked Felix. 'She only does voluntary work, because she wants to be around for us.'

'My mum does,' trilled the girl. 'To set an example.'

'To pay the school fees, more like. *My* father hasn't had to pay for *my* education.'

'How come?'

Felix tapped his nose with one finger. 'It's not what you know, it's who you know.'

It was the carelessness of his arrogance that did it; I felt a tugging sensation deep within me, as though some tethered force was beginning to strain at its moorings.

A large black car was parked across the entrance to Cathedral Passage. The girl climbed into it without much of a goodbye. Felix continued down the alleyway, the school wall high to his left, the back walls of the terrace running to his right. The city itself seemed designed for that boy's convenience. I fell into step behind him, synchronising our footsteps so that the sound of my own shoes on the flagstones would not alert him to my presence.

Felix was halfway along the passage when the bells began to ring out for five o'clock and suddenly the dark force inside me came loose. I ran to push him face-down onto the cobbles. The clarinet case flew out of his hands and fell open on impact with the floor, the components of the instrument rolling and bouncing on the stones. Felix, still in the prone position of his pratfall, reached to grab a little black cylinder; I stamped on his fingers. I was possessed. I had never done anything like this before and I wondered why not, because this feeling was a primal savage high. A boiling river that flowed from a place too deep to name poured through the levee of my anger at Felix. Despite my inexperience, instinct told me the best places to hurt him. My violence was disproportionate to my size and Felix's terror blinded him to the ease with which he could have overpowered me. The clock was still striking the hour; each knell a corresponding injury, a foot to the ribs, another to the face. Felix had curled into a ball, his hands over his head. His pale chin provided an ideal target for a kick but at the last second he moved, and instead of the expected crack there was a squelch as the flesh of his face surrendered to the toe of my shoe.

Softness brought me to my senses where resistance had not, and I stopped.

I seemed to have a gargoyle's eye view of myself, standing before Felix as he whimpered through his fingers. What had I done? What had I done? What had I *done*? Fear and regret poured into the place so recently vacated by anger, and cowardice, too. When the first blood seeped through Felix's cupped hands, I left him moaning on the ground and ran through the gap in Cathedral Terrace.

Rowan MacBride was putting a bag of rubbish in the bin outside his house; he looked up, but I was halfway across the Green before recognition had a chance to dawn and anyway, my face was hardly foremost in his memory. Across the Green I stopped to recover my breath and try to make sense of what I had just done. My instinct was to cover my tracks; whatever rogue criminal spirit had possessed me for that terrible minute in Cathedral Passage had evidently deposited some kind of folk wisdom before it had left me. I ducked into the British Heart Foundation shop and picked a pair of nearly-new size four trainers from the shelf. They were a perfect fit. My old shoes, which I now saw glistened red around one buckle, I threw into a rubbish bin just outside the city centre.

The policeman turned up on my doorstep at the same time as me. His gleaming badge identified him as PC089.

'You on your way back from the Cathedral Quarter, by any chance?'

A fresh wave of fear engulfed me. 'Me? No.'

'We'd best talk this through with your mum anyway. Is she in?'

It was the one certainty. I knocked four times. 'It's all right, Mother, it's only the police.'

'How many times?' she said, when she saw my uniformed escort. 'Darcy is *home-schooled*.' Three miles away, the Cathedral clock rang out for evensong, and I watched the realisation dawn that they wouldn't pick anyone up for truanting at this time of the day. 'What's happened? Has someone hurt you?' She tucked my hair behind my ear, looked to the policeman.

'May I come in?' said PC089, shoving his way through the door. He took in the shabby room, eyeballed the books as though trying to decide what on earth they could be. My cheeks burned as he glanced down at the carpet, where my mother's fallen hair had begun to mesh itself into a loose, dark weave. 'PC Jon Slingsby, Saxby Constabulary. We've had a report of a child being mugged in Cathedral Passage.'

'Oh, my God, *darling*!' and then, 'Do we have to go to the station?'

'Darcy isn't the victim.' He turned to me. 'We have eyewitness reports of you being at the scene.'

My mother turned her gasp into a laugh just in time. 'When is this "mugging" ' – those quotes again, only this time she smiled them around the words – 'alleged to have happened?'

Slingsby pulled out his notebook. 'We can pinpoint the exact time of the attack to 5 p.m., because the clock was chiming the hour.'

'Well, that's easy. We were here, together, doing our prep,' said my mother, waving a hand towards my study. She lied for me without hesitation because she thought she knew me to be incapable of violence.

'Prep?'

'I suppose someone like you would call it homework. Although it's *all* homework really. As I told you, we have all Darcy's lessons here. I can give you the number of the local education authority, we're in constant touch with the inspectors. Look, is this an actual *arrest*?'

My empty guts churned; I wished she wouldn't call his bluff.

'Not yet,' he said. 'We're waiting on a positive ID from the victim.'

When he had gone, my mother unhooked her smile and shivered.

'What in heaven was that about?' she demanded. 'And what are you wearing on your feet?'

I was about to explain and apologise when a hammering on our front door shook the windows in their frames. We peered through the nets at the street. A black Range Rover was parked at an acute angle to the kerb, the front wheel on the pavement, driver's door open. Rowan MacBride was standing directly underneath us, his face dark with rage. I felt my mother's hand slacken on my shoulder.

'Kellaway! Darcy Kellaway! I *know* it was you, I know I saw you. You've been hanging around outside my house for months. Don't think I haven't noticed. If I'd had any idea you were going to . . . I mean, I knew you had a strange sense of entitlement, but this . . . what the *hell* has *Felix* done to *you*?'

The street came alive at the drama. The students opposite actually sat themselves in the window, swinging their legs over the edge of the sill. Rowan's academic authority carried no weight on a street like ours, used to the genuine menace of bailiffs and drug pushers; this was light relief to them. 'When my son is out of hospital, I'm going to the police again. We won't let this go until charges have been brought against you and have stuck. A civil case isn't out of the question. In the meantime, if you come anywhere near my family again, if you come anywhere near my *school*' – at the mention of the word 'school' the little claw on my shoulder resumed its grip – 'I will dial 999 without hesitation, do you understand?'

Again he stared into the blank glass of the ground-floor windows, as if expecting an answer. Finally he gave a little slump of defeat and returned to his car. The audience dispersed. Mother turned on the bedside lamp. The dull gold glow threw her face into a relief map of hills and caves.

'I don't know what came over me,' I said. 'He was swinging this stupid clarinet all over the place and bragging about how he didn't even have to pay for his school fees, and I just thought, it's so unfair, that he should get to go there and I—'

'He had a clarinet?'

'What's that got to do with—'

'And he definitely said that his family haven't paid for his education?'

'Yes, but—'

'And when you went to the house, MacBride said, didn't he, that the scholarship had gone to a musical prodigy?'

I could almost hear her synapses fizzing. She punched her palm. 'Of course. Of *course*! I ought to have worked it out myself.'

'Uh?' She was leaving me behind, the way she sometimes did when she raced through a text I'd never seen before.

There was a loaf of bread on the sideboard. To my utter astonishment she pulled off a big hunk and began to chew.

'He'll have given the scholarship to his own child!' she said through a dry mouthful. 'Academics are notorious for nepotism, closed shops, old boys' networks. The minute they get found out, they close ranks and sling mud. God knows, I should know that better than anyone.'

I flinched: even an oblique reference like this put me on high alert, but she was high, soaring on a current I couldn't see. I let myself believe that her conclusion was the correct one: the world was full of things she understood better than I did.

'You're going to have to be clever about it from now on,' she said.

She'd lost me again. 'Clever about what?'

'*Revenge*, darling! They stole your intellectual birthright. Of course you're right to be angry, to want to get your own back. But it ought to be cerebral. Anyone can go in with fists flying. Violence is down there with sex and drink, and . . . and *shit*. They stole your future. They stole your *future*, Darcy. How can a few cuts and bruises, only the body, which is *nothing*, atone for that?' It was the means, not the end, of my behaviour that she disapproved of. From her words I was able to wring forgiveness that made the incitement that followed easy, logical, necessary. 'You're going to have to do better than that. Seek revenge, but make it like-for-like. This isn't boxing. It's chess.'

Her eyes shone with an enthusiasm that cancelled my misgivings. I gave myself up to the pursuit of our new common goal. I lay awake for hours, excitement and fear conspiring against sleep. I wondered what we would have to do, what we could take from that family, to ever make it enough.

16

To find evidence of the original corruption would expose MacBride for his hypocrisy. My mother and I were agreed on that. She began by writing to the school and asking if we could see a copy of the records for the scholarship that year. While we didn't expect MacBride to be so stupid as to commit to paper hard evidence of his corruption, we were confident that some slip, some omission would lead us in the right direction. She exchanged increasingly terse letters with a secretary, probably in MacBride's thrall, who told her unequivocally that the Cath was under no obligation to make its records public.

We agreed that our only option was somehow to infiltrate the establishment. We did try to enlist Kenneth in our plans but he was hurtfully dismissive of them, trivialising my mother's conclusions as fantasies. Without him, we struggled to hatch plans that I could carry out alone.

While my mother directed our play, I was, when it came down to it, unaccompanied on the stage. I alone carried the performance.

I saw Felix and Tara in the market place on a December afternoon. The square was tastefully sprinkled with Christmas lights that picked out their bright hair. Brother and sister were wired together by the earphones from Tara's CD player. Felix seemed to have dropped a couple of inches from his height and the swagger had left his step. He didn't swing his shopping bag but held it close to his chest. They stopped to buy horse chestnuts from a steaming brazier. I drew closer. Tara had put on a little weight, and grown taller. She wore her hair in two pigtails, creating an unfortunate Brünhilde effect. Felix's hair had grown longer, to hang in front of his eyes. A breeze lifted the wing of his fringe to reveal a hollow of shiny red skin that whirlpooled to a glistening orifice where his right eye had been. At the sight of it, I lurched so violently that I turned around to see who had pushed me but there was no one there. My left foot tingled as if recalling the contact it had made with his flesh. Rowan MacBride's accusing voice seemed to play in discord with my mother telling me that I had been right to get my own back on Felix. I throbbed with shame and confusion, but also a sense of my own power. I think I cried out. I prepared myself for recognition, accusation, conflict, but Felix's blank half-stare passed through me and out the other side again. I was still nobody to him.

Their indifference shielded me in an invisibility that allowed me to follow them back to Cathedral Terrace. When they got home, Tara yanked Felix's earphone out.

'Ow! Fuck *off*,' he said, and flicked her on the forehead.

'*You* fuck off,' she said, flicking his head back before unlocking the front door. A dozen fobs swung from the keyring. Felix pushed past Tara into the house and her bulging carrier bag burst, sending bubble bath and chocolate wrappers, clothes and CDs everywhere. She scrabbled to pick them all up before kicking the door closed behind her. The key stayed in the door.

I waited a few minutes for Tara to realise her mistake, or for a passer-by to notice and knock, but it started to drizzle. Umbrellas went up and heads went down. With a hammering heart, I crept up the rain-darkened steps, and retrieved the keys. Sheltering under a plane, I examined the bunch at close quarters. Amongst the charms and trinkets were four keys, one so small it must fit a window lock. A blue plastic fob had the number 4035 written on it in ballpoint. There was a while-u-wait key cutting place on the other side of the Green; I was there and back within fifteen minutes, high on my own daring. I tiptoed up to the front door and slowly, soundlessly replaced Tara's originals in the keyhole, and went home to show my new set to my mother.

We studied those keys until their tiny metal ramparts were imprinted on our minds. She wrote the number 4035 in her notebook even though I had committed it to memory at first glance. 'I expect it's the number for her bank card,' said my mother, 'To make it nice and easy for pickpockets to clear her bank account as well as get into her house. I don't know what qualities the girl inherited from her father, but cunning wasn't one of them.' She steepled her fingers and pressed them to her brow. 'There will be something in that house that shows that Felix isn't entitled to his education. Modern life always leaves a paper trail,' she said, gesturing to the box file that held everything from our birth certificates to our NHS cards.

The more specifically she talked about it, the more ridiculous it seemed.

'Let's not get our hopes up,' I said. 'That stuff's probably all in some office in the school somewhere. If they even kept it.'

'Well, darling, you're hardly going to find a signed confession, are you? But bank statements, school correspondence, there will be *something* that we can use, even if we have to get an expert to follow the trail. Now, let's think. We can't take it to the school authorities. It's likely that the board is complicit in the corruption. The local newspaper is the obvious choice. Or a *national* newspaper? The *Times Educational Supplement*, perhaps, or the *Guardian*. Once we've exposed the scandal, if they pay us for the story, they'll be out of the school, we can appeal, we might even be able to pay your fees ourselves.

We could get you in well in time for A levels, darling. What do you think?'

Animation and happiness were so rare that I could not help but humour her.

'Yes' I said. 'They'll rue the day.'

17

Was there a busier house in Saxby than 34 Cathedral Terrace? There was always someone coming, someone going, adults, teenagers, old people. Sometimes I would wait for hours in front of an empty drive and unlit windows, I would gather my courage, and just as I stepped from behind the plane tree the front door would swing open and one of them would appear, or the car would pull up outside and all five of them would emerge. It seemed the place would never be empty.

Far from resenting the delay, I would have postponed the trespass indefinitely. My mother was buoyant with hope, happy in a way that I had not seen her since the years before my application to the school; if this was a delusion, I was happy to nurture it. It is better to travel hopefully than to arrive.

But there was still the outside chance that my mother's hunch was right, and I finally breached the threshold late on a Saturday afternoon, eight hours into an all-day vigil. My copied key slid in as though oiled but immediately a shrill repetitive beep sounded, increasing in frequency and volume. On the wall I saw a little white box gemmed with emerald and ruby lights flashing in syncopation, the words 'INPUT CODE' flicking across the dot matrix and seconds counting down to zero. The beeps were approaching a continuous screech when I realised it was a burglar alarm. I neutralised it with four seconds to spare, using the code from the keyring. I was in.

I explored the red sitting room first, where huge framed posters for art exhibitions in European cities shared wall space with real oil paintings. A silver-framed print of the family, windswept and laughing outside a big black barn that looked like a church without a steeple, had pride of place on the grand piano.

The fridge in the basement kitchen was obscenely well stocked. There was a huge year planner on the wall above the bin; the present date was struck through with the word 'Devon' written across the next four days in pink highlighter. The chart marked the rhythm of the household. Everything was written down, from Felix's orchestra practice and Sophie's term dates to the day the cleaner came (I made a mental note to keep out of the way on Wednesday mornings) and Tara's modern dance lessons. Lydia spent the second Friday of every month at Saxby District Magistrates' Court. Was she a *magistrate*? It didn't seem modern, or feminine: but then I had drawn most of my ideas about the magistracy from Fielding and Dickens.

I scaled the stairs, then worked my way down through the bedrooms. The desk in Felix's bedroom had another chair by it, as though someone else habitually helped him with his homework. I opened his geography exercise book. An essay about land reclamation in the Netherlands was so badly written I had to stop reading after the third paragraph. This was not a boy who deserved a scholarship.

Under Tara's bed I found a little red safety deposit box covered in band stickers. The smallest key on my bunch opened it to reveal a shiny ravioli of condoms, and a half-smoked packet of cigarettes. Tara was only one academic year older than me, but already she had crossed the threshold into the adult world that my own underdeveloped body suggested would never be mine.

Sophie was the eldest by some years but the gymkhana rosettes and talcum scent gave her bedroom the innocence of a child's rather than a girl on the verge of womanhood. A University of Durham sweatshirt hanging next to her old school hat was the only clue to her age.

On a mezzanine level opposite a bathroom was a room that seemed to be the administrative heart of the house, lit by a little stained-glass window set high in the wall. An embroidery sampler cross-stitched with the word 'Mummy' was propped in the corner of the large pine desk. A cherrywood bookcase with scrolled edges bulged with box files labelled *Children, School, Insurance, Car, Choir & Church, Health, Campaigns, Current Account, Savings & Investments, Pensions, Court, Devon, Moorfields Eye Hospital.*

I went through these files systematically and with diminishing excitement and confidence in my mother's theory. *School* was nothing more than reports. *Children* was a batch of birth certificates, christening cards, child benefit numbers and so on. *Current Account* did not contradict her theory – a year's worth of statements and cheque stubs showed not a single payment of school fees – but neither did it confirm it.

After that, each file held increasing irrelevances. By the time I got to *Campaigns*, I knew that Lydia MacBride sat on a dozen committees, one against a new housing development outside the ring road, another against a mobile phone reception mast somewhere called the Otter Valley, and that she was, rather too late, lobbying the council to install CCTV in Cathedral Passage. In despondency I turned to her bookshelves. Paperbacks and classics sat beside textbooks about the justice system and psychology and youth offending. Cruel as her husband and children were, I could find little to despise about Lydia MacBride.

The Cathedral clock rang seven o'clock, and I had promised to be home by half past. My mother was gracious in the freedom she gave me – she did not want her prison to become mine – and I could not abuse that grace by missing an agreed curfew.

I rearranged the papers as I had found them, feeling an echo of the way I'd felt the time I'd had to tell Mother that my appeal to Rowan MacBride had been rejected on the doorstep of this very house. I reset the alarm and let myself out through the back door using the old-fashioned Chubb key, slinking through the courtyard and the back gate into and along Cathedral Passage.

She was understandably disappointed when I didn't come home with something more concrete, but I think I went some way to appeasing her by making my own chart with the information I had cribbed from their calendar. This also enabled me carefully to plan future intrusions.

'It's all right, we've got another couple of days until they come back.'

I found nothing more that weekend, but got to know the house so thoroughly that I could have searched it in the dark. I always visited in the day, when no light from within would signal my presence. I used the rear entrance, like a servant. I went there as often as I could, made searches and dispiriting re-searches of that office, but to our increasing despondency, nothing ever turned up.

To counter my growing sense of impotence I began little interim revenges on all of them, tiny surges of power that kept me going until the ultimate retribution. Some were just for fun, such as repeatedly loosening the bulb in the reading lamp next to Rowan's bed, or spitting in their food.

Other revenges were less petty. In the blind alley of Cathedral Passage I saw Tara kissing another pupil from the Cath, a good-looking black boy. The sight of them made my skin sizzle. The next time I was able I checked her deposit box and was not surprised to find that she was now buying her contraception in packets of twelve. Using the smallest needle from the sewing kit in Lydia's study, I carefully pierced the rubber all the way through each prophylactic, taking great care to smooth the foil back down again afterwards. That day, triumph made me careless and I let myself out of the front door for the first time in weeks. On the street I almost literally ran into PC089, the one who had questioned me over Felix's attack. A split second earlier and he would have seen me descend the steps.

'Fancy seeing *you* here,' he said. He had changed since our first encounter, his face somehow giving the impression of accelerated ageing without a single line or grey hair. 'Scene of the *alleged* crime. I never forget a face. Or a name, Darcy Kellaway.'

I could feel his eyes on me all the way down Cathedral Passage, long after I had turned the corner.

18

'What are these stains, here on your trousers? They won't come out,' said my mother, holding up my grey woollen trousers to the light. Strange dark patches traced the stitching of both pockets.

'I don't know,' I said, flushing hot to the skull and turning my face to the wall so she could not read me.

'Very curious,' she said but her tone was flat. She was staring at the wall, wearing her new permanent expression, the wide-eyed baleful look of a marmoset. Her body had become more simian, too, a fine black lanugo downing her matchstick limbs.

As she developed ever more elaborate ways to avoid eating, my cunning kept pace with hers. The public library had a small shelf of cookery books and I returned time and again to a French recipe book whose lists of ingredients were rich with butter and cream. I was used to learning by rote and it was no challenge to memorise lengthy and complicated recipes. She checked my till receipts so I had to steal the little pats of butter that came free in cafes and pubs. I hid them the way that Tara MacBride hid her cigarettes and her contraception, balancing them on top of the lintel on the front door and smuggling them up the stairs in my sleeve and then, with sleight of hand, unwrapping and sliding the yellow slab of fat between the folds of a chicken breast, doubling its calorific value, over-seasoning it so that she would attribute its unfamiliar richness to garlic and fresh herbs. I would pocket the foil wrapper again before she saw what I was doing, and that was how the grease had stained my trousers. I resolved to stick to my black tracksuit bottoms from now on, confident that it would not show up on the thick black cotton. I hated to deceive her, I hated it with all my heart, but I had no choice.

'Let's do some work,' I said, to break her trance as well as change the subject.

'Yes!' she said, and reached for a text we had studied so often I could all but recite it.

'*An Ideal Husband*? Again?' I said. 'Why can't we do something new?'

I got off the bed, went along the bookshelf, let the *Complete Shakespeare* fall open. '*Coriolanus*. I've never even *read* it.'

'That's rather more visceral than I'm equal to.' She closed her eyes and I wondered if she was about to drop off again. She had developed the sleeping patterns of a baby, twelve hours at night and naps in the day, too.

'OK, OK,' I said. 'We'll do the Wilde.'

I can't remember precisely when it became clear that the pupil had surpassed the teachers, that my education had stalled. My mother was straining at the limits of her stored knowledge. We had exhausted the literature and history she knew: before she could teach me further she had to crib it herself. Kenneth's lessons too had been repetitive for years and we were now reduced to the study of the algorithm he was working on to predict the numbers under the latex coating on lottery scratchcards. I could not suppress the unfaithful thought that one reason she had been so anxious for me to gain entry to the Cath was not my advancement in the world but an awareness of the limitations of my little tutor-family.

Matters were worsened by a schism in the tiny faculty. They were in passionate disagreement over two things. The first was her refusal to take the steroids the doctor had prescribed to strengthen her heart (which had, ironically, grown flabby, a common symptom of anorexia). The second was the visits I paid to Cathedral Terrace. My mother kept faith that somewhere in that house was evidence of the corruption that had derailed the life I was destined to lead, and Kenneth was not as sensitive or protective of her feelings as I was. He broached the subject with a directness that was at best clumsy and at worst cruel. 'I know what you're doing,' he said. 'Rowan MacBride, he doesn't stand for all academia, you know. He's not who you think he is. Heather, give it up.' The colour left my mother's face as if someone had pulled the plug on her blood supply.

'This is not about me. This is about Darcy, and what has been stolen, and what needs to be restored. This is about a family who are out to crush us.'

'They're *not* out to crush you. You've got absolutely no evidence that any funny business took place. It's all in here!' He tapped her head. 'It's making you both ill.'

'Darcy has never had a day's illness,' said my mother.

'How can you call *that* healthy?' he said, jabbing his finger my way. 'You're starving puberty out of the child! Jesus, Heather! What is it, some kind of sick insurance policy against what happened to you? Do you know, some days I'm *this* close to calling social services, telling them what life is *really* like up here.'

Kenneth did not come up to our rooms for a very long time after that. He never did call social services, and I still saw him after that but lessons were conducted in cafes, beer gardens and occasionally quiet corners of various Saxby bookmakers while the women behind the counter turned a blind eye. When conversation ran aground, we shared newspapers – front pages for me, back pages for him – and endless bowls of chips. If Heather was trying to starve puberty out of me, then he was trying to force-feed me into adulthood. I tried to refuse the junk food he bought me, but could not make a convincing excuse without betraying the truth. It was no secret that I was learning to cook but I was tempted to tell him about the butter and the calories I was sneaking into her body. I wanted to tell him to get him off my back and also, I think, because I wanted praise for my resourcefulness in teaching myself a new skill. But to confide in Kenneth would have felt disloyal and besides, to acknowledge the problem would have been to admit that I could not solve it alone. And I was making tentative progress. My clothes had in fact become interchangeable with those of my mother, and I was fairly sure that that was because I had grown, not because she was shrinking.

'I know you're going along with all this to keep your mother happy, but sometimes I wonder if you're starting to believe it yourself,' he said one day, over curly fries and ketchup in a pub that televised horseracing. 'You know you can't . . . call something into being, just because she wants it, if it doesn't exist.'

Those tiny facial muscles that serve only to hold back tears suddenly flexed and held. I did not dare speak, afraid that I would betray her, or myself. It was the same thing.

'I didn't mean to upset you. I'm sorry, I've never been very good at things like this. What I'm trying to say is . . . your mum, she isn't very well, she never has been. This whole wild goose chase, it's not logical. I mean, what if you get caught? They could send you to a borstal. How's that going to further your mother's cause of raising a bloody Oxford don?'

'I'm very careful,' I said in a clogged voice. 'And I *might* find something, one day.'

'I know you don't really believe that,' said Kenneth.

I shrugged and sucked the soggy potato from the crisp shell of the chip. I had long given up trying to make Kenneth understand. He didn't know what it was like to come first with someone. He didn't know what a responsibility it was. He would never understand that this quest, fantasy or not, had bound my mother's love to me the way dreams of my future had done throughout my childhood. I had been doing it for so long that it was my constant companion, the way a lonely child is trailed from room to room by an imaginary friend.

19

The lush vulgar smells of high summer competed with fumes from the traffic that congested the Green but in Lydia MacBride's study the air was cool and still. At first I took the book on her desk for a Bible; big, brown, leatherbound. A gold buckle hanging open at its waist revealed itself on close examination to be a four-digit combination lock. When I opened it and saw not the expected printed pages but handwriting I knew that what I held was holier than any sacred text. It seemed to pulse in my hands as though it, not me, was the live thing.

> *Three days before the operation and he tells me he doesn't want the surgery. The new eye won't fool anyone, he says, he'll still have the scar, so what's the point? Two years seeing the best doctors in England, his injury finally healed well enough for the eye to be fitted, all that money on consultancy charges, the research, all those trips to London, driving round and around the Old Street roundabout, the A–Z balanced on my lap. All for a custom-made fibreglass eye that cost a fortune – it would be a year's school fees, for some – and he doesn't want it.*
>
> *When he told me, I didn't say anything but when he had gone to school I locked myself in the bathroom and screamed into a towel. I don't show my anger anywhere but on these pages. As far as Felix and the rest of the family are concerned, he has my support. What I*

*really want to do is shake him and ask him if he knows how much
this has all cost me, in terms of patience, in terms of time and, yes,
in terms of money. I know we can afford it – at times like this, when
large sums need to be found quickly, I no longer feel guilty about the
way his education is funded.*

My skin was pricked all over by a million tiny needles. Did
this mean my mother was *right*?

*No, more than the money it is the rejection – of my help, of me. He
doesn't let me in any more; he's so closed, so sullen and sarcastic
where he used to be cheeky and playful. Tara has also withdrawn,
spending all her time in her room or with her friends. Sophie is under
strain too and that I'm afraid is my fault. Rowan and I decided to
shield the younger children, but I told her everything. She is mature
for her age but I shouldn't have used her as my confidante.*

I didn't see what was so inappropriate about Sophie acting
as her mother's confidante – it seemed rather odd, this
concept of the mother – child relationship being a one-way
street – and found nothing to explain or qualify. In fact, the
diary was bafflingly vague throughout. No further allusions
were made to Felix's method of entry into the Cath. This
did not read like the diaries I was used to, Frank and Pepys
and Byron, which were written to be read. This journal was
a rambling interior of a fine but undisciplined mind, pages
of unstructured emotion that, devoid of context, contrived
to exclude the reader.

I returned to the first page I had read, which remained the
most relevant. My mother would know what to make of the
writing, but how should I get it to her? My instinct was to tear
the page out or at least to score it close to the spine so that
its removal was hard to detect – but that would alert Lydia to
the fact that someone had read her words. And as amusing as
it was to think of her accusing her children of spying on her,

it might somehow lead to my own detection too early in the process; it was not worth the risk.

Few people had decent home printers or photocopiers then. I took the book to the local library. On the street, the sense of justice and entitlement I had felt in the house evaporated and I felt edgy and guilty, as though I had kidnapped a baby.

The Xerox machine in the library was a huge, space-age gadget that took scans of documents and was connected to a computer. I asked the dreadlocked librarian whether the machine kept a record of photocopied pages and was relieved when he shook his head. A smooth, warm double-page spread of photocopied handwriting slid into the tray.

In Lydia's study, I replaced the diary exactly as I had found it, down to the angle of the pen. My mother was in bed when I got home, under the covers despite the heat and wearing an expression I had come to know and dread: part challenge, part pre-emptive disappointment. I had folded the page in half, and handed it over like a birthday card.

'Lydia MacBride keeps a diary,' I said.

She opened it, read it, glanced up at me with a smile, read it again. The eagerness on her face was so raw I was almost embarrassed for her.

'Oh, clever brilliant darling!' She threw back the bedclothes as though finally something had warmed her from the inside. I felt a corresponding internal heat, as though some hot liquid was slowly being poured into me, cancelling the chill guilt of my incompetence, and knew that I must do whatever it took to preserve this feeling.

'This will be the first page of our dossier. On its own it isn't quite proof enough, but I'm sure you'll find something more concrete in the others.'

'The others?'

'The other diaries, Darcy. People who keep journals don't

just do it once. They do it all the time, their whole lives. You did check that there were more, didn't you?'

I hadn't. But there *were* more. In fact when I went back, a couple of weeks later, the diaries were the first thing I saw. They had been hiding in plain sight, lined up behind the scrollwork on the top of the cherrywood bookcase so that they literally looked like part of the furniture. I climbed onto the desk to get a better look. There were perhaps a dozen identical volumes; whichever one I had read was indistinguishable from its neighbours. I picked up the one on the end and saw, as I had feared, that these were all locked. I tried all the children's birthdays (digging out their birth certificates was half a day's work in itself), the MacBrides' wedding anniversary (ringed with a mawkish loveheart on their wall planner) and the obvious combinations like 1234, but got nothing.

Lydia's sewing kit proved its versatility for the second time; a thin, curved needle, possibly part of a sewing machine, slid under the numbers and beckoned itself around. To begin with I wiggled it pointlessly, but I soon fell into a kind of trance; I was absolutely still apart from my fingers, the tips of which quickly grew red, bulbous and sore. The thought of my mother's face if I was successful kept me going; after an hour I was covered in sweat from the exhausting concentration required. By the time the last catch sprang open, I was panting. The disappointment was crushing. The diary on my lap was from 1987, years before our lives had crossed and entirely irrelevant to me. When she wasn't wondering at the beauty of the children she had created, or extolling her deep pride at being made a magistrate, she wrote a bewildering amount about food she had cooked and food she had eaten. Occasionally, she stuck a recipe, torn from a magazine, onto the page.

No challenging or dry academic text had prepared me for the tedium of Lydia MacBride's diaries. She teased me with false starts and red herrings; the word 'confession' leapt off the page like a caught fish only to degenerate into a tedious avowal of a minor misdemeanour.

Cathedral Terrace
September 23rd 1999
I have just come from a funeral service that made me feel I wanted to go to confession. Diana Font. Only 50: breast cancer. She is the first of my peers to die, and once I would have called her my best friend. Shock and sorrow were the initial reactions but hot on the heels of those was guilt. Diana was the only other girl from my school to go up to Cambridge and, after graduation, the first of our set to get her own flat, on the Whiteladies Road in Bristol. The rest of us, living in various digs, all thought her terribly grand, although not quite as grand as she thought herself to be. She fancied herself as a matchmaker, and held frequent supper parties where she would inevitably sit me next to some dullard and herself alongside a bright young man she hoped to ensnare. One New Year's Eve she paired me with an overweight bore I had met the previous time. I couldn't bear the thought of it, and swapped the place cards so that I was sitting next to someone called Rowan MacBride, who arrived late, unfastening his bicycle clips. Diana was too busy fussing with cocktail shakers and a hostess trolley to notice the switch. By the time she realised, we were all seated and she could not change the arrangement without looking churlish. It wasn't until I saw the devastation on her face that I understood she'd been serious about him, and I felt desperately guilty. But what could I do? It was love by the main course. It is one of the only secrets I can ever remember keeping from Rowan. At first, I was embarrassed by my subterfuge and by the time I was secure in him, it was a habit.

Strange how the guilt resides even when regret does not. How good it feels to get that off my chest! I forget how it is with writing, the power of it to give perspective. Often, to let the genie out of the bottle is not to grant it life but to see it dissolve into mist. I suppose

> *that sooner or later everything I have ever done will end up here, this*
> *fragmentary memoir, this scrapbook of a life.*

Lydia's over-sensitive conscience gave me hope with one hand and despair with the other: hope, because any fraudulence regarding my scholarship *would* eventually be committed to paper. Despair, because what if it was going to take another thirty years?

I read her last line again and again, trying to extract from it a promise that there were other confessions to come, like lemon ink over a flame.

20

While practice got my safecracking technique down from half a day to half an hour, Lydia did not make it easy for me. The volumes were in no kind of order, and not externally differentiated, and I often picked the same lock twice. It was months before I hit on the idea of marking the volumes I had already read by making tiny scratches on the binding, and soon afterwards I hit upon the 1998 diary. I read it from cover to cover but there was no mention of Felix's entry to the school apart from a long, rambling passage about how grown up Lydia's baby boy was and how smart he looked in his school uniform. My mother interpreted the omission almost as a confession in itself. 'Why hasn't she written about it?' she said, poring over the now-ragged page I had copied.

'It's not that kind of diary. She doesn't write it in order. I found an entry written this year, about meeting her husband in the seventies. She's all over the place. That's why I have to read all of them. She goes backwards and forwards.'

'You'd think she'd have the grace to cross-reference and index it all. You can tell she's not a true scholar.' There was a strange flicker about my mother's lips that erupted into a loud 'Ha!' By the time I identified it as laughter, it was over. 'It's suspicious, don't you think?' she asked, drawing her knees up under her chin. 'It's conspicious by its absence. You don't just gloss over something as momentous as sending your children to one of the best schools in the country. If it had happened to us I would have *begun* a diary, I would have written a *book* about it. What do you think, Darcy? Is it because his acceptance was a foregone conclusion? Because they're too clever to incriminate themselves, even in a secret diary?'

Or maybe it was because the stolen scholarship and campaign of persecution were little more than the fabrication of a paranoid and disintegrating mind. The disloyal thought had come to me so quickly it must have been nearer the surface than I had dared to admit. Instead of that answer I gave her more reassurance.

'Don't worry,' I said. 'I won't give up.'

And nor did I. I continued to visit and continued to report back, although no discovery ever came close to expanding upon the promise of the original. I got so used to scanning those diaries for evidence that key words, such as Felix and school, leaped out at me from any text, the way your own name resonates when called by a stranger in public. It was, then, ironic that after all that time scanning the words for Felix's name it was my own that leapt from the page at me and made the world lurch to a standstill.

2nd November 1997

Hallowe'en was a gruesomely appropriate day to put a face to the name Darcy Kellaway. I was shopping in town with Rowan and Sophie when Rowan stopped to stare at a dun little face hidden under a hood. It was the teeth that gave it away; they really are astonishing, inhuman, sticking out like the Jabberwocky's. They're all you see.

'Is that . . . ?' I began but Rowan's face was all the answer I needed. I began to quiver with rage. How could that dark, ugly little gnome steal the beauty from my golden boy? Some primal maternal instinct raged in my veins. We were next to the ancient arch on the precinct; I could have toppled it with one push.

'I'm going to say something,' I said.

'Leave it, Mummy,' said Sophie. 'What good can it do?' But

she too was shaking when she put her hand on my arm to guide me away.

Ever since that sighting, I have been plagued by an anger so consuming I can only compare it to the first months of sexual desire. I enjoy horrible uncharacteristic revenge fantasies in which Darcy Kellaway is brought before the bench and I use the full force of my power to pass the highest sentence possible. On other occasions it is Kellaway's face that is ruined, that the notion of an eye for an eye manifests itself and somehow my son's bright blue eye is restored. Or perhaps there are other Kellaways I could hurt, loved one for loved one. In my darkest daydreams I am the one springing forward, weapon in hand, meting out the vigilante justice for which I routinely condemn those who come before the bench.

The pain inflicted by her vicious description was so acute I knew I could not pass it on to my mother. I had closed the diary and was about to put it back on the shelf when, twenty feet below me, the front door opened.

'Surprise!' someone called. In shock I let the book drop to the floor.

'Hello?' came the voice. '*Hello?*' The voice was young, female – Sophie's. What was she doing here? She was scheduled to be in Durham. I waited for her to go into the sitting room, then ran down the stairs and out of the front door which I didn't bother to close behind me. I flew across two lanes of moving traffic, stuck to the edges of the Green, not daring to look back.

I relaxed a little more with every day that passed, convinced that if Sophie had seen, and recognised, me the family would have sent their pet policeman round again. Still, it was weeks before I went back, even to look. Even from across the road I could see that the locks had been changed. New chrome glinted where once was dull brass and there were splinters in the encircling wood.

★   ★   ★

I found Kenneth in his favourite betting shop. He wasn't expecting me, and when he saw me his face stretched in shock.

'What?' I said. It had been a few weeks since we saw each other.

'Are you eating properly?' he said.

'Yes,' I said, 'I'm cooking every night.' I had not lied as such. I continued to cook for my mother but was cutting back on my own consumption. Strange upsurges of unfamiliar energies that felt like power had been troubling me lately and things were starting to change: hair where there used to be skin and clothes that seemed to have subtly altered their cut overnight. I had tried to pour everything I had into my work, but still the changes were coming. After the way I had let her down by failing to win the scholarship, I could not press this fresh disappointment on my mother, let alone turn to her for a solution. Instead, I followed her example of controlling what I ate to master my own body. If she noticed what was happening to me, she didn't remark upon it, and by the time Kenneth addressed my state, in his usual oblique way, I had already lost half a stone.

'We'll get a fish supper after this race,' he said. 'I don't want you going the same way as your mother.'

The race began, he was distracted by hooves thundering across a screen, and his attention was gone. When it was over, he scowled, then screwed up his betting slip and threw it like a snowball across the room.

'I won't be going back to Cathedral Terrace again, you'll be pleased to know,' I said. His expression brightened.

'High bloody time,' he said. 'I can't tell you how relieved I am. You're lucky you got away with it for as long as you did. But how did she take the news?'

'Are you insane? I can't *tell* her.'

'What are you going to do? Pretend to her that you're still going back, still researching her imaginary project?'

I looked down at the counter and fiddled with one of those funny little half-pens the bookies always had.

'Oh, *Darcy.*'

'What can I do?' I said. 'It's all that's keeping her alive.'

But no one, no matter how wilful, can live off hope alone. Every time I 'returned from Cathedral Terrace' empty-handed, my mother diminished a little more. Over the next few months she grew frailer and frailer until she became like something from one of her beloved Victorian novels, a consumptive heroine, dreams dashed, a bloodied cough away from death.

21

'An apple?'

She shook her head.

'A soldier of toast? *Dry* toast?'

Another shake.

'A little bit of egg? *Please.*' In desperation I named one of my secret foods. 'What if I made you herby chicken?'

'*No!*' she said with such vehemence I wondered if she was on to me. I swallowed, hard.

'What about sushi?' Her expression changed and I knew she was considering it. 'What about just a bit of sushi? You know, salmon the way I did it last week, sliced really thin. No dressing or anything, just lemon juice. Not the rice. No fat on it at all.'

She nodded her head. 'Yes. I think perhaps I could manage a mouthful of that.'

'Stay right there,' I said, unnecessarily. Her world had shrunk to a path between our bed and the bathroom.

Our local shops didn't do fresh fish, or not the kind you could make into sashimi, so I had to walk to the new Tesco on the other side of the city. The round trip would take me the best part of an hour but I didn't mind. To buy food that she would swallow and keep down I would have walked to London on bare feet.

The air was crisp and the city was calm. The snaking plume

of my breath led me via Cathedral Green. I glanced up at the terrace but didn't linger, unsure when the new supermarket closed. I needn't have rushed: a sign on the door said that it was open twenty-four hours a day. Something about the infinite possibility of this made me optimistic enough to buy a multipack of four yoghurts as well as the slab of fish; my haul had a promising heft in my hand.

I crossed the Green for the second time as the clock struck nine. This time I did take a moment to check in on the MacBrides. I had given up even the pretence of honouring my mother's obsession, but after all this time I still felt bound to them. In fact, the longer my mother stayed angry at them for having 'stolen' my education, the angrier I grew that they *hadn't*. I wanted a peg to hang this hatred on.

Only Lydia seemed to be in, reading a book in the sitting room, a glass of white wine on a side table. I couldn't see her any more without remembering what she had written. I tried to purse my lips over my teeth.

The cool quiet night provided the perfect acoustics for the scream. It seemed to be coming from behind the terrace, perhaps the very spot where I had attacked Felix. The next thing I knew, a hooded figure shot through the gap in the terrace, a spilling bag tucked under its arm, cleared the street in three strides then disappeared into the dark shrubbery of the Green. I bent down like anyone would have to see what had been dropped; it took a few moments to identify the plastic triangle in my hand as the sheath for the blade of a knife; the words 'Kitchen Devil' were etched on one side.

I don't know who raised the alarm but there was a squad car there in what seemed like seconds. The noise summoned a few of the residents to their steps with murmurs of 'Oh, dear lord,' and 'Not again,' and 'What'll it *take* for them to install bloody CCTV in that passage?' Among their number was Lydia MacBride, still with her book in her hand.

I let the sheath fall to the ground, and prepared to run, turned on my heel and found myself at eye level with the polished silver buttons of a police uniform. The number on the officer's shoulder was 089.

'Darcy Kellaway.' He retrieved the sheath and put it in a plastic bag. 'Where's the rest of the blade?'

'It's not mine!' I said. 'I just picked it up to see what it was. The person running off dropped it.'

'Let me guess, hooded top, couldn't see anything in the dark, average height?' said PC089.

'*Yes!*' I said indignantly. 'The top had a sort of orange piping around it. I can't be the only one who saw.'

'I saw what happened,' said a soft voice to my left. I turned to see my saviour and looked directly into the blue eyes of Lydia MacBride.

Recognition was mutual and instant. Anger lit her up. I recognised her expression, I had seen it on my own mother's face and I had known it from within, too. I could feel the heat of her hatred, as clear in person as it had been expressed in her diary.

'I didn't see anyone but you,' she said, her tone entirely without inflection.

'No!' I said.

How could she lie like that, so coolly? It gave new credence to my mother's theory about my exclusion from the school, and guilt for doubting her burrowed its way up through my fear.

'Thanks, Mrs MacBride. Would you be prepared to come down and make a statement to that effect?'

'Oh, yes.' Now her lips were twitching as though trying to suppress a smile.

'You're lying! She's lying! You can't have seen me do anything because I didn't *do* anything. You're only out to get me because I—' I stopped myself just in time. They both raised their eyebrows. Lydia MacBride lost her battle with her smirk.

'Yes?' said PC089. 'No, didn't think so. Darcy Kellaway, I am arresting you on suspicion of aggravated street robbery. You do not have to say anything—'

'Please, I've got to take this to my mother,' I said, waving the carrier bag of salmon around. 'She needs to eat, she's starving.'

The policeman rolled his eyes. 'This is Saxby, not Ethiopia.'

'But you've seen her,' I said, then realised that of course that had been years ago, when she was in relatively good health. I appealed directly to Lydia MacBride.

'Please, please don't do this, it'll kill her,' I said, unsure whether I meant the stress or the starvation, but she had already turned her back on me. 'It'll kill her!' I said, as the heavy cuff was slipped on my wrist.

In the short car journey to the police station, my very real terror could not quite cover a stirring of anticipation for the moment when Lydia MacBride would be arrested for perverting the course of justice. Underneath the worry about my mother's distress, I was already nostalgic for the moment I would tell her what had happened.

I half expected Lydia to be waiting for me at the police station, wearing handcuffs that matched my own, but the holding area I was bundled into was empty except for me and a custody sergeant in owlish glasses.

'How old are you?' she asked in an accusing tone, as though my age was a indicator of guilt.

'I'll be seventeen on my next birthday,' I replied.

'Fuck's sake, you look about twelve. They must've known you was underage. They're supposed to give me notice if I need to call in an appropriate adult.' She rolled her eyes to the ceiling then turned back to me, speaking slowly, as though to an idiot. 'You're a *ju-ven-ile*. That means—'

'I know what juvenile means.'

'We need to get a grown-up to sit with you while we read you your rights and that. D'you live with your mum?'

'I told them all this! My mother's not well, she couldn't come out.'

'Dad?'

'Get my uncle.' I dictated Kenneth's number. 'Tell him to tell my mother where I am, I don't want her to worry about me.'

From the slamming car doors outside I deduced that the cells were alongside, or perhaps underneath, the yard they had brought me into. I was bundled into a room painted a lurid yellow that existed nowhere in nature, and left there. Where was Kenneth? The hot, greasy stench of processed food curled through the hatch and my treacherous tastebuds secreted saliva.

'Room service,' said a voice and a cardboard box was posted through the hole. The label said 'wood fired pizza'. The contents looked like a slick of phlegm hacked up onto a bloodied medical dressing. I tried to push it back but the hatch could only be opened from the outside. When, after an age, the door finally opened, the figure behind PC089 was not Kenneth in his sports jacket but a fat middle-aged woman in a salwar kameez.

'Hello, dear,' she said. 'Don't worry, I'll explain it all to you.'

'Who is this? Where's my uncle?'

'Who?' said PC089. 'Oh. Right. No, we couldn't get through to him. Zima's a social worker.'

But if Kenneth wasn't coming then that meant my mother didn't know where I was. Perhaps they would let me call her; she might be worried enough by now to pick up the phone, and I could come up with a little white lie to give her peace of mind until I could make it home with the vile, wonderful truth about Lydia MacBride.

'I need to call my mother, right now.'

'All right, dear,' said Zima.

Somewhere outside a door clanged. PC089 was called away, spoke in urgent whispers, came back into view. 'I'm sorry, I've wasted your time,' he said, but he was talking to Zima, not me.

'Is anyone going to tell me what the *hell* is happening?' I said.

'Turns out you were telling the truth,' said PC089. 'We found the victim's credit cards on someone else during a subsequent arrest. Batten down the hatches, they're bringing Ricky Jinks in now,' he said to the custody sergeant, who rolled her eyes.

'Again?' she said.

PC089 turned back to me. 'You're released without charge, this time.'

Now the opposing emotions were relief and rage.

'I presume that your next arrest will be Lydia MacBride? The eyewitness who placed me at the scene. Let's see, there's wasting police time, bearing false witness. I know that the rest of her family are corrupt to the core, but *she*'s the worst of the bloody lot.' PC089 bent to my level. I could count the pores on his nose.

'Don't even think about it. I would take the word of any member of that family over you, every time. I don't know what you've got against them, but I haven't forgotten what—'

We were interrupted by a commotion, a gate opening, and more uniformed officers came in with the handcuffed form of the man in a black hooded top with an orange trim.

'Ricardo! Welcome back,' said the sergeant.

'Get to fuck,' sniffed the man who could only be Ricky Jinks. He was a eugenicist's dream, with that peculiar flat dead face that those born into poverty and stupidity seem to share. I shivered to think that I had been bracketed, even temporarily and in error, with someone like this.

'Can we offer you a lift back?' said the sergeant, picking at the scabs of my unwanted pizza. 'All the stretch limos are busy but we can drop you back in a squad car.'

'Sarcasm is the refuge of an unoriginal mind,' I said.

'Charming!' she said. 'I can see *you* get your manners from your mother.'

I stopped. 'How do *you* know what my mother's like?'

'I spoke to her earlier, didn't I? When I couldn't get through to your uncle?'

'How did you get her number?'

'I rang directory enquiries.'

'But we're not in the phone book.'

'I'm being sarcastic, aren't I? Must be my unoriginal mind. I'm a *police* officer. How'd you think I got the number? It took like a million rings for her to answer, and when I told her where you was and what you was in for, she hung up on me.'

I pictured my poor mother in that room, the ringing telephone that would to her have been as stressful as a battering ram, the summons to the station that she would not have been able to obey.

I ran back to Old Saxby Road, the city flashing past me, the buildings rapidly becoming younger. I was through the street door in seconds, didn't bother with the lights, found footholds on the cluttered stairs by instinct and memory. Light oozed through the keyhole.

'Mother, it's me!' I said, as I let myself in.

She lay on her back on the floor, her right hand a claw upon her breast. Her outdoor shoes with their unmarked heels were paired at her feet and her old coat lay on the bed, picking up where my imagination had left off and mutely relaying the sequence of events – the telephone call, the terror, the impossible attempt to leave the room, the weak heart admitting defeat on her behalf. I dropped to all fours, touched the hollow of her cooling cheek. And then it is as though a blackout blind was pulled down over my eyes; I remember nothing more, and have only the words of others for what happened next.

22

Kenneth told me that he had arrived back from two glorious days at the Cheltenham racecourse to find his answer phone flashing red with a dozen messages. The first few out of the concatenation of a dozen conflicting summonses were left by my mother, followed by a couple from social services, then a handful from the police who had custody of me, and finally the same police officers with their imperative tone subdued. Saxby police station seemed to be the common factor, so he had wheezed his way there, and after much argument with confused officials, they were able to redirect him to the Intensive Care Unit in the secure wing of the Wellhouse. There I lay sedated on an intravenous drip, suffering from post-traumatic shock, severe dehydration and chronic malnutrition.

The nothing people had apparently ignored my screaming, but it had been loud and prolonged enough to raise the students over the road from their sloth. They had called the police and an ambulance, who escorted me to the Wellhouse, where I was held under Section 2 of the Mental Health Act.

After a week or so – and here, returning memory begins to dovetail with the accounts given to me, and at last I can begin to trust the story again – I was taken off the drip and moved into the secure ward proper, which was not a single ward as such but rather an entire wing, with segregated dormitories and showers but communal living, counselling and educational spaces that I was expected to share with various casualties of society ranging from the addicted to the insane.

At first speech was difficult. The word 'mothermother-mothermothermothermothermother' looped in my head like tinnitus. It was impossible to drown out but with practice, over the weeks, I learned to accompany it with normal speech, the way a pianist's right hand plays the treble and the left the bass. When I had regained my articulacy I used it to explain to anyone who would listen that the MacBride family were as much to blame for my mother's death as if they had collectively gripped the hilt of a knife and stuck it between her ribs. Time and again I told my inscrutable psychiatrist, Dr Myerson, the whole story. I explained how the scholarship had been stolen from me, choked on my guilt when I confessed how I had doubted her, shared the irony of my new awareness that now, in the light of Lydia MacBride's deception, my mother had been right all along.

'And *why* do you think an entire family would want to persecute you and your mother?' she asked.

I saw my necessary omissions like Vaseline on the lens of my story. And besides, the secret of what I had done to Felix was irrelevant, given that it had all begun with them.

'I wish I knew,' I replied.

When I wasn't in conversation with Dr Myerson, I was obliged to take part in an excruciating practice called Circle, which consisted of the inmates sitting in a horseshoe of plastic chairs, sharing their moods and their progress, crying and drooling. If this was group education I was glad once again to have been home-schooled. One of the education inspectors who used to visit us had told my mother that the biggest drawback of my education was that I did not get to mix with others. Would my life at the Cath have resembled this, living cheek by jowl with strangers, no privacy, the drip-drip-drip of small talk preventing clear thought? I had never before had to interact with more than two, occasionally three, people at a time and in Circle I felt like a novice juggler trying to keep a dozen balls in the air at once.

To avoid meeting my fellow patients' eyes, I spent a lot of time looking out of the window. I liked the view out onto the hospital lawns, trimmed above with the quaint cityscape of the Cathedral Quarter; the sight of the spire was reassuring even if the bells were out of earshot.

My new next of kin came once a week: Kenneth was ill at ease in the communal lounge and at each visit he brought bad news like other relatives brought grapes. The first bulletin was that the council had already taken over our rooms on Old Saxby Road, and that in the event of my recovery it was to Kenneth's flat I would be returning. A couple of weeks later, he dropped the bombshell that the coroner's report had been filed and that an inquest had found the cause of my mother's death to be a massive cardiac arrest, probably the result of chronic anorexia nervosa. The next time we met he told me that my mother had been cremated without me. 'We had the funeral,' he said. 'I didn't know what was for the best, how long you were going to be ill for. I'm so sorry, kid. Up at the crematorium. It's nice there, in the rose gardens. I'll take you there as soon as you're up to it.'

I didn't need a municipal rosebush to remember my mother by; I carried her blood in my veins and my mind too was a vessel that she had filled with everything she knew and everything she believed. The energy with which I had loved her had warped into hatred of the family who took her from me. The longer I was incarcerated the grander my retributive fantasies became; they began as face-to-face confrontations with Lydia MacBride and escalated until I was burning down her house with her family locked inside. But the more I pressed the truth upon them, the more entrenched the medical staff grew in their belief that I was in the grip of delusional psychosis. The freedom necessary for my pursuit of justice seemed a long way off.

In fact, liberty was handed to me not by one of the medical

staff but by a lumbering alcoholic called Steve with whom I had established a kind of mealtime symbiosis. What I couldn't finish, he would happily shovel down.

'Are you eating that?' he said one lunchtime, and speared a perfectly circular fishcake from my plate without waiting for my answer. I toyed with the salad in my mouth, letting a single lettuce leaf turn to velvet and dissolve against the flat of my tongue.

'What's up with you, anyway?' he said.

'I'm just so frustrated, stuck in here. There's so much I've got to do outside, and I'm not getting anywhere.'

'Why don't you just tell them what they want to hear?' said Steve.

'Because all I've got is my word against theirs. If I back down, then I've literally got nothing.'

'Suit yourself,' said Steve. 'Are you going to have that custard?'

A while later when my case came up for review, I decided to 'recover'.

It cost me to betray my mother, but eventually I asked Dr Myerson if I could see her death certificate once more. She smiled into her clipboard and, two days later, brought me a photocopy of the certificate which I pretended to study, deliberately staring so hard at the words that they swam and blurred. A few days later I told her that I accepted that my mother had died of natural causes. 'I'm a bit embarrassed about all that stuff I said before. I don't really believe that the MacBrides killed her,' I said. 'I don't suppose I ever did, really. I was just looking for someone to blame. I'm sorry I threatened them. I'd never do anything like that, not really. I feel a bit foolish, to tell the truth.' The words burned like bile but I knew that my mother would understand and approve; if ever there was a case of the end justifying the means, this was it.

For weeks, I repeated variations on this theme every day.

It was a triumph over the brainwashing process; rather than override my certainty that Lydia MacBride was my mother's murderer, it ringfenced it. Every time I said the word 'MacBride' I hardened against the family a little more. Every time I retracted my threats, I saw myself marching straight from the Wellhouse to Cathedral Terrace and picking up our confrontation where it had left off.

After seven weeks of false statements, I was diagnosed as having had a single extended psychotic episode from which I was in full recovery.

'Good news, Darcy,' said Dr Myerson. She swigged from the bottle of mineral water she always carried. 'You're ready to go home. There are a couple of conditions, of course. The first, which is standard practice, is that you come and see us as an outpatient every day for the first couple of weeks. And the other is that you'll have to keep your distance from the MacBride family.'

'What do you mean exactly by keep my distance?' I asked, my elation punctured.

'You made some very serious threats against the family, Lydia MacBride in particular, when you first came in here,' she said. 'The family have requested that a protection from harassment order be granted against you. A restraining order, to you and me. You're not allowed to go within fifty metres of their home, or of them.'

My mouth dried out.

'But you said I was *better*! I am better! How many times have I told you I didn't mean it, that it was just the grief talking?'

'For what it's worth, I agree with you,' said Dr Myerson. 'But this is out of my hands, it's a police matter. And if you're better, it shouldn't matter, should it?' Was she trying to trick me?

I was not foolish enough to voice my conviction that the minute I was released from the Wellhouse, the MacBrides would contrive to turn up wherever I was, thus forcing me to breach my order – and I didn't doubt that Lydia would brief her magisterial cronies to impose the harshest of sentences on me.

'No,' I said, my lips cracking as they parted. 'No, I suppose not.'

My desire for revenge did not dim, but they were doing everything they could to reduce my opportunities. The prospect of retribution seemed as remote as passing through the solid stone of the old city walls.

23

As threatened, Kenneth collected me on the day of my release. 'Hello, kid,' he said. 'Came straight here. Didn't even have time to cash my slip, even though it came in at twenty to one.' It was the nearest Kenneth would ever get to a declaration of love. But when you have been everything to someone and they have understood you better than you understand yourself, fondness and good intentions are worse than nothing.

Kenneth's basement flat was a map of his mind. Copies of the *Racing Post* and tattered almanacs were stacked to head height against every wall. The carpet of used scratchcards on the sitting-room floor explained the perfect pewter crescent of scraped foil under his left index fingernail.

In the spare room, the bed linen still held its creases from the packaging. Piled books – my mother's – formed a Manhattan skyline against a papered wall. The Russian dolls and a manicure set were in an open shoebox. 'I didn't know what were your clothes and what were hers, so I just hung all of them up together,' he said, gesturing to a wardrobe I knew I would never open. 'Don't know if they'll fit you now, anyway. Although I have to say you look better for having a bit of meat on your bones. Well. Shall I open some Scotch?'

It was half past three. Kenneth poured us a finger each into cut crystal tumblers. The first small sip rinsed my sinuses with fire but he gulped it like water. The alcohol enabled the small talk that was necessary to prepare the ground for the important things we had to discuss, my plans to avenge my mother's death, how he must be on my side now that the law was not. I had so much to say to him but none of the right words. There was an awkwardness between us that was new. Of course we were used to hours in each other's company but always with the stipulation that I would be back in my mother's care before long. The bottle drained like the world's slowest hourglass, although I could not go beyond my second tumbler. Presently he raised his glass in a lopsided toast.

'Here's to your future,' he said. 'Today is the first day of the rest of your life, as they say. So glad to see you're on the mend, put all that nonsense about your mum and that family behind you.'

I was incredulous. It was one thing to dupe Dr Myerson, but for *Kenneth* not to see through the ruse . . .

'Kenneth, I can't believe this. We're not talking about a school place any more. We're talking about life and death. We're talking about *murder.*'

'Oh, Darcy, *no.* I was at the inquest. I know what I heard.'

'And I know what I saw when she framed me for that mugging. She was out to get me.'

Kenneth snorted dismissively.

'You forget that I *know* that family, Kenneth, I've been to their house, I've read . . . I *know* how they think.'

Now he sighed. 'I wish you could see this as an opportunity, Darcy, a chance to make something of yourself. You've effectively been your mother's carer since you could walk. Don't you realise that? Everything you've done has been for her benefit. I'm just saying that now you've got a chance to let go of all that crap and—'

'Forgive me if I don't see my mother's death as an opportunity for personal growth,' I snapped. Kenneth poured another finger of whisky; his pink eyes made him look more like a white rabbit than ever.

'You're twisting my words again. I'm just *encouraging* you to see that there's more to life than Saxby, and that stupid bloody school. You're old enough to – well, you're not that much younger than your mother was when she—'

'We're not going into *that*.'

Kenneth drummed his fingers on the bottle, bit his lip, then retreated into a silence that I could not translate. After a while, he put the television on to watch the racing results, a sedative drone of names and numbers that soon had him snoring in the armchair.

I crashed into the shop-starched bed, my mind whirring. Kenneth had, in his clumsy way, made up my mind for me. He had been wrong to suggest that my mother's death had freed me to become myself; I knew that I would never truly be myself again, that some vital piece of me was lost forever. If nothing could be the same, *everything* had to change. I knew I could not stay. My ambitions, for so long centred on this city, would have to turn outward for a while.

For all his efforts in the spare room Kenneth had forgotten to put up a curtain, and dawn broke in at six the next morning. I didn't take a single book. It was the first glimmer of the ethos that would guide me through the months ahead, the idea that survival depended on becoming another person, not just away from Saxby but away from everything that she had wanted for me. I palmed the smallest matryoshka, folded my birth certificate into my pocket and slipped the uncashed betting slip into a carrier bag full of virgin scratchcards, which I took with me when I let myself out of Kenneth's dank little flat and joined the first trickle of commuters making their way towards the station.

The further Saxby receded the stronger I felt. I resolved to change everything, from my name to the way I looked. I was not running away from my responsibilities to my mother's memories; I was honouring them in a different way. I vowed to return when I was a match for the MacBrides, more than a match for them. If that turned out to be a life's work, so be it. I had the patience of a saint, or its opposite.

24

Kenneth's betting slip yielded £5,000 cash which I divided into piles of £100 in the sterile surrounds of the Paddington Travelodge. I used the edge of a coin to work my way through £400 worth of scratchcards. The revenue of £127 undermined Kenneth's algorithm but bought me my first few nights' accommodation.

Now what? I couldn't stay in the hotel room. I was buzzing with a need for action unlike anything I had experienced before. In the nineteenth-century novels we used to read, people were frequently overwhelmed by bereavement, taking to their beds for months on end. I found grief to be a dynamo. I was never busier than during my mourning; the construction of a new life is a full-time job and leaves mercifully little time to dwell on loss. I had money to live on but I needed to work. I craved busyness, purpose and physical exhaustion.

At first, I was worried that my inexperience would work against me. The world of employment was as alien to me as it had been to my mother, who had of course never done a day's paid work in her life. I was equipped only for one thing, and that was to teach, to keep alive the knowledge that she had passed down to me. I had naturally gleaned enough of the system to know that, without qualifications, my knowledge was worthless.

In fact, the opposite was true. Adult ambitions and capabilities had been smouldering inside me, growing stronger for being suppressed in favour of my mother's needs. Who would have guessed that I had it in me to walk the streets until I found an employment bureau, armed only with my name and my National Insurance number? I filled out a form that had boxes for me to list my achievements as measured by the blinkered parameters of examination boards. The blank spaces of my educational record brought home for the first time how badly prepared I was for survival. She had not taught me how to live, only how to know, but I could not blame her: that was all she knew, too.

The pretty woman behind the desk looked me up and down for a full minute. She lingered on my teeth for a second too long before saying that she did not think front-of-house work would be for me, and that hospitality would be the best industry to try. Still, I emerged from the agency with a zero hours contract as a commis chef at a French restaurant on Ealing Green.

The lot of a commis chef involved chopping, cleaning, stirring and carrying raw meat in my bare hands across a steaming, noisy kitchen crammed with hot bodies. Nobody else in the kitchen had English as a first language, for which I was grateful. Engulfed by my oversized, shapeless chef's whites, hair hidden under a hat, I was invisible, spoken to only in one-word sentences. After six days of working fourteen-hour shifts I was given one day off. Idle hours were dangerous; no matter how busy I kept there were moments every day I could not control, like the seconds between waking up and opening my eyes when the full force of loss slammed into me.

I got the tube to Oxford Street, pushed through the throng to buy my first ever brand-new clothes. I had my hair washed, cut and blow-dried in a real hair salon. I was still nobody's idea of good-looking but if I remembered to keep my lips together I could now achieve a kind of neutrality. Every time I tended to my appearance I was alert for inner change, for the first signs of atrophy of my character and intellect. I felt the stirrings of something, but it did not feel like degeneration. I bought a copy of *Loot*, a *London A–Z* and a mobile phone, and began to look for somewhere else to stay. I saw half a dozen studio flats in Hanwell and Isleworth, all variations on the theme of my childhood home. None were beautiful, only half were affordable, all were acceptable, but landlords and estate agents all wanted references, copies of bank statements, credit histories. I had nothing but a sob story and a stay in a secure hospital to recommend me.

The seventh place on my list was a big Victorian house, on a quiet Ealing street opposite a park with a bowling green. The door was opened by a vast man of Mediterranean appearance and Australian accent. When we shook hands, mine was like a child's in his.

'I'm Vassos,' he said, and then, gesturing to a tiny brown woman behind him, 'and this is Carmel. Come in.'

The house was like a zoo, with a zebra-skin rug, leopard-print cushions and a jungle of plants in big stone pots. There was leather everywhere – the sofa, the chairs, the bed – even a solid wall of the sitting room had been quilted then stretched over with hide, and studded, as though the construction of a padded cell had been abandoned. The calmest room was the one they called their office, where the only colour came from a solid wall of oversized paperbacks.

'Carmel's my partner in business as well as in life,' said Vassos, showing me a mirrored room containing a small trampoline, exercise bike and treadmill. 'We're fitness instructors at the big tennis club up at Chiswick.'

His shoulders filled the narrow stairway to the attic. The room had a double bed with a peacock feather print on the cover, a widescreen television and an ensuite wet room. 'You're probably wondering why a room this good is as cheap as it is. Truth is, you'll be more of a house-sitter than a lodger. We work pretty mad hours and we go away a lot, a hell of a lot

– we're branching out into boot camps, yoga retreats, detox breaks and all that – and we need someone to make the place look lived-in, and to look after Misty for us.'

On cue a horrible, hard grey cat sauntered into the room and started to wind itself around my legs.

'How lovely,' I said, internalising my shudder.

'Aw, she likes you, she does,' said Carmel. Her broad Irish accent came as a shock after the rich mahogany of her skintone. Zooming in, I noticed patches of white in the webbing between her fingers and around her hairline.

We all followed Misty back downstairs where Carmel and I had herbal tea and Vassos had a protein shake.

'Are you named after the Darcy in the TV programme?' said Carmel.

'The novel.' She looked blank. '*Pride and Prejudice* was based on a book by Jane Austen.'

'*Was* it?' she said, wide-eyed. 'I didn't know that. I've only seen it on telly.'

'So, what do you think?' said Vassos, somehow managing to make it sound like a threat, but from what I had seen of the London property market, I wasn't going to get a better offer.

'I like it, I'd like to live here. But I've only just left home after losing my mother . . .'

'Ah, bless,' said Carmel.

'. . . so I haven't got references or anything like that.'

Vassos looked solemn. 'I'm sorry about your mother, although I am taking a punt on giving board to someone without background.' He stroked his chin. 'Now. I'm a Neuro-Linguistic Programming Master Practitioner. Do you know what that means? That means I can read people as well as inspire and manipulate them, and spot a liar from ten paces. It's like trusting your instincts, but on an *informed* level. And my gut' – he punched his solid abdomen – 'is telling me you're good for it. What do you think, Carmel?'

'Oh yeah,' said Carmel. 'Grand.'

'Welcome to the madhouse!' said Vassos.

'Thanks, Vassos,' I said.

'Call me Vass,' he said. 'I'm a busy man. Life's too short for two syllables.'

I took a deep breath. 'While we're on the subject, I prefer to go by my middle name, Matthew,' I said. 'Matt, for short.'

25

I had chosen the ideal place in which to rebrand myself. Vass and Carmel were the most fascinating people I had ever met, although not for the reasons they thought. On the fridge they had pictures of themselves in their late teens. Carmel's adolescent complexion had an eau-de-nil tinge, while Vassos had been skinny and knock-kneed. Their shared goal was self-improvement, and their vast library of books were all to this end – not the enriching literature I had read with my mother, not even the sanctimonious, cod-spiritual texts that Lydia MacBride had favoured, but books that taught the reader how to become a better person in a *quantifiable* way that showed results to the outside world. Their authors were CEOs, dietitians and psychologists and their subject matter body language, manipulation, business strategy and endless, *endless* diet and exercise guides. I read a book every other day, and on Vass's laptop taught myself to use the internet.

Vass was big on a process called 'modelling' – identifying someone whose qualities and achievements you admired, then aping their behaviour until it became second nature. I looked to Vass himself, not because he was someone I longed to be – he was, for all his self-importance, just a nothing person with money – but because he was there and he was, in his own way, a success. It was far easier to start again from scratch and adopt wholesale Vass's alien values than try to pursue my mother's ambitions for me. This was the way men acted, I realised, although I often wished I could ask him why, like an actor asking the director for his motivation.

True to their word, Vass and Carmel were rarely at home but the time I did spend in their company was intense. My efforts to make myself a blank canvas had been so successful that they could not resist making me their pet project; she designed me a nutrition programme, supplementing three balanced meals a day with nutrient-rich shakes and powders, while he took me to his gym and taught me how to use the weights. There was nothing either of them could do about my height – I never got past five feet six – but they masterminded an otherwise complete transformation of my body below the neck. With every pound I put on, I commanded more respect. Strangers no longer spoke to me as though I were a child.

So that I could save enough money for the orthodontistry we all agreed was necessary, they found me a part-time job, for my days away from the restaurant, manning the reception in their gym. They called it cash-in-hand and I wondered if they knew quite how true that was, as I pocketed the odd pound here and there that people paid for pure protein in chocolate bar or milkshake form. Two or three times a month, sales reps came to flog new miracle muscle builders or fat burners. I was fascinated by the low rhetoric of their sales patter, and took their business cards with curiosity. Their world of glamour and profit was so far from the life I had been groomed for that it held an exotic appeal.

One white-skied Tuesday afternoon, a rep called Bradley Rider barrelled through the double doors, intent on persuading me to invest tens of thousands of pounds in a variety of machines from a laser that promised to tighten upper arms by means of cryogenic freezing to an 'ultrasound massage' that purported to be a painless way to melt fat. He didn't stop to think that a receptionist might not have access to funds beyond what he could take from the till and didn't listen when I tried to explain that; he had spread his catalogues across the counter and was a few minutes into his pitch when Vass came in. When Vass saw what Brad was peddling, he virtually threw him out by the collar.

'Not in *my* gym! Piss off to Knightsbridge or somewhere else people have got more money than sense. Don't insult me, mate.'

'All right, all right. Your loss.' Bradley Rider left with an upturned collar and a defensive shrug.

'What was all that for?' I said, or rather I tried to say: I had only been wearing my new dental plate for a few days and my tongue had yet to accustom itself to the false ceiling in my mouth. 'You should've seen the figures he had. If his projections and those returns are true you'd have been printing money after the first few months.'

'It'd be a fucking goldmine,' conceded Vass. 'But that's not the *point*. He's selling dreams, not results. People are desperate to believe there's a magic bullet, but the *only* way to reduce body fat is by nutrition and exercise, or to have someone to cut you up on the operating table and suck it all out.' He banged his fist on my counter. 'Anything else is just exploiting when you should be *educating*. It shows contempt for the body, contempt for human intelligence. What that bloke's doing goes against everything I stand for.'

'*He* seemed pretty convinced by the science behind it all,' I said. 'He reckons he can extract fat through the skin.'

'Bollocks! The only thing he's extracting from people is money. I might not have a penthouse, but do you know what I have got?' He put his paw on his massive chest, looking near to tears. 'Integrity, Matt. Integrity. It's the one thing they can't steal from you. People like him make me . . . man, I need a run.' He shouldered the doors to the cardio suite.

Bradley Rider had left a single brochure behind on the counter. It had a business card stapled to the front of it, which I slipped into my pocket.

In spring 2003, Vassos and Carmel finally departed for Australia, leaving me in charge of their house and their cat. Misty's food allowance – it ate only wild, line-caught fish and free-range organic chicken – was more than enough to feed a human being. Like a car, it had a kind of log book that acted as proof of pedigree and ownership, and a bold idea came to me. I took a series of photographs of it in various poses all over the house, and once I was sure I had enough to slowly feed them a diary of it, sold it to a rare breeds dealer for £600. The ease of this emboldened me to sub-let the house to a family, placing an advert in *Loot* and drawing up a contract from a boilerplate on the internet so that there was no estate agent to ask for my proof of ownership or to take a cut of the cash. It was simple, but that didn't mean it was easy. On the morning the contracts were signed, I was sick twice, although after it was done I felt only euphoria I rented a studio a few doors down for one-third of the income I derived. With that money, I could afford to leave the restaurant and the gym and work full time for Bradley Rider, selling his fat-busting ultrasound machines to beauty salons and health farms all over the south-east.

The reason the job sounded too good to be true, I soon realised, was because it was. Without my income from Vass and Carmel's house I would have gone under: Bradley employed me on a commission-only basis, and it took me a long time to perfect my sales patter and turn a profit. When I did make a sale, Bradley's royalty as licensee swallowed the lion's share of the proceeds. My frustratingly meagre accounts were submitted quarterly to Bradley's accountant, a Southall wide-boy called Rikesh, who was, in Brad's words, 'just the right side of dodgy'. Rikesh had been delisted from the Institute of Chartered Accountants for some nebulous borderline fraud, since when his popularity with clients like Bradley had reached an all-time high. I met him just once, the day we set up my limited company. 'For when you hit the big time,' said Rikesh. 'You want to be able to funnel your cash through a company. Trust me, self-employment is for part-timers, losers and women. What are you going to call it? You can make up a brand name, or just your own name followed by Ltd.' If I could not escape my association with Bradley, I might as well capitalise on his reputation. 'Matthew Rider Ltd,' I decided.

Although Rikesh knew my birth name, he never once referred to me that way. The only people who wrote to me in my own name were banks and utilities. No letter from Kenneth ever came. Every few months I would be pulled up short by the awareness that he had made no effort to find me, but I was too busy to let that sting.

The growth of my little company was accelerated in 2004, when Bradley was sent to prison for trading whilst bankrupt. Rikesh transferred his loyalty from Bradley to me with admirable speed and offered to put up the capital to help me buy the UK distribution rights for the entire range of machines at a fraction of their market value. 'I'll give you a better rate of interest than any bank,' was how he sold the arrangement to me.

'I don't get it. What's in this for you?'

'You wait till you see my bill,' he said.

'But you don't want a stake in the business?'

'Nah. Cashflow, mate. Cashflow.' Cashflow, I was learning, was Rikesh-speak for 'Don't ask, don't tell.'

Bradley's incarceration added a zero to my company's turnover, and the next year another. I evicted the family in Vass and Carmel's house, moved back in while I looked for somewhere to buy and wrote to Australia with the double-barrelled bad news of my intention to leave and of Misty's demise (a hit-and-run: people are *bastards*).

I soon found and bought outright a good two-bed, two-bath flat in a gated community in Ealing with a gym and a pool in the basement. I worked out for two hours every morning, slowly assuming the sculptured shape that is modern society's idea of neutral. When the dental plate came off it left me with just a millimetre's overbite. My new smile transformed everything from the size of my nose to the set of my jaw and my journey to fully inhabiting the flesh was almost complete. Rather than my mother's intended immunity to beauty, I had a heightened vulnerability to it. I felt a flicker of betrayal every time I was moved by a pretty girl in summer clothes. But I could not ignore the truth that the further I turned my back on the ideals that had been instilled in me, the more successful I became. Why should sex be the exception?

The first few times I paid, a premium price for a premium product, a red-haired girl in a good room at the right end of the King's Road. It was confirmation that a parallel dimension of pleasure had always existed alongside the ascetic world of my upbringing and if, afterwards, I felt the urge to apologise to my mother it was more in a spirit of commiseration than regret that I had crossed this threshold. I always used the same agency but rarely the same girl twice. Although I could not imagine reconciling the sweat and power of sex with the tender understanding I still missed, I eventually found the confidence to complement the professionals with amateurs. Many of these girls were keen, but when adoration is the benchmark, admiration seems so weak and watery. What was worse, none of them seemed to have a spine, a purpose, a creed, and as such, their expectations and demands were mercurial and bewildering. My mother's linear, constant approach to life, I soon realised, was the exception rather than the female rule. *This*, I thought, was what she ought to have warned me of: not the harmless transaction of the physical act but the bewildering power struggle that accompanied it.

Despite this, I did want to find someone. A woman seemed to be the only thing missing. I had the business, the property, the car; and after all, the truth that a single gentleman in possession of a good fortune must be in want of a wife is so universally acknowledged as to be the only Austen most people can quote. In that sense, I was a victim of my own success. Being a self-made man has its drawbacks. I had so carefully constructed Matt Rider, the outer doll who enclosed all the others, that the casing had sealed permanently. Darcy Kellaway, and all his childhood avatars, were in there, but the only way to access them would be to smash the outer shell.

26

Although success is a consuming business, of course I still thought of the MacBrides; for my first few years in London they were a constant background crackle, like static. My initial research was patchy and frustrating; the internet was still a dial-up dinosaur. However, the *Saxby Courier* became a surprisingly early adopter of the web, with a rudimentary online edition that included every word of the print edition, no matter how parochial the piece. The Cath featured heavily, from stories about the cricket team's performance to their Christmas carol concert; there was even – to my dismay – an open letter from Rowan MacBride asking bright children from all backgrounds to apply for the Mawson-Luxmore scholarship.

I matched every accomplishment of the family with a parallel achievement. A profile piece about Sophie's new and glittening career in publishing, hot on the heels of a first-class degree, inspired me to pursue a huge contract with a nationwide chain of gyms. When Rowan MacBride was promoted to Headmaster, I leased my machines in a spa hotel group, and was able to pay off the mortgage on my flat. Lydia's name cropped up in the occasional court bulletin and campaigning websites.

At first, the youngest two MacBrides had no online presence but social networking was a gift. Using a thumbnail photograph culled from an American university website, I set myself up a Facebook account, joined a group called the Old Cathians and requested the friendship of all its members. Over half of them responded positively: so much for the intellectual elite. When I had a hundred friends of my own, I approached Felix and Tara. He declined: she accepted within seconds. The photographs on screen showed a very different person from the chubby teenager whose bedroom I had plundered. My mother, whose voice was always present in a static hiss all of its own, would have quoted Austen herself: 'It sometimes happens that a woman is handsomer at twenty-nine than she was ten years before.'

Tara was still in Saxby, was single, worked as a teacher at a state primary school and was mother to a ten-year-old boy called Jake Owusu MacBride. Kenneth would have been proud of the speed of my mental arithmetic as I thought back to my old game of pushing the needle through the latex. *Jesus.* They grow up so fast . . . Jake was a good-looking mixed-race boy, tall and broad for his age. His father, presumably the boy I'd seen Tara kissing in Cathedral Passage, was nowhere to be found on any friends list. The Cath's ethos of instilling honour in its pupils had obviously not worked on everyone. Tara's profile was updated almost hourly, riddled with emoticons and exclamation marks, but I spotted a crosswind of loneliness and vulnerability under the prevailing breeze of happiness.

Sophie was not on Facebook but featured heavily in Tara's photograph albums. She had married a dark, rangy man whose impressive body hair must have indicated virility, as she seemed to be almost constantly pregnant. The couple were always surrounded by little boys, so many it was as though they were real and running around my ankles, dizzying me. So that was where a first-class degree got you. Through the mutual friendship of Tara's profile I was able to peer through the chinks into Felix's. He had shot up and filled out, appeared to go to a lot of fancy dress parties and worked as a furniture restorer. So that was what had become of my scholarship! I felt my blood turn to boiling oil. The old fixation came roaring back into the forefront of my mind, the volcano's eruption all the more violent for its dormant years. Those expensive educations, all those advantages, and what had the MacBride children done with them? They had become a teacher, a shopkeeper, and Sophie, the finest mind among them, was little more than a brood mare. How *dare* they waste their privilege? Didn't they *know* what some people would give to have an education like that?

One September, Tara posted a picture of Sophie's eldest two, Toby and Leo, standing in front of the school gates in their crop green uniforms, all teeth and apple cheeks. I enlarged the image, stared at it until the smiling faces seemed to break into mocking laughter that sounded just like Tara's and Felix's had years before. That noise echoed in my ears until it seemed to be coming from outside my head. I slammed the laptop closed.

When I could bear to open it again, I created a new file. I made a list of every detail I could gather. Names, ages, addresses (where I could get them), occupations, routines, vulnerabilities. I put them into a spreadsheet, just as, years ago, I had cribbed the details from their wall planner and written it down by hand.

The following January, Rory Allen, a brash, foul-mouthed Dublin hotelier and a good client of mine, bought an old Jacobean manor house ten miles outside Saxby with the intention of converting it into a health farm. He wanted to show me around, to brag as much as to entice me into partnership, I suspected. I hesitated; of course I had planned to return to the area one day, but this had forced my hand before I felt ready. Was I strong enough yet, was I rich enough? The weight of my wallet did not provide its usual comforts. But Rory pressed invitation after invitation on me, and he was too important a contact to refuse.

As I clipped the brow of the hill that hid Saxby from the rest of the world, I was astonished by how much the place had shrunk. How could somewhere that small ever have contained all the ambition in me? A little outcrop of houses had sprung up outside the ring road. I remembered Lydia's campaign against the city's sprawl; I could not have been more delighted by the violation if I had laid the bricks myself. I orbited the city in a C-shape and drove on to the outlying countryside beyond.

The manor house hotel had potential, and I was happy to shake Rory's fat hand on a deal. It was rush hour when I got back into my car; the traffic announcements said that the Saxby ring road was gridlocked after an accident, and advised motorists wanting to cross the city to travel through it. Cathedral Terrace was unavoidable. My restraining order had long expired but with every revolution of the wheels my nerves stretched a little closer to breaking point. The traffic was slow enough for me to see that the drive was packed with cars and lights were on in every room, but I could not identify the figures in the windows. The years melted away and I felt so young that I doubted my place behind the wheel. The chant started up that had been silent for years: mothermothermothermothermother. Sweat sprang from my palms and made the wheel hard to grip; I was relieved when the traffic cleared and I could pull away from the terrace towards the Cathedral. Fresh perspiration slicked my brow when it looked as though my route would take me down the Old Saxby Road, but fortunately a new one-way system diverted me down a parallel street.

After that, it got easier, the way things do after the first time. I would have had cause to return anyway. Rory wanted me involved in the design as well as the supply of his fitness suite. I would visit once or twice a month and, until the manor house was habitable, I stayed in a motorway Travelodge. Apart from its location, it differed little from the one I had stayed in on my first nights away from Saxby. It was a ten-minute drive into town, and the perfect base from which to plan my expeditions. I grew bold, shadowing Tara from the meshed gates of Saxby Community Primary to her Monday night yoga class. I found Felix's fusty little shop and browsed the decrepit furniture he had apparently restored, both relieved and disappointed when the man behind the tatty counter told me he was out making a delivery. Sophie was too tedious to bother following and Rowan too sequestered – he seemed not to leave the Cath for days on end – but Lydia was the easiest of all, sitting as she still did on the bench in Saxby Magistrates' Court once a month.

The Court was a fan-shaped, art-deco building, modern by Saxby standards and rather beautiful. The central lobby was dominated by huge opaque windows dissected by brass crosses and the courtrooms were lined with walnut. The raised public gallery was unpoliced and either empty or sparsely populated by gum-chewing family members and the odd journalist busy with the staccato Arabic of shorthand.

The first time Lydia took to the bench I got a shock, like touching an electric fence. She had aged well, I thought: her hair was still fair and they all had that very fine white skin that does not fold or jowl but develops only feathery wrinkles that are invisible from a distance. If anything, her eyes had grown even bluer. She was always chair, conferring with the magistrates at her elbows then speaking for them, assuming the importance of the Lord Chief Justice as she doled out fines to speeding motorists and town-centre drunkards. Her hypocrisy turned my stomach and filled me with awe at the same time. Once I faked a coughing fit, drawing her eyes up to the gallery. They met mine briefly: no recognition glimmered in hers. Only I knew that her authority and status were undermined by her stupidity, not recognising her nemesis when he sat in the gods above her.

My long-term plan remained to find and publish her confessions, to destroy her reputation and that of her husband. Perhaps that would have been gratification enough when I was seventeen, had I been well enough to pursue my revenge in the immediate aftermath of my mother's death. But I had changed since then, and my anger had had time to stew. Now, it was not enough simply to unearth the truth about my mother's death and Felix's education. 'The way to hurt any parent is through their children,' my mother had said; well, then, I would pay back the sum of my mother's pain and mine, with Lydia MacBride's children as interest. I wanted to take down two generations: like for like.

Public humiliation, the destruction of a reputation, was a hard-nosed bullet, the kind that enters the body cleanly and exits the same way. I wanted a soft bullet, the kind that spins in its trajectory to shred the flesh from the inside. Anger continued to ferment, but it had not yet matured; while the idea of revenge held strong, its nature remained amorphous.

27

October 2011

Defendants at the Magistrates' Court tended to wear either sports gear or suits, but the girl in the dock was in leather and denim. She was the raw materials of beauty; long, dark, cavewoman hair, huge eyes dirty with make-up. Even her cheap, badly cut clothes could not disguise the perfect proportions beneath. She could easily have got work at an escort agency, although it was hard to determine her age: she could have been anything between fifteen and thirty-five. She gave her name as Kerry Stone, confirmed her address at a bail hostel, then shrank into silence while barristers played legal ping-pong above her head.

She was before the bench on charges of harassment and as the prosecution laid out their case I found myself for the first time being absorbed not by Lydia MacBride but by the drama played out on the walnut stage. Kerry Stone had allegedly been stalking a ten-month-old boy called Conor Watson, whose mother had frequented the children's playground where Kerry spent her empty days. At first the child's mother had been touched by the extra attention Kerry lavished on her child but the odd gingerbread man had turned into surprise gifts which had turned into offers to babysit and those, when rejected, had mutated into unwanted after-hours visits and hourly telephone calls through the night. Kerry would materialise whenever Conor's mother took him out of the house, offering to push the pram or take him to the park. In a statement read out by the prosecuting barrister, Mrs Watson explained that she was being treated for anxiety, lived in fear of an abduction, and was staying in Ireland with relatives until Kerry could be restrained. The defendant's chin stayed on her chest throughout the prosecution's speech. I willed her to look up, desperate to see that face again, but she remained slumped even as her own barrister took the floor and entered a guilty plea.

'It is important that the bench is aware of the extenuating circumstances of my client's offence,' said the barrister. 'Kerry has been suffering from post-traumatic stress disorder after losing her own unborn son in a violent attack at the hands of her partner, one Dean Prescott of Saxby, in her seventh month of pregnancy. Prescott is now serving five years for attempted murder; in addition to this loss, the injuries sustained meant that Kerry had to have an emergency hysterectomy. Had she carried her own baby to term, he would have been the same age as Conor Watson.' The defendant put her hands to her face; only the pendulum swing of the huge gold hoops in her ears showed that she was crying. 'While this does not excuse Kerry's behaviour, it does go some way to explaining it, and we ask that the bench consider this when sentencing.'

'Has she been receiving any kind of counselling?' asked Lydia, with fake concern.

'She has,' replied the barrister, 'and she's in touch with the Women's Haven, they're a charity who work with vulnerable women to help them—'

'I'm aware of the Women's Haven, thank you,' said Lydia. She cast her eyes to the gallery. 'Is there a representative from the charity here?'

'No,' admitted the barrister. 'You know what resources are like.'

'Indeed I do,' said Lydia MacBride. The three magistrates

bent their heads together for an intense conference. When they parted it was of course Lydia who spoke.

'We understand that the defendant has no family ties to this part of the country. We note that and that the child's parents have considered leaving Saxby, their birthplace. In fact the mother and child are currently staying with family abroad. The welfare of the child is naturally paramount, and so our sentence to you is that a protection from harassment order be made. The zone of the restraining order is to be extended to encompass all of the Saxby district council area.'

What was it with this place and restraining orders? That was typical Lydia MacBride, typical *Saxby*, to throw open the city for the rich and privileged while barring anyone who had not been born into that elite. They had barely progressed from the mediaeval practice of locking the city walls at night.

'Help will be given to rehouse you somewhere else. Ordinarily you would be asked to leave immediately but as the family are not present you have a few days' grace with this.' She bounced a look off the magistrates at her elbows. 'Seventy-two hours should do it. I'm familiar with the charity and know that they have connections elsewhere in the country. I am sure they will be able to find you alternative accommodation somewhere far from the Watsons.' She put down her pen and lowered her glasses. 'I *do* feel for you. I am a mother myself, and cannot begin to imagine the pain of the circumstances in which you lost your child. We hurt and feel through our children, even if we never meet them, in ways that those without families can never begin to understand. But the fact remains that you have no relationship with this child, and that although you profess to be fond of him you're actually causing him considerable distress. It is as a *mother* that I put his needs first.'

Kerry Stone finally looked up. 'You *bitch*,' she said. In that second, she became a sister of circumstance, another victim of this woman's prejudice. I suddenly had to speak to her for reasons that went far deeper than attraction.

Lydia's glasses went back on. 'I'm going to pretend I didn't hear that, but anything more and I will see you back here for contempt of court.'

The public gallery was on a different floor to the main courtroom. As Kerry's barrister escorted her through a door, I bowled my way out of the gallery and descended a curving brass staircase to find them in conversation.

'She's taken Conor away from me. He was all I had. She might as well have taken him out of my arms.'

The barrister's voice was stretched tight with forced patience. 'Kerry, Conor was never yours. You *know* that.'

'I would never have *hurt* him. I *love* him.' Her eyes narrowed. 'I'm going to get her back for this.'

The taut voice snapped. 'Kerry! Now you're really being ridiculous. It takes three magistrates to make a ruling, she was just the spokesperson and anyway, she's very compassionate compared to some on the bench. You could have done a lot worse than Mrs MacBride. Frankly, I think it went well for you. You could have been given a custodial sentence. You didn't even get community service.'

'Where am I supposed to *go*?'

'You heard the JP, the hostel will give you a hand. Look, Kerry, I've got to go, I'm in the family court this afternoon. Good luck with everything, OK?' She squeezed Kerry's upper arm briefly, then barged past me, muttering under her breath, 'Thank you for securing my freedom, Alison, thank you for getting me off the hook, Alison.' At the door, I saw her wipe her hand on her skirt.

Kerry Stone pressed herself against the court wall and cried some more. I bent my knees so that I was crouching before her.

'All right, all right, I'm going, I'm going,' she said.

I caught her hand; acrylic nails, pink with white tips, had been there long enough for the ragged cuticles beneath to show. 'No, I'm not moving you on. I want to talk to you. I think you and I might have something in common.'

She took in my expensive clothes. 'You and me?' she said.

'Would you like to go for a drink?' I said.

The wine bar was in a cellar not far from Kenneth's old flat. Descending the flagstone steps into the area was like going from day to night with no dusk; its darkness was lit with candles in bottles and the nooks of its vaults were filled with ostentatiously cobwebbed barrels. Racked, rare bottles of wine were kept behind bars.

Kerry went straight to the toilet; I thumbed the wine list, thick as a novella, then played safe by ordering a bottle of Moët. I filled my glass first and raised it in a secret toast. My superstitions then, as now, were limited to the little talisman I carry in my pocket, but I could not escape the thought that fate had delivered Kerry to me just when I needed someone.

Kerry came back, face clean. Early twenties, I guessed, or a hard life in its very late teens. Hers were the kind of good looks that peak early. Without care and attention, without prompt intervention, they would be gone before she was thirty.

'Drink this,' I said. 'It'll take the edge off your shock.' She swigged from the flute and held it in her cheeks for a second, like a child drinking cola.

'So what've we got in common?' she said, her face as inscrutable as her voice. She lacked the self-consciousness that most beautiful women have. So much the better.

'I'm going to tell you a story about Lydia MacBride,' I said. 'Forget what your barrister said, about how it takes three magistrates to make a ruling. I've been watching her in that courtroom for a long time, and what she says goes. Nothing she does is an accident.'

For the first time in years I repeated the story I had so often shared with Dr Myerson. Unlike the Wellhouse staff, Kerry never once told me I was delusional, or that it was a coincidence. I had not felt so listened to since my mother was alive.

'Come back to London with me,' I said impulsively. My heart danced. As when I had laid into Felix, I had that same sensation of being outside myself looking on. 'You've got to leave Saxby anyway. Why not come back with me?'

'Oh. OK,' she shrugged. I attributed her lack of gratitude to the shock.

'I suppose being swept off your feet by strange men bearing champagne is an occupational hazard when you look the way you do,' I said, although I suspected it was more likely to be half a cider and a packet of crisps. Everything from the way she held herself to the way she drank suggested she was unused to luxury. I doubted anyone in her past could compete with what I had to offer.

I pulled up in the middle of an estate just inside the ring road. Kerry entered a 1960s tenement and returned in under a minute. Her life's accumulated possessions fitted in one of those cheap plaid laundry bags, which billowed like an airbag in front of her in the passenger seat. On the journey back to London we shared more of our histories, exchanged the vocabularies of our childhoods: to her, the world of study and scholarship was as alien as children's homes and foster families were to me. As we approached the city, conversation gave way to quiet. I had forgotten how companionable silence could be.

28

Back in Ealing, I offered her a shower, showing her the en-suite in the guest room and getting out two white towels, one smaller than the other, as though I was used to visitors. While she was in there I threw all of her clothes into the washing machine, condemning them for being too cheap, too black, too lacy, too synthetic.

The thrum of the machine drowned out her presence and then suddenly she was there, swathed in a towel, wet hair snaking darkly over her shoulders.

'Where's my stuff?'

I gestured to the machine and patted the sofa next to me. I untucked the corner of the towel, ready to retreat at the first sign of resistance, but there was none. I unwrapped her like peeling notes off a wad. I had to catch my breath. Her body made a mockery of my livelihood. That perfect fluke of fat and bone, firm and soft: you could strap most women to a machine for a year and this wasn't waiting to emerge from underneath. Her papyrus skin was flawless but for a faded vertical stretchmark under her navel, intersected by a scar just above the neat triangle of pubic hair, to form an inverted cross. She was reticent at first, but with a little encouragement grew more vocal, the way I liked them to be.

It was the first time I had ever slept with a girl who knew my background. With anyone else, that would have made me feel weak, but not with Kerry. I was so lucky with her: because of Dean Prescott and the other men who had gone before me, it was like riding a horse who expects to be whipped and so jumps at the slightest tug.

'Why did you put up with him?' I asked her.

'It was all right at first, you know. He was a good laugh, and he had loads of mates, and that. And he had a really nice flat, it had views right over the countryside so even if you were stuck in all day you never got that feeling of being in prison. I used to like waiting for him to come home at night, rolling him a spliff and having it ready for him. But then he did his back in and he couldn't get work, and he was at home all day, and he started to take it out on me; just digging at me all the time. I thought it'd get better if I was pregnant. I thought a baby might give him a reason to lay off the gear and get a job. And for about five minutes it was, after I'd done the pregnancy test. But then, as soon as I started to show, it got worse. That's when he started whacking me about.'

'So why didn't you leave him *then*?'

She was incredulous. 'Because you've got to give a baby its dad, haven't you? At least a *chance* of a dad. Hardly anyone I know has. I wanted my baby to be different.'

'Some mothers can compensate for the lack of a father. If they love enough, if they're strong enough.' I was of course talking about my own mother but that was not Kerry's interpretation. She nuzzled into me.

'Dean would have never said anything like that,' she said. 'You get that I could have been a good mum. You see it, don't you?' A pause hung between us until she bridged it. 'You'd never have hurt me like that if it was our baby, would you?'

If Kerry had been able to conceive, I'd have worn three condoms to avoid impregnating her, but, 'I'd never do that to you,' I said, reaching for her hand. Promises leave the lips like breath when there is no question of their being kept. The crying started up again. I tracked the tears' progress down her cheeks like racing raindrops on a window pane.

'What is it?' I said, when they grew too many to count.

'If only I'd met you before,' she sobbed. 'Just two years earlier. If only we'd known each other then. Life could have been so different.'

She had little choice but to be financially dependent on me; at twenty-three, she had literally no skills and her work history was chequered and sporadic. As my live-in partner she was entitled to no unemployment benefit and I would have been too proud to claim it if she was. Because she asked for nothing – her only desire was both priceless and impossible – I took pleasure in giving her everything. I educated her on the broadways of Sloane, Regent and Bond Streets, passing on the lessons of reinvention I had taught myself a decade before. I took her to a hairdresser who taught her how to spin silk from cotton, gave a Fenwick's personal shopper carte blanche and my Black Amex. I could not part her from her gold hoop earrings but even they had their own charm, an anomalous reminder of the gypsy I was beginning to tame. At home, I taught her basic civilities such as how to make real coffee in my espresso machine, and I cooked to re-educate her palate. I didn't need her to eat haute cuisine every night, but I did need her not to turn her nose up at anything that didn't come with ketchup.

When I had to travel she was content to stay in watching TV talent shows and reality TV imports from America. Entire days passed with me making calls from my office while she watched back-to-back episodes of *The Real Housewives of Beverly Hills* and *Jersey Shore*. She was bewitched by a channel called Home & Health that screened back-to-back documentaries about motherhood, every aspect of the condition from miracle conceptions to multiple births. If the reality shows were opiates, these were stimulants, rousing in Kerry a flash of the same hysterical passion I had glimpsed when she had shouted at Lydia from the dock. At first, she was consumed by her grief, desperate to talk for hours about her lost babies.

'Kerry,' I would say to her. 'You've got to stop this. It's not good for you to talk about it.' I had to be cruel to be kind: the sooner she moved on, the better for both of us. That side of Kerry was not a broken horse but a wild one. Hers was a double tragedy; not only did she have all that pent-up pain and passion, but it had nowhere to go. It could not be converted into ambition on her own behalf, for the worst had already happened to her. It was only right that I harnessed that energy, channelled it away from her useless grief and into my own scheme. Even if her grief had come with an accompanying plan of revenge, the force of my own obsession was such that no relationship I had would ever be able to accommodate anyone else's. I called up the telecoms company and had Home & Health blocked from my subscription.

In some ways Kerry was a distraction from the MacBrides – my time and energy were of course finite – but in one crucial respect she redoubled my intentions. Before I met her, the war on the family had been a cold one. In ten years, I had barely progressed beyond studying them, and I had not shared my intentions with another soul. The moment I told Kerry my story, the thaw began.

March 2012

I was in my home office, the first coffee of the day – she was getting better at making it – steaming on my desk. I delved into my emails. Every morning several Google alerts were waiting in my inbox; I had saved scores of searches, one for each of my products and projects, one for each of my professional competitors, one for each of the MacBrides, one for the school, one for my own name and another for Kerry's. The business searches yielded results most days: as for my parallel project, I was lucky to get one a week. That morning, though, Lydia+MacBride generated dozens of links to the same story. She had been named in the New Year Honours list.

The *Saxby Courier* had the most in-depth coverage, under the headline, 'From JP to MBE'. The accompanying photograph was new. She had finally begun to show her age, or perhaps it was the black robe she wore, rather like Rowan's academic gown, that bled the colour from her face. She was in her study; I recognised the carved cherrywood bookshelf, although the walls had been repainted. Lined up behind her, out of focus and unidentifiable to the ignorant eye, were two rows of thick brown diaries. I ran my fingers along them as though I might be able to pluck one from the screen.

'Well, well, well,' I said.

My voice summoned Kerry from the sitting room.

'Is the coffee OK?' she said, and sidled onto my lap. Her lips moved as she read the text underneath, and I correctly anticipated her question, 'What's an MBE?' she said.

'It's a Queen's honour,' I said. Kerry remained blank. 'It's like a prize. It's a good thing, though: the higher she rises, the farther she falls when I take her down.'

'You still haven't told me what we're going to do to get our own back,' said Kerry. 'Are you any closer to getting them diaries yet?'

'*Those* diaries,' I corrected. I saved the new picture in a file called 'MacBrides_Collective', and flicked through the other photographs I had captured from Tara's Facebook account. I stopped on a recent one of the whole clan wrapped up warm and holding sparklers.

'It's a shame really, that they hate you so much,' said Kerry. 'It'd be easy enough to hurt them if they loved you. D'you want another coffee?' She slid off my lap and went into the kitchen, where presently the espresso machine began to belch and hiss. I remained motionless but for my right hand clicking through the album, coming to rest on a snapshot of Tara, Jake and various other parents and children at sports day. Tara still seemed conspicuously single, and the germ of an idea began to form. Kerry's words echoed in my ears. 'It'd be easier if they loved you.'

Yes! No. *Could* I? It would solve everything. It was audacious, but if I was successful the rewards would be proportionally spectacular. I thought of Kerry and, in a further burst of inspiration, I clicked onto the cache of photographs labelled 'Felix', filled the screen with thumbnails and it hit me for the first time that I had never seen him pictured with any kind of girlfriend. Kerry could have her own role to mirror mine.

She returned with my cup; quickly I filled the screen with a spreadsheet. I was letting my imagination run too far ahead of what I knew to be possible. I could not possibly ask Kerry to dive in before I had even tested the water.

29

April 2012

When I got to the church hall, Tara had already made herself a
space at the front of the class. From a tattered sausage-shaped
bag made out of sari material, she unfurled a pink yoga mat
and spent the minutes before the class began in the downward-
facing dog position, arse in the air, palms and soles in contact
with the floor, evidently aiming for some future rather than
present grace.

Afterwards we were all given liquorice tea that looked and
smelled like plant fertiliser.

'Great class,' I said to Tara. 'I feel inches taller.'

'You're very bendy for a big man,' she said. I raised an
eyebrow; her cheeks became embers. 'What I mean is, you get
all these big blokes in here who can lift their own bodyweight
on a bench press but when it comes to balance and flexibility
they're all off kilter, they're not used to using their own
bodyweight as resistance . . . God, I'm rambling. What do you
think of the tea?'

'Disgusting,' I said.

She laughed. 'It's very cleansing. I'm on a detox.'

'That's a shame. I was going to ask you if you wanted to go
for a glass of wine or something with me. But I don't want to
be a bad influence.'

She blushed again. 'I'd love to. It's just, I've got to get back
to my son.'

'I understand,' I said, and left it there. I counted in my head, one, two, three, four—

'Next week, maybe?' she said. 'A retox?'

'I don't want to keep you away from your little boy.'

'Oh, he's not that little. He could actually feed himself, but I've got nothing in . . . He's fine if he *knows* I'm not going to be around. It's only spontaneity that's tricky. I'm Tara, by the way.'

'And I'm Matt,' I replied, pouring my liquorice tea into an oversized cheeseplant pot. 'I'll hold you to that drink next week.'

The following week, she had painted her toes seashell pink and was wearing perfume, and I knew things would go my way. Over a glass of nasty pub wine she told me things I already knew about her and I told her things about myself, some of which were true.

'If you live in London, what are you doing here in Saxby?' she said.

'Last week, it was business,' I said. 'I've got an interest in a new spa hotel not far from here, and I'm on the lookout for staff. Far better to take a yoga class than to interview a yoga teacher.'

'And what brings you back this week?' she said, running her finger around the rim of her wineglass. The feed line was so obvious I was almost embarrassed by my reply.

'You.'

She smiled. 'Jake's staying with my parents tonight.'

Half an hour later, we were entering her flat. I barely had time to register the interior – textiles everywhere, rugs, throws and kilims on the walls as well as the floor – before her hands were on the buckle of my belt. Half a minute later, with one hand on each of her shoulders and her feet crossed at the small of my back, I felt a thrill of trespass comparable to my first time in Cathedral Terrace.

As Tara slept, I explored her flat. The fridge was a solid wall of photographs of the MacBrides. Shelves were crammed with ethnic knick-knacks from Buddha heads to African masks via Indian woodcarvings with tiny little gods and goddesses. A diary like Lydia's lay on its side, heavy enough to bookend a row of paperbacks. I tried not to raise my hopes yet felt them plummet when I opened it to find the pages entirely blank.

Tara woke me the next morning with a cup of tea.

'Are you around later?' she asked. 'Jake's got cricket practice after school, so I'd have the flat to myself for a couple of hours.'

'I'm a busy man,' I said. 'I've got an empire to run, I've got a nation to save from morbid obesity. I need to be back in London this afternoon.'

'Next week?' she said.

'I'd like that.'

I drove back to London on autopilot. My thoughts were all of Kerry, and how I was going to sell this scheme to her. She would understand the desired outcome – my dreams were hers – but the method? If only there was some way of keeping her onside, some big declaration that would show her that this thing with Tara was nothing more than a means to an end. If only you could wrap an idea in a gift box, if only persuasion were as easy to bestow as a necklace or a—

The solution occurred with such startling clarity that I swerved in the road, as though the idea itself had driven out in front of me without signalling.

30

The registrar gave a little preamble, said something about how the success of a marriage was not about gazing into each other's eyes but looking towards the same horizon. I could not have put it better myself.

My bride was a Klimt painting made flesh in her sequinned gold shift, her hair a soft dark hood. She had even swapped her cheap gypsy hoops for similar circles of tasteful hammered brass. She spoke her vows with careful, deliberate diction. After the ceremony we had a sushi lunch. It took Kerry three glasses of champagne before she could muster the courage to eat the sashimi and then it was done with much laughter and clumsiness.

'Mrs Kerry Rider,' she said, admiring her left hand. 'It suits me.'

'The name, or the ring?'

'Both.'

Technically, of course, she wasn't Kerry Rider – she had just pledged her life to Darcy Kellaway – but she knew the name my mother had given me was something I saved only for the gravest of occasions. I did not press the subject: the last thing I wanted was for her to change her own name. When the time came for her to move in on Felix, there must be no outward signs of our connection. I knew from experience with Tara how much concentration it took always to pay with cash or my company account card, never keeping anything that spoke my real name in my pocket or wallet, hiding my driving licence in the boot of the car. I watched Kerry inexpertly stabbing a rice ball with a chopstick, eyes crossed with concentration. I would be asking enough of her as it was.

'Thank you,' she said, suddenly. 'I never thought I'd have a wedding day. A lot of men wouldn't want me, you know.'

'Because . . . ?'

'Because I'm damaged goods, aren't I? My past's a right old mess.' Champagne and happiness had led her to drop her guard; her vulnerability was actually charming.

'So's mine. That's why we're a good match. That's why it bodes well for the future.'

'And you really don't mind that I can't have children?'

'I take back what I just said about you understanding me.' I cloaked the truth in jest, then grew serious for my lie. 'I only mind that *you* mind.'

It was still early afternoon when I carried her on sea-legs over the threshold of my flat. Consummation was swift and urgent in the newly matrimonial bed. She rolled on top of me so that her hair was a stole over her shoulders and mine. I reached up to tuck it behind her ears and trace with my thumb the perfect contour of her cheekbone. 'Matt?' she said 'Maybe now we're married . . .' Her breath was crisp with champagne and her words were liquid, but when I raised my eyebrows she broke off eye contact with me; alcohol could only embolden her so far.

'Go on, spit it out,' I said. She shifted, sending a shiver down the length of me.

'Why don't we just let it all go?' she said into my chest.

'Let what go?' I said, with patience that did not feel sustainable.

'All this MacBrides stuff. Look how nice life is when we don't talk about them, when it's just us. You haven't mentioned them all day and it's been so much better. Why don't you just leave it? You know what they say; the best revenge is living well. We live well, don't we? So why don't you channel all your energy into that? Into making a family with me? Do you know how easy it would be for a couple like us to adopt a baby?' Now that the cork was out of the bottle, the words kept pouring. 'It's easy if you've got money. We wouldn't have to wait years for my court order to run out, or take on a kid, we could get a new *baby*. We can afford to do it abroad, can't we? There's *millions* of babies out in places like Pakistan or Mexico.' I kept quiet and gave her a chance to stop talking. 'I saw a thing the other day about Chinese girls whose parents just abandon them. They're crying out for people like us.' I was rigid with anger at her ingratitude. After all I had done for her. After everything I had *given* her. Eventually she sensed the tension and began to falter. 'I'd do all the work, all the looking after. It wouldn't be any extra stress on you. It's not as if I do anything all day—'

I hooked a finger into each of her earrings. She realised what I was doing a half-second before I pulled. Her screaming was disorienting but I managed to throw her off me before too much blood could spill. The bed linen was ruined, a messy parody of the virgin bride's bloodstained sheets. I was too angry and hurt to look at Kerry properly, but I gave her a towel to clean up the worst of it and called a taxi to take her to the A&E department of Northwick Park Hospital. I pulled on some sweats and waited in the sitting room while she made herself decent.

I changed the bedsheets and lay back on clean cotton to watch the static screen of my bedroom window. I stared at treetops and rooftops until daylight softened into a violet dusk that was abruptly dispersed by the vulgar pop of an orange streetlight. I was pinned to the bed by shock, stunned by the way Kerry had withdrawn her support, swift as a magician whipping a cloth from under the set table, and just as illusive. If she was not on my side, who would be? If she was not my ally, what was her worth to me?

I was still in my trance when her key turned in the door. By then it was no longer our wedding night. She stood in the darkened doorway of the bedroom. Even in the streetlamp's glow I could see that her earlobes were dressed with gauze and her neck was streaked with what looked like rusty water.

'I'm so sorry,' she said, before I could get a word in. 'I didn't mean to upset you. Of *course* we'll carry on. Please don't leave me, please don't throw me out.' Her apology melted my anger. I waited a beat, in case there was more. 'Please, Matt. I love you. I'd do *anything* for you.'

She crawled onto the bed and collapsed into my arms.

'It's OK,' I said, stroking her hair, now lightly infused with the stale antiseptic smell of the NHS. 'I know it won't happen again.'

31

'No Jake tonight?' I asked, uncapping two bottles of beer and handing one to Tara.

'He's at my parents' again,' she replied. Her earlobes were perfect petals with one single pink pinprick in the centre. 'He's seen me hurt by men in the past, and that hurts him, so now I have a policy of not introducing him to anyone until I know it's going to be serious.' She said this in a neutral tone, making it impossible for me to deduce whether I potentially fell into that category or not. Intimacy was elusive, perhaps inevitably, given that I was limited in what I could share with her. Tara was more cautious than I had originally guessed, giving back only what I offered first.

I let my fingertips trail, as though idly, over her bookshelves, alert for the leather brick of the diary. I knocked something off a ledge and had to jump to intercept it.

'Good save,' said Tara. I looked down at my catch. It was a hexagonal wooden shield with a gold plaque in its centre, an award given to Tara and Jake for raising money for a charity that supported young people with sickle cell anaemia.

'That's how Jake remembers his dad,' she said. 'He had sickle cell.'

'*Had?*'

She looked at the trophy. 'He died while I was pregnant.' I thought of the clinch I'd seen them in. He hadn't looked anaemic then, he'd looked bursting with red hot blood. 'We didn't know each other that long.'

'I'm sorry to hear that,' I said. I no more wanted Tara's diseased school boyfriend entering the narrative of my life than I did Conor Watson and his unborn predecessor, but was curious to see whether this vulnerability had passed down a generation.

'I don't know much about sickle cell. Is Jake . . . ?'

She shook her head. 'No, you can't get it unless both your parents carry the gene, and it's almost unheard of in Caucasian families. Jake's in rude health. *Too* rude, sometimes,' she said with a rueful smile. 'Still, the Cath – sorry, that's the big school up near the Cathedral – is already sorting him out. He started the prep last year. He'll go up to the big school when he's thirteen.' I put the award back on its perch and picked up the diary instead, just to have something to do with my hands; anything that involved the Cath obviously had my full attention. 'We all went there,' she continued. 'I had all these lefty ideals about him going to state school, which was fine when he was little and I was teaching there and I could keep an eye on him, but funnily enough I found my principles changed rather when he went to the local comp; it was all a bit much for him and he got himself terribly bullied at first, because he talks like we all do, rather than the other kids there. And then in the second term he sort of fell under the influence of this vile Year Ten boy. It started when Jake let him shave a Nike swoosh into his hair, which was bad enough in itself, but the next thing he was talking like some godawful rapper, then he came home smelling of cigarettes and before I knew it they were getting him to carry their bloody marijuana for them. That was all they wanted him for, just to be their little mule, because they were nowhere to be seen when the police picked him up.' Her voice wobbled a little. 'So my parents and Will and Sophie got involved, and to cut a long story short,

Jake's a public schoolboy now.' She shot me a defensive look, as though she expected me to judge or challenge her. Perhaps I would have, if this had been a revelation, but all it did was confirm what I already knew about the way the MacBrides closed ranks to protect their own. 'I suppose I was trying to prove some kind of point, although I don't know what, and I don't know why I thought I could use Jake to do it. Mother of the year, that's me. Anyway. The Cath'll be the making of him. He needs structure and discipline, he needs a bloody *uniform*. I tell you what, the quickest way to turn a liberal into a Tory is to give her a teenage boy to bring up.'

I swilled my beer around, held it in my mouth long enough for it to sting my gums. 'I don't mean to be rude, Tara, but how can you afford that on a teacher's salary?'

'The MacBrides have ways and means.' She tapped the side of her nose with her bottle. It echoed the gesture Felix had made in Cathedral Passage, but this time I had enough discipline to control the bubbling rage. 'What have you got there?' she said, looking at my hand with an unsuspecting smile.

'I don't know, I hadn't looked,' I said. 'Sorry, is it your diary or something?'

Tara took the book, transferred its weight from palm to palm and let the blank pages fan open.

'My mum gave it to me. She thinks it'd be good for me, uphold the family tradition. I can't be arsed though. I mean, who keeps a diary these days? If you want people to read it, you blog, and if you want to go down memory lane, you just go on Facebook.'

'But your mum keeps one?' The effort of keeping my interrogation light was demanding, like a drunk person trying to appear sober.

'She's Saxby's answer to Samuel Pepys. She's always written, from when I was little. All in books like this. She's always threatening to write a warts-and-all memoir.' She giggled.

'What's funny about that?' I said.

'Clearly you've never met my family,' she said. 'My mum, skeletons in the cupboard? Hardly. She's so . . . *good*. She's so patient, and forgiving. You've no idea what it's like, having to live up to someone like that, especially when I'm so, y'know . . . Not that I'd have her any other way. The world would be a better place if everyone had a mother like mine.'

32

Kerry was in the bedroom working on her hair. The warm female smell of her, mixed with the sweet chemical fizz of hairspray, diffused into steam that filled the corridor. She had changed her hair so that it fell over her ears. It affected her whole posture, shoulders forward and spine round. I wished she wouldn't slouch. It made the expensive clothes I had bought her look cheap.

I closed the office door behind me and made a call to Rikesh. I had a few things to run past him: an increased investment in Rory's spa hotel – I had given him a proposal a few weeks before – and I wanted to see if the company could justify renting a flat in Saxby, ostensibly so that I could be near the place. Rikesh greenlit both ideas.

'It's going to mean a lot of paperwork and some creative accounting but if you pull this off, you'll be a very rich man. Richer, anyway. Any other big schemes or scams on the go? Remember what I always say, I'm like a defence lawyer, I can't help you if you don't tell me the truth.'

Rikesh was beginning to grate, but to disentangle myself from him would be a risky and complicated process that was probably best delayed until after I had dealt with the MacBrides.

'Well – there is one thing you probably ought to know, not that it makes any difference. I got married a couple of months ago.'

Rikesh sang the bassline and chorus to 'Another One Bites the Dust'.

'Very funny,' I said.

'You won't catch me getting married, not until pre-nuptial agreements become legally binding in this country, anyway. There's lots of ways of getting rid of girlfriends. There's only two ways to get rid of a wife, innit? Just ask Henry VIII. I'm only joking. It doesn't have to be all bad. Does she work, this wife of yours?'

'No.'

'Well, what did she do before she met you? Has she got office skills?'

The thought of Kerry sustaining any kind of career was laughable.

'She can't even turn on a computer.'

'Ah, we can put her on your payroll anyway. Call her a PA, you can draw out more money from the company without paying higher-rate tax. Marriage does have *some* advantages.'

'Thanks, but I like to keep Kerry separate from my work.'

'Well, then, you shouldn't have married her, should you? She can take half of whatever you've got now. This is what comes of acting without consulting Rikesh. Look, I'll get her put on, it's easy, I'll send you the paperwork. She doesn't have to get involved, just sign a couple of pieces of paper. You might as well exploit it.'

I put the phone down, angry at Rikesh's over-familiarity and his crude reduction of the situation. His words had hit home. Of course I had known that I was giving Kerry access to half my worth, but I had been so caught up in the gesture that I had overlooked the practicalities. Kerry would have done this without a ring; she would have done it for a warm bed. That's the problem with having a vocation: the grand plan often overshadows the details. I conceded that Rikesh was right in one respect. If I had made the gesture, I ought at least to get my money's worth.

I stood in the bedroom doorway, watched her run the

straightening irons through her hair with a sizzle and a hiss. When she saw me over her shoulder in the mirror, her delight was quickly lost in apprehension, the way it seemed to be these days. I stroked her hot hair, taking care to keep away from the irons, which the digital display told me were at 200 degrees. She set them down carefully and turned them off at the plug.

'I've made a decision,' I said. She swung around to face me, her face primed for bad news. 'I've thought long and hard about this. I just know the only way to find out what I need to know is through those diaries. I've tried everything to get at them, and the only way is go through the family, but they're completely closed. And also, it's about *like for like* revenge. They split and destroy families, so that's what we've got to do, too. It has to go beyond just the diaries. We're getting revenge on everything, taking down the whole family. There's a duality to it, do you see? Two sides of the same coin.'

Her brow furrowed in consternation. I'd lapsed into Darcy-speak again, a fatal mistake with Kerry, who needed the plainest language possible – while I'd long stopped hoping for understanding from her, comprehension was necessary.

'Basically, the closer you are to someone, the deeper the wound.' I picked up her hair irons, still hot, pointed them like a sword and took a step backwards. 'It's like, I can't hurt you from here . . .' In the next second, I took a full lunge close to her and held them millimetres from her skin. 'But from this distance, I could do you some real damage. *Now* d'you get it?'

She shrank away from them until she took up almost no space at all.

'What are you going to do?' she whispered.

'I'm going to get at her children. I'm going to start with Tara, I'm going to make her fall in love with me, and then I'm going to let her know who I really am, at the same time that I tell them all what Lydia did to me.'

Kerry's lip began to tremble. 'But what about—'

'I know what you're thinking. Hear me out. It'll be completely separate from us, it won't change things. It doesn't affect us at all. I *married* you, didn't I? I won't *mean* it with Tara.'

'But you're not going to *sleep* with her . . . ?'

'I'll have to make it convincing. Come on, Kerry, have you forgotten what that family are like? It's the perfect way to get access to those diaries *and* really ram home what they did to me.'

'I'm sure there's another way we can get those books, Matt. Why can't we just break into the house and get them?'

'Breaking into the house is a criminal offence. It could be used against us, it would make us into common criminals and we're better than that, I'm better than that, the whole point of this is that they see I'm better than *them*. I don't want to break the law. Just their hearts.'

'And then what? Once we've told them? Do we get on with life as normal?' She looked away from me and started to run some stuff through her split ends.

'Not normal,' I said. 'Better.'

I could see she wasn't convinced so I played the trump card that she had dealt me herself. 'I'll be different, on the other side of all this,' I said. 'I won't get so stressed, I'll be much more open to doing new things. We might even try for that adoption.'

She froze with a thick black skein of hair between her palms. 'You're serious?'

'Why not? But this is the thing: until the MacBrides are dealt with, I won't have the energy to devote to a child, will I?'

'No, yeah, all right,' said Kerry cautiously.

She had spoiled what was coming next: I had intended to tell her what she was going to do with Felix but now that would have to wait while she became accustomed to the idea of me and Tara, and to the thought of a baby. In the meantime, I laid some groundwork. I found a flat in Saxby; nothing fancy, just a studio on the outer edge of town. I bought a couple of things that might convincingly pass it off as Kerry's – nothing special, nothing that would be above her standards, just some Ikea candlesticks and a canvas box print of Van Gogh's *Almond Tree in Blossom* over the bed. It would, I was sure, act as a sweetener for her when the time came for her to play her own mirror role. Whenever she broached the adoption, I stalled her with the single word, 'Afterwards.'

In fact I had to keep 'afterwards' vague, even to myself. The rest of my life was a glittering city just over the brow of a hill – but it remained abstract, amorphous. Not until I was close to the summit could I commit to making plans for life after the MacBrides.

In my London neighbourhood, there was a place with a tuxedoed mannequin in the window that called itself a Spy Shop and sold cutting-edge espionage technology to private detectives and suspicious spouses: men who had never outgrown their James Bond phase. Using the company credit card, I bought a state of the art pen-shaped pocket scanner that read documents line by line and copied them into fascimiles of the original. I carried it everywhere I went, so that the next time I saw those diaries – and there would be a next time – I would be ready.

33

Six months after I gatecrashed Tara's yoga class I was formally introduced as her new boyfriend to the MacBrides.

'Do you want to come for lunch at home next week?' was how she put it.

'I thought I was going to be here anyway?'

She laughed. 'By *home* I mean the house I grew up in. It's on Cathedral Terrace, you know, those houses on the edge of the Green. We all go back there a couple of Sundays a month.'

'*All?*' I said, hardly daring to hope. 'Are you threatening to introduce me to your family, Tara MacBride?'

'It's about time, isn't it?' she said, throwing me a smile that I caught and returned. I had almost given up on this longed-for invitation; despite what I had said to Kerry, closeness to Tara was slow coming and hard-earned.

The only progress prior to this had been meeting Jake. Tara had introduced me as her 'friend' but he knew exactly what that meant. There was an obvious parallel with his life and mine at that age, a single mother and her son living in a small flat in Saxby, but there the comparison ended. Jake was surrounded by friends, cousins, team-mates, even girlfriends. He was as socialised as I had been isolated, as physical as I had been weak, and, I had to admit a few minutes into our first conversation, as ignorant as I had been studious. He was one big physical impulse; from fidgeting to eating to playing sport, he was never still. He lived in his body where I had been in denial of mine. Had it not been for my background in sports science we would have had nothing to say to each other; fortunately he was interested in intelligent nutrition that would give him the edge over the other children on the pitch. After Jake's brief stint as a drug-dealer's protégé, Tara refused to differentiate between protein shakes and anabolic steroids, and I smuggled sports drinks and fuel bars into Jake's pockets. 'You're so cool, Matt,' he said to me. He did not contrive to hide his admiration for me, or any of his enthusiasms. I could see how, ironically, it would have been Jake's wholesome, naive quality that would have carried him to the fringes of youth criminality; it would have made him so attractive to the boys who were looking for someone to exploit.

Immediately after the invitation to Sunday lunch was made, I was so thrilled that I would have access again to those diaries that I didn't consider the family who stood between us. As Sunday grew nearer, excitement was eclipsed by a dread that I would be discovered. In reverse order, I was concerned about Sophie recognising me, then her parents, and my chief worry was that Felix might have some kind of dramatic flashback and suddenly identify me as his attacker.

I studied my face from every conceivable angle, searching for a feature that would give away the boy I had been. I deliberately passed mirrors by, then rounded on my own reflection at the last minute to see if I could snare a glimpse of my former self. It never happened, but I could not trust my own judgement. I needed a second opinion.

Re-entering the Paddy Power betting shop was surreal. The once-shiny facade was dulled and dripping with pigeon shit. A make-up artist had painted wrinkles onto the face of the woman behind the window. The furniture inside had shrunk and so had the men. He was short and shrivelled; the sports jacket that had once strained to contain him now hung like a too-big blazer on a schoolboy. His eyes darted between two races on televisions suspended from the ceiling. I sidled up to the counter next to him.

'What do you fancy for the 2.17 at Goodwood?' I asked. Kenneth looked at me with less interest than he had shown the screens.

'Oh, now you're asking,' he said. 'The going's hard today, so . . .' and he reeled off a list of horses with preposterous names.

'Thanks,' I said. I placed myself right in his eyeline, giving him one last chance to identify his surrogate son. This time he did look at my face, his eyes tracing the triangle of eyes, nose and mouth. I smiled, all the while studying him, alert for a flicker of recognition. I saw only puzzlement.

'Everything all right, then?' he said, in the patronising tone he used to use with my mother. I knew he had no idea who I was.

'Everything's great,' I said, and left the shop without placing a bet.

I arrived with Tara and Jake to find Rowan and Lydia waiting for us on the top step of the house. Hellos were said and my trembling hand was shaken. In the entrance hall, Will extended a hairy, lean forearm and said, 'Hello, old boy,' in an exaggerated Wodehouseian accent that I suspected wasn't far from his true voice. I had the same feeling I used to get with Vass: that here was a walking instruction manual on how to be a certain type of man. But where Vass had kindled in me the glow of superiority, Will provoked its reverse. Sophie flicked on a fake smile that disappeared when she thought I wasn't looking. A little boy with white-blond hair headbutted me on the knee.

'Oh, Leo,' said Lydia. 'Give the poor man a chance to cross the threshold. Do you like children, Matt?'

I gave her a perfect, even smile. 'I do,' I said. 'But I couldn't eat a whole one.'

They all laughed as they let the wolf into their fold. I despised them for being so easy to fool, but part of me was disappointed that they could not project my current likeness onto my childhood self. It made me feel that the shadow I had cast across their family was light and shallow, engulfed by the one they had cast across mine.

I did not have to pretend not to recognise the place: the house had evolved sufficiently for my curiosity and disorientation to be real. The grandchildren had claimed it as their own: toys were everywhere. Even their crude paintings were on the wall, replacing those their mothers and uncle had created years before. The kitchen had been refurbished, granite and chrome updating the pine units, and extended so that a new dining area with a glass roof took up much of the courtyard garden, which was cluttered with ride-on toys. A basketball hoop was attached to the back wall that gave onto Cathedral Passage.

We had wine in the dining room while Sophie and Lydia bustled around the kitchen. I couldn't sit still, and got up to examine a glass-fronted drinks cabinet which contained only brandy, perhaps a dozen bottles of the stuff, from Rémy Martin and Courvoisier to Hennessy Black.

'Will's pride and joy,' said Tara, sidling up to me. 'For God's sake don't ask him about them, you'll never get him to shut up.'

I was about to ask Tara why Will's pride and joy should be stored at his in-laws' house, but the brandy buff himself came in wearing a striped apron, his cheeks rosy. 'Grub's up,' he said. At the heaped and steaming table, Rowan interviewed me for the second time.

'Have we met before?' said Rowan. My blood froze. 'You're not one of my old boys, are you?'

'No,' I said. 'No, I'm definitely not one of your old boys.'

'Well, thank goodness for that. I pride myself on never forgetting a single one of my pupil's names, after they're in my care. I thought I was losing my touch. *So.* Tara tells us you're an entrepreneur.' An expression of suppressed snobbery rippled across each of their faces. 'What exactly is the nature of your enterprise?'

'Fitness, nutrition, beauty, that sort of thing.' In the context of lunch in Cathedral Terrace, I saw my career through my mother's eyes, and could not muster my usual pride.

'I never got that myself,' said Felix. 'I mean games, yes, but exercise without the sporting element? It always struck me as a little odd.' I think he suddenly saw how rude he was being. 'I mean, I'm sure there's a market for it.'

'There is,' I said. 'A bloody good one.' I fought the ridiculous urge to stand up and recite the first book of *Paradise Lost* or discuss the foreign policy of James I.

'Tara says you spend a lot of time on the road,' said Will. 'I don't know how you stick it. My office are sending me to London every Monday and Tuesday for the foreseeable. I stay in the same hotel every Monday night. I don't even bother unpacking my suitcase some weeks. I feel like what's-his-name from *Death of a Salesman.*'

'Willy Loman,' I said, Darcy briefly raising his ugly head. Rowan gave me a sharp look, not of recognition, but surprise.

'You shouldn't complain, not in a recession,' said Lydia.

'True, true,' said Will. 'That's the other thing, Matt: how do you stand the insecurity?'

'Actually, I thrive off it, and the rewards make it all worthwhile.' I saw from their faces that that had come out all wrong. My wealth seemed to have turned against me, making me less, not more of a man in their eyes. I felt stung, as I suppose one would at a betrayal from a close friend. I felt the early-warning prickle of extreme thirst for the first time in years, and drained my cup to prevent a coughing fit. I pushed back my seat, and remembered just in time to ask, 'Excuse me, where's the loo?'

'First-floor landing, first door,' said Tara through a mouthful of roast potato.

The desk that had been in Sophie's room now served as a telephone table in the tiled hallway. The wood was soft with age. There was a sharpened pencil, black with The Lomond Hotel written on it. On impulse, I used its point to gouge my given initial on the desk. The staircase seemed narrower, doubtless because I was so much broader. My heart was kicking at my ribs as I regarded the study door, all that stood between me and Lydia's diaries. The handle turned without resistance to reveal a little boy's bedroom, with a Thomas the Tank Engine duvet, a globe night-light and a huge poster of a spaceship on the wall.

'Wrong one!' said Sophie, coming up behind me, in an echo of her interruption of a decade before. The toddler on her shoulder had a wet patch on the groin of his trousers and a smell hinted of worse to come. She softened a little. 'It's easily done. All the doors are the same, and all these corridors and staircases. Even I get it wrong sometimes, and I've lived here for thirty-five years.'

The brandy bottles and bubbles suddenly made sickening sense.

'*You* still live here? You *all* live here?'

'God, no! It's enough of a squeeze with just us. And it's about to get squeezier,' she said, patting her stomach. 'Mum and Dad live in an apartment in the school, have done ever since Dad was made head and I was expecting Toby. All their stuff was carted out of this house and into the flat, all our crap was shipped in, and the cycle begins again. Do excuse me,' she said, wrinkling her nose at the soiled child, and closed the bedroom door behind her.

In the bathroom I ran my wrists under the cold tap, willing my pulse to return to its resting rate. The diaries may as well have been in the vaults of the Bank of England if they were walled inside the Cath. I pressed my head against the cool bathroom mirror, bullied my panic into submission. It would be fine: I could do this. This was my life's work; there were bound to be setbacks. The diaries would come to me eventually. I had to believe that. In the meantime, I would concentrate on the other branch of my campaign. I had more than enough to work with.

34

I drew from my desk drawer the black pencil imprinted with the Lomond Hotel crest and dialled the number.

'Will Woodford, I'm just confirming my reservation for next Monday?' I said, trying not to overdo the impersonation. I heard the click of fingertips on a keyboard.

'We'll look forward to seeing you then, sir,' said the receptionist.

'I wonder if you could give me a room overlooking the street, quite low down,' I said.

'Not a problem. Will that be all, sir?'

I put down the phone and fired up my computer.

The agency that had supplied me so well in my first years in London was still going, now with a slick new website and prices to match. I recognised none of the girls on their books. Briefly I flicked through my remembered images of the ones I had used, allocating graduation, marriage or deportation as the reason for their retirements. First I narrowed the pool down to the aspirant actresses; there would be a certain amount of improvisation and dramatic licence required to ensnare Will. As it turned out, that restriction barely skimmed off ten per cent of the girls. If all those who claimed to be drama students really were, RADA must be thronged with whores. Then I was unsure whether to hire a girl of Sophie's type or her opposite. I had read that married men, if unfaithful, tended to go for women unlike their wives but Will seemed the kind to have a type and I wondered whether a younger version of Sophie might be a better shot. I vacillated between icy blondes and dusky beauties, finally trusting to my own experience and the pleasurable novelty of contrast between Tara and Kerry. The girl's working name was Annabel, but her dark olive complexion and almond eyes marked her out as an Aisha or a Layla or a Yasmin.

The Lomond was just off Piccadilly, its lobby over-stuffed with over-stuffed furniture, its dining room over-stuffed with over-stuffed Americans and decorated with antlers and watercolours of Highland scenes. I met Annabel in the snug bar at half past six.

'First things first,' I said. 'I'm not the client.' I showed her a picture of Will on my phone. She was not quite experienced enough to hide her disappointment but brightened when I told her that, if she was successful, I would double her fee. I gave her her script and we ran over it a couple of times.

'What if he doesn't go for it?' said Annabel.

I thought about telling her I would still ensure I got my money's worth but didn't want to disincentivise her. 'Don't worry. He will.'

Will entered the bar at seven, ordered a pint of beer and stared into it without drinking. His top button was undone underneath his tie and he needed a shave.

I was hidden in a winged chair in the corner, able to watch everything through a mirror. The Lomond was the kind of place where a man is invisible behind his tumbler of whisky but a woman will turn every head. When Annabel walked in, for a second she looked so obviously what she was that I was afraid the barman would ask her to leave, but he met her request for a glass of Laurent Perrier and a double Bache Gabrielsen without demur. Will looked up at the name of the drink but barely gave the girl a glance, even when she took the bar stool next to him. I called Annabel's phone, ringing off as the connection was made.

'Oh, no! What a shame! I was so looking forward to seeing you.' I was impressed: her disappointment was not obviously feigned. 'I've just bought you a brandy and everything. Well, never mind. I'll see you soon.'

She placed her phone on the bar and turned to Will.

'Do you like brandy?' she said.

'Oh, ah, oh . . .'

'It's just that the person I bought it for isn't coming now and I can't stand the stuff.'

'I don't think it's . . .' He cast about the room as though looking for someone to rescue him. I pressed my spine harder against the back of the chair.

'Please, I'd like to.' Annabel slid the glass across the bar to him. Once his lips were on the glass there was an inevitability to it all. She ordered him another three brandies, half-finished her own champagne. Her hand brushed his knee and she let it rest there. When he drew his room key out of his pocket to sign for the tab, I paid my own bill with cash and took up my place with my camera in the window of a Starbucks across the road.

Annabel took direction beautifully: she left the light on and the curtains open. She was clever, too, positioning herself to hide her own face while exposing as much as possible of him, the precise actress hitting her mark.

She was back downstairs by ten o'clock.

'Job done. He's in a bit of a state, though,' she said, counting the notes without removing them from the envelope. 'Started trying to justify it all the minute he'd come. He loves his wife, he would never do anything to hurt her, but he couldn't believe his luck when I came onto him and it's just been so hard since she'd been ill, postnatal depression, and he just gives and gives and yada yada yada . . . Some of them get turned on by guilt, it's half the point. He's not one of them. Can I see the pictures?'

I handed over the camera. 'Nice piece of kit,' she said, then scrolled through the images and checked the trash folder to make sure I hadn't stored any that showed her face. Our taxis took us in opposite directions.

Back in the flat, I locked myself in the office and printed the photographs, black and white, 10×8, and slid them into a stiff envelope. I addressed it to Sophie Woodford at 34 Cathedral Terrace, Saxby, then tucked it in between slices of paperwork in a file so tedious that no snooper would be tempted to look inside. I thought of them as cash savings, safe in the bank but easy to access. The intention was to produce them with a flourish when I broke the rest of my news, but there was no telling, once I'd finally found those diaries, how fast I would have to move.

35

We plunged down winding lanes so steep that it felt as though the car was going deep below sea level. Shadows swam like fish across the windscreen. Then a sharp right down a ditch-trimmed track, and there it was, the heathen chapel of Far Barn. This was where the MacBride children had played while I was learning poetry by rote.

I took in the solid wall of books, the fire where a television should be, the low sofas strategically arranged so that no matter where you sat you were forced into facing someone else. A strange noise fought its way out of my throat.

'You can shout for help as loud as you like,' said Tara. 'In Devon, no one can hear you scream.'

'Ha!' I said. 'Just testing the acoustics.'

She disappeared into a little room off the kitchen and fiddled with the thermostat.

'OK if I go for a run before dinner?' I said, squinting through the kitchen window. 'How far can I go?'

'I don't know. A mile or so? You'll hit a fence at some stage. If you get chased by a cow at any point, you've gone too far.'

The run was all wrong from the first stride. I couldn't get my footing well enough to build up speed. I literally stumbled across various decaying outbuildings scattered across the land. It took me half an hour to reach the fence, making a nonsense of Tara's estimated mile. On the way back, I took time to stretch at the little cottage. The doors and windows were all sealed up with plates of some kind of metal that was almost too cold to touch with my bare hands. I tried to prise one open, to look inside, but it was as stuck fast as though it had been soldered on. I looked closely at it, and saw that the grille was not actually bonded but lowered onto a sort of peg on either side. It took strength to lift it up and off. I doubted a woman could do it. There was nothing interesting inside, just a dank sort of room with another low little chamber leading off it. The ground inside was silver with frost. I hooked the grille back on its pegs and it fell like a portcullis.

I anticipated with pleasure the smell of onions and the sizzle of a good steak but was greeted at the border of the garden by a bitter, charred smell. A pan smoked on the range and Tara was a tiny shape in the vast sitting room, the phone at her feet, her face raw and tearstained. When she saw me she leapt to her feet and threw herself against my chest.

'We've got to go back to Saxby, now,' she wailed.

'What's the matter?'

'FelixjustrangMumsgotcancer.'

'*What?*'

A bubble of snot inflated and deflated in her right nostril. 'My mum's got . . . ovarian cancer. It's in her lymph nodes, it's in her spine, it's . . .' I lost her to a succession of hiccups and shrieks. 'She collapsed and she's been taken into hospital. She didn't even tell Dad. She's going to *die*, Matt!'

'What's the prognosis?' I said.

'Felix said it could be this week.'

I was actually speechless with the injustice of it.

'I don't *believe* this is happening,' I let slip. Tara's interpretation was typically solipsistic.

'Oh, Matt, thank God for you, thank God for someone to lean on.' Wet blue eyes gazed through spiky blonde lashes. 'What have I done to deserve you?'

36

I parked in the ambulance bay at Saxby Wellhouse. It was next to the gardens that gave onto the psychiatric ward. I noted that I was about twelve years late for my outpatient appointment. Usually I would have found that funny but my sense of humour had deserted me. In fact, I don't think it is an exaggeration to say that I was in as much agony as Tara was.

She blew her nose for the hundredth time that hour.

'Do you know where you're going?'

'Yes, she's in a private room in the oncology department.'

Of course she was. I watched Tara disappear – tiny as a wooden doll – through the great doors, to join her family at her mother's deathbed. The impulse to abandon the car where it was, run after her, tell all of them everything, nearly overtook me. The diaries were in the school. Lydia was in the hospital. Only one of those places was accessible to me. I was faced with the impossible choice: did I bring my imperfect showdown forwards, or did I wait and execute perfect revenge after her death?

My phone had been switched off for the journey. When I turned it back on, the screen was measled with little red dots: texts, emails, voicemails, missed calls. While I was staring at the screen wondering which to tackle first, the phone buzzed in my palm. It was Rikesh.

'Where've you been, man?' he said. 'I've been trying to get hold of you for hours. You haven't been picking up your letters, have you?'

What did he expect? I'd spent the few days before travelling to Devon in Saxby, using Tara's flat as a base while I oversaw the construction of the gym at Rory's hotel.

'Your accounts are *months* overdue. If you don't get them to me this week you're going to be hit with a massive fine.'

'Then I'll pay the bloody fine,' I said. 'I've got other stuff on the go.'

'You might not mind the fine but believe me you don't want to be investigated and if you default once more that's what you're looking at. Can you get the VAT stuff over to me in the next couple of days, at least?'

'I'm not in London.'

'Then get your missus to send it.'

The thought of Kerry sifting through my filing cabinet was even more stressful than the thought of leaving Saxby. I travelled the well-worn groove of the motorway. At home, Kerry was in front of the television. I caught the phrase 'British couples who go abroad to adopt' before she leapt up from the sofa, fumbled for the remote and turned the set off. Her hair was undone and in thick waves and she was wearing my dressing gown. She looked awful without make-up, eyes all piggy and puffy.

'I didn't know you were coming home today,' she said.

'Clearly not,' I said. 'I'm not. I just need to pick up some stuff, then I've got to get back to Saxby.'

'Again?' pouted Kerry, and followed me into my office. I gathered the VAT file from its place in the cabinet, slid it in a Jiffy bag and addressed it to Rikesh.

'Shall I make you a coffee?' she asked.

'I've got to catch the post office before the counter shuts,' I said. 'This has to go recorded delivery.'

'And then you'll come back?'

'Kerry, were you *listening* when I told you what was happening in Saxby? We're at a crucial stage. She could die any minute, and I don't know what's in those diaries, I haven't got a confession from her, I don't know whether to tell her who I am, or what. Have you got any *idea* of the stress I'm under right now?'

'I know what's good for you when you're stressed,' she said. She sidled up to me, slid my dressing gown off her shoulders and put her hand on the crotch of my jeans. I shrugged her off. Sometimes she felt like a plastic bag over my head.

'Look, Kerry, this is important,' I said. 'I thought I had your support on this.'

'You do!' she said, but I was already leaving, package under my arm. 'Come back! Please, Matt, I hate being on my own here, please, come back! It's only because I miss you. Please! Come back!'

Compared to Kerry, I sometimes thought, life with Tara was almost relaxing. Even my marriage was Lydia MacBride's fault. She was, after all, the one who introduced us.

I stood behind the bus shelter outside the Wellhouse. The blank diary filched from Tara's bookshelf was in a supermarket carrier bag at my feet. It was a desperate bluff but I had no other ideas. Hadn't Lydia written, years ago, that everything she had ever felt would eventually end up in her diary? Why, then, should I not hasten the only entry that mattered to me?

I watched Tara and Sophie hug their father goodbye outside the Wellhouse. Rowan disappeared back into the coffee shop next door to the hospital. Through the plate glass window I saw him join a long queue. I left my hiding place and ran to the oncology ward, knocking as a precaution. Felix opened the door.

The room smelled like bile and flesh that was already beginning to rot. The scent pulled me back with force to our rooms on the Old Saxby Road, my mother lying on her back. Death was in the room as sure as if he was sitting in one of the empty chairs at Lydia's bedside.

'You've missed Tara,' said Felix. 'She and Sophie have gone to pick everyone up from school.'

'Oh, right,' I said. 'Felix, are you all right? You look a bit pale yourself. Why don't you go and get some fresh air?'

'I don't like to leave her alone,' said Felix.

'She won't be alone,' I said. 'She's with me. Come on. You look very pale.'

'Yeah, maybe a ten-minute breather won't do me any harm. I'll go and find Dad, I think he's gone for coffee. Want me to get one for you?'

'No, I'm good.'

'Cheers, Matt,' said Felix, patting my arm on his way out.

Lydia's hair had grown out around her face, prematurely and erroneously making an angel of her. I looked at the tempting pillow but that thought was dismissed the second it arrived. Let her die as my mother had, terrified about her family.

I poked at her arm until she woke up; you could see the effort it cost her to open her eyes, and then it took her a few seconds to identify me. Her eyes passed over my face unfocused but as soon as she saw the book she became completely lucid, as though the saline drip in her arm was delivering a hit of adrenalin, not morphine. 'How did you get that?' she said. I felt a corresponding rush: I'd hit a nerve, here. Whatever else happened today I at least had confirmation that somewhere a diary existed. I no longer felt as though I was calling her bluff.

'I had to pick some stuff up for Rowan,' I said. 'It was just lying around.' She grasped for the button that would raise the bed into a recline. 'Lydia. I can't tell you how disappointed I was to read this. I wouldn't have thought you could be so cruel.'

'Oh, hell,' she said, hands going limp. 'I don't know why I wrote it down, I meant to destroy it, and then the next thing I knew I woke up and I was already in here. Tear it up, Matt, get rid of it.'

'I can see why you don't want it made public.'

'Never mind the *public*,' she said. 'Can you imagine what the family would think of me? Can you imagine what it would do to Tara? You wouldn't want her to see it, would you, Matt, I know you think the world of her.' I reached in my pocket for my mobile phone to record her confession. My hands grabbed cloth; I saw the phone plugged into the charger in my car. I was furious at myself. 'If you've read it, you'll know how sorry I am. You'll know I didn't mean for them to die.'

This pulled me up short. 'Them? Only my mother died. Only Heather Kellaway died.'

'Yes, and then there was the boy,' she murmured.

I massaged my forehead. She wasn't coherent, after all – although in a way she was right, she had killed Darcy Kellaway, forced the conception of Matt Rider.

'No, you stupid bitch, *I'm* the boy,' I blurted, but Lydia's eyes were closed and her mouth slack, the window of clarity abruptly curtained again by sleep.

Felix and Rowan were back, Starbucks in hand, sandwiches in paper bags, faces concave. I dropped the book into my carrier bag just in time.

In the corridor outside, I clung to the positive. Through my own carelessness, I had not recorded the confession. But Lydia had confirmed the existence of her diaries and effectively appointed me their guardian. It felt as though she was giving me her blessing.

37

I lay on virgin sheets. The Van Gogh blossom print over my head had been in season when I hung it back in May. Now its white flowers and blue sky were another reminder of how long it had been since I bought the flat. If Lydia had not become ill when she had, Kerry would be in here by now, working, under my supervision, on Felix. It was so unfair the way the goalposts kept shifting.

I went to the hospital every day, my phone always charged, in my pocket, and set to record at the touch of a button. I had by then decided that, if necessary, I would force the confession in front of her family, but that last speech I extracted from her had, for all I knew, been the last she ever made. Her mind was now a ransacked library of non sequiturs and fragmentary sentences. Through the jumble of her words it was evident that she was in distress, a state that her family said had inexplicably come over her a few days before. It must have been down to me, and I drew comfort from that.

I was unable to be alone with her, although we established one last private connection. While Lydia's family mumbled around her, her eyes suddenly found their focus on mine. There was a pleading in them that she could not have achieved with language. I'm trusting you, those eyes said, to protect my family, to destroy those books. There was a secondary plea for a reassuring smile, for some signal from me that I would do what she wanted, that I would keep her secret. I stonewalled her. Her eyes twitched about wildly in panic or recognition or both, then a bubble of morphine made its way into her vein and she was under again. The corners of my mouth were tugged upwards by a force I could not fight, and I had to leave the room.

'I got all your stuff for the VAT return,' said Rikesh. There was an uncharacteristic hesitancy in his voice that concerned me.

'Everything OK?' I asked.

He forced a laugh. 'I was about to ask you that, actually. I think you sent me something by accident. A spreadsheet that doesn't mean much to me, but it's got some very strange things written on it. A sort of . . . like you're keeping tabs on someone. And you've put through some expenses from a spy shop, whatever that is. Are you adding Private Eye to your many talents?'

My stomach shifted, as if I was in a car going too fast. 'Oh, that. It's just . . . I was just having a laugh. I wouldn't take any of it seriously. Just, you know.'

'Right,' said Rikesh. 'I'll bin it then, shall I?' I heard paper being scrunched into a ball. 'I take it this isn't the only hard copy. I think we sent the other stuff on for you.'

'What other stuff?'

'I don't know, some parcel or something had got in with all your files as well. Lucy took care of it. Lucy? What was that thing in Matt Rider's records, can you remember where it was going?'

'It wasn't a parcel, just a large letter,' came a tinny voice. 'An address in Saxby. Went in the first class post, should've got there today.'

My heart swerved. In my mind's eye I saw the carelessness with which I had bundled everything up, a result no doubt of the exhaustion caused by leading a double life.

'Fuck!' I shouted.

'Dodgy spreadsheets, letters in the wrong places. Maybe you need a holiday, mate.'

'Maybe I need a new accountant.'

There was a sort of shocked chuckle on the phone.

'I'm going to put the phone down now, and after that I'm going to call HMRC and revoke your right to act as my agent.'

Rikesh responded in the voice of an automaton. 'I really would strongly advise against you managing your own accounts . . .' Then he snapped back into the wideboy I knew. 'Fucksake, Matt, what's brought *this* on?'

'Actually, Rikesh, I haven't been happy with your services for some time now.'

He spluttered. 'My services? My *services* are faultless. My *services* are the only reason you haven't been investigated by HMRC a dozen times over the last few years. My *services* are the reason you've halved your tax bill by channelling your income through your wife. And I haven't even put your rates up for three years even though every quarter you file a more erratic set of accounts and every quarter I pick my way through it until it all makes sense.'

'I'd be grateful if you could send back all the paperwork you have as well as my final bill,' I replied. I could hear his breathing, rapid and shallow.

'Fine. You know what? Whatever. I don't know what's going on, Matt, but I hope you get the help you need.'

I slept badly that night. Short of breaking into Cathedral Terrace – and there was no way I had waited so long and built myself up only to end it so crudely; I could have done *that* half a lifetime ago – there was nothing I could do to stop the post from getting to Sophie. In my wish-fulfilment dreams I experienced the visceral pleasure of seeing her face when she opened the envelope. They were so vivid they kept waking me up. I was only half-asleep at 5 a.m. when my telephone rang. It was Tara, telling me through tears that Sophie had given birth to a little girl at three in the morning. Fifteen minutes later, at the other end of the hospital, Lydia had died.

38

Fauré's Requiem was sung in full by the Saxby Cathedral School choir and the vast nave of the Cathedral was swollen with mourners. The great and the good of the city squeezed into the short pews, spilled into the aisles and onto the flagstones and the grass outside, paying their ignorant respects to Lydia MacBride, JP, MBE, liar, murderer. The air was thick with their tributes, their cumulative whispers roaring in my ears. I saw faces I recognised from the streets of my childhood. PC089 was there, his apt black uniform now of the dress kind, the rank of Sergeant visible on his lapel. I saw him deep in commiserative conversation with Rowan. At the wake, in the Cathedral Hall, the four remaining MacBrides were still points in the milling crowd of mourners. I pictured myself tinkling a fork on a glass, giving my speech. The theatricality was tempting, but it was not yet time.

Jake's paternal grandparents had flown over from Ghana; he all but ignored them, following his mother around, a protective hand on the small of her back. She kept giving him little pushes in their direction but instead, he came to me. There was a half-moon of fuzz on his upper lip and I wondered if Tara was expecting me to teach him how to use a razor. Let the boy find out with a face full of lacerations, just as I had done.

'I've got fuck all to say to them,' he said, gesturing to the African couple. 'It's so fake. It's so *hypocritical*. They're not sad for me or for my grandma, they're just here to remember my dad all over again. Like Mum isn't fucked up enough over all this. I didn't even know my dad and they want me to get involved in all this bullshit charity work. They don't *know* me, though. Not like my real granny did, not . . .' His eyes began to brim. This time when he sidled back to Tara, she kept him close by.

I loaded a china plate with slab of poached salmon and a puff of salad and carried it to a table. The empty chair next to me was filled by Will.

'Old boy?' he greeted me.

'Old *boy*. How are you bearing up?'

'Hard to tell, to be honest,' he said. 'It's all so . . . everything at once, you know?'

He gestured to Sophie, centre stage in the middle of the hall, the baby a fat white larva on her shoulder. The way she looked at everyone but her husband told me that she had indeed seen my photography. I felt the waste keenly, like a bitter loss. The frustration at not having been the one to deliver the photographs was only partly tempered by the knowledge that they had clearly hit home. And still the couple were together. What did you have to *do* to this family to break them up?

'The boys are with a neighbour,' said Will, never taking his eyes off her. 'I hope we've done the right thing there. I mean, Toby might be up to it, but it's so hard to make a call between him and Leo, and obviously with Charlie being so . . . I mean there's no *way* . . .' He pushed his food around his plate a few times. Once or twice he took a breath as though about to speak and then thought better of it. I held my own tongue: something about his expression suggested to me that he was on the brink of sharing a confidence, and I even dared to hope that he was going to give me the inside story on the secondary tragedy striking his marriage. Instead, he gave me an embarrassingly transparent display of joviality.

'Feels strange to see all the old faces again,' he said. 'Makes me feel guilty, like I haven't done my homework.'

'What do you mean?'

'Half the people here used to teach me,' he said. He pointed with his fork. 'That's my old games master, Mr Potts. That's Mrs Hilton, she taught Latin, and I'm sure I took history with that old guy in the tweed. What's his name, now? It's on the tip of my tongue.'

'*You* were a pupil at the Cath?'

'Well, yes. That's where I met Soph, although we didn't get together until we were at Durham.'

'I had no idea,' I said. I pressed my fork through the fish and into my plate with force, daring the china to shatter. 'I'm quite the odd one out, not having passed through the hallowed gates.'

'Oh, don't feel badly about that. Between you and me, old boy, I've always felt like a bit of an impostor myself. I only got in through the back door.'

I knew what was coming next.

'I was a scholarship boy. I think they felt sorry for me. It was just me and my dad at home, not the best of times after we lost my mum, you know.' He coughed into his napkin for punctuation. 'Anyway, since I've been with Sophie, the MacBrides have been all the family I could ever ask for.'

A little scuffle at the far side of the room had caught his eye. A woman with thin white hair was trying to take the baby away from Sophie, who all but hissed in her face.

'Ah, hell, I'd better . . .' said Will, and loped across the hall after his wife.

39

We sat in an old-fashioned tea room on Winchester Street, a cake stand laden with tiny sandwiches between us. A scratchy recording of the Andrews Sisters played through a discreetly concealed loudspeaker; in cloyingly close harmony they begged the listener not to sit under the apple tree with anyone else. A poster above our heads urged us to keep calm and carry on, a command repeated to the point of nagging on tea-towels, posters and mugs. Kerry was enraptured by a noisy toddler in a high chair at the next table. When he left with his mother, I was the only male in the place.

This Victorian parade, a down-at-heel area on the western edge of town, had rebranded itself as Saxby Vintage Quarter. The only shop that remained from my childhood was the cycle shop, and even that had had a retrogressive makeover, a sit-up-and-beg bike with a wicker basket in the window display. As well as the tea room, there was a sweet shop with sugar canes and bonbons in glass jars, half a dozen vintage clothes shops, a second-hand bookshop, a hairdresser's called Pin-Up with red leather seats and pictures of Rita Hayworth and Vivien Leigh in the window. Directly opposite us was a shop called Spirit of the Blitz that sold reclaimed and antique furniture, reproduction prints, toys and accessories. In an uncluttered corner, Felix was sandpapering a chair.

'There he is,' I said. Kerry's eyes started to fill.

'Not again. Kerry, your *make-up*.'

I'd done her up in the kind of thing that I thought would appeal to Felix, although it did nothing for me: hair swept to one side, eyeliner, shirtwaister dress. Her scarlet lipstick was a desert rose in the sallow plain of her skin.

'I don't want to do it. I don't like his funny eye.' I felt sorry that Kerry had to sleep with Felix, especially when she was used to me; and at least with Tara I wasn't writhing around with a monster. I took the fold of notes from my wallet, laid twenty down on the table and gave her the remainder.

'That's nearly a thousand pounds, there. Even at his inflated prices there ought to be enough for you to buy something that needs delivering, something you couldn't get up the stairs yourself. Ask him to deliver it himself. He's got a van, I've seen it. What did we rehearse?'

She absently stroked the scar tissue of her earlobe. 'I've just rented a new flat, and I want to do it up, make it a bit more personal, but I don't know where to start, and I'd like some advice.'

'Good girl.'

'What about those diaries and that, do I ask him about them today?'

'No! For fuck's . . .' I clenched my fists underneath the table. 'Kerry, how would he know that you know about them? That's the last thing you do. All you need to do is just . . . make him like you. If he talks about his mother, listen, and report back to me, but that's it. I don't want you ad-libbing.'

'What's that mean?'

'No making it up as you go along.' I took both her hands in mine, to still them. 'You're not going to let me down, are you? Just think about afterwards.' She shook her head and nodded it at the same time. 'Good. Well, you look very pretty.'

That, at least, coaxed a smile from her.

The street outside was sunny. I pressed myself into an

alcove between two shops. Kerry pushed Felix's shop door. A brass bell jangled and he jumped up to serve her. I could see the drawing up in height, the tentative smile on his face, the forelock being tugged over his missing eye. Suddenly it mattered less that language was not Kerry's strong point. She was, after all, at her best when she did not speak. I saw that the seduction, at least, would take care of itself.

While Kerry was staying in Saxby, I took a room in Rory's manor house, the newly renamed Saxby Falls. Rory was weeks away from opening; half the guest rooms were still plasterboarded cells but the gym, pool and spa were finished, machines already installed and staff from beauticians to chambermaids to chefs practising their trades on Rory and a rotating squadron of human guinea pigs, of whom I was one. From my window on a clear night I could see the amber-sequinned circle of the city's ring road.

He joined me at breakfast one morning; he was a poor advertisement for the lifestyles he peddled as he piled his plate high with heart-furring meat and eggs.

'Swear to God half the bookings I'm getting are on the strength of your machines,' he said. 'If it carries on like this they'll have paid for themselves within six months.' It was the longest I had ever heard him speak without uttering an obscenity. 'Here's to lazy, gullible fat fuckin' bitches.' He raised his coffee cup in a toast, then set it down, sloshing coffee over the tablecloth. 'I don't suppose I could make you an offer? Buy you out?' he said.

'No way,' I replied automatically, although even as I spoke, my internal motor was whirring. Selling the business was not something I had thought of, but already I could see various advantages to making a clean break.

We spent the rest of the breakfast in silence, punctuated by the clicking of BlackBerry keys and the odd lip-smack from

Rory. He cleaned his plate in the time it took me to eat half my spinach and egg-white omelette. He pushed back his chair and threw something across my plate. It was a starched cotton napkin with a long number scrawled across it in ballpoint, four zeros at the end that suggested the switchboard of a large company.

'New phone number?' I said, trying to decipher the city code.

'No,' said Rory. 'That's how much I'm willing to offer for your business. Think it over.' He downed his coffee. 'Enjoy your fuckin' rabbit food.'

A waiter poured freshly squeezed orange juice from a pitcher into my glass. I stared at the number the way other men read the *Financial Times*. With money like that I could start again once I had finished with the MacBrides. I could really start again this time, safe in the knowledge that my work with them was done. Until that was over I wouldn't know whether, this time, I would build a new identity around Matt or strip myself back to Darcy. What was certain was that Kerry would not be part of it. The second the revelation was made, her usefulness expired. I raised the glass of glowing orange liquid to my lips. Its sweetness turned to vinegar as it hit me that half the sum before me was legally hers.

September 2013

She was crying again. Tears had become her default setting. At least now they had a focus other than babies.

'Are you like this with Felix? He's going to think you're a nutcase.'

'No,' she said. 'It's all right when I'm actually *there*, it's just that afterwards I come and see you and . . .' She dissolved again.

After a while, I got used to it, the way you do with a car alarm in the street outside your window.

I met Kerry almost every day; it was safer for her to take a taxi to see me at the hotel than it was for me to risk being seen with her in Saxby. Every time, she asked me if we were any closer, if the diaries were in hand, when it would end.

'You're not being unfaithful to me,' I said. 'How can you be, when you're acting on my instruction? It's only cheating if you're doing it behind my back, without my permission.'

'I just don't think if you loved me . . .'

'It won't be long now,' I said. 'You're doing really well.'

In fact, she was more successful, more swiftly, than either of us could have anticipated. Twenty days after I had sent her into Felix's shop he had told her that he was falling in love with her. While I did not doubt Kerry's loyalty, I was less sure of her ability to sustain the deception. I knew what she was like when she was nervous. She grew gauche, she gabbled, she said things she shouldn't. To slow this process it was necessary to reduce the amount of time she spent with Felix. We began to spend weekends in London again. There, Kerry's telephone cheeped like a hungry chick. 'He's got it bad, hasn't he?' I said, as she turned off the handset. 'I can't wait to see his face when he finds out what's happened.' This progression lent my campaign against the MacBrides a feeling of momentum and urgency and I cultivated the rest of my life accordingly. I didn't accept Rory's offer, so he made me another, better one, buying out my entire company. I combed my way through the contract myself before signing. It was stressful managing without an accountant or financial adviser – I was having to do all the research myself, and was reminded of those early days in Vass's house, reading all his business books – but I knew that I wanted as few ties to my old life as possible. When the deal was done I would have no business partner, no assets, no responsibilities – only the money. I was ready to move. There was a definite feeling that things would soon come to a head.

★ ★ ★

Jake had gone to the cinema to text his friends all the way through a film, and Tara and I were in her flat, in bed. I was present in body only, my mind whirling, and the faster it turned, the harder it became to think in a straight line. My uppermost thought lately had become the riddle of how I might get into Rowan MacBride's apartment. I asked if he needed anyone to help him deal with Lydia's things: he said he could not bear to touch them. I asked if he needed any jobs doing about the place. He told me not to be silly, that that was what the school caretaker was for.

I even got desperate enough to consider burglary. I managed to wheedle the apartment's location from Jake – it was, of course, in the heart of the establishment, overlooking the central courtyard – but when I tried to find out from Rowan what kind of security they had in place, he shrugged and said that it was all Greek to him. I even offered to pick Jake up from school, hoping that a spontaneous tour of the grounds would ensue, but he told me that he couldn't think of anything gayer. Was there any other way I could insinuate myself into the building, in some kind of official capacity? The school often had visiting speakers, but the Cath did not shape its young men and women to become entrepreneurs. The irony was not lost on me that I could probably have walked into any English lesson and taught the subject in greater detail and with more sensitivity than a master of thirty years' standing.

The right idea was in there, if only Tara would stop bloody *talking*. I closed my eyes the better to tune her out but short of wrapping the pillow around my ears there was little I could do to block out her strident voice.

'It's Tar Barrels soon,' she was saying. 'Between you and me, I thought we'd give it a miss, what with it being so soon after Mum, but Sophie thinks it'd be good for Dad, for all of us, she reckons if we don't do it this year we might never do it again, and it'll become like a *thing*, like getting back on a horse, and it's half-term week, it'd be such a shame for the boys to miss out on it. It was such a lovely part of our own childhood. So I suppose I agree with that. And she thinks it might be nice to scatter Mum's ashes there, thinks it'll help Dad move on. Well, I guess she thinks it'll help *all* of us move on, and – *anyway*. Dad's got to vacate the flat, and he's going to bring all the stuff that he can't fit in storage down to the barn, and store it there. Loads of Mum's things that he's found squirrelled away and can't bear to part with. Old diaries . . .' I felt my windpipe constrict. 'Are you all right? What's wrong with your mouth?' She reached across to the bedside table for a glass of water. Half of it went on my chest. 'That better? You gave me a fright there, I thought you were choking. OK, so, yeah, diaries, photo albums, all the stuff he'll never look at again . . . Hellooo? Earth to Matt? Are you free, or what?'

'Yeah, I suppose,' I said in a voice that sounded even to me as though someone had their hands around my throat.

Back at Saxby Falls, I had champagne on ice waiting for Kerry. For the first time in months she did not arrive in tears. She knew when she saw me that something good had happened, and her own face lit up in reflection.

'You've got them!' she said.

'As good as,' I said, popping the cork. It hit the wall and Kerry jumped and pressed her hand to her breastbone. Clearly the stress of maintaining the pretence with Felix was tightening her strings. The glasses I filled were nine-tenths froth but I raised them anyway. 'The end is nigh. We're all going to spend the weekend in their holiday cottage, for Bonfire Night. Tara just told me that Rowan's bringing the diaries. They're actually bringing them to me, they'll physically be in the same place the whole weekend! I *told* you it was worth waiting for. I *told* you that when it came good it would really come good.'

I drained my glass, feeling the sparkling liquid fizz down

under my collar like a long fuse, but Kerry left hers untouched.

'What do you mean, we're *all* going to be there?'

'You've got to get yourself invited, it should be a piece of cake if he's as keen on you as you say he is.'

'You and Felix in the same place?' said Kerry. 'What if it all goes wrong?'

'Well, it *is* going to go wrong, from their point of view, isn't it? But from ours, don't worry. Once I've got those books I'll be in complete control.'

Kerry drank her champagne in silence.

'What are you thinking?' I said, tracing my thumb along her cheek, feeling the folded tissue of her earlobe.

'There's going to be a baby there, isn't there?' she said, eventually.

That was the first time in a long while that she had mentioned babies directly. Only a couple of months earlier I would have pulled her up on that, told her how self-serving she was, reminded her that there was no room for her petty obsessions in this marriage. But now I didn't even bother to respond. If anything she had done herself a favour, and made it easier for me to let her go.

40

There was no sign of Rowan's car outside Far Barn, just that ridiculous black minibus that Sophie insisted on driving everywhere. While Tara fumbled and dropped her keys, I yawned my way through Jake's complaints about the back seat. He wouldn't have that problem on the return journey.

The children were out of the way when we got there; it was just Will and Sophie sitting on opposite sides of the room, a bottle of wine on the coffee table between them like a mediator. We'd barely got comfortable ourselves when from overhead came a thunder of footsteps followed by an awesome retch and a splash. Rowan was here already and was, to Tara and Sophie's great consternation, insensibly drunk. All he'd done was to start a meagre little bonfire outside – presumably to scorch the ground for the real bonfire the following night – talk some nonsense and then tread ash all through the house on his way upstairs, but from the way the sisters were talking you would think he had run naked through the house wielding a machete. One of the advantages of the MacBride children's cosseted upbringing was that it took little to distress them.

While the others were opening bottles I crept upstairs to where he lay snoring, gut hanging out of his trousers. I did a quick search of his room. There were books and clothes and the promised photograph albums but nothing in the way of the diaries. Had he had a change of heart? No – only yesterday he had told Tara that he intended to spend the weekend reading Lydia's journals. I kept my cool. The barn was large and the weekend was long. Panic now and it had all been for nothing.

Conversation downstairs had a thrilling banality, the dullest of practical exchanges laden with meaning. The more I knew about the pattern of our weekend, the better I could choose my moment. (Of course, this would also be determined by when exactly tomorrow I could access the diaries, but that one unknown element made it all the more necessary to arm myself with related information.)

When Sophie went upstairs to check on her father, Tara said to Will, 'Who's out tomorrow night? Which cars are we taking?'

'It depends how many kids we're bringing. No way Sophie's going to take Edie there, but I think Charlie might be coming. We took Toby when *he* was four, so . . . anyway, Sophie will probably stay behind with one or both of them, so we can do it in two cars. Why?'

'Just wondered how many designated drivers we'd need,' replied Tara. 'It's a shame that Soph misses out. I mean, part of the reason for coming down was to give her a bit of a break, wasn't it? Are you sure she couldn't be persuaded to let someone babysit?'

'Are you offering?' Will raised his eyebrows.

'Any other year I would. But Matt's never been to the festival before, and someone needs to keep a rein on Jake.'

'Well,' said Will. 'It was a nice idea.'

There was naturally a moment of apprehension when Kerry turned up. Felix's eyes followed her around the room as though she would disappear if he blinked. She had decided to play the whole thing as a kind of mute. Jake and Will expressed their obvious attraction to her in opposite ways: Jake staring slack-jawed, Will barely looking at her. Sophie and Tara's reactions were harder to gauge beneath fake, bright smiles.

Saturday, 2nd November

Far Barn was thick with childhood, spent and active. Tara, Felix and Sophie's young years were ubiquitously memorialised; every picture, book, object, had attached to it an anecdote of their idyllic upbringing. The place seemed to be literally crawling with children. The baby that had been a bug on Sophie's shoulder was mobile now and constantly underfoot. She stared at me with blue eyes that were an heirloom from her grandmother. The entire family revolved around her. Her warring brothers united to dote on her. Her grandfather couldn't pass her by without ruffling her hair, and even Jake stopped surreptitiously taking pictures of Kerry's breasts with his mobile phone for long enough to spoon mush into her mouth, although he drew the line at changing her nappy. Kerry, of course, was captivated. The child made me uneasy. It was not natural for someone that small and unformed to have so much power over so many people.

Jake was a little smart-arse at the breakfast table. I think the fact that he literally owed his existence to me made cheek from him harder to bear than it would otherwise have been. I had not yet decided whether to play that card. It would be a shame to waste it, but I could not see quite where it would fit into my revelations. Like so much else, it depended on what I found.

The family made it difficult to search the house. If the boys weren't playing sardines in tottering wardrobes, Rowan was rifling through drawers, checking pockets and feeling radiators. I took Rowan's car key, but the only books in his dusty Range Rover were ancient motoring atlases. I needed to enlist Kerry's help, but time alone with my wife was as elusive as the grail of the diaries.

When we were all getting ready for a woodgathering expedition from which I could not convincingly excuse myself, I snatched thirty seconds alone with Kerry and made her go out in her flimsiest shoes, knowing she'd be forced to turn back. With the house almost empty, she'd have a better chance of looking for the diaries. I winced at the thought of the expensive suede being ruined, but wrote off the investment.

On our return I was first out of the mud room, kicking off my shoes and running up the stairs. Sophie was alone in her bedroom. I found Kerry in Rowan's, not scouring cupboards but cradling the baby on her lap. Four little guys in paper masks stared blankly ahead.

'Find anything?' I said, but the sarcasm was lost on her. 'I take it you've been busy looking.' She at least had the grace to look shamefaced.

'I did try to talk to Sophie about them, but I didn't really know how to bring it up, and then she found her mum's jumper and . . .' The baby gurgled.

'What are you wittering about?'

Kerry reached to pull open the drawer beneath a wardrobe and gestured to a spangled mass of wool pushed into one corner. 'That. Sophie wants to keep it. Her mum knitted it when she was pregnant with Felix.'

I raised my hand in warning; Kerry offered me her cheek to protect the baby's head, which only made it worse. I forced myself to breathe evenly.

'Kerry. *Kerry.* Don't forget who she was. She's not some cuddly granny in a fluffy jumper. She killed my mother. It's imperative that we find those books this weekend, it's Saturday lunchtime already and we still haven't cracked it.'

'Yes. No. I know.'

'Thanks for nothing,' I said. The baby started to cry. 'I'll do it myself. Make it stop that noise. Can you take it away, so I can hear myself look?'

I plundered the room, looking under the bed, pulling drawers, even unrolling a rug. If the diaries had been there, I would have found them. An icy panic began to lap at my ankles. Just for a sense of achievement, on the way out of the room, I pulled the jumper onto one of the guys, wrapped that in a moth-eaten blanket, carried the whole thing downstairs with the other three and gave it pride of place on top of the bonfire.

Sophie's paroxysm was awe-inspiring. This red-faced, tear-stained harpy was a stranger, who plunged her hands into the fire and threw accusations like stones. It was a rare glimpse of what the MacBrides were like when they lost control; even in grief, they had all been quiet and dignified. The only thing that stopped me fully relaxing and enjoying the spectacle was that Kerry was its subject. I was on edge, worried that she would respond and give us both away, but she doggedly adhered to her policy of silence.

The charred atmosphere filled the ground floor of the house long after Sophie had gone upstairs to wash and calm down. Around the kitchen table, Rowan, Will and Tara spoke about Sophie's mental health, telling me a secret story about postnatal depression and child abandonment that jarred with the smug, superior image Sophie showed the world. I made the right noises of sympathy and concern to hide my burgeoning anger; the confidence now only highlighted the exclusion that had preceded it. Tara had not, then, trusted me as much as I had thought.

Will banned everyone from the kitchen while we got to work. He poured cream into ramekins, I attacked the langoustines, calamari and scallops until the air was thick with fish and fire and garlic. My dish took minutes to prepare and hours to simmer, and I stood at the stove, stirring occasionally, in a half-trance. It was dark outside, Saturday afternoon was turning into Saturday night, the diaries were somewhere in the house and still I had not found them. They must be in one of the unlikely, dusty recesses of the barn; the garage perhaps, or the greasy nooks of the kitchen and storehouse. Every minute that passed, I had less time to spend with the books. Once found, the work was of more than a moment. I would have to open them – now, I had no compunctions about excising the locks to save time – but then I would have to skim-read an unknown number of volumes before preparing my presentation – and all this entirely undetected. Short of asking Rowan where they were, how was I to access them? The heat and the stress were making me dizzy and when Will began to test his new culinary toy, the air become intolerably hot and dry and I had to get out of that kitchen.

The crisp outside air was welcome for the first minute or so. After that, the sweat on my skin cooled unpleasantly, and I wandered over to the remnants of the bonfire, took the big iron bar Rowan had been using as a poker and began to rake through the embers. The things that had burned in our main fire were reduced to almost nothing – a zip and some strings of melted white plastic, a little stone circle that demarcated the smaller fire that Rowan had lit the night we arrived. I poked the pool of ashes aside, ran the tip of the poker along the rocks, enjoying the mineral click of iron on stone. I stirred the pool of ash; the floor of the fire seemed to be tiled with some kind of dull metal. I bent closer, blinking through the smoke. When I saw what I had exposed I leapt back as though I'd touched their surfaces.

They had been tarnished and dulled by flame but their shape had not been affected by the fire. There were several dozen little padlocks, all broken up. Here was all that remained of Lydia MacBride's diaries. For years I had run hot and cold, been both confident and doubtful about these books, and here was the ultimate confirmation. What they had contained was so incriminating, so disturbing, that Rowan had burned the lot and then drunk himself into oblivion.

Little charges of electricity went off inside my skull and in the pit of my belly. I felt scorched through, as though there was no water in my body, only an angry ball of fire licking the inside of my skin. My eyes were even drier than my mouth, my lids rasping with each blink. I could have done with tears, but it was too late for that. The only weapon I had was my identity and Kerry's, and what were we – who was I? – without the context of Lydia's confession?

Even my sense of self seemed to be splintering, shards of the boy I had been piercing the man I had made, so that I could not tell who was in control, Darcy or Matt.

At supper, I must have spent half an hour chewing the same ring of squid. For once I was glad of their habit of travelling in a pack down memory lane, glad no one asked me to join in as they reminisced about childhood holidays and times shared with their mother, more slow steps in the constant process of her canonisation.

I had eyes only for Rowan. Whenever his wife's name was mentioned discomfort flickered on his face and I *knew* he knew her elusive secret. His spoken word was now the only possible substitute for her written one. In fact, it would be *better*, as I knew how it would pain and humiliate him to recount the truth before his children. The more inscrutable Rowan remained, the more determined I became. If only I could get him to say it. There must be *something* that would make him talk, but I was tired, and I was in shock, and I could not think what that thing might be.

I was the last awake. When I was sure the others were all asleep, I went back out into the garden. I looked up at the black mirrors of the back bedroom windows. I loosened the bulb in the sensor light so that I would not be floodlit and worked by the light of the breakdown lantern from the boot of my car, balanced on the ground. I dug with my fingers like a mole, combing through earth and ash for surviving scraps of Lydia's writing, shining the torch into the bare branches in vain, vain hope. What was I really expecting? A perfectly preserved page, setting out her guilt, miraculously untouched by the flames? At three in the morning I gave up, and returned to the sitting room.

I drained the dregs of a Grenache and opened a Pinot Noir. Regret smothered me. I rued all the risks I had not taken. Why hadn't I broken into the house, or forced my way into the apartment at the school? Why hadn't I made a scene in the hospital? Between us, the morphine and I might have coaxed a confession from her. But no. I had fucked those opportunities up like I had fucked up the one golden chance life had ever given me. I felt twelve years old again, weak with disappointment and pathetic in the face of an undefiable authority.

I placed an empty glass upside down on the table, put my fingertips on its base, as though about to perform a seance. I wished more than anything that my mother could come back, just for half an hour, long enough for us to talk about everything that had happened since she had left me. She would have known what to do, she always did. It was only without her that I came up with these schemes that painted me into lonely corners. She wouldn't even have to talk if I could just touch her. She could even, I thought, tears brimming, release me.

Overhead, Edie started to cry. Not loud enough to wake the sleeping, just a weak repetitive bleat swiftly subdued by the soft soothing low of Sophie's voice. *Mothermothermothermothermothermothermothermother.* My fingers slipped on the glass, and I swear it wasn't my doing. It was as though my mother's spirit tossed a lifeline of inspiration to my drowning brain. Threaten that child and Rowan would admit to anything. She was the beating heart of the family. To rip her from their breast would be the perfect revenge. Like for like. Family for family.

41

Beside me, Tara sighed and rolled over, taking half the bedclothes with her. I had not slept. Despite my exhaustion I was wired with dangerous energy.

That nobody suspected me was of course an advantage but I needed a bold statement to draw a line between the person they thought they knew and my true self, with all his terrible ambition and capability. The obvious thing was to remove the child somewhere, create an initial stir of terror before somehow producing her – I thought with a smile of a magician producing a rabbit from a hat – and making the physical threat that would loosen Rowan's tongue. Of course I could not do that alone, but I knew someone who could. I knew someone who would do anything for some time alone with that baby. I forced myself to slow down. I had made that mistake before, making rigid plans that ran too far ahead of circumstance. For now, I needed to concentrate on getting Kerry alone with Edie.

Tara began to stir and I pretended that I was waking up too, taking the arm she threw around my shoulder and pulling her close to me. Her body felt liquid and boneless, while every muscle in mine was clenched. This was the last time I would ever wake up next to her. By the time she next went to sleep, this lazy, careless morning would have been recast as the prelude to a nightmare.

'Morning!' I said.

'Tar Barrels day!' she said. 'My favourite night of the year. You're going to love it.'

'I hope so. It'll be nice, all the family out together.' She beamed to hear me say that. 'It's a shame Sophie isn't coming out,' I ventured. 'I was listening in on Will and you talking the other night, about babysitting and stuff. I just think it would do her good to get out of the house.'

'I couldn't agree more,' said Tara. 'Especially after yesterday's meltdown. But what can you do?'

I shrugged and left the thought to fester. From then, it was a question of five minutes alone with Kerry. The offer of babysitting had to seem to come from her, even though I would be the one in ultimate control.

The valley was thick with a horrible drizzly mist that frizzed up Kerry's hair as we wandered up to the old ruined cottage. I kept trying to catch her eye but her method acting had gone too far for that; she was avoiding me in a way that almost looked deliberate. Sophie was burdened by her smallest son, the creepy one, so Edie was passed from person to person. Only when it was my turn did Kerry approach me. She took the baby from my rigid arms and folded her deep inside her coat. I was frustrated that the child had to be present – I wanted Kerry's full attention – but this was better than nothing.

Jake stuck close behind Kerry and I wondered if we would ever shake him off, but eventually the sight of her bottom began to bore him and he ran to catch up with his cousins.

Now we brought up the rear of the party, abreast but separate. I had to be careful that no one could see us, two ostensible strangers, in intense conversation. Boys zipped around us, visible, invisible, in and out of pockets of mist. Every time Sophie glanced back at Kerry, as if to check she had not spirited the child away, I was reminded of the

challenge in hand. When the little boy in Sophie's arms began
to whine, I grabbed Kerry by the elbow and pulled her behind
a vast oak.

'He burned them,' I said, talking quickly and clearly. 'Rowan
burned the diaries, and with them all my chances of ever being
believed.'

'But without them . . .'

'I know,' I said. 'Don't worry, there's a plan B. It involves
your little friend here. We're going to take her on a trip away
from the barn.'

Kerry's expression was transformed, as though someone
had pressed her 'on' switch.

'To *live* with us?' she said, her face glowing. My heart sank.
What was worse, her insanity or her stupidity? She was a
danger to society. How did she think we would possibly hide a
kidnapped baby? I wondered again what I was doing trusting
her with such an important plan. I used up my last reserves
of fake patience.

'No, Kerry,' I said. 'Not to *live* with us. That wouldn't work.
What we need to do – are you listening to me? What we need
to do, is get you to babysit tonight, and then while we're all
out, you take Edie away to show them we all mean business.
I'll come back and get you both and then we pretend we're
going to hurt Edie, just to give Rowan enough of a scare that
he tells me what I want to hear.'

Kerry put one hand over the baby's head and stepped back
away from me.

'No, no, *pretend*. Just pretend. Like all of it's pretend.' I
checked that no one was looking; in fact they were barely
visible. Still, I positioned us further round the tree for extra
cover. I put my hands on Kerry's shoulders, chased her eyes
around with mine until she was forced to lock onto my gaze.
It was crucial that she understand this perfectly. 'It's going
to look very real, and it's going to be frightening, but it's got

to be that way because otherwise Rowan won't tell me what Lydia did. I might have to pretend – *pretend* – to threaten you, too. You'll just have to go along with that, and look scared.'

'We're not really going to do anything bad to the baby?'

The child looked up at me, Lydia in infant form. 'Absolutely not,' I said. 'But it is vital that they *believe* something bad is going to happen to her if Rowan doesn't tell them all what Lydia did. Once I've got that confession, once they all know what kind of person their mother really was, that's when we get in the shot about who we really are, and then . . . And then, at last, it's all over.'

'They'll just stop us. There's more of them than there are of us.'

Kerry was not usually this argumentative or paranoid. It must be the stress of the double life. I had thought about this long and hard. It was the mainstay of my plan.

'I don't think they will.' I opened my jacket to show her the weapon I had chosen. 'They won't be able to get near us.'

'What's to stop them just calling the police on us the second we've gone?'

'Edie?' called Sophie, an edge to her voice.

'All present and correct!' I shouted.

I took my hands off Kerry's shoulders and we walked again, side by side now. I spoke to her out of the corner of my mouth.

'I'll have Rowan's confession then, won't I? I'll have my phone in my pocket, recording every word he says. I'll tell them that if they call the police I'll post it online. It's always charged, I'll start recording it the minute it all kicks off, I'm not making that mistake again. They'll know that to call the police out for a baby that's completely unharmed, when I've got that on them . . . No, they won't do it. Trust me,' I said. I looked up. 'Here comes Sophie now. Ask her if you can babysit tonight. Tell her it would be nice.'

Kerry took the baby back to Sophie. I saw her ask the

question with hesitation, and I could tell by the way she began to twist her earlobe, as though trying to separate the healed flesh, that it was not good news. Everything rested on Tara now. She took Sophie by the arm and leaned in close. I hoped the seed I had planted that morning had begun to germinate.

Half an hour later, Will and Sophie emerged from the mud room. They both wore washed-out but genuine smiles and said that, actually, if it was still OK, they would take Kerry up on her offer to babysit and Sophie would come out to the Tar Barrels. The little boys bundled onto their parents as though they had been given a gift they had long wished for, but never really believed was within their reach.

While various MacBrides tore about the barn looking for lost mittens, gathering pound coins for the fairground and, in Sophie's case, prepping the baby's room, I ran through the falling dusk to the cottage, where I raised the grille, laying a few blankets inside as a concession to comfort and care. In the kitchen, I took my paring knife, sharp as a diamond, located the telephone cable's entry point just outside the kitchen window, and sliced the outer wire so that the live ligaments inside were exposed. Then I sawed through them to sever the connection. I checked that no one had reattached the bulb in the outside light.

While they piled into the car, I ran over the plan with Kerry one last time.

'OK. So we're all coming back just after eleven. That means that at half ten, you go and hide. I tell you what, I'll set an alarm for you.' I programmed the phone to vibrate at the appointed time. 'It's important that we give them a scare, remember?' Kerry nodded. 'You remember the cottage we saw, that one that Felix used to play in?'

'It's got a big cage over the door! I'll never open it.'

'You won't have to. I'll have done that before I leave. There's a knack to opening it. It's not easy to raise the grille up but it's easy to pull it down, you can do it one-handed. It's nice and warm, I've made it comfortable.'

'Will it be dark?'

'Well – yes, but you want the baby to go to sleep, don't you?'

'I won't put her down in the cot,' said Kerry. 'She can just fall asleep in my arms, then I won't have to disturb her when we get up and go.'

'Whatever. And then you just wait, and I'll come and get you both. You don't come out for anyone but me.'

'And then it'll all be over?' she said.

'Yes,' I said. 'It will all be different afterwards.' Reflexively, my hand went to the knife in my pocket. The success of my plan would make Kerry redundant, and whatever path my new life took there was no room for her in it. I almost felt sorry for her.

42

It was inconceivable to me that people would go to something like this Tar Barrels festival voluntarily and, once there, behave as though being rammed shoulder-to-shoulder in filthy narrow streets was something to be enjoyed. Here, the mist had thinned almost to transparency yet I would have been grateful not to see most of what was on offer. It was like a scene from a Viking raid only instead of fleeing the burning village the crowd continued to pour into it. People hung from upstairs windows, laughter and song spilled from pubs and houses. The smell of bodies and beer and hot dogs and fire assaulted the nose and disorienting cheering rounded street corners like wind. I watched in contemptuous disbelief as the MacBrides smiled and hugged each other and greeted old friends with kisses and waves. As the crowd pressed against the buildings to make way for some village idiot giving a piggyback to a ball of flame, Felix hoisted a small boy onto my shoulders. Instinct told me to fling the child into the crowd, but I controlled myself even when he found handholds in the hair at my crown. It would not do for me to come this far and lose my temper with a child.

Salvation came in the form of a leering yob who shouted something about Felix's face, and I thanked my thirteen-year-old self for providing me with a get-out clause now. As Felix stormed off to the pub, I handed the child back to its father. I stretched my hands up, reached first to the left and then to the right as though warming up for an aerobics class. Something in my back went click, like a twig underfoot. 'I'll go and make sure he's all right,' I said, nodding towards Felix. As soon as the others were out of sight, I stopped following Felix and shouldered my way out of the crowd.

There was a church at the top of the village and the surrounding streets were lined with Georgian houses in ice-cream colours. I sat in the relative calm of the churchyard. A plaque there commemorated the town as the birthplace of Samuel Taylor Coleridge. No wonder he took to drugs. Up there the mist returned, like a chiffon scarf loosely held six feet above the ground. It was far easier to breathe. I projected onto the flickering sky images of my life leading up to this point; myself at various stages, from underfed child to nervous young man to whoever the hell I was now.

At half-past nine, I went to the Lamb and Flag, the pub I had seen Felix enter. He was swilling a pint of dark ale in a plastic glass on the pavement outside, deep in conversation with a bearded yokel. He waved me over and introduced me as his 'brother-in-law, or as good as'. I had expected him to drown his sorrows, but he seemed entirely sober and I was glad; I did not want alcohol to numb any of what would come next. We spent a good hour wandering around looking for the others, through a fairground and briefly along a riverside and over a bridge next to which a huge bonfire blazed so fiercely that to stand too close was to feel your ears and nose begin to melt. At a quarter to eleven, we gave up looking for them and began the trudge back to our cars, my heart beating faster for reasons unrelated to the steep trek up the hill. I had told Kerry to leave the barn around now, and hoped it would not be too early. The press of bodies and the bonfire and the exercise meant it was difficult to gauge the true temperature. If she left too early, she might grow too cold and return too soon. The blankets I had left for them at the cottage should stop this happening, and my brief experience carrying the child earlier that evening had taught me that they generated heat disproportionate to their size, but still . . . If they were in the sitting room when I returned, the logistics would be much more complicated. I would have to somehow create a separate space for me and my hostage without raising suspicion; how much more powerful if I brought her in, let them think for a second that I was restoring her to them, and then played my card.

When we got back to the car, everyone was waiting around that space cruiser bus Sophie insisted on driving. I did a quick head count: as well as me and Felix there was Will, Tara, Rowan, Jake, two of the boys.

'Where's Sophie and Charlie?' asked Felix as I rounded the minibus to see a strip of bare grass where there should have been a BMW Z4.

'Where's my *car*?'

'Don't be cross, but I let Sophie drive it home,' said Tara, directing her reply at me. 'Charlie was playing up something rotten, he was really frightened by it, she had to take him home.'

Fuck fuck fuck fuck *fuck*. Tara misread my expression and put her hand on my arm. 'She's a good driver, she'll be fine.'

'When did she go?'

'An hour or so, I'm not sure.'

I sat in the passenger seat and pressed my temple to the cool glass. It took an age for everyone to match the maypole of dangling seatbelts to their correct buckles.

Will was driving at fifteen miles an hour. 'I knew I should have taken him back, Soph will have *hated* driving in this.'

'Yeah, but then Sophie would have had to drive this bus through the mist rather than Matt's little car,' said Felix. 'She'll be fine. She'll be doing an inch a minute. We'll probably overtake her.' I prayed that he was right.

If they had already gone, though . . . Sophie could have

made the search herself, found Kerry and Edie waiting in the cottage. Under interrogation Kerry might have broken, told Sophie everything without my even being there. Or she could have discovered them missing, got to a place with reception, and called, if not the police, then at least one of her family, who were presumably an emergency service themselves as far as she was concerned.

Behind me, Tara's phone buzzed. My heart leapt into my mouth. In the passenger mirror I watched her pull out her phone. It was evidently an innocuous text from a friend because whatever she read made her chuckle, then set the phone down again. From then on, I held my breath until we began the descent into their valley. I kept my eyes on my own phone and watched with relief as five bars flickered into four, three, two, one, none.

A couple of minutes later the car came to an abrupt halt, throwing us all forward in our seats. Will, squinting into the mist, had seen what it took the rest of us a second or two to grasp; our path was barred with a diagonal light, two lights, they were—

'That's Matt's car!' shouted Jake. 'Matt, that's your car!'

'Oh shit, *Sophie*!' said Will. He unbuckled his belt and leapt from the driver's seat without bothering to kill the engine. 'Matt, there's a torch in the glove compartment, can you get it for me?' he threw over his shoulder.

I picked my way after him, torch in hand, closely followed by Rowan and Tara, who was trying in vain to restrain three curious and frightened boys. The car's back end was in the ditch. It was empty. The doors were closed. The problem of Kerry and Edie's whereabouts was now joined by another. If it did all go according to plan, my getaway car was stuck.

'It's unlocked,' said Will, trying the passenger door. 'That's good, isn't it? All the windows are intact, they can't have been thrown through solid glass. What the hell *happened* here?'

'Please God they're in the barn,' said Rowan. 'Please God they're not hurt.'

I hoped he was right, but for different reasons. Just because we hadn't passed her on the lane didn't mean anything. Fuck. Fuck, fuck, fuck.

'Children, back into the car, now,' said Rowan. I was almost amused to see that he was talking to all of us.

All the lights in the barn were on, white squares chequering the black. The front door was wide open. Sophie was silhouetted in the middle, wild hair, wilder eyes. The emergency was clearly not over and while the others doubtless assumed that this was related to the crashed car, I tried desperately to gauge the true situation before they did. 'Tara, can you get the boys to bed, please?' said Sophie. Tara marched to scoop Charlie from the sofa and bundled the other children upstairs so quickly and with such determined conviction that I wondered if I had missed some rushed exchange of précis and instruction between the sisters.

No one saw me slip around to the side of the barn. There, I tiptoed and craned to the cottage to see if they were where they ought to be but it was almost hidden even in daylight, and tonight visibility was down to about ten yards.

Back in the sitting room, we heard the solid sound of Tara closing the bunker door behind her and then Sophie said, 'They've gone.'

Will started firing questions at her, and she dissolved into nonsense. I unravelled her words; she hadn't yet made any contact with anyone outside the barn. Clearly, she hadn't searched the cottage. Concern was turning to suspicion, fast. To buy myself time to think, I made a big show of getting involved in the search and did a quick tour of the upstairs of the barn.

Downstairs, Rowan and Will were ignoring Sophie to

struggle with the telephone. This distraction bought me a few seconds more. I needed to ensure that everyone stayed in the barn, so that when I brought Kerry and Edie back I could make my threats to the assembled family. It was no good if one of them was on the loose. They all needed to hear me at the same time, and besides, I wanted them all where I could see them.

'Right, I'll go and use my mobile,' said Will. I tensed. Events were spiralling away from me. I had to stop Will making that call. He asked her how long they'd been missing, and Sophie snivelled something about there being no one there when she'd got back.

'Hang on a sec, Matt,' said Will. I shot back in from the kitchen. 'I'll go and call for help,' he said, 'and then I'll go out in the car and look for them. If I give you a lift to the top of the lane, do you think we can get your car out of the ditch and you can take it around and do a separate scout?'

'Of course,' I said desperately. 'Anything, whatever.'

43

I hoped that Sophie had not run my battery out, leaving those lights on. Will had the phone in his grip but couldn't dial the most famous number in the country. His hands slid all over the place as we made our way up the drive. I was about to take the wheel when he dropped the phone, then broke into noisy sobs. 'My baby girl, they've taken her, she's got her, why would anyone take her?' He retrieved the phone from the footwell and began to stab at it again.

'Hold it together, Will, can you?' I said. A brilliant new idea came to me. 'Look, you keep driving, I'll make the call. Slow down, will you? No rush if I'm talking.'

I wrestled the handset from Will. It was the same kind as mine, the same one we all had, a touchscreen with a virtual keypad that was slippery with his tears and the sweat from his palm. I pressed 9 three times, making sure he saw me do it, but hung up before the connection was made. 'Police, please,' I said. I flipped on the heater to mask the silence on the other end of the phone. 'Yes, I'd like to report an abduction, please. Someone's taken my, uh, my niece, Edie Woodford. She's nine months old.' I paused for a few seconds. 'Far Barn, Otter Valley.' I gave the postcode then went quiet for bit. 'Yes, I know, but . . . nine o'clock. A white sort of babygrow thing. She was with a babysitter, a girl called Kerry . . .' I caught myself just in time. 'I don't know her last name. No, they haven't got a car.' I pulled away from Will, pretending to put my other finger in my ear so that I could concentrate on the call I was taking. Something hove into view before us: it was my car, the headlights still on, and my time was up. I made a show of ending the call with a note of urgency and pre-emptive thanks just as Will pulled to a halt in front of my car and braked, killing the engine.

'They're going to go straight to the house,' I said, I calculated: how long would I need? 'They said it could be twenty-five minutes, on a night like tonight.' Will was shaking in the driver's seat. 'Will,' I said. 'Come on. Rowan and Sophie can give them all the information they need, I reckon. I think we should keep going. Let's get my car out, we can both cover enough ground.' I handed him back the phone. In his position I would have checked the screen. He put it back in his breast pocket without even glancing at it.

We pushed the car together. Mud and dust flecked Will's face. I wondered if mine was the same.

'Thanks so much, Matt,' said Will. 'Right, no time to waste. If you turn right out of the lane, that's further into the valley. It's a dead end so you can't get lost. You can cover it and come back in maybe twenty minutes.' The act of righting the car had focused Will. Now, with every word, he distanced himself from the wreck he had been minutes before. 'I'll turn left, retrace the route we took back from Ottery.'

I thought fast. The deeper into the valley Will went, the less likely he was to have a phone signal.

'Maybe I should take the Ottery road,' I suggested. 'I've never done that drive down into the valley. At least if I'm retracing my steps, I'll have my bearings. Let's face it, it doesn't matter if I disappear for hours. But Sophie will want you back at the house, the police will probably want to talk to you.'

Will drummed his fingers on the roof of my car before making his decision.

'You're right. Good call, mate,' he said. He got behind his

own wheel and I followed in the slipstream of his tail lights, devil's eyes in the dark.

Will took the right turn, I made a pretence of taking the left, and, when his lights had dimmed to nothing in my rear-view mirror, I did a U-turn, driving back down the lane that led to Far Barn. It was all downhill and even without power or lights I could nudge the car down by taking my foot off the brake. When the lights of the barn came into view, I turned off-road to scoop a curve in the direction of the cottage. I had to turn my sidelights on for this and hoped that no one was out looking yet, that no one would see me. The outline of the cottage was just visible. I engaged the parking brake and took a few seconds to catch up with myself.

All was not yet lost. If they were all still in the barn, if no one had yet got to the cottage, if Will did not check his telephone or call the police to chase them up, if he did not return, I could still do this. I closed the car door behind me with the softest of clicks, took my torch and marched towards the cottage with my boyhood self and my mother, an army of three.

ROWAN

44

Rowan had never known anything like this, not since the pea-soupers of his early childhood. Toby tried to trace a picture on the car window, not understanding that it wasn't condensation that made the window opaque but the mist outside. Will was tense, hunched behind the wheel in silent concentration. Matt rode in the front passenger seat, evidently in a sulk because Tara had let Sophie take his car. Jake was plugged into his machine in the back seat; a quick tinny rhythm was just audible above the car's purr. At Rowan's left side, Leo was slackening into sleep. First had come the uncharacteristic stillness, and then an arm had pressed itself against his and now a hot little head was periodically thudding against his shoulder, mouth relaxing to display teeth still not quite to scale. Rowan raised an arm and put it round Leo's shoulder. The boy was too old for cuddles, really, but he might not get the chance again. One couldn't say, any more, how lovely children were to hold and to be near.

He stared at the blind window and silently congratulated himself on surviving the festival. He had endured the sympathies and condolences and every time someone had paid tribute to Lydia he had nodded and thanked them and swallowed the scream that had been crouching in his throat since Friday. Scenes from that afternoon kept coming back to him; the courage it had taken him to break open the first diary, the heartbreak of revisited memory and then, in the last book, those four confessional pages written so late into her life. The blue inked loops of her admission had given lie to the values she had preached, the values she, *they* had instilled in their children. His instinctive reaction had been to tear those pages from the book. He had screwed them up, and then he had hit the bottle in a way he hadn't done since his undergraduate days. Hours later, his blood still rich with port, the same compulsion that drove him to burn book after book also drove him to retain the incriminating pages, to unscrew and smooth them, to reread and reread until he had committed it all to memory and then thrown them onto the fire. Hadn't he? The memory of the terrible words curling up and dying on his little pyre had a slightly unreal air about it, like a scene from a late-night film, watched through a doze from an armchair.

Will turned the car into their lane with great care and the headlights cut a tentative swathe through the fog. Fifty yards or so later – hard to gauge distance, with visibility so poor – the brakes were engaged, hard, and from that moment it was shouting and chaos and movement, examining the abandoned car, frantic searching and desperate speculation that continued even once it had been established that they were not there. They might have stayed like that all night had Rowan not commanded them all back into the car. Will took the rest of the drive at speed, the children unrestrained in the back seat. Sophie stood in the doorway with a look on her face that told him something more than a pranged car was the matter. Will was talking to Sophie but her eyes were fixed on Tara's. She asked her to get the boys to bed, and Tara seemed to extract a world of meaning from that one simple instruction. Rowan was both frightened and impressed by her brisk authority as she plucked Charlie from the sofa, gathered the other children together and marched them straight up to the bunker. Then Sophie told them, in a whisper that spilled into sobbing the second the bunker door was closed, that Edie and Kerry were missing.

The low points in Rowan's life all seemed to have been nothing but a rehearsal for the way he felt now. Lydia's collapse and the cruel swift loss of her, his parents' deaths, Felix's attack; he had thought each one unbearable, but now knew he could take them all on the chin, simultaneously, if it would cancel the horrific present. Better to lose his wife a million times, better to watch Felix cry a river of blood, better to stare at his parents' open graves forever than to see Sophie's arms hanging helpless and empty like this.

'*Daddy*?' she said.

'I'm calling the police,' he said, but when he lifted the receiver there was no dialling tone. He tapped the earpiece, tried again, repeated the movements with increasing panic and a rising sense of impotence. 'It isn't working.'

'I *told you* that!'

Matt, who had gone straight into search mode, reassured them that there were no signs of foul play upstairs and immediately departed to check the rest of the house. The way Matt's nervous energy manifested itself in physical release only seemed to Rowan to highlight his own paralysis. As if from a distance he heard Will ask how long they'd been gone, and Sophie unable to give them a time. Will called Matt back from the kitchen. 'I'll go and call for help and then I'll go out in the car and look for them,' he said. 'If I give you a lift to the top of the lane, do you think we can get your car out of the ditch and you can take it around and do a separate scout?'

'Of course. Anything, whatever.'

Seconds took hours to pass. In the sitting room, Felix was now enduring Sophie's hurled accusations like a man in stocks. Eventually she drew breath and he had a chance to speak.

'Isn't it just as possible, isn't it actually *more likely*, that someone came and took both of them?'

Rowan looked around the barn.

'Felix, if that's the case, where are the signs of struggle? You heard Matt, there's nothing upstairs. You can pick up a little baby and carry her without her permission,' he looked at Sophie, 'I'm *sorry*, darling – but you can't do the same to a grown woman. It really doesn't look as if anyone else has been here.'

'It doesn't make any sense,' repeated Felix. 'I'm as confused as you are, I just . . . I *know* Kerry.'

Sophie's voice grew shriller. Rowan dropped to his knees and gave the phone one more try, shaking the receiver and running his finger along the length of the cord to check for snags in the wire. He found nothing. The old machine had never let them down before. The icy thought sluiced him that this disconnection might be his fault, that he might have failed to write a vital cheque to the telephone company. He did not remember a red bill but Lydia had always been the domestic administrator and so much had slipped through his fingers since she had gone. If the delay in calling the police proved crucial, if he were even partly to blame he would never forgive himself, if he bore any responsibility for whatever had happened . . .

Felix's voice roused him to action, telling him that he would take the orchard if Rowan did the trenches and beyond.

'Right behind you,' said Rowan. He got to his feet, knees crunching like gravel as he rose. Sophie's footsteps sounded overhead as she combed empty bedrooms for her lost child.

45

As Rowan scrabbled in the kitchen drawer to match old batteries to older torches, his mind drifted strangely. How useful it would be, he thought, if we had a dog. Dogs could track people through thin air. One saw it all the time, on television. When the children were little they had pestered him constantly for a pet, but the house in Cathedral Terrace had been all wrong, the garden too small, and he knew that he would have been the one to walk the bloody thing every day. If only he had given in. Perhaps having a dog would have become a habit, and they would still have one now. A golden retriever, faithful, friendly, each of their scents implanted in its memory.

But there was no dog, and he could only imagine one for so long before the real narrative toppled his daydream. Felix couldn't be right that someone had made off with both of them; the conclusion was inescapable that the girl had taken Edie. But why? The path of his thoughts forked in two. In one direction lay the theory that it was in Kerry's interests to keep Edie safe, to nurture her. He found himself praying that kidnap, in the old-fashioned sense, had been the motive, that soon the demand for money would come and they would pay with everything they had and more. Or perhaps she had taken Edie for her own, to steal, to *raise*. He had read grotesque tales of young women using the birth certificates of dead children and imposing their identities onto abducted babies. How long does it take a child Edie's age to forget her mother? Six weeks?

A year? These thoughts were heartbreaking but preferable to those that paved the other path, a dark trail down which pain was being inflicted, some kind of abuse was occurring. He slammed closed the door on the sickening scenarios in his mind's eye.

He finally married the right torch to the right battery and cast his eyes to the ceiling. Tara and Jake had certainly been up there long enough to get all three younger boys off to sleep and keep them in the bunker. The baby monitor had been set to mute but the flashing green bars showed that the bunker was far from silent. Rowan willed the frantic dancing lights that indicated the tumble of boyish chatter to subside into the slow flickering rise and fall of a mother's soothing tone. When Tara had settled the children he would have to break the news to her. He steeled himself; Tara loved Edie like a mother, and Jake was more devoted to her than her own brothers were. How could he tell them she was missing? How could he do it? The loose floorboard at the top of the stairs sighed. Rowan was disgusted by the selfish little contraction of relief he felt when it was Sophie.

His daughter's skin was grey and her eyes were punched far back in her skull. He winced as he realised that she wore her mother's death mask, that the same changes had occurred in Lydia's face in her last days. Rowan tried to close an internal door on this image too, but his head was teeming with unwanted thoughts and sickening imaginings and all such doors were straining at their hinges. The best he could do was to drop his eyes from Sophie's face.

She was holding a piece of paper in her hand. For the briefest fraction of a second he thought it was pages from Lydia's diary. His heartbeat, already racing, escalated a little more, and did not return to its previous rate even when he saw that the paper was not blue but ivory and the markings were not handwriting but green printed borders framing black type.

'Dad?' said Sophie, thrusting it into his hand. 'Dad, is it the same . . . It's got to be . . . I don't understand.'

He saw the name before he recognised the nature of the document. It came into sharp focus and then the letters that formed it seemed to expand and come off the paper until they were ten feet high. The torch fell from his hand. The batteries slid out and rolled noisily across the kitchen floor. Rowan sank down into the kitchen chair with such force that something splintered.

'A sister?' said Sophie.

Rowan held the driving licence to his nose as though its meaning would become clearer at close quarters.

'He was an only child.' Rowan was entirely sure that Kellaway had been alone in the world, no relations at all but that pitiful mother and that strange bachelor – cousin? uncle? – who had accompanied him to the interview.

'How long since we've seen this name? I haven't thought of him for what, fifteen, sixteen years? What could this have to do with *her* taking Edie?' How could Rowan tell her that he had seen it days before, written in her mother's own hand, without telling everything? Until he knew what it meant, until he could connect the old nightmare with the current one, he must hold his tongue.

'A *cousin*? A wife?' pressed Sophie. 'But then . . . why would he send . . . where's *he*? What do you think? Dad, *say* something.' Rowan shook his head hard as though by dislodging the wrong ideas the right ones would have space to breathe. 'I mean, do you think Felix knows who this is? Who Darcy Kellaway is?'

'I don't know. We were very careful to keep the details about Kellaway away from him. No way would Felix get involved with someone who was connected with him if he knew what it meant. No, I'm sure he's as confused as we are. And Sophie, I'm sorry, I don't know what it means, I can't begin to know. The police will help us, I'm sure.'

The clock struck midnight.

'Where are they, then?' said Sophie, her voice rising to a screech over the chimes. 'Where are the helicopters, the dogs? Where are the blue lights and the search parties?'

'They'll be on their way now,' said Rowan. He spoke with conviction but wondered whether that could possibly be true yet. It seemed an eternity but in fact it had only been ten minutes since Will and Matt had driven off together. His mental abacus began to click. It could take up to five minutes to get a reliable telephone signal, another five to have the conversation, God knows where the nearest police helicopter was based. Exeter? How long to man it and launch it? The only police station he could think of was on the other side of Ottery, a little cottage station really, glorified security guards, and anyway run off their feet on this, the busiest night of their year. Perhaps they could be summoned immediately but traffic around the town would be gridlocked as people drove home from the festival. On these single track lanes and in this mist, a squad car couldn't tear through over the speed limit like they could in a city. So let's say five to make the call and to be on the safe side twenty to arrive. They could be here in ten minutes, they could be here in fifteen. 'They'll be here by quarter past, I'm sure,' he told Sophie.

Quarter past twelve, the next chime of the clock. Fifteen minutes, nine hundred seconds. A manageable, survivable period of time. During it, he would be able to sustain the belief that the arrival of the police was not an end in itself but simply an end to this, the first stage of the nightmare. Rowan had compartmentalised time like this since Lydia's illness. The only way to deal with tragedy was to break it down into tiny units, to put the process into blocks of time: visiting hours, the length of time taken to die, the days between the death and the funeral, the span of the car journey to the crematorium, the chasm of days between her wake and the end of his own life.

Sweat made a second skin of his shirt but he kept his jacket and jersey on, ready for anything.

Sophie began to look under the sofa seat cushions time and again, as if the missing might be hiding there like old coins and finding them was only a question of thoroughness and persistence. Rowan folded the driving licence in on itself again and again until it was a little wedge. He unfolded it, repeated the action. He counted six halvings, and wondered if it was true, then, that you couldn't fold any piece of paper more than seven times. He shook his head again, harder this time. Why did his thoughts keep running off like disobedient children? The baby monitor finally displayed the flatline of silence. The landing sighed again. Now Tara and Jake came down the stairs, so quickly their feet barely made contact. What was *he* doing up? Rowan had presumed he would have been sent to bed with his cousins. But there he was, like his mother still in his coat and boots. Their flushed faces were stricken with terror of the unknown. Rowan almost envied them their ignorance.

'We stayed until they were all settled,' said Tara. 'Dad, what the hell's happened? Has there been an accident? Charlie seems fine.'

'Edie's missing,' said Rowan, flinching in tandem with Sophie. 'Along with Kerry. They weren't here when Sophie got back. Will and Matt have gone to get the police.'

'Oh, no,' said Jake. 'Mum!' He looked to his mother but Tara had pulled her sister close and the two women had both begun to speak at once, one murmuring explanations while the other simultaneously offered platitudes. This was what Sophie needed, not her clumsy father with his ineffective attempts at fixing the phone and his inability to explain the Kellaway connection. Tara's presence made him redundant in this room and freed him up to search.

'Girls, I'm going out to help Felix,' he said.

'I'll come with you,' said Jake. Rowan panicked: he wanted to be alone, to gather his thoughts in the light of Sophie's revelation, but more importantly to talk to Felix alone, whether to extract information or provide it he was not yet sure. He had already forgotten Jake's presence, his existence. The poor boy had been hopscotching from boy to man to boy all weekend, and Tara now relegated him to the status of a child.

'No, you stay here with us, Jakey. I don't know what's happening, I don't know if you'll be safe out there.'

'I want to help,' said Jake. 'I *need* to help. Grandpa, *tell* her.'

Rowan understood that even at his age, Jake was feeling the same masculine urge for action that made his own legs twitch. In the midst of all this hell, he still had room for a surge of pride in his eldest grandson. Shameful, painful to recall that when Jake was born, his alien colouring had given Rowan cause to wonder if he would ever truly be able to think of him as a MacBride.

'The more people looking, the quicker we find them,' said Rowan.

'Jesus, hell, all right,' said Tara. 'But stay on our land, OK? Promise me you'll stay on our land?'

Jake gave one of the smaller torches a whack on the table. It glimmered into life and he followed its slim beam into the garden. Rowan trailed the boy. At the kitchen door he hesitated before turning on his heel. He had to ask.

'Tara, does the name Kellaway mean anything to you?'

Tara's expression was curious but uncomprehending. She shook her head. He left Sophie to explain it to her sister, heard a mumble from Sophie and then a sharp intake of breath before Tara asked, 'What the fuck?'

Rowan wore so many layers that it took a full minute for the outside temperature to register. It was now cold enough to make a baby wake and howl in protest, but where were the cries? He tried to improvise a strategy. Will and Matt might be out in their cars but the rest of them had to assume that the missing girls were still close by. Where might they be? Where would *I* hide? Felix had said he would scour the orchard and Jake was already down in the trenches, his torch picking its way through the little maze.

Rowan strode towards the outbuildings. With every step his breathing felt a little easier, although the longed-for clarity of thought seemed as remote as ever. Even Darcy Kellaway's face in his mind's eye was an out-of-focus photograph, those teeth the only clear feature, and the threat of his deliberate menace was all the more terrifying for being only partially known. He looked over his shoulder. Already Jake's torch was half-obscured, the cat's eye flash that one would see on a clear night diffused until it was just another light ghost.

Rowan was momentarily unsure where to go. Something had happened to his internal compass; he had lost his true north and the magnet was pulling in the wrong direction. That dog would have made light work of this. If only he had let them have the bloody dog.

46

He suddenly had the sharp hearing of a man half his age, over-sensitive to everything, from the knocking of steely branches to the rustle of dead ferns and puff of heather under his boots, and a soft but persistent crackle that sounded every time he swung his arm. Something had burrowed its way between the waxed linen of his jacket and the polyester lining. The same impulse that had made him undertake a frantic search of the house the morning after his binge now led him to frisk himself all over, until he finally located the source of the crackle. He was almost relieved to see the driving licence. He hadn't even been aware of putting it in his pocket, but he tucked it back in and continued his search.

He was astonished to find that he now took a perverse comfort in thinking about Lydia and what he had read. It helped him to cope with the intolerable crisis, the way digging one's fingernails into one's palm can stop one crying over a bigger pain.

Someone somewhere cleared his throat. Rowan swung his torch around and found its beam intersected with another, faint shafts scoring a misty X. Felix was on the other end of it. As Rowan stepped in closer, he saw that his son had been crying. Even in the half-light Rowan could see the livid blotches on his face. Tears always seemed worse coming from Felix. Of course they were awful coming from a man anyway but on the rare occasions Felix cried he did so harder than anyone else, as though his left eye were over-compensating for its dead twin. They stood opposed for a moment, frozen in the makeshift searchlights.

'What did the police say?' asked Felix with a catch in his voice.

'Still no sign of them.'

'Maybe they've got her already, or maybe Will's found them, or Matt. I should have brought my own phone out here. You can get a signal on the other side of the wood. I didn't think.'

The only way they could see each other's faces was to shine the light into the other's eyes, adding to the interrogatory nature of their conversation.

'Felix, something's come up that makes me . . .' He was lost for words, feeling his authority diminish with every second's hesitation. 'This isn't easy for me to ask . . . What's Kerry's last name?'

'What? It's Stone,' said Felix, his eyebrows meeting.

'Not according to this,' said Rowan. Slowly he panned his torch across the document. Felix's face changed from pain to confusion and back again. 'How do you explain this, Felix?'

There was a pause and Rowan saw that it wasn't just the name that was bewildering. 'I didn't even know she could drive. This must be someone else's. It hasn't got a photograph on it or anything, has it?'

'Sophie found it in Kerry's bag,' said Rowan.

Felix looked again. 'Kell-a-way,' he said, sounding it out as would someone who had never heard the name before. Rowan felt a stab of disloyalty for suspecting his son, but had he not learned this weekend that we do not know anyone else, no matter how much we love them?

'Her name's Kerry Stone. This must belong to some other Kerry, mustn't it? What else could it be? And why would she lie about . . . and what would it have to do with what's happened with Edie? Dad, what's going on? I don't understand!' Felix's voice jumped an octave. 'Dad, where is she?'

'Which one?' said Rowan before he could help himself.

Felix looked as if the blow would fell him.

'Edie, of course! How can you ask me that?' he said, and in that second Rowan knew he trusted his son entirely. 'If anything bad happens to Edie because of me, or whatever, I will never, ever forgive myself.'

Rowan opened his mouth, prepared to tell Felix who Kellaway was, but held back. Until he could connect the fragments of logic that were swirling around his mind and pin them down into something that made sense, anything he said to Felix would raise more questions than it answered.

'Look, where had you searched before you found me?' said Felix, wiping his nose on his sleeve.

'Nowhere,' said Rowan, glad to be back on the surer terrain of planning and action. 'I came straight to you. Jake's doing the trenches and the wood house and the drive,' although now that Rowan voiced it, he wasn't sure that Jake had agreed to undertake all these, or if he had just presumed it.

'I don't know whether we should stick together or go off separately.'

Rowan closed his eyes, the better to map the territory. 'Let's do the outhouses together, then go back to the house. Surely the police will be there by then, and they'll be able to tell us how to search more effectively.'

'If we haven't already found them by then,' said Felix with unconvincing certainty.

Either the mist was beginning to disperse or their eyes were getting used to this strange white inversion of darkness that was not light. The odd distant firework penetrated the tension but of the longed-for sirens and blue flashing lights there was no sign.

They looked in every tiny, roofless, crumbling outbuilding, each double-checking the other's surveillance out of desperation rather than doubt. When he found himself lifting a sheet of corrugated iron that Felix had examined only seconds before, Rowan was reminded of Sophie pulling the sofa cushions apart. A sense of absolute impotence almost caused him to abandon the search, whilst another part of him knew that he would continue for as long as it took, that if Edie did not turn up then the following springtime might find him here, bearded and ragged, still searching the places that never could have held her in the first place.

Rowan squatted on his haunches and shone his torch into a waist-high, dry-stone outhouse originally intended to store coal. Its door was too narrow even for Kerry's slight frame.

'Don't bother with that,' said Felix. 'No way could they both fit in there . . .' His voice trailed off, and Rowan wondered if it had occurred to him, too, that they might not be looking for both of them.

They checked the old cottage last because they were so sure that Kerry could not have breached it. Rowan himself had made it a fortress to exclude the small and weak. He shone his torch from a distance of ten yards. The grilles at the windows and doors were all secured.

'We'll check it close up anyway,' he whispered to Felix, but before they could approach the crumbling structure, they saw a third beam from somewhere on the far side of the cottage. Rowan leapt back and extinguished his torch. Felix, at his side, did the same. In addition to their own heavy breath was the definite sound of someone else puffing, as though after exercise. Abruptly, the panting stopped; they had been seen, or heard. Without verbal agreement, father and son bypassed the cottage and approached the beam. The third light remained on.

'Kerry?' said Felix, his voice rather more tender than Rowan would have liked. 'Is that you? It's OK, it's me. We're not angry, just come out.'

A dark shape shifted. Rowan knew from the footfall alone

that it wasn't Kerry. His stomach plummeted at the sight of Matt, whose torch was pointed up at his chin as though unambiguously to declare his identity.

Matt's first attempt at speech didn't work; his tongue made a strange clicking noise against his palate, as though he had gone for days without water.

'It's only me,' he said eventually. 'Sorry I was quiet, I thought you might be her. *Them.*' His face was creased, as though the full horror of it had only just struck him.

'I thought you were going off in the car,' said Felix.

'I am,' croaked Matt, gesturing with his torch. The silver paintwork of his BMW, fifty yards or so away, caught the light and sparkled. He must have driven off-road to get here. 'I mean, I *was*. But I didn't really know where I was going, and you can't see much anyway, so I thought I'd be more helpful if I just came back here.' He shone his torch in the direction of the cottage, tracked by Felix's beam. 'I've checked that place out, head to toe. There's no way anyone can get in there.' He coughed and made that noise again, triggering a half-formed memory that Rowan swept aside. No more irrelevant, distracting thoughts, *please*. He forced his focus back where it was needed.

Felix scratched his head. 'I don't know, I still think we should be covering the roads. If you couldn't get very far maybe that means they haven't, either. Maybe I should go with Matt, so that if we find them, I can talk to Kerry.'

Was Rowan reading too much into Felix's choice of words, or was his son suggesting that he was coming round to Kerry in terms of an active kidnapper rather than passive victim? Whatever the case, Rowan reflected that Felix might well be the last person Kerry wanted to talk to. It was Felix she had deceived. She might actually find it easier to deal with a relative stranger, a comparatively neutral party like Matt.

'Felix, you know this land like the back of your hand. I'd rather have you on foot, at least until the police get here. We need to *find* them in the short term, and talk later.' Rowan turned to Matt. 'If you do see anything, just get the baby. Nothing else matters. Just get the child and bring her home safely.'

'Of course,' said Matt, evidently kicking himself for his misjudgement. He returned to his car, inched it across the uneven ground carefully, his engine so soft that he seemed to dissolve into the night.

Before Rowan and Felix had a chance to talk further there was the sound of a new engine. Someone was coming down the lane, not tentatively but very fast, deliberately announcing their presence.

'The police!' said Felix. They abandoned their amateurish search and ran back to the barn, to hand over their horror to the experts.

47

Rowan and Felix reached the house as the distressingly familiar car pulled up. Tara and Sophie were standing in its path, their silhouettes like matchstick figures. Will leapt out without bothering to kill the lights or the engine. He was mud-spattered from head to toe, presumably from the effort of pushing Matt's car out of the ditch. A wiped letterbox of flesh framed his eyes.

'Where are the police?'

'We thought you *were* the police,' said Tara thickly.

'What are you doing back here? Why aren't you *looking* for her?' cried Sophie. 'Get back out there! Or I'll go! Give me the car keys, you're useless. I'll do it myself.' She made for the car, but Will held her by the shoulders. He spoke into her hair, but his words were audible to all.

'Soph, the police have been called, don't worry. But I can't drive like this. I can't see a thing, I lost control of the car twice. Matt's still on the lookout, or at least I hope he is.'

'He is,' confirmed Felix.

'This is a job for the professionals. They'll be here any second now. They should be here already.'

'What, we're supposed to just *sit tight*?' said Sophie. 'I'm not having that.'

'They'll be here any second,' said Will. 'They'll need to know everything that we know, won't they?' He strode into the kitchen and went at his face with soap and water. The others sat around the kitchen table. Tara retrieved the baby monitor from the sitting room and placed it on the kitchen table. Felix and Sophie circled the table. Rowan slumped uselessly at its head.

'What do we know, though?' said Felix. 'We don't know anything, we don't know what's happened, whether they went off on their own or someone came and got them or what. We don't know anything. Unless Kerry's name has something to do with it.'

Will dried his hands, blackening the tea towel. 'What do you mean, Kerry's name?'

Sophie's eyes passed the responsibility to Rowan. He had to clear his throat twice before he could speak.

'Sit down,' he said to his children.

'I couldn't possibly—' began Tara.

'Tara, this won't take long. Sit *down*,' said Rowan. Tara sat. Will dropped onto the bench beside her. They looked like children in detention. Outside, Will's car continued its patient purr.

'It'll all come out when the police get here anyway,' he began. 'Better you hear it from me, first, now.'

'Dad, you're scaring me,' said Felix. He looked to his sisters for reassurance but neither of them would meet his eye.

Rowan took the driving licence from his pocket and spread it on the kitchen table. Everyone craned to read it.

'This is Kerry's,' he said. 'Sophie found it in her bag. Her last name isn't Stone, as Felix thought, but Kellaway. It's a name I knew a long time ago. Darcy Kellaway was a boy who applied for the Mawson-Luxmore about seventeen years ago. He didn't make the grade, but somehow developed a conviction that you were awarded the scholarship in his stead, Felix.' Rowan walled up the memories associated with the word 'scholarship', and pulled his focus back into the moment.

'*Me?*' said Felix. 'This has all got something to do with *me?*'

'Let me finish, please, Felix. Kellaway was a . . . strange boy, given to delusion and paranoia and, I'm afraid, eruptions of violence. He's the one who attacked you, Felix.'

'*Christ*,' said Will.

'I thought no one knew who attacked me?' said Felix.

'We *knew*, they just couldn't make the charges stick, and I'm afraid we kept it from you. You needed to concentrate on getting better . . .'

Felix clapped his hand over his missing eye as though registering its absence for the first time. 'Did you know about this, Sophie?'

Sophie, who had been looking out of the door, turned her face back to the table and gave a curt nod.

'Tara?' Tara carried on with the slow head-shaking movement she had been making for the last minute or so.

'Sophie told me just now,' she said. 'I had no idea.'

'So what's this got to do with Kerry?' said Felix at the same time that Will said,

'Rowan, how does this relate to what's happened to Edie?'

'I wish I knew,' said Rowan. The clock struck half past midnight. Surely it would literally be seconds now before the police arrived. Time enough to tell his family the rest of what he knew.

'A few years after your attack, Kellaway had another run-in with your mother.'

'With *Mum*?' said Tara, disbelievingly. Rowan spoke fast, hoping that his tone was enough to pre-empt questions about Lydia.

'I told you, the boy was delusional. It turned out that he was still harbouring a grudge and he made some ugly threats against the family. But then he disappeared, for years he disappeared, and I never dreamed he'd come back, I never dreamed . . . but it seems as though Kerry's some kind of relative. It's an unusual enough name that coincidence seems unlikely. It makes this all seem premediatated, planned, even.'

'How can it be planned?' said Will. 'Kerry wasn't even going to look after Edie until this afternoon, when we all persuaded Sophie to come out.'

'Unless she targeted me from the very beginning,' said Felix slowly. 'Unless she knew who I was from day one.'

'Oh, *bollocks*,' cried Tara. 'What, you think she seduced you just so that one day on a weekend she didn't even know she was coming on she could steal a baby that isn't even yours? Don't be ridiculous, Fee. People don't do things like that, fake entire relationships. It's a coincidence, this name thing, it must be.'

'I'm just telling you what I know,' said Rowan. 'If Kellaway is involved it means that . . . I mean, we don't know what their relationship is. We thought he was an only child . . .' He trailed off, unable to give his children answers to the questions he had raised himself.

Sophie's fist came down on the table, making everything shake. Everyone turned to look at the baby monitor; it remained blank.

'Where ARE they?' she said. It was clear that she meant the police as well as Kerry and Edie.

Rowan's brain was beginning to flag. He felt as though he was having to maintain a sprint velocity over the course of a marathon. 'Exactly what did the police say, Will?' he asked. 'It's been forty-five minutes. What exactly did they give as their arrival time?'

'I don't know, I didn't have the actual conversation,' said Will. 'I mean, it was my phone, but Matt had to make the call.'

Somewhere deep inside Rowan, a connection was made. A current travelled, agonisingly slowly, between knowledge and understanding. If only he could hear himself think. A sixty-second silence would do it, but Sophie punched the table again with a force that threatened to shatter her frail fists.

'You didn't even *talk* to them yourself? Jesus *Christ*, Will.'

'What does it matter, so long as the information gets through?' said Will. 'Matt gave them a good description and everything, he gave them the postcode . . .'

'You're her *father*. It was your responsibility.'

'I was trying to save time! I was on my way to get the car out of the *ditch* you drove it into!'

'So this is *my* fault?'

Jake appeared in the doorway, silhouetted by the fog lights of Will's car.

'Anything?' Tara asked him. He shook his head.

'I went everywhere,' he said. 'All round the trenches, orchard, the wood house, everywhere you said. I'd have stayed out, but the batteries went.'

'Oh, Jakey, go to bed, darling,' said Tara. 'I don't want you getting mixed up in this. It'll all be all right in the morning.'

'Are you serious? How can I sleep, knowing Edie's in trouble?'

'Don't argue. Bed.'

'No. I want to *help*,' said Jake. He looked at Rowan. 'I tried to go to the cottage but it had already died by then,' he said, pressing down the switch to illustrate the torch's uselessness.

'We did the cottage,' said Rowan.

Cottage.

The word was the trigger his subconscious mind needed to make contact with his lucid thoughts. Rowan recalled that strange alien choking noise Matt had made and knew exactly where he had heard it before. Suddenly, vividly, he was superimposing the man's face over that of the boy and, for all the differences, the fit was perfect.

Oh God no.

Oh God, no no no.

Not this close to home. Not for this long.

'Will, did Matt use your phone?' said Rowan, and in

response to the uncomprehending nod, 'Give it to me, please.' The handset was identical to his own, and it was easy to scroll through the most recently dialled numbers. The last call made had been to 999, but the conversation had only been two seconds long.

48

Will blinked at the phone. 'I don't understand.'

'Will? Dad?' said Sophie. Her teeth had started to chatter. Rowan showed her the phone.

'It looks as if Matt dialled 999 on Will's phone and then hung up. It looks as if the police haven't been called at all.'

Everyone started shouting at once. Rowan blocked the discordant 'What the hells' and 'Oh Christs' and turned to Will.

'Call them again. Go to the top of the lane and call them again. Give them Matt's name and say he misled us that he'd called them the first time.'

'Why would he . . .' said Will, staring stupefied at the screen.

There wasn't time. 'Just go and call them again, do whatever they tell you to.' Will scrambled from the table and ran back to the car, whose key had never left the ignition.

'Where are you going?' screamed Sophie as the retreating headlights left the kitchen in relative darkness.

Now that it was too late, Rowan wondered if he should have kept Will back for the time it took to share what little he knew, but before an internal debate could begin, the questions started up again, his children's words tumbling unintelligibly over each other. Only Jake, in his corner, was shocked, or confused, into silence.

'Why would Matt *do* that?' said Felix. 'Why would he not call the police, why would he lie to us about going after them?'

'It's a mistake,' said Tara. 'He's going to be *mortified* when he realises.'

Rowan looked at each of his children in turn.

'I'm so sorry. It's *him*. It's Matt. Darcy Kellaway is Matt's real name.'

Sophie collapsed against Felix, who himself looked close to folding. Tara placed both palms on the tabletop and let out a horrible sardonic laugh.

'So now you're saying that not only has Kerry been pretending to go out with Felix, but Matt's pretending to go out with me as well? What's wrong with you, Dad? What the hell are you doing, inventing these little farces while your granddaughter is *missing*?'

'Tara, I don't know what it means, I don't know what he's been playing at, but—'

'*Playing*? Dad. Look. I know you want an explanation for this but you're really clutching at straws here. I *know* Matt. His name is Matthew Rider, I've seen it on his credit cards, he virtually lives in my flat, I sleep with him, I *know* him.'

'That's what I thought about Kerry,' said Felix.

'There you go! How do you know it's not her, behind it all? How long have you known Kerry – what, a couple of months? I've been going out with Matt for nearly *two years*.'

'Tara,' said Rowan. 'I remember him, I met him.'

'Well, you haven't remembered him at any point previously over the last eighteen months, have you?'

Rowan sighed heavily.

'He's *changed* himself. He's had his teeth sorted, and he's filled out and he . . .' The real reason for recognition seemed surreal, now that he was going to voice it. 'Look, I had two conversations with him when he was a boy, and both times he made this strange sort of throat-clearing noise, a choking that came out of nowhere. I'd never heard anyone make that noise again, but then Matt did it up at the cottage. That's why I'm so sure it's him. I know it sounds strange, I know it sounds ridiculous, but—'

'No, it doesn't,' said Tara. She suddenly looked exhausted and her voice sounded drugged. 'I know exactly what you mean.' Rowan watched as his daughter's faith fell away from her. She locked eyes with Felix. They have made fools of us both, they said in silence. I know what you are going through because I am going through it too. Rowan felt his heart break twice, two discrete fractures in such rapid succession that they felt like one.

'What does it mean, Mum?' said Jake. 'Who *is* Darcy Kellaway? Has Matt got Edie?'

Tara stretched out her arms to Jake, then pulled him close around his waist. Their embrace mirrored the way Sophie clung to Felix further along the bench. Tara's right hand scrabbled about on the table until she found Sophie's. Rowan desperately wanted to be held himself but there was no one left over for him.

'No, but listen, this could be a good thing,' said Felix.

'How the bloody hell do you work that out?' said Tara.

'If they're all together, Kerry won't let the baby come to any harm. You know how much she dotes on her. That's *if* she's gone of her own free will. Don't look at me like that, Tara, no one knows anything. And they can't be far away. I mean, it's only, like, ten minutes since we saw Matt get into his car . . .' A new awareness crept across his face. 'Oh, Jesus. I persuaded him to go. What if they were in the *car*?'

'You *saw* him?' said Sophie, chopping her way out of Felix's embrace and staggering to her feet. 'You didn't say you'd *seen* him.'

'I did,' replied Felix. 'When Will said Matt was on the lookout I confirmed it. I didn't make a big thing of it because I didn't know who he was then, did I? Yes, he came back from the search to . . . oh, *Christ*. He came back from the search he was *supposed* to be on. If he was taking Edie and Kerry with him, why would he come *back*? And why was he looking in the cottage?'

'They couldn't get into the cottage, it's like Fort Knox,' said Rowan with conviction. 'I saw to that myself.'

'It's – it's not, actually,' said Jake, shamefacedly 'If you slide up the metal rather than pulling it you can get in and out quite easily. Well, you can get in, anyway. I dunno if you'd be able to get out from the inside if it was down.'

'How do you know—' began Tara, but was cut off by Felix.

'We've only got his word for the fact it was empty. We didn't look that hard, did we, because we met Matt and we bloody took his word for it. Oh, shit, what if they were there after all? What if he was coming back *for* them? We saw him leave but we didn't see how far he went. He'll have had to come back for them.'

They were all in the garden in seconds, torches in their hands and round their wrists. The change in temperature fogged Rowan's glasses. He took them off to rub them and saw his children scramble up the gentle slope of the garden. Twenty-five years before, this had been a rock face to them. Now they moved in a grotesque imitation of their younger selves at play. They were halfway to the back wall before Tara realised that Jake was with them.

'What the hell are you doing here? Get back into the house.'

'You need me to show you how you get the thing off the cottage.'

'Felix will work it out. Jake, get back into the house.'

'I want to find Edie!'

Tara put her hands on his shoulders. 'Look, we can't leave the boys on their own, can we?'

'*You* look after them, then. You're a mum.'

Patience came hard to Tara at the best of times and Rowan admired her control now.

'I need to talk to Matt, if he's there. So does Dad. And obviously Sophie needs to be there for Edie. We need an *adult* to stay back, to tell Will what's happened, when he gets back with the police. Can you do that for me? Can I trust you, Jake?'

The word 'adult' had swung it. Jake nodded, clearly gratified to be given the responsibility.

'OK, I want you to get back into the house. Wait outside the bunker with the rest of the boys, make sure no one gets in. If anyone comes in who you don't know, lock yourself in with them. OK?'

Jake blinked.

'OK, Jake? This is important.'

'I get it,' he said.

Felix and Sophie plunged into the cloud but Rowan hesitated and tugged on Tara's sleeve. 'Is this a good idea, leaving him in the house on his own? What if Matt comes back for him?'

'Dad, I can't believe I'm saying this, but I expect they're long gone by now. And I meant what I said, Will's going to need someone to tell him where we've all gone, and the police, too. And we don't know what's on the other side of the hill. If the worst comes to the worst I don't want Jakey to see anything more than he already has.'

If the worst comes to the worst. Rowan's heart tightened again. The idea that there might be worse to come tonight was almost more than he could bear.

49

They had raised their voices in the house. Now, as though by consensus, they all spoke in whispers, despite the covering rustle and hush of leaves and branches.

'If he's there, we'll tell him the police are on their way for real this time,' murmured Felix.

'Let's play it by ear,' said Rowan. 'For all he knows, Will never came back and we still don't know what he's done.' He allowed himself a second's grimace at the irony. They *didn't* know what he had done, not really. The chunks of information they had were somehow less than the sum of their parts.

A lifetime of doing everything together served them well now; they fell into step and seemed to breathe with one breath. How far was it to the cottage? One minute? Two? It was not the kind of thing one ever thought to measure. The soft white glow emanating from the cottage took an age to come into focus.

Felix was the first to kill his light and immediately Rowan did the same. All four stayed still to allow their eyes to adapt. The metal grille, which had been secure against the old doorway minutes ago, had been lifted off the main door of the cottage and leant against one of the windows. Light shone through the holes in tiny spindles.

Sophie tried to break into a run but Tara grabbed her.

'Look, we don't know what we're going to find,' she whispered. 'Let's take it easy.'

Rowan and his children approached the cottage slowly and in silence, as though playing Grandmother's Footsteps.

They drew near its blind side, the open doorway sideways on. With no window in the facing wall it was impossible to tell how many were inside. The spindles of light were unbroken, suggesting that whoever was in the cottage was still. Because they knew the MacBrides were coming, and were waiting? Because they were restrained and could not move? Because they would never move again?

'We should have brought something,' said Felix as they approached the threshold. He did not have to explain what he meant. Matt worked out, he lifted weights, he was strong and fit. Even outnumbered he was a force to be reckoned with. Rowan kicked himself for not making them bring one of the shovels from the garden. The torch in his hand, purchased as much for its light heft as its strong beam, would be useless as a weapon and Felix's wasn't much better.

'Maybe we should just wait here until the police arrive,' breathed Tara.

'No way,' said Sophie. 'They could be another half-hour.'

She broke free from Tara's grasp, rounded the building and disappeared through the door. Without discussion or (on Rowan's part at least) forethought, the others spilled in behind her. Now they were all in the empty shell of the cottage, staring into the brilliant white eye of an electric lantern that rested in the centre of the floor. It was designed like an old-fashioned storm lantern, so that it strongly illuminated one spot rather than throwing a circle of light all around. Rowan had never seen it before. It didn't come from the house: it was too powerful and new to be theirs. A couple of cigarette butts – a little swoop of disappointment in Jake tugged at his terror – were ground out on the floor at the lantern's base.

Rowan picked the lantern up and made for the little low bedroom.

'Hello?' he said. 'Edie? Kerry?'

Before their wedding, Rowan and Lydia had once trysted

in there; he recalled the dimensions of the place, not high enough for a man to stand up in but perfectly able to accommodate Kerry and Edie. He ducked into the doorway, trying to quell the violence of his heartbeat. Inside, there was nothing but dead leaves and dust. The light at the end of the tunnel abruptly turned into a solid brick wall. He backed out, straightened himself up, turned the lantern to face the main doorway.

'No,' he said.

Sophie's mouth became a perfect circle and she seemed physically to deflate. Had Felix's arms not encircled her waist she would have fallen to the floor. Only by following the line of her gaze did Rowan see the reason for her silent scream.

Matt's broad form filled the narrow doorway. The cottage had been built for undernourished peasants, not strapping modern men. In his left hand he held something small and shiny, wrapped in a rag. The beam of the lantern on the floor illuminated him full in the face and he blinked in its dazzle. Rowan saw him now through the lens of his new knowledge. The teeth had been done, as he'd surmised, and naturally the extra weight changed everything, and of course the short hair made a difference, but – my God, how did I not *get* that?

Matt's face wore an expression of panic – literally, blind panic, in the seconds while he was too dazzled by the glare of his own light to see who was inside the cottage. Slowly his eyes adapted and the MacBrides came into focus. 'You!' he shouted. He kicked at the doorway and a jagged stone shot from its pointing. 'Fuck!' he said, and began to shake.

The knowledge came to Rowan like a trickle of cold sweat down his spine that Matt, or Darcy, or whatever this monster wanted to call himself, had no more idea where Kerry and Edie were than they did.

50

'Matt?' said Tara, softly, in a half baby-voice that Rowan recognised as the kind shared between lovers. 'What's going on? Where's Edie?'

Matt – would calling him by his real name provoke or placate him? – did not respond. The tantrum of moments before was replaced by a kind of surface serenity that was more chilling than any loss of temper. The rag in his hand slipped to reveal, in his grip, Will's blowtorch. He looked down at his hand, faintly bemused as if wondering how on earth it had got there. One of the girls – or was it Felix? – began to snivel.

Sophie dropped to her knees, making a soft thud as she connected with the earth and entered the makeshift spotlight. Her hands were pressed together. Rowan wondered if she was about to start praying and prepared to kneel himself and join her.

'Please,' said Sophie. 'Where's Edie?' She unclasped her hands and raised muddy palms to Matt. 'I'm begging you.'

'I'd love to be able to help you,' he managed eventually. 'But to tell you the truth, I'm fucked if I know. They were supposed to be here, but it doesn't look like they've kept the appointed rendezvous.' He looked at Sophie. 'You don't seem to be very good at keeping hold of your children, do you? Let's have another look. Let's throw a bit of light on the subject.' He made a tiny movement of his thumb on the blowtorch's trigger switch. The blue and orange flame was a dragon's belch and the fierce dense noise drowned out thought. All of them took a step or two backwards, Sophie shuffling on her knees. Their bodies were pressed against the walls, in the pitchy hollows of the cottage that the lantern could not reach, yet they each remained little more than a flame's length away from Matt. There were four of them and one of him, but he had them entirely surrounded.

He released the trigger and the flame was momentarily extinguished; the world seemed darker and quieter in the relative absence of light and sound. The scent it left was one Rowan had not smelled since he gave up cigarettes in the seventies, the sickly sweetness of lighter fuel.

Felix was next to the barricaded window. In his peripheral vision Rowan saw his son fiddle with the grille in a desperate attempt to see if escape was possible that way. Matt saw it too. He pointed his weapon at Tara and said to Felix,

'If you move another muscle, I'll burn your sister's face off. I'll do her eye to match yours.'

'*Where is my baby*?' cried Sophie.

Matt threw out another jet of fire, aiming the torch vertically this time so that it licked the crumbling beams of the ceiling. There wasn't much wood left in the structure but Rowan guessed there was enough for a blaze to take hold. Will was going to call the police, but not the fire brigade. For the first time that evening – for the first time *ever* – Rowan feared for his own life. Just as his distress over Lydia had been eclipsed by terror for Edie, his current horror obliterated both those concerns. This new fear was a physical force and an unstoppable one. His body temperature increased by degrees; his skin was crying out for cold air but to remove his jacket could be interpreted as a threat by Matt. He sweltered in silence.

'Matt, please,' said Tara. 'Why are you doing this?'

Matt took his thumb off the trigger. 'Ask your father. We go way back.' He glanced at Rowan. 'She likes to call *me* Daddy, by the way. You know. In bed.'

Rowan tried not to react but his suppressed flinch turned into a full-body shudder. If he tried to say something clever it would be the wrong thing. How could one ten-second sentence compete with a seventeen-year grudge? How could reason triumph over obsession? 'They already know who you are.'

'Oh, I might have fucking known. You couldn't even let me have that moment, could you? Is there *anything* you won't take from me?'

Rowan sensed rather than saw the confused looks his children exchanged. 'Please, calm down, Matt . . . can I call you that? If you'd prefer me to address you as—'

'Don't you *dare*. Don't you fucking *dare*. You're not fit to say that name!' Matt sent spittle flying through the air, each torchlit globule seeming to contain a word. 'You *killed* that boy, you and your family. I had *one chance* to make my mother happy and you stole it. So you could keep your smug little world complete. To keep people like me away – I know what you think. I know what you're like, you and that evil wife of yours. Don't even get me started on *her*.'

The burning pages of Rowan's recollection recoiled from the fire, threw off the curling flames at their edges and smoothed themselves flat. That Matt might be in possession of the facts about Lydia was almost as terrifying as the weapon in his hand.

'If you believe that we stole the scholarship from you, I understand your anger,' he said, hoping that he could keep the conversation hinged on this earlier aspect of Matt's delusion and avoid a return to Lydia's later involvement. 'But I promise you, that's not the way it was.'

'Bull*shit*,' said Matt, a thick vein cording the length of his neck. 'You didn't pay for their school fees.'

'No,' said Felix. 'I got a free place because of my dad's job. We all did.'

'Bullshit,' said Matt, but less convincingly this time. 'You've all had years to concoct a cover story.'

'It's not a story,' said Rowan. He remembered watching a documentary about hostage negotiators and the people who try to talk suicides down from their ledges. The trick, he thought, had been to make people focus on future events, to disengage them from their immediate environment. 'You're welcome to come to the school and find out for yourself. All the records are in there.'

Records: Rowan could almost smell the dust in the archive room, picture the manila file that held Kellaway's scholarship application and his history. The perspiration that plastered his shirt to his back and chest found a new outlet, springing from his brow and rolling down to blur his vision. He did not get a chance to develop his improved negotiation skills, or test their efficacy; Sophie's interruption was shrill.

'Please, please, please, *please*, where's Edie? Is she still . . .' Rowan could see the effort it took her to form the words. 'Is she still *alive*?'

Her loss of control seemed to restore coolness in Matt. He casually tossed the blowtorch from one hand to the other. Damn, thought Rowan. Felix and I could have overpowered him then if only we had been quick enough. If only we could establish eye contact out of Matt's sight line.

'Who knows, if Kerry's got her? She's a bit funny around babies, she doesn't quite know when to stop,' said Matt, in a tone of voice that suggested he was wondering what he'd done with his keys. He placed his thumb on the trigger.

'Edie!' screamed Sophie. The name reverberated off the bare stone walls.

Outside, a small shrill voice sounded for a splinter of a second.

With lightning reflexes, Matt depressed the trigger again to release the ferocious, disorienting roar. It was impossible now to tell where the disembodied voice came from, whether it really had been the baby. Rowan's only certainty was that the sound had been outside the cottage and that to reach it they would have to overcome an impenetrable wall of fire.

51

Rowan tasted salt on his upper lip. Three voices were in frantic competition with the roar of the torch. Tara begged Matt to turn off the flame. Sophie screamed for Edie, over and over again. Felix shouted Kerry's name. Even Rowan, in the midst of it all, had to struggle to distinguish the words. To anyone outside the cottage, to anyone on the other side of the flame, the screams must have been wordless animal noise.

It was impossible to see what was happening behind Matt, only that he kept flicking brief glances over his left shoulder. Once the back of his head stayed in view for two full seconds. 'Now!' said Rowan, gripping Felix's forearm, but before Felix could reply, 'Now what?' Matt was watching them again and the torch was trained in their direction. Sophie scrambled to her feet and made a suicidal charge towards the flare but the heat threw her back as though it had picked her up and flung her. She too was learning that mind over matter only goes so far, that the body will resist mortal danger independently of the heart's desire.

Then, for an instant, Kerry's face appeared behind Matt's left shoulder, two black eyes that glittered in a wan oval. The image was gone before Rowan could begin to believe in it. Had he really seen her? Had any of the others?

'Kerry?' shouted Felix.

'Kerry!' said Matt, his voice sharp with imperative.

'Edie?' cried Sophie. 'Did she have Edie?'

Matt craned his neck to the left, but he was looking in the

wrong direction. Light poured over his right shoulder to reveal Kerry, a pace or so behind him. Her image shimmered in the heat, but Rowan could see the state of her; there was a black smut on her cheekbone and a dead leaf was caught in the nest of her hair. And there, nestling into her neck, was Edie, or a rolled blanket that promised to contain her. A wordless prayer whispered its way through Rowan's veins. He glanced at Matt; he was still looking the wrong way, but as long as he held the blowtorch they could not dare to take advantage.

Kerry pulled the top of the blanket down, slowly and deliberately, to reveal by the lantern's dazzle the shining white dome of Edie's head. Time ceased to play out slowly and stopped altogether. The only sign of urgency was the frantic pulse of the baby's fontanelle. Rowan felt his own heart rate keep pace with it and could not allow himself a second of relief. Kerry's expression was a terrifying void that made it impossible to guess what her game was. Could she be showing them the child safe and well to reassure them, or to taunt them before taking her away or harming her?

Rowan sensed a change in Sophie beside him and knew that she had seen Edie too; she emitted longing so strong that one could almost see it, like the trail left by a sparkler. Don't say anything, Rowan silently willed his daughter. Don't tell him where Kerry is. Please do not point him in the direction of the child. The voice, when it came, was Felix's.

'Kerry, for God's sake, don't just stand there. Take the baby and get the fuck away!'

Rowan barely had time to curse his son before Matt whipped his glance around, managing to keep his weapon trained on the family even as he reached his free hand behind his back. With his body in the way, the light was no longer in their favour. The dark scuffle was disguised by flame and the MacBrides were a captive audience of the monstrous shadowplay before them. All Rowan could be certain of was that Kerry was not quick enough for Matt as he grabbed the girl by the neck and banged her head hard on the stone door jamb. Now time distended itself, as in slowed-down footage of crash test dummies floating through the windscreen. Kerry slid down the frame with a slowness that would have looked deliberate and mocking had it not been for her eyelids flickering closed and the livid red mark on her forehead. It took a single second that lasted for years for Matt to pluck the bundle from Kerry's loosening embrace and hoist it onto his shoulder, inches from the flame. The baby opened her eyes, saw the fire, and gave a delighted smile, as though nothing in the world could be more charming than a deadly jet of flame inches away from her skin. She put her fingers in her mouth and sucked them, hypnotised. Kerry lay across the threshold like a heap of rags, her face pressed into the earth. Was she still alive?

'Oh, my God. What have I done?' said Felix, too low for anyone but Rowan to hear.

'Matt, please,' said Tara in that same pathetic voice. 'Just let me have Edie and then we can sort this out.' Rowan saw the layers in Tara's face: love, hate, anger, fear.

'Shut up! Don't move!' Matt ordered. Kerry stirred and his boot pressed firm on her neck. 'That goes for you, too,' he said. Her body bucked reflexively then stilled obediently.

Rowan watched his children. Felix squinted into the flickering shadows beyond Matt. Sophie's gaze never left Edie. Tara was focused entirely on Matt.

'Babies are *heavy*,' said Matt, shifting under Edie's weight, momentarily sending the flare up to the ceiling again. Rowan found himself assuming the starter's position from his old athletics days, ready to pounce; immediately, the finger of flame was trained on his chest. 'Do your children know about their mother? I mean, do they know what she was really like, underneath the community service and the do-gooding and the honours and all the rest of that hypocritical *shit*?' Matt's voice rose to a shriek. Edie raised her own voice in sharp discord and the torch's trajectory became haphazard. 'I mean, are you going to tell them or shall I?'

Of *course*, thought Rowan. What else could he have wanted? His last thought as he cleared his throat to speak of the insignificant thing that would rewrite their history, was to thank God that the grandchildren were in bed, that at least none of them would ever know.

Rowan braced his feet against the floor. Should he preface the truth with a disclaimer about how much Lydia had loved them all? They already knew that but it seemed important to remind them before he began.

'Come on, spit it out,' said Matt. 'Or I'll have to do it for you.'

Rowan felt his mouth working, but no words issued. It was as if his vocal cords had been sliced through. He tried again but was frozen awake in the familiar dreamscape scenario of the silent scream.

Matt's mouth twisted into a wry smile. 'The thing about your mother—' he began.

A pale oblong seemed to move through space as if of its own accord, its grace belying its speed and the strength of its impact on Matt's temple. The blowtorch went out. Matt swayed, backwards, forwards, to the side. Felix took a fullback's dive to intercept the falling baby just as her head was about to hit the ground. The blowtorch slipped from Matt's hand and thudded onto the cottage floor before rolling into a dark corner. Matt swayed, his legs gave way and he collapsed, his body landing crossways over Kerry's. The pale object rose back up and came down on the same temple, this time shattering the skull it had dented on first impact. The noise was at once soft, like rotten fruit hitting the ground, and hard, like the breaking of a branch.

Jake let the weapon drop and examined his palms with the wince of someone who has just caught a fast ball he didn't see coming. Rowan's old cricket bat lay at his feet, the Cath school colours banding its neck and a proud rosette of blood on the willow.

52

Felix placed the screaming Edie into her mother's trembling arms. Sophie unwound the swaddling and inspected the little fingers individually like a midwife checking a newborn. The blanket was woven through with twigs and patched with mud but the child herself seemed incongruously clean and mercifully unmarked. Her babygrow was spotless and her white hair looked as though she were straight from the bath; the only sign of neglect was a dangerously bulging nappy. Sophie pressed her nose into Edie's cheek, speaking in tongues through tears; her hair, loose and messy, covered both their faces. A reverent silence fell. Rowan watched, humbled by the perfect fit of them. He allowed himself briefly to cherish the illusion that this longed-for moment was a truly happy ending. But when Sophie unbuttoned her shirt to feed Edie, he was forced to look away and the spell was broken.

Tara pushed past, vaulting the heaped doorstep, and ran to Jake, who stood staring straight ahead with his hands at his sides, like a lead soldier. Tara clamped her arms around his unyielding body. 'It's going to be fine, we'll get through this, it's going to be fine,' she said in a hysterical tone which grew less convincing with every shrill repetition. How was it going to be fine? How was *anything* ever going to be fine? Jake's stature might have been that of a man and his pose the rigid stance of the military but his face was a little boy's and when he spoke, even his voice seemed to have regressed to its pre-adolescent pitch.

'He was going to hurt Edie. I couldn't let him, I had to stop him.'

'It's going to be fine,' Tara started up again. 'It's going to be fine. I promise, Jakey, it's going to be *fine*.'

Rowan wondered if they would have to slap her face.

'Jesus *Christ*,' said Felix. Rowan followed his gaze to the cottage door and saw that the dark mass on the earth was starting to shift and stir. Instinctively, he kicked around in the dark for the blowtorch. His toe found something metallic that rolled a little on contact. He bent to pick it up but touched the nozzle; the heat seared his fingerprints and he dropped it, somehow managing to swallow his swear word. Felix had not gone for a weapon but to the lantern, which he trained on the doorway. The pain in his fingertips all but forgotten, Rowan let out a low moan of horror.

Kerry was crawling out from underneath . . . oh dear *God* . . . she was crawling, with intense effort, out from underneath Matt, shrugging off his weight and dragging herself onto the old path, where she lay in a C-shape. Her hair was clotted and her forehead was smeared and her cheeks were freckled with blood.

'Felix . . .' she began, and stretched out her arms, whether to Felix or to the baby it was impossible to tell.

Felix crouched to Kerry's level, took her by the wrists and pulled her to her feet. For a sickening moment Rowan thought he was going to kiss her. The look on his face was one of hurt but underpinned by something else, something more terrifying in this context than anger. Surely Felix's reservoir of love for Kerry had been abruptly and permanently drained by everything they had just found out? Surely it was shallow enough for that? She tried to place her head on his chest but to Rowan's relief, his son recoiled. The bones of Felix's knuckles gleamed white in the dark as he made his fingers into handcuffs and held her at arm's length. He was keeping her away from Sophie, who was only feet away on the cottage floor, eyes closed, unaware of or unable to deal with anything other than her daughter. Kerry mouthed the words, 'I'm sorry.'

Rowan turned his attention to the horrible, necessary task of examining Matt. He stooped over the prone figure. Matt was face down and apparently motionless; Rowan watched his torso for the involuntary movements of the lungs. The ribcage appeared entirely still but Rowan would not have been surprised to find that through sheer force of will Matt could have held his breath for minutes on end. Rowan was aware of fervent hope bubbling inside him, but could not have said whether he wished that the boy was dead or that he had survived. He felt for a pulse at the wrist and had confirmed that he had known since the second impact.

'Have I knocked him out?' asked Jake. The horror on Tara's face told Rowan that she knew, too. Standing on tiptoe, she put her hands over his eyes the way she had when he was little and something scary came on television. Rowan levered his hand under Matt's shoulder and rolled him onto his back. From behind him came a sexless cry. The top left quarter of Matt's face was missing. A shattered mosaic of bone was meshed in his sticky hair and the blood that had poured from his nostrils was laced with a pearly white ichor. His mouth gaped, the tongue obscured by what looked like a black mess of tar. No cloud of breath issued from it.

'Is it bad, Grandpa?'

Rowan's instinct was to buy a few more seconds of his grandson's innocence with a lie, but he had to rise above it.

'Jakey, he's dead.'

Jake screamed into Tara's shoulder; her whole body seemed to absorb the sound.

'*Good,*' came Sophie's voice from inside the cottage. She got to her feet without breaking the baby's latch and stood in the doorway. 'Too bad you didn't get *her* as well.' Anger had distorted Sophie's features from sweet Madonna to vicious thug. She took a step towards Kerry and spat in her face. Saliva hit Kerry square in the eye but she did nothing to wipe it away. He saw Sophie twitch as though she wanted to strike Kerry but that would have meant letting go of Edie, and Rowan had the impression that it would be weeks, months, before even the briefest of separations between mother and child took place.

'I can't breathe in here,' said Sophie, putting a muddy forefinger into the sleeping baby's mouth to break the seal. She pulled up her bra cup and wrapped Edie into her coat. 'I need to get her home, I need to get clean. I need to get away from all *this*. Dad?' She put out her hand. Rowan took it. She negotiated the slippery ground around Matt and stepped over his body with an expression of detached care, as though crossing a stile or a cattlegrid.

Only Kerry and Felix remained inside the cottage. Rowan had absolutely no idea what they were going to do about Kerry. 'I'm sorry, I'm sorry, I'm sorry,' she kept saying to Sophie, to Felix, to Edie, to all of them. 'I'm sorry, I'm so sorry.'

Rowan was almost vibrating with anger at Kerry, and the thought was inescapable that if it had not been for Jake, if he had been on his own, the temptation to send her the same way as Matt would have been real and dangerous.

Her professions of remorse meant nothing and anyway, it must soon dawn on her that the balance of power had just tipped in her favour. The criminal had turned witness the second Jake had struck. 'I'm sorry, I'm sorry, I'm sorry,' she whimpered. Her repetition was its own echo in the tiny space.

'Shut *up*!' said Felix, and then to the rest of them, '*Shh*! What's that noise?'

The voice in the mist was unidentifiable until the repeated word became clear.

'Sophie!' came Will's voice. 'SOPHIE!'

'Will! Edie's here! It's all right, she's here!'

'Oh, thank Christ,' said Will. 'Keep talking, will you, and shine a light if you've got it. I haven't got a torch, I can't work out where you are.'

All of them cast their torches into the branches but nobody spoke.

'What's wrong? Is she hurt?' said Will. 'Talk to me, Soph.'

'She's fine,' said Sophie. 'She's fine, she's perfect . . .'

Only those of us who know everything, thought Rowan, can hear the unspoken 'but'.

There was a scuffle of footsteps on the other side of the ridge and Will emerged, shielding his eyes.

'Turn off the bloody floodlights, let me see her!' The torches were lowered. 'Oh, sweetheart, oh, *Edie*.' He wrapped his wife and daughter in a crushing embrace, then pulled away to repeat the same process of examination that Sophie had carried out in the cottage. 'She's OK,' he said, appearing to count her miniature fingers. '*Is* she OK? She *is* OK!' He brushed Sophie's tearstained cheek, leaving an earthy thumbprint on her skin. 'Are *you* OK?' Sophie nodded. Will laughed, evidently mistaking her silence for relief. 'Look, we'd better get back to the barn. I waited until I could see them coming over the hill and then I came up here.'

'Who?' asked Sophie.

'The police, of course. I told them about Matt not making the call, and Kerry, all that. That's what I'm saying, we'll have to go down now so they don't arrive at an empty house. They're just a minute or two away.'

53

'What?' said Will, looking at their stricken faces. 'Tell me!'

Rowan fumbled for the right words to explain that, in the time it had taken Will to summon them, the police had gone from an institution of trust to a source of fear. The words did not come; he had to let the torch tell the inexpressible truth. The beam glanced over the shattered skull and came to rest on the stained cricket bat. 'Oh, Jesus Christ,' said Will. 'What *happened*?'

Like actors taking their cue, Kerry and Felix emerged from the cottage into the waiting spotlight. Now he was holding her hands behind her back. Rowan had never seen anything on Will's face compared to the look of hatred he shot Kerry; he recognised from his own reaction the way Will made a split-second decision to file Kerry away, deal with her later, and understood the effort it must have taken him.

'Rowan? Soph? Please, what happened here?' He began to stroke Sophie's hair but without tenderness; there was something compulsive about the repetitive gesture, reminiscent of a man pacing the floor. She clapped her hand over his to still it.

'I didn't mean to kill him!' burst Jake.

'*Jake?*' said Will in disbelief.

'He *had* to,' said Tara, who had dredged some composure from somewhere. 'Matt had us all cornered inside and he was threatening Edie. Jake came up from behind and knocked him out. He could have killed her, Will. He could have killed all of us. He'd got hold of your blowtorch. He was aiming it at us. He was going to use it on Edie.' Will blanched and closed his eyes; he could have been about to faint or gathering strength, it was impossible to tell. It was impossible to tell anything about anyone any more, and probably always would be. Rowan had a sudden and desperate urge to lie down and close his own eyes.

'But . . why would Matt want to hurt Edie? I thought Kerry took her?'

Oh, hell, thought Rowan. He doesn't know. He didn't know who Matt really was because I sent him away to phone the police.

'Matt wasn't who he said he was,' said Tara. 'Him and Kerry knew each other. They did it together.'

'What the *fuck*?' said Will. His eyes snapped open, their focus on Kerry intense.

'He was . . . someone from a long time ago,' began Rowan. 'Someone who had a grudge against the family.'

'A grudge?' echoed Will. 'Against *this* family?'

'Fucking hell, have we got time for this now?' shouted Tara. 'The police are going to be here any second.'

'I'll fill you in on the walk back,' Sophie told Will.

'What's going to happen when they get here?' said Jake.

'We're going to decide what to do now,' said Tara. It had not, until then, occurred to Rowan that there might be more than one course of action.

'Don't worry, Jakey. The police will handle it,' said Will. 'We'll tell them everything, whatever it is. They'll understand. We'd better go.'

He turned on his heel, shepherding his wife back in the direction of the barn. Rowan had to break into a trot to keep pace with them.

Tara and Jake tottered behind as though in a three-legged race, she evidently as reluctant to let go of her child as Sophie was hers.

'No way, Will,' she said. 'Will! Slow down. Let's talk about this. What will they do to him? He's *thirteen*.'

'You're not seriously suggesting that we hide this from the police?' said Will, without breaking his stride. 'We've got a dead man on our land. It's not the kind of thing you can just sweep under the carpet. This needs to be dealt with.' He stopped and turned to look at Kerry. 'This woman and her . . . whatever he is, they took my daughter away. How would you feel if it had been your child?'

'It's my child *now*,' said Tara. 'It's exactly because my child is involved that I want us to handle this between ourselves. I can't let him go through court.'

Sophie took Will's side, but her voice lacked conviction. 'If we tell them about Matt, about his history with the family, the police will work it out. Who are they going to believe, the abductor with the fake name or the blameless teenage boy with all his family around him?'

'Hardly blameless, Sophie,' said Tara urgently. 'Not in the eyes of the law. He's got a record.'

Sophie sighed and shifted Edie on her shoulder. 'Oh, Tara, that's completely different. He was being bullied, there were extenuating circumstances . . .'

'Sophie, we're not talking about a bit of dope, here. We can't get Jon Slingsby to turn a blind eye to this, can we? This will be a different force, people who don't know Jake, his history. This is serious, this is . . .'

The word 'murder' hung above their heads like a guillotine.

Rowan felt their disagreement as a stitch, savage in his breast. He was almost grateful that he could not catch his breath to intervene. Nothing in his life had prepared him for this. It might be different for those born into a different class, they might be equipped with the resources for this sort of thing, but it was not the MacBride way.

Will looked over his shoulder at Tara. 'There's been enough

anarchy already this weekend. The police need to come and take Kerry away. They'll just talk to Jake, we'll all tell them what happened, and they won't press charges.'

'Don't be so fucking naïve! Of *course* they will. Whatever, there'll be some kind of process . . . they'll still want it all to go through the proper channels. It's obvious to us that he didn't do anything wrong, but they're outsiders, they don't *know* him. They don't know his background, everything he's been through. Come on, Will, I know how much you care about Jake. We can let them deal with Kerry without dragging Jake into it, without telling them about Matt.'

Jake remained still, but flared his nostrils like a frightened horse about to buck. The way Will looked at him, heavy with the kind of tenderness one would expect from a father to his own son, showed that Tara had got through to him. Rowan knew that Will was forcing down his principles in favour of something truer and closer to home, because something similar was happening to him.

'What about Kerry?' said Will. 'I take it *she* knows, the way you're all talking so freely in front of her. What's to stop her blurting it all out?'

'I wouldn't do that, sweartogod,' spluttered Kerry, then yelped as Felix tightened his grip on her wrists and said,

'Forgive me if we don't exactly take you on your word on that one.'

'Please don't tell the police on me!' said Jake. 'I only wanted to stop him hurting Edie, Auntie Sophie! I mean, I really *liked* Matt.'

Tara saw the glance Sophie and Will exchanged and pounced on it. 'Any of us would have done the same thing if we'd been in the right place. You know you would have. Your boys would have done it, if they'd been here, if they'd been Jake's age, if they'd been strong enough. Dad, tell her, please? Tell them?'

Five faces turned towards Rowan; even Will, so assured, now stood in temporary deference to the head of the family. Over the years Rowan had been accountable for hundreds of children and yet he now understood that he had never before come close to knowing the meaning of responsibility.

'Just . . . will you all just bloody *stop* for a second, and give me a chance to *think*,' he shouted, digging his heels into the earth. They were at the top of the garden. From here, the drop to the lawn looked almost vertical. Rowan stood, aware of how pathetic he sounded and desperately willing his warring thoughts to coalesce. He had an ingrained deference to authority but knew the police were far from infallible. Dare he trust them with his grandson's future? Everything Jake had was going into keeping him upright. He was old enough to try to be strong, but lacked sophistication to disguise the effort. Rowan saw in the boy the man he was turning into, responsible and considerate and accomplished, all the more impressive when one considered the disadvantaged circumstance of his birth. How could they derail him from this path, only so recently established?

The growl of an engine sounded in the far distance. Another thought began swiftly to crystallise. Say they did tell the police everything that had happened, say they gave Jake up, showed them the body and told them who Matt really was, what then? Their investigations would probe why he had borne this vendetta against the family, and who knew then what might come out? Lydia had written that she cared less about public opinion than her children's but she had not seemed to realise, or at least not to mention, that for her actions to be made public would necessarily be for her children to learn of them. If Jake's golden future was tarnished, it would take the MacBride name with it. Rowan knew, somewhere deeper than principle or pride, what they must do.

'We can deal with this as a family,' he said as they approached the barn. 'We don't need them to know that Jake was involved in any of it.'

There were sharp inhalations, sobs, a dry scraped gasp that might have come from Jake himself.

'But *how* will we—'

'I'm *thinking*, Will.'

Light had caught up with sound now: blue lights far along the lane turned naked branches into steel. Even allowing for a slower than normal speed, they would be here in three minutes. The family entered the kitchen through doors that had remained wide open. Sophie made straight for the baby monitor on the table. It registered no sound but she pressed it to her ear like a seashell. 'I can hear them,' she said. 'I can hear them breathing,' and she sank into the chair at the head of the table. Under the strip light of the kitchen Rowan noticed for the first time the extent of their dishevelment. Kerry's contamination was far worse than had been apparent at the cottage, a stippling of blood over her skin and God knew what embedded in her dark jersey.

'Wash your hands and face, will you?' Rowan asked her. Felix marched her to the kitchen sink; the suds foamed pink.

'Let me get this straight,' said Will. 'If we're going to somehow shield Jake from all this, how are we going to explain away the dead bloke up at the cottage?'

The values by which Rowan had raised his family had been destroyed. He had minutes, perhaps seconds, to come up with a new set and instill them in his children. Sheer force of circumstance was his inspiration. 'We're not,' he said.

Will was aghast. 'Rowan, you're not serious.'

'They're looking for a baby, not a man.'

'What if they want to question him?' pressed Will.

'We'll say it was crossed wires, that he's still out looking. Once they see that Edie's here, why would they? What reason will they have to go combing the outbuildings?'

'But he *will* still be there,' said Tara.

'Yes . . .' Don't make me say it, thought Rowan. It's bad enough that it has to be done. Please let's not put *this* into words.

'We *can't*,' said Will, but his voice was already slack with defeat.

'For Jake,' Sophie said. 'Tara's right. Our boys would have done the same. I can't bear the police crawling all over our lives.'

'Do I have a choice?' said Will.

'Darling, please, don't be like that,' said Sophie. 'If we're going to do this, we need to do it together. You're as much part of this family as anyone.'

Will laced his fingers together and pressed the heels of his hands deep into his eyes. 'Fine. Well, not fine, but . . . Jesus *Christ*. What a mess. Look, I'm going to check on the bunker, OK? I'll be right back,' he said.

The car outside grew closer. Rowan guessed it would be about a minute away.

'Oh no,' said Sophie. 'Jake, your *top*.' The boy had a smear of blood on his white T-shirt in the shape of his beloved Nike swoosh.

'Oh fuck!' said Jake. 'What am I going to do? They're going to put me in prison!' He pulled off his jacket and went to take off the T-shirt, all elbows, tangling himself up in his own clothes like a toddler, and getting just as distressed.

'Tara, he needs to go upstairs,' said Rowan. 'It's not fair to ask him to stay calm in front of the police.'

'I don't want to be on my own! Mum?'

'Grandpa's right, Jakey. Just while we talk to the police. Go and wait in my room. Stay there until we tell you to come down.'

'What if they come after me?' he said. 'What if Kerry tells on me?'

'I promise, I won't,' said Kerry. 'Felix, I *promise* I won't.'

'Short of gagging her, I can't think what we're going to do with her,' said Tara, as if Kerry wasn't there.

'I swear on my life,' said Kerry. 'I brought the baby back, didn't I? That shows you can trust me.'

'It shows nothing of the sort,' barked Rowan.

'What if I get her out of the way, too?' said Felix. 'She can't say anything if she's not there.'

Rowan thought hard. The story that was taking shape in his mind depended on having Kerry around. It depended on trusting her. To accidentally report an abduction was a believable parental overreaction. To explain Matt away would be difficult, but possible. But for the accused abductor to disappear as well was unequivocally suspicious. Or was it? The clean lines of innocence and guilt had blurred and dissolved. Who was he, now, to say what looked suspicious and what didn't?

'*Please* don't make me go upstairs on my own,' said Jake, dangerously close to losing control.

'I'm sorry, Jake,' said Rowan, temporarily diverted from the problem of Kerry. 'It's not a choice.'

Tara got up to escort her son and overrode her tears to speak. 'Darling, I'll be up with you as soon as I can. We're going to take care of it all, OK?' Rowan and Tara stood at the kitchen door, watched Jake climb the stairs. He seemed to grow smaller and younger with each tread. At the top of the stairs, they met Will coming in the opposite direction. Will put a hand on his nephew's arm, drew him into a brief hug and whispered something in the boy's ear that made him gulp, nod and hold his uncle even tighter. As Will descended the staircase, Jake paused to study his face in the landing mirror before disappearing through Rowan's bedroom door.

'How are they?' Sophie asked Will.

'Sparko, all of them. How the hell do they sleep through that? I mean, I know you can't hear anything in there, but how come they didn't sense it? The air feels *live*.'

Outside two car doors slammed. A police radio crackled.

'We still haven't decided what to do about *her*,' said Tara, fixing Kerry with a Medusa stare. 'There's no point in getting Jake out of the way if she's still here to land him in the shit.'

Soft footsteps sounded outside. The family stared at the open kitchen door.

Rowan drummed his fingers on the table. Now, with seconds to spare, the decision was easy to make. He would just have to find a way to explain Kerry's absence. 'Yes, take her away,' he decided. 'Take her up to your bedroom and keep her there until we come and get you. I'm sure we'll clear it all up in a couple of minutes.'

Felix had loosened his jailer's grip on Kerry and now took her elbow in a foolish act of vestigial trust. Rowan had no idea what to make of the meekness with which Kerry let him steer her away. In the sitting room, Felix exclaimed in surprise. She's given him the slip, thought Rowan, and pushed back his chair. Will too rose from his bench. But before either of them could give chase, Felix and Kerry returned. Their strange embrace was broken and they were accompanied by two uniformed police officers. The sergeant was in late middle age and the constable, a small Asian woman, was about the same age as Tara. Their faces were composed in twin expressions of professional concern and compassion.

'Sergeant Andrew Hough and PC Maya Rayat,' he announced. 'Responding to a 999 call reporting a missing child.'

'They came in through the front door,' said Felix unnecessarily.

Hough sniffed the air like an animal. Rayat tried to look at Felix's eye without making it obvious.

Rowan put out a hand to the sergeant and saw that it was encrusted with earth. Suddenly, he seemed to smell the metallic edge of blood; he withdrew his hand just as the officer extended his own.

'Sergeant, thank you so much for coming out. But I'm afraid it's been a false alarm.' He stepped aside so that they could see Edie slumbering on Sophie's shoulder. 'As you can see, the baby is here and she's perfectly safe. It's been a horrific hour, but it was just a case of bad communication. A family misunderstanding. We were literally just about to ring you again and call off the search.'

'Right,' said Hough. He looked Rowan up and down, took in his filthy clothes.

'It's been quite a search party, as you can imagine,' said Rowan. 'Stumbling around in the woods like fools!' He forced a smile.

Kerry had positioned herself behind Rayat. Her eyes flicked between the officers to make sure she could not be seen, then she pulled up her sleeve to examine a smeared bracelet of blood on her left wrist. Felix's fingers had left a mark on her forearm. She rubbed her jersey over the stained skin so that the blood was absorbed. Whether she was signalling cooperation or distancing herself, only the next few minutes would tell.

54

'Oh, that's such good news,' said Rayat. 'Better to be called out for a found child than a lost one. Better every time.' She crouched down next to Sophie, stroked Edie's hair. 'Hello, you. Have you been on a bit of an adventure? Oh, she's *gorgeous*. Those *eyelashes*! I've got one her age at home. I can't imagine what you've been through this evening. The thing about false alarms is you don't know they're false alarms until later, it feels real at the time, doesn't it?'

Sophie kept staring at Rowan. He wished she would stop. It looked odd, unnatural.

Sergeant Hough seemed less pleased. 'We've got a chopper with a thermal imaging camera already on its way from Bristol for this.' Rowan wondered if the others were thinking the same as him; Matt would be giving out heat for some time yet. How long *did* it take for a body to cool? How long had he sat with Lydia until her hand had grown— 'Mind you, it's the worst night for a heatseeker. It'll all look like join the dots tonight. Big bonfires, kids setting fire to bins, pissheads sleeping in ditches, pissheads *shagging* in ditches. Still, kid's here, that's the main thing. I'll have to cancel now, anyway.'

Hough harrumphed and began to pace the kitchen. He stood at the back door, next to the corner where shovels and mops, brooms and a ladder leaned against the wall at a 30 degree angle. A wicket and stumps lay in a little pile on the floor. The absence of the cricket bat suddenly gripped Rowan as the most incriminating absence in the history of detection, and he braced himself for the interrogation as to its whereabouts. 'Any danger of a cup of tea?' said Hough. 'So my journey wasn't completely wasted?'

'Sure,' said Tara. In her haste, she swept a stack of pans off the top of the stove. They clattered to the floor; the noise was like a hail of bullets. Rowan hoped his glance at the baby monitor was surreptitious. The boys might have slept through raised voices but that noise would wake, if not the dead, at least sleeping schoolboys.

Tara handled the kettle and mugs with hummingbird fingers. 'Milk and two for me, milk and none for her,' said the sergeant. The kettle's boil was deafening, making conversation impossible. Had it always been like that?

'Well, listen, let's just tidy this all up. I can write it up and go,' said Rayat. 'Who made the call?'

'Me, Will Woodford, Edie's father.'

'God, you must be so *relieved*. OK, so my notes say that we've got a suspected abduction of a child by someone called Kerry Stone.'

Rowan cut in, hoping desperately that Kerry would keep her vow of silence. 'That's Kerry, next to you. As I said, it was just a misunderstanding. She took the baby for a walk without telling us—'

'What, at night, in this fog?' said Rayat, eyeballing Kerry.

'Well, quite,' said Will. 'We weren't expecting it either, so when we came back from the Tar Barrels early, we naturally panicked. You know how it is.'

'And your relationship to the baby is . . . ?' Rayat asked Kerry.

'She's a family friend,' interjected Rowan. Should he keep answering for Kerry? He knew it sounded odd. But what was the alternative? Who knew, once the girl began a dialogue with this woman, what she would say? It was impossible to tell which of her various truths would float to the surface.

'Right. So that accounts for Kerry. So, Will, my notes here say that on the call made at 11.59 p.m. you stated . . . and forgive me here, because you were a bit emotional, it's not quite clear, that someone called Matthew Rider had tried to call us originally? So why didn't he?'

Rowan held his tongue. To answer on Kerry's behalf was one thing: to speak in Will's place would definitely arouse suspicion.

'Oh, that was also a, ah, a misunderstanding,' said Will, flushing scarlet. 'It was more that I think I just thought he had. You know. Heat of the moment.'

Tara had made enough tea for everyone. She served the police officers first and PC Rayat nodded in thanks. 'So you both thought that you'd made the call but neither of you had? Seems a bit odd, that you left something as important as that to chance, don't you agree?'

There was steel beneath this woman's softness, like a skull beneath skin. Will wore a gloss of sweat. 'Like you said, I was emotional. Isn't the main thing that Edie is here?'

'Firstly, of course you were, and secondly, I can't tell you how happy I am about that, but questions are asked back at the station and I just want to tie up all the loose ends. I still have to make a report, since we've been called out.' She brought the mug of tea up to her lips but didn't quite sip from it. 'Which of you is Matthew?' she said, looking at Rowan and Felix. And then it was all over.

Idiots. They were all idiots. They weren't cut out for this sort of thing. Of course the police would want to talk to Matt. Of *course* they would. It was so *obvious*, now. His original plan, to tell her that Matt was still out looking, was useless if Rayat insisted on waiting for him to return. There was no way out of this. Worse – yes, it could still get worse – Kerry looked as though she was about to say something, and Rowan was all out of ideas to stop her. He watched helplessly as she nudged Felix in the ribs.

'Come on, Matt,' she said. 'Speak up.' She stepped back into her shadow.

'Sorry,' said Felix eventually. 'I think I'm still in shock. Yes, we, um, we got to the top of the hill where there's a mobile signal, and in all the fuss and panic I thought he'd called you and he thought I'd done it, and, you know, just, crossed wires.'

Rayat's eyes narrowed. 'It's a pretty big thing to get your wires crossed about. A missing child and you weren't checking who'd made the call? If it had been my daughter,' she said to Will, 'if I'd been in your shoes, I'd have stopped at *nothing* to make sure that call got through.'

'Don't think I don't know that! I *know* I fucked up. I doubt I'll ever get over it.' Will's voice broke on the last word. Rayat's expression changed. She might not know the true context of his outburst but there was no denying its sincerity.

'Yes', she said. 'I'm sure you do. One thing I was wondering about; why did you have to go all the way to the top of the valley anyway? Haven't you got a house phone?'

'It's not working,' said Rowan. 'I let the bill run out, we're not here very often,' understanding only as he spoke that the dead telephone was no more due to his own neglect than the failure of the outside light bulb had been.

'Sooner they get that bloody mobile mast up around here the better,' said Hough, whose pacing had landed him in the doorway. 'Even our radios barely work down here. Speaking of which, I need to radio back to the station, get them to cancel that helicopter, redeploy the cover back to Ottery. Hang on, you've got a hill here. Let me walk a bit further up, see if it's any different.' He shone his torch into the darkness, a finger of light pointing the way up to where Matt's body lay.

'It's a bit treacherous out there,' said Rowan. 'You'd probably be better off trying to do it from the lane outside.'

'Fair dos,' he said. 'Back to what's left of the festival.' He drank his milk-and-two down in one and put the cup in the sink. Rowan's eyes were drawn to the hand soap; a faint rosy lather still clung to the white slab. He held his breath until Hough retrieved his hat from the table. 'You ready, Maya?' he said.

'My heart was in my mouth on the way over here,' said Rayat. 'Never had to deal with anything like that before, to be honest. I'm relieved. Not as relieved as you are, though. I bet you'll sleep well tonight.' She stopped by Felix. 'You sure you're not family, Matt? You don't half look like the others.'

Felix shook his head.

Hough chucked Edie under the chin on the way out. 'I don't want any more trouble from *you*,' he said.

Will's answering laugh was far too loud.

They waited in perfect silence until the sound of tyre on track was an echo in the memory. Felix was the first to leave the table. He opened the drinks cupboard, reached down the brandy and poured a good slug into each steaming mug, hesitating only over Kerry's. Rowan drank it down. The spirit seemed to take the liquid beyond boiling point. It scoured his insides.

'Are you going to get Jake?' Sophie asked Tara.

Will put his hand on Tara's arm. 'I think it's best if we get this all sorted without Jake, it's a conversation for the adults only. I won't pretend I'm happy that we lied to the police, but it's done now, and I stand by it. We *all* stand by it. Isn't that the point of family?'

Rowan could not have been prouder of Will if he was blood.

'*She's* not family,' said Tara, gesturing to Kerry.

'I promise I'm not going to say anything, ever,' said Kerry, to bitter protest. 'Didn't I just prove that? Didn't I just cover for you? I don't want anything more to do with this no more than you do. Look, all the people who might notice he's gone are in this room, he didn't have no one else in his life. I won't even report him missing. I'm *glad* he's gone, I was terrified of him!' she beseeched Tara, then Sophie. 'I don't blame you if you don't believe me, but I was always on your side, never his.'

'How bloody *dare* you . . .' began Sophie.

Kerry spread her hands wide. The lines on her palms were maroon threads. 'I couldn't say no to him, I didn't know what he might do, but I was never going to take her away from you. I was always going to bring her back. I would *never* have hurt her.'

The clock struck once.

55

Will cleared his throat. 'Look, Kerry can wait, until the morning at least. I was thinking more about the *immediate* future. It's one o'clock in the morning. Our boys will be up in a few hours and there's no way I'm involving them in any of this. We need to clear things up.'

'No, hang on a minute,' said Tara, setting down her mug. 'I've got to get Jake, if we're talking about that. He must be worried sick. And I think he does need to be involved, now the coast is clear. He needs to see the consequences of what's happened. Not to punish him, just for, you know, closure.'

'Are you sure?' asked Sophie.

'No, not remotely,' said Tara. 'I'm not sure about anything.'

Rowan felt a swell of guilt follow her out of the door. He was suddenly revisited by the memory of the father of a pupil who was experiencing rare bullying at the Cath. He'd come to see Rowan in his study and said, 'Makes you wish you could suffer on their behalf, doesn't it?' He wished now that he could shoulder Jake's guilt for him.

'This doesn't seem like a scene from my life,' said Felix offering the brandy around again. Sophie shook her head but Rowan and Will gratefully accepted another shot.

Tara returned, her mouth working and her hands twisting the hem of her sweatshirt. 'He won't come out of my room. He says he wants to be on his own. I'm not going to let him, obviously, I've only come down to let you all know. I don't know about you, but I don't think I'm ever going to sleep again.' A nervous giggle spilled over into crying. 'Oh God, what am I going to say to him in the morning? How am I going to get him through the rest of his life?'

'You'll manage,' said Sophie. 'You're a brilliant mum, you'll get there. And he's got all of us as well, hasn't he?'

'What was I thinking, letting that bastard into our lives? I'm such a stupid cow.'

'Oh, Tara, honey,' said Sophie. 'You weren't to know. How could you know? How could *any* of us know? I'll come up with you. Charlie's going to wake up in what, six or seven hours? And Toby and Leo won't be far behind him. Those boys need us.'

Half an hour earlier, when Edie was still missing, Sophie had depended on Tara for physical support. Now Tara shuffled like an invalid with Sophie as her crutch.

Will collected an armful of picks and shovels from the garden. He took the square shovel for himself and handed Felix a newer version of the same. The spade he gave Rowan had a rounded point. A child's plastic spade, part of a seaside set, remained. Kerry knelt to pick it up.

'Shall I take that one?' she said pathetically. 'I could help you.'

'Why, do you want to build a fucking sandcastle while we bury your – what *was* he to you, anyway?'

'Husband,' she murmured through her fingers. 'Please don't hate me for it, Fee.' She reached out to touch the cheek below his empty eye socket. Felix raised the hand with the shovel in it and for a moment Rowan thought that he was going to strike her. Kerry evidently thought so too; she did not cower but ducked to the side, with the practised reflexes of a boxer who is always on guard for the next jab. It gave the possibility of truth to her claim that she had acted in fear. Felix lowered the shovel, gazed at his hands as if they were someone else's.

'You must think I'm the biggest prick ever,' he said without looking up. 'I bet you had a right laugh about me.'

'I'd never laugh at you. It started out pretending but, Felix, it changed. I love you now.'

Felix winced. 'Please shut up, Kerry. I think you've insulted me quite enough already.'

'It's true! That's why I took Edie, I was keeping her safe from *him*. I did it *for* you, to show you I was on your side, yours and your family's. I did it because I want to *be* with you.'

Now he made an incredulous noise that was half-laugh, half-gurgle. 'Be with me? I can barely even look at you! After what you put my sisters through? No way, Kerry. Just shut up and stay where I can see you for now. I'm going to help my dad and Will sort out this . . . *shit* . . . I'll deal with you when the sun comes up.'

Kerry followed them into the garden. The mist had lifted a little and a soft-focus crescent moon helped to improve visibility. The ridge that separated the back of the garden from the surrounding land was now discernible, white light from the lantern rising over a fuzzy horizon.

'Are we really doing this?' said Felix.

'What choice do we have?' said Rowan.

They left their shovels at the edge of the trenches and were almost at the ridge when a cracked voice called him back.

'Dad?' Tara was silhouetted in the doorway of the kitchen.

Jake, thought Rowan. What if, while Tara was downstairs – how could they have been so *stupid*? – he had done something rash? Why didn't I hide my dressing-gown cord, thought Rowan, why didn't I take the bleach from the lavatory, why didn't we all hide our razor blades? He ran towards his daughter.

'What is it? Is it Jake?'

'No, he's all right. I mean obviously he's *not* all right, but . . .' She was wearing pyjamas. She carried a black holdall in one hand and had a tangle of clothes tucked under the other. Rowan nodded down at the bundles. 'What's all that?'

'These are all Matt's things,' she said, handing him the holdall. 'You might want to have another bonfire.'

'Oh. Lord. Right. Good idea.'

'And then what you're wearing too. Our stuff's already in here.' The topmost garment, Rowan now saw, was Jake's bloodstained T-shirt. Tara's eyes blazed with fear and pleading and a terrible, compromising gratitude. Looking into them was like staring into the sun. He had no choice but to drop his gaze.

56

Kerry shadowed the men on the short journey to the cottage, and Rowan kept to himself the superstitious conviction that Matt would not be there when they arrived. It was not that he doubted Matt's death, rather that so much had shifted in the last few hours that it would barely surprise him to learn that ghosts were real. But there he was, on his back as they had left him. The lantern cast a white aureole around his hair. From this perspective his face appeared intact, his profile perfect. I ought to have recognised that face, thought Rowan again. I ought to have *divined* it.

Stooping to a crouch, Rowan rolled Matt onto his front so the mash of his features could not be seen. He did it carefully, almost as one might roll over a sleeping child one did not wish to wake. The body rocked to a standstill and Rowan was suddenly possessed by the urge to kick the lifeless form all the way down the garden like a football. He overrode the impulse; in these grotesque circumstances it seemed more important than ever to set an example to the younger men.

'Right,' said Felix, wiping his hands on his jeans then rubbing them together. 'Let's get it over with. Who's going to take the head end?'

'We could just take him by the feet, and see how that works,' suggested Will. 'Rowan, maybe you could bring the rest of the stuff.'

Rowan took the slimy bat, holding it gingerly by the neck. The cooled blowtorch he placed in his jacket pocket.

Felix and Will took a boot each and dragged the body face-down over the heathery earth. Rowan picked up the electric lantern and lit their way, but the others were clearly struggling, and every time Matt's head passed over a tree root or rock it bounced at the neck. A foretaste of bile rinsed Rowan's mouth.

'This won't do,' he said. He shrugged – what was more blood on his jacket? – wedged the bat under his arm, and the three of them switched to a wheelbarrow arrangement, Felix and Rowan taking an armpit each, Will with a foot in each hand. They fell into careful step. It was in a similar formation that the three of them had carried Lydia's coffin into the crematorium. Jake had been the fourth pallbearer. The memory was searing.

'Dad, you've stopped,' said Felix. 'Come on, we're nearly there.'

When they reached the garden, the incline forced them to carry the body at an angle, head lower than the feet. The slope took one last sharp dip before levelling itself out, and as Matt's body was upended at a tilt of 45 degrees, the contents of his trouser pockets emptied themselves. Silver, brass and copper coins rolled across the grass and lay glinting like treasure trove. Rowan made a mental note to retrieve them after the initial task was done.

At the edge of the trenches, he wedged the lantern into the crooked elbow of a pear tree. Will dropped into the widest, deepest part of the ditch. He was over six feet tall, and the ditch only came up to his elbows. 'How do the boys get in and out of this?' he said, feeling up and down the smooth walls. 'We're going to need to dig deeper, by a good two feet.'

Felix passed Will a shovel, then jumped down with another one.

'Dad, maybe you could get to work filling in the rest of them?' said Felix. 'Backfill it with compost and if that isn't enough we can start digging into these banks.'

Rowan peeled off his jacket and hung it on a branch. Within half an hour he had shovelled every leaf, twig and branch in the entire compost heap, as well as the remains of the bonfire and some rubble from the side of the wood house. The trench was still only half full and by that time, Felix and Will had finished digging to the required depth and were free to help him loosen the solidified piles of earth all over the garden.

Rowan was grateful for the physical demand, channelling all his anger and fear into the shovel, turning great clods with every action. His jersey came off, his shirtsleeves were rolled. Within an hour, Will was bare-chested, his sweat turning to vapour. The men worked in silent complicity, culpability settling more evenly over each family member every time the earth was broken, every time the soil was spread.

A sudden flare and a *woof* broke the silence. All three men started and turned to the source of the light. Kerry stood before a sputtering makeshift bonfire, Rowan's own coat around her shoulders, blowtorch trained on the black holdall and a pile of clothes like an empty guy.

'Tara said to burn his stuff,' she said. 'You should put his phone on here. Or at least wipe it. He was going to record you, when you said about—' She stopped herself mid-sentence, looked at Rowan, realised she had almost given the game away. Rowan felt sick; what did she know? What had Matt told her? Whatever it was, she wasn't going to say it, or she wasn't going to say it yet.

'I think it's in his inside pocket, in his jacket,' she said. Rowan unzipped Matt's jacket, felt warm flesh between the ribs as he fumbled for the telephone. A little red icon on the screen told him that it was thirty-five minutes into a voice recording. Whatever Matt had been planning to record, he had inadvertently captured the sound of his own death.

'Want me to wipe it?' said Kerry. Did she think he was

stupid? He might not understand how young people could broadcast this kind of thing around the world in seconds, but he knew that they could and they did. He did not hand the phone to her but bowled it underarm, straight onto the fire where it was consumed in a crackle and a spark.

Kerry tossed the cricket bat after it. At first the flames danced over its surface, caramelising the blood before starting to consume the wood. The light it created made her face no less inscrutable. Rowan's heart sank. The problem of Kerry was looming larger as the morning approached. What were they going to do with the girl? She could not maintain this ridiculous pretence of being on their side forever. Was Felix supposed to keep her with him for the rest of her life? She yawned and rubbed her eyes in a gesture that reminded him of Charlie.

'I'm going to get her out of the way,' said Felix. 'Kerry, go to bed. Come on.'

Again holding her hands behind her back, but in a looser lock this time, he led her into the house through the kitchen. The light went on in Felix's bedroom window, a yellow square in the roof that gave no view of the interior.

'What's the point of having her out of the way if she's watching us?' said Will.

'What can she see that's worse than what she's already seen?'

Felix returned a couple of minutes later. Rowan peered at his son for signs of softening but if anything Felix's face was set harder than before. 'She'll keep until the morning,' said Felix.

'What if she does a runner in the night?' said Will.

'I wedged a chair under the door handle,' replied Felix. 'She won't be able to get out without making a hell of a noise.' He dug into his pocket and pulled out the keys to all their cars. 'And this is just in case she *does* manage it. I wouldn't put anything past her after this. I should've known, shouldn't I? I should've *known* that someone like her would never go for . . .' His voice fractured, and his head dropped into his cupped hands.

The trenches were completely filled, bar one six-by-six-by-two-foot cavity. They threw him in as they had dragged him, face down. One of his boots came off in Rowan's hand, pulling the sock with it, leaving his foot bare.

'I can't . . .' began Felix.

'Yes you can, old boy,' said Will. 'We all can.'

'Thanks,' said Felix ruefully. 'But that's not what I was going to say. I was going to say, I can't believe this is the boy who kicked my eye in.'

For the first time Rowan really connected the cooling empty flesh of Matt's body with the child he had known. Of course he had known it, had known on some level from the moment he had seen the name on Kerry's driving licence, but now the emotional realisation caught up with the intellectual understanding and the aftershock was as great as the first tremor.

Soon all that remained visible of Matt was a single pale round heel, a full moon that diminished to a crescent and was then totally eclipsed as the turned earth covered it. Rowan wished he could throw his own memories in after it, seal them underground forever.

When the trench was level with the garden, they went over it all with their shovels, trying to make it look natural.

'I think that's as good as it's going to get,' said Will, throwing his spade down.

It was far from satisfactory. The deep clay had become mixed in with the surface loam. The foundations of the old house were as clearly demarcated as they had been when they were ditches. To Rowan's guilty mind it was an obvious grave.

'The kids won't be happy,' said Felix. 'What are we going to tell them in the morning?'

'I've been threatening to fill them in for years,' said Rowan. 'I don't know, we'll tell them there was a landslide or something. Leo's quite into landslides at the moment. It'll settle eventually.' It wasn't the younger boys' reaction that concerned him but Jake's. If only grass could grow overnight, if only the garden could be restored to innocence, if only Jake could be convinced upon waking that it had all been a terrible dream.

Will examined his hands and said, 'Out, damned spot.'

Rowan looked up sharply but Will wasn't trying to be funny. 'I know this changes everything. This changes me, this changes us, the family . . . but I can handle it. I'm strong. I'm an adult, I'm already fully formed. But what the hell is this going to do to Jake? What does this mean for him?'

'This – what we've done here, I mean – should go some way to showing him that we share the blame,' said Felix. 'Well, blame's not the right word. That we share the consequences. I think it's less "Out damned spot," more, "I am Spartacus." '

He smoothed the surface of the earth with his boot. 'I keep thinking about all these moments when it could have gone the other way, you know? Like what might have happened if the police had been a bit more probing, or what if we hadn't all gone into the cottage.'

'Or if I'd made the call properly the first time around,' said Will.

Felix took the blame like a baton. 'Or, let's face it, if I'd never got off with Kerry in the first place.'

Or if I had given a different child a chance, thought Rowan.

'What did Matt mean by saying you had something awful to tell us about Mum?'

Lying to the police had been desperately inadequate preparation for lying to his son. He was caught; if Felix challenged him, Rowan felt he would break down, and if Felix believed him, it would be a pane of glass that must stay between them forever.

'I've no idea. He was just trying to get a rise out of me. He'd have said anything. Come on. You know your mother. She wasn't a dark secrets sort of person.'

'No, of course. That's one of the few things we *can* rely on.' Felix let his spade fall to the earth.

In the mudroom, Felix and then Will took off their clothes and bundled them into a bin-liner in accordance with Tara's instructions. It was the first time Rowan had seen his son naked for about fifteen years. It paled in comparison to the terrible intimacy that bound them all now.

'I'll take the downstairs shower, if you want the one upstairs?' said Felix, taking a clean, if threadbare, towel for himself and handing another to Will.

'Sure. Thanks,' said Will. 'Shit, Fee. Have you got to share a bed with Kerry now?'

'I suppose so,' said Felix. 'I have to share a room, at least. I need to make sure she stays put.'

Rowan waited alone in the mudroom until the stilling of the pipes and the ceasing of footsteps overhead told him that the young men were both in their beds. He heard the horror-film creak of Felix's bedroom door. Doubtless he would take the floor while Kerry had the bed.

Rowan removed his own clothes, wrapped himself in the last towel and in the garden threw them and the black bag onto the smouldering fire. He lurched up the stairs, cold enough now for gooseflesh to sleeve his arms. In the family bathroom he had a shower so hot it gave him pins and needles.

He walked the corridor in the merciful dark. Below him, the grandfather clock struck half-past five. It must have been decades since he had stayed awake this long – even by Lydia's deathbed, sleep had come to him in five-minute snatches – and he wondered how long this buzzing, manic energy would last. Tara had said she would never sleep again.

He did not turn his bedroom light on, felt under the pillow for last night's pyjamas. He lay flat on his back under the blankets for a while, and then with a crack and a whoosh, the internal dam broke in Rowan's memory and he could hold back history no longer. He closed his eyes and let it flow.

After Felix's attack, Rowan had been equally crushed by the frustration of not being able to press charges against Kellaway and desperate to understand what could make someone react so violently to a disappointment that dozens of children had borne with dignity. He had known that he must learn to live with the first emotion but, to appease the second, he had visited the annexe of the library that housed the Mawson-Luxmore applications going back thirty years. If he was entirely honest, he'd failed to remember much about Darcy Kellaway's interview. The examination paper had been more memorable, an unusual sensitivity to poetry discernible even through the rather stilted and archaic language of his essay. Rowan had in any case strongly suspected that the key to Kellaway's outburst lay not in the boy's spoken or written words but in the documents attached to the application. For the first time in his tenure as admissions tutor, he had taken out the accompanying file. He was surprised by its heft, and transferred it from hand to hand before opening it. He had always made a point of ignoring the letters that accompanied the children's applications, preferring to judge the child by the performance on the day rather than risk being swayed by the persuasive prose of a good prep-school master, or prejudiced by the inexperience of an inner-city primary schoolteacher against a child from a less privileged background. But the heft of Kellaway's file had suggested something more than the usual Record of Achievement and letter of recommendation.

The first page had borne the insignia of Saxby Council Social Services. Rowan had tried to remain neutral as he read the boy's wretched story. It had read like a synopsis from Dickens. He had lived alone with, and been home-schooled by, a mother herself a veteran of state care. At twenty-one, Heather Kellaway had spent six months in a psychiatric hospital near Oxford, where she had been a student of English literature and at which university her parents had both been dons. She had suffered a complete nervous breakdown after her tutor was accused, tried and acquitted of her rape. Her parents had disowned her immediately. The university did not send Heather down, but she did not gain her degree: eight and a half months after the alleged rape, Darcy was born. Heather had followed a distant cousin to Saxby with the newborn Darcy, who had barely left her side since. The boy was described as intelligent, with a reading age of eighteen, but nervous and introverted, and more than usually dependent on his mother. Someone had scrawled in the margin, 'And vice versa – possible young carer status?'

It pained Rowan now to remember how he had closed the file and left the library unswayed. He had felt compassion for the boy, of course he had, but what could one do? Even after Felix was attacked, Rowan had not regretted sticking firmly to the principle of meritocracy. He had told himself time and again that one simply could not let emotion come into it, it would be like grading an examination according to a pupil's manners rather than his ability. Part of him was even confident that he had done the right thing in rejecting the application. If Kellaway had been admitted to the school, would they have been able to tame him or would he have been a force for destruction within the institution? It was impossible to say, and hindsight always knew best.

The fact remained that, in the 1997 intake, the Mawson-Luxmore had gone to the most accomplished child. Arthur Li had been a virtuoso violinist, the kind of instinctive musician one saw only once in a generation. He had deserved the scholarship. A sleeping memory was shaken awake: Arthur had left the Cath for the conservatoire at the Guildhall two years into his time at the school. He was currently with the Birmingham Symphony Orchestra. He would have been fine wherever he ended up.

Now, his grandson a murderer and his children's worlds shattered, Rowan's regret was bitter. He turned onto his side. The old bed rocked and she came rolling towards him just as she had in life, though the soft warm flesh that had always soothed him to sleep was now encased, small and cold and hard. He pressed the chilly urn to his lips, suffered the anodyne kiss of metal.

'Oh, Lydia,' he said. 'What have we done?'

It was the first time he had ever cried in front of her.

57

Rowan awoke with a jolt and a drumming heart after less than two hours' sleep. Immediately his eyes were open he began to hurl himself on the jagged shards of what had happened. Had it really been he who had ordered his family to hide a man's death from the world? Last night's solid conviction that the best way to protect Jake was to hide the truth from the police had lost its substance. Perhaps it was not too late to involve the law, to get everything out in the open, to retrieve some kind of truth? But no; the lies, the buried body . . . this was a border that could only be crossed once, and in one direction. He had dragged his family into an abominable other world in which they must make a new home. An all-over ache pinned him to the bed; it was as though his bones were fusing into one giant mass, leaving him immobile.

It was with great effort, and a series of clicks and cracks, that he rose. The darkness outside had not quite lifted, yet in a way, the night seemed longer ago than his childhood.

Sophie and Tara's bedroom doors were open and the beds empty. Felix's remained closed. There was still the problem of what to do with Kerry. What would Felix say to her when they woke? What would anyone say today? What had been said already between the conspiracy of mothers downstairs?

Rowan's empty stomach gave a warning growl as the warm nutty smell of fresh coffee curling up the stairs made him salivate. He was astonished to find that the animal reflexes of thirst and hunger were still working.

Everyone was in the kitchen but Felix and Kerry. The children were a reminder of the world as it had been the day before. The boys were lined up at the table eating cereal and Edie in her high chair, oblivious to her nocturnal adventures. Sophie and Tara were always talking about how sensitive children were to changes in adult moods, but his grandchildren made nonsense of that theory. It was as though the adults occupied a stratosphere of guilt and grief and fear while, below them, the children continued to breathe the same innocent air as yesterday. The contrast was almost unbearable. Sophie looked in need of a hundred-year sleep. Will looked in need of a shave and a drink. Tara looked in need of a blood transfusion. Jake's face was the picture next to 'anguish' in the dictionary. His smooth brow was corrupted with a series of wavy lines and his mouth was set in a brittle straight line. Guilt had diffused into all of them, made them strangers to themselves yet more intimate with each other than any family, no matter how close, should ever be. Rowan knew that the days, weeks and months to come would bring a new chapter in the family's history. He would do everything in his power to ensure that growth, not decay, was the outcome of this mess. And his first words in this brave new world?

'Good morning.'

'Morning, Grandpa,' chorused Sophie's boys. Tara managed a weak 'Hello.'

Rowan could not bring himself to ask his usual questions about how well everyone had slept. He was frightened by the sudden conviction that, if he did, that would set the tone for the rest of time, and that a series of shallow interactions would replace their relationships.

'Jake's got a hangover,' said Leo, with solemn respect for

this most grown-up and masculine of states. 'We've all got to be good around him.'

Jake gave Rowan an almost imperceptible shake of the head.

Outside, light finally filtered through the lingering mist.

'Time to go outside!' said Leo, rising to his tiptoes to retrieve the back-door key from its hook. If Rowan had known he was tall enough to reach it, he would have hidden it. A yard into the garden, Leo came to a halt so sudden that Toby ran smack into the back of him.

'Oh, Grandpa! What's happened to the trenches?'

'We filled them in last night. I noticed that they weren't safe.'

Leo glared at the adults. 'No way! I hadn't got to the end of the last game. I was going to win it. Can't we dig them out just for the rest of the day, and then we'll do it back again?'

'Maybe we could play MacBride cricket instead,' said Toby. 'Are you up for it, Jake?'

'I don't feel like it,' he said in a voice that sounded as though it hadn't been used for years.

'Oh, *Jake*. Why'd you have to get a hangover? Maybe we can get Matt up to play?'

Jake started to tremble, and looked to Tara for help. Tara's eyes passed the buck on to Rowan, but it was intercepted by Sophie.

'Matt's gone back to London,' she said, briskly. 'For business.'

'How come his car is still outside, then? And what's it doing all the way over in the trees?'

The car. Of course it would be visible now that darkness had lifted. What would they do about that? Leave it to rust in the garage that only they ever used? Bury it, drive it into a lake? *Burn* the blasted thing? Rowan wanted nothing more to do with fire.

Sophie drew in a deep breath before replying. 'He got a taxi, very early, before you were all up.'

'A *taxi*?' said Leo, as though he had just been told that Matt
had chartered a private jet. He turned to Toby. 'See, I *told* you
he was rich. We'll have to play MacBride cricket, just us.'

Toby reached behind the kitchen door. 'Where's the bat
gone? Is it in the garden? Leo, did you leave it in the garden
again? That's Grandpa's bat, you can't just chuck it on the
ground and leave it there.'

'I *didn't*!' said Leo. 'I haven't touched it.'

This time Will stepped in. 'It'll turn up. These things always
do.' Rowan wondered if the burden of explanation would be
passed around the family forever.

Leo kicked a lump of clay across the ragged lawn. 'No
trenches, Jake's wrecked, no Matt, no bat. Today's *rubbish*.'

Charlie's little voice rang across the garden with a cry of
'TREASURE!'

Toby and Leo cast off their boredom and ran to join him.
Will, whose face had curdled like milk, hurried to supervise
his sons as they scrabbled for the loose change that had fallen
from Matt's pockets. Rowan swept the garden, fully expecting
to see a phone, a discarded shoe, some unimagined object that
could explain and incriminate.

'Dad, do you reckon it's Roman?' said Leo, holding up a
muddy disc.

'Yeah right, because Roman money would totally have a
picture of Queen Elizabeth II on it,' said Toby.

'Shut *up*. I reckon we should dig up the whole garden, see if
there's any buried treasure. Jake, do you want to get involved?'

'I told you,' said Will. 'Go easy on Jake today.'

Jake joined Rowan and leaned back against the outside of
the barn. To the innocent observer it might have looked like a
classic tough-guy posture but to Rowan it looked as though
Jake depended on the wall to keep him upright.

'It's like they're targeting the questions at me,' said Jake. His
voice was rigid, as if he was worried that any emotion might

creep in. 'I know they don't know, but you'd think they did. Is it going to be like this forever? Because I don't think I can cope, Grandpa.'

The dam having broken last night, now the effort of holding back tears was like holding up a car with one hand. With great self-consciousness, Rowan employed a phrase he had heard the boys use. 'We've got your back.'

'Yeah, you say that, but ... *fuck*,' said Jake, and rubbed his eyes, and then immediately, 'Sorry.' He was apologising for the language, and Rowan took that as proof of Jake's essential decency, which almost transmuted into a kind of innocence.

'You didn't have a choice,' said Rowan. 'Anyone would have done it. You saved your cousin's life.'

'I saved Edie's life the first time I hit him,' said Jake. 'When I whacked him the second time, that was because of what he did to my mum.'

'Are you sure?' said Rowan, recalling how quickly the second blow had been delivered, unable to countenance any further depth to Jake's guilt. 'I'm not sure you were thinking in those terms. It seemed to me that it was much more reflexive, much more defensive, than you're giving yourself credit for.' Jake's face was impossible to read. Rowan had no idea whether he was making things worse or better. 'Maybe the stuff about your mum, you're just thinking that now you've had a few hours to mull it over.'

'Well, she blames herself for all of it, for letting him ...' Jake's lips began to wobble.

'Grandpa!' shouted Leo. 'I've found a two-pound coin!'

'I'm talking to Jake,' said Rowan, more sternly than he intended. Leo's face creased in an effort to understand why he was being told off, then he turned on his heel. 'Oh, Leo, I ...' Rowan remonstrated with himself: the last thing he needed was to upset the little ones. Jake picked up on it.

'No, you go after him, go and play with them. I need to go and look after Mum, anyway.'

Rowan clapped Jake on the shoulder. 'If you ever want to talk . . .' but Jake had shrugged him off.

In a perfect footprint (whose?), Rowan found a five-pence piece that he handed to Leo, who bit into it as though testing for forgery. Something else was palpable through the sole of Rowan's boot and he toed at the loose earth to investigate. Rich colours were dulled beneath a dusting of soil. It looked like one of the painted eggs the children hunted at Easter. He stooped to retrieve it and found that it wasn't an egg, but a little wooden doll, the Russian stacking kind – what were they called, babushkas? He left the boys to it, came back into the kitchen, rinsed the doll under the tap.

'Is this Edie's?' he said to Sophie, who flicked a glance at it and shrugged. 'It is now. Watch she doesn't choke on that.'

Edie examined the doll and then gummed at its head. Rowan watched her closely as he poured himself a coffee.

'Well, *she's* clearly fine.' He nodded at the baby. 'But what about you?'

'Don't ask me. I'm waiting for the anaesthetic to wear off. I think we all are. I had a good chat with Tara before you came down. We've agreed that we'll treat today just as something to be survived, and then tonight, when the kids are in bed, we'll talk this through properly. Try to come up with some kind of, I don't know, strategy, for helping Jake. And each other. How are you, Dad?'

'I don't know,' he admitted. Edie held up her arms to him. 'Let me take her for a bit.'

'But I can't—'

Rowan felt he would collapse and weep if he did not feel the weight of the child in his arms. He infused his voice with all the leftover authority he had. 'Sophie, come on, it's *me*. You've got to let someone else hold her one day.'

Sophie's brisk smile could not disguise the reluctance with which she let Edie go.

Rowan took Edie into the sitting room and played with her on the sofa. He no longer cared who knew of the delight he took in the sheer warm physical fact of her. Each hair on her head was a miracle, as was every tiny new tooth. She offered the little wooden doll, now coated in spittle, to Rowan. He set it down on the side table.

Upstairs, there was a rumble of footsteps and Felix appeared on the landing in his pyjama bottoms, pulling on his dressing gown as he went.

'Where is she?' he said. 'Where's Kerry? Is she in the kitchen?'

Rowan's heart screeched to a halt. 'I thought she was in with you.'

Felix's widening eye formed perfect concentric circles of pupil, iris, white.

'She was gone when I got up. *Shit.* Where is she, Dad?'

KERRY

58

The mist was lifting but there were no signposts and it was impossible to know which way was east, for escape. Felix had tried to teach her how to get her bearings by the sun but she had never grasped it and anyhow dawn was still hours away. The road was gently curved, its sides banked with naked branches. She walked until she found a long, straight stretch where she could see and be seen. When the low hum of the engine came, she stood in the dead centre of the road, thumb up.

Twin suns punched holes in the fog, dragging behind them a large red van. It did not slow and she prepared to run into the hedgerow, realising too late that she was almost invisible, camouflaged in the dun and midnight shades of other people's clothes. She had thrown on Rowan's waxed jacket from the night before and it was big enough to wrap round her twice, sleeves dangling past her fingertips.

The van jolted to a standstill. Its passenger window opened to reveal a friendly face framed with wild curly grey hair.

'Christ, are you OK, love?' said the woman. 'Are you hurt?'

A strange, warm, farmyard smell and a man's voice came from inside the cabin. 'Tar Barrels last night, weren't it?'

The woman smiled. 'There's always a couple of stragglers the morning after. Bit of a heavy one?' Kerry nodded. 'Where are you headed, love?'

'Anywhere I can catch a train to London,' she said.

'We're doing all the little delis today. I think Bath's the first big station. We can drop you there if you like?'

'Yes please.'

The inside of the van stank, a curdled version of the pure sweet milk smell of Edie. It made Kerry gag.

'That's what I call a gut reaction,' said the man, laughing. 'Goat's cheese. It's a bit much on a delicate stomach, I know. There's nothing I can do about that, I'm afraid. Still, I'll drive careful over the potholes.'

The couple laughed. Kerry had laughed once, with Felix. Now it was all she could do to breathe. She put her head in her hands.

'It's like that, is it?' said the woman.

'We haven't been to the Barrels for years, have we, Jan?' said her partner. 'It was a lot more informal when we were your age, less of the health and safety brigade. Lot of police up there now, were there?'

The faces of Sergeant Hough and PC Rayat hung in Kerry's mind.

'I suppose so,' she said, breathing through her mouth.

The conversation petered out and left her on edge for their next question. The word 'widow' fluttered inside her mouth like a crow and she was afraid that if she opened her lips it would fly out, squawking its terrible truth. For all that, it was not the widowhood that pained her and it was not Matt she was beginning to mourn.

She had believed, at the start, that she was in love with him, but it had been the old story, like with Dean; gratitude dissolving into fear so slowly that you could only tell it was happening when they were kicking you downstairs while you were pregnant, pulling your earrings out through your flesh, making you sleep with other men. You didn't realise that it didn't have to be like that until someone was curling around you in bed, playing you his scratchy old records until the sun came up, telling you that he hadn't known it could be like this, asking where you had been all his life, saying he loved you after three weeks and a day. You didn't know sex didn't have to be a noisy performance until someone gentle quietly coaxed from you something that was all the more powerful for its silence.

Lovely, sweet, Felix with his funny eye and a whole world of tenderness and insecurity behind the clownish exterior. She had known he was different from their first conversation but hadn't known to call it love until that morning, a few weeks in, when she had felt him reach across the bed for her in his sleep. In seeking comfort he had given it. And what had she given him in return?

After a while, the roads ceased to rise and dip and the misty night became a crisp sunny morning. As she grew accustomed to the smell in the van, another odour crept under its top note; like pennies, or meat. She looked down to see a clump of something dark in her hair, and remembered the warm porridge of brains leaking out onto her skin and soaking into her clothes. Kerry closed her eyes and tried to paint over the hideous pictures of the night before with safe and beautiful images, the upturned faces of babies from Vietnam and Sri Lanka and Malawi, but their huge dark eyes turned into trickling wounds.

She heaved again, this time an instinctive reaction from a place too deep inside to control. The cheese people exchanged worried looks and both the windows slid down. Felix had shown her a film that claimed the weight of the human soul was 21 grams, and that at the point of death the body became lighter by exactly that amount, but she had felt the moment the life had gone out of Matt and his body had seemed to double, treble in weight as he left the world, as though he would crush her to death. Perhaps it would have been better for everyone if he had.

They passed signposts, service stations, villages gone as soon as glimpsed. She didn't know what was going to happen – she could barely process what *had* happened – but instinct told her that the thing to do now was to survive this journey out of Devon and back to civilisation. Wait it out. How much easier it had been to wait with Edie in her arms, how much patience she had had with a sleeping baby, how the time had passed differently then.

She pictured the inside of the barn, how it must be looking, where they would all be. She felt bad for the position she would put them in when they realised she was gone. If she was them she would assume that as Matt's wife she had gone to raise the alarm. She had promised them she wouldn't, but they wouldn't believe her. Felix was probably parked up on some country lane, trying to call her on the phone she had thrown on the fire. She cursed herself for not making a note of Felix's number, but the only place it was stored was in her own mobile and of course the landline was no good even if she had the number. She had to get word to Felix, one last conversation, to reassure him that whatever else was going through his mind, he need not worry that she would betray him. She would take Matt's death to her own grave.

At Bath they parked on a short-stay single yellow line and asked her to mind the van while they went out to make their deliveries, offering to pick her up a coffee on their way back. Through the windscreen she saw a sign for the station and she got out and ran, hoping she had not left anything to identify herself, hoping that if they remembered her at all it would just be as the girl with the hangover.

She had enough cash for her train ticket and, in London, for her tube fare from Paddington to Ealing Broadway. On the short walk to the flat, she caught sight of herself in a full-length shop window. The clothes that had been all wrong for the country were no longer right for the city. Underneath her borrowed coat, her expensive outfit was streaked with blood and earth.

The flat was clean and silent and she had the ridiculous notion that no one had broken the news to it. In the kitchen she drank from the tap, then tore her clothes off, leaving them in a pile at the bottom of the washing machine. She showered, leaving her hair to dry wavy the way he hated it.

Writing Felix a letter seemed both the safest way of reaching him and the surest way of putting her point across without interruption or misunderstanding. If she did not give her address and maybe went into the West End to post it, there would be little chance of him finding her. She would send it to his flat above the shop.

She entered Matt's office, sat at the desk, drew a blank sheet of paper from the printer and a pen from the desk drawer. The task was intimidating; apart from jobseeking exercises at the hostel, Kerry had never written a letter.

The pen didn't work. She turned to rummage in the filing cabinet. In it, documents swung in foolscap files, bank statements, letters, demands and receipts from HMRC. Darcy Kellaway and Matt Rider existed side by side in there as though they were business partners. There was money stuff, house stuff, Matt Rider Ltd stuff—

Kerry froze. She had known for months now the true extent of Matt's wealth. She had once overheard him tell Rikesh that she couldn't even turn on a computer and so his desktop was the equivalent of an unlocked door. She had filled countless empty days by rifling through documents real and virtual, staring at Matt's spreadsheets and his boxed and annotated documents for so long that the numbers had begun to make sense. There was no mortgage on any of his properties, she had never been able to spend all of her allowance and she was a co-signatory on Matt's current account, swollen after the sale of his business. She could live like a queen for years on the money she knew how to access, and like an empress with the money that was locked into the other accounts and bonds. Perhaps she would get in touch with that Rikesh, and tell him that Matt had done a runner. She knew they had parted on bitter terms.

With enough money she could afford to adopt a baby on her own. Not here, but abroad – she had watched enough documentaries on the Home & Health channel before it stopped broadcasting to be an expert on the subject. It was a tortuously drawn-out process, you had to leave the UK for months, but that might be a good thing. The people in those orphanages in Pakistan or China would not know about the mess she had made of her life. They would be dazzled by the love she had to offer and the cash she had in her purse.

She would have to siphon the money gradually, without attracting attention. Legitimately to claim Matt's money as an inheritance would mean to declare him a dead man, or at least a missing one. It would mean going to the police. And what could she tell them? She thought again of the police officers and the grilling they had given Will even when there was no longer an emergency. What if they put her under that kind of scrutiny? She was not educated like the MacBrides, she did not have that kind of inbred confidence that would allow her to talk herself out of situations. She could be sneaky when she had time and space to think, but face-to-face confrontations had always terrified her. Even in the barn, when she had saved the day by presenting Felix to the police as Matt, she had known how easily they could have caught her out. She wouldn't trust herself not to leak some detail that might incriminate Felix and his family. She could not run that risk. She located a ballpoint in the bottom of the filing cabinet and returned to her blank page.

'Dear Felix,' she wrote. And then what?

The pen skittered in her hand and her stomach growled.

The fridge was empty apart from a half-drunk litre bottle of Diet Coke. She drank it down in one, belched brown foam, retrieved a pizza from the freezer and switched on the oven.

She smelt her clothes before she saw them, waiting in a pile in front of the washing machine. There was the coat belonging to Rowan, there were her jeans all stiff with mud, the cotton vest that had begun the weekend white. She would never wear any of these clothes again and for a while toyed with the idea of throwing them all in a bin in the street, but what if someone *was* watching her? The sooner she got everything clean the better. She pulled her purse from the pockets of her jeans. The jacket had half a dozen pouches, some hidden so deep inside the garment that she had to pull apart the lining to retrieve scraps of paper, a tissue, a penny, crumbs of soil, tiny stones, blades of grass.

Denim, cashmere and waxed linen shared the same hot wash. Kerry tried not to think about what the detergent was scouring from the fabric. When the garments became a spinning blur she turned her attention back to the spoils of her clothes. She stacked the coins and smoothed the receipts. A little dun knobble unfurled to reveal itself as a Scottish twenty-pound note, brown with age. The crisper of the larger papers was her own provisional driving licence. She had packed it along with the rest of her stuff the first time she had gone to the flat in Saxby, something to remind her who she really was, but had never thought to take it out of the bag. The third she smoothed to reveal four pages of handwriting, faded cornflower ink on duck-egg paper.

17th January 2013
Guilt eats one away like a cancer. Maybe that's why I'm ill. Perhaps if I had made my confession beforehand, I would be well now. I'll never know.

It takes superhuman strength to form the words, but I can't put it off any longer.
~~He first came into our lives~~
~~To begin with we actually had sympathy for Darcy~~
~~The name Darcy K~~
~~It wasn't until~~
~~It all changed when~~
~~Felix was in his last year at the prep when~~
The first time I heard the name Darcy Kellaway was the day the scholarship letters went out.

When Kerry realised what she was holding, the paper seemed to grow hot under her fingertips and her hands began to shake. Dean had given her a gun to hold once, for a laugh, and she had hated it, felt its terrible power and known she was not equal to it. These pages made her feel as she had then, burdened by a responsibility she had not asked for and did not want.

59

Of course Rowan was used to distraught parents calling at the school but it was the first time a child had turned up on our doorstep. The boy had come to demand his place in the school, Rowan said. 'Confrontational' was how he described him.

'Did he threaten you?' I asked.

'Not as such, but there's definitely something a bit ... wrong with him. Not intellectually, he was very articulate, quite able. A sort of ... lack. It's hard to define.'

A few weeks later, Rowan said, 'He's been hanging around the house.' It was funny, I didn't have to ask who he meant. 'In that alleyway. Outside the school gates. He was in the bloody tree opposite the house yesterday. It's really unsettling.'

'How unsettling?' I said. 'Draw-the-curtains unsettling or call-the-police unsettling?'

'There's nothing the police could do. Possessive as I am about Saxby, it's all public land, he wasn't trespassing. I'll ignore him. I'm sure he'll get bored with it soon.'

'What does he look like?' I said. I wanted to be on my guard. Rowan tried not to smile.

'You'll see the teeth about twenty minutes before you see him. Poor little sod.'

It was another month before he struck. When Rowan saw Kellaway run past the house he was about to confront him, but before he could, Felix crawled from the passage with his face bloodied.

Kerry couldn't call the way she was feeling shock, or even surprise. It was too numb for that. If anything, she felt stupid, as though she should have somehow known that Matt had been the one to attack Felix. She felt a lover's anger refracted through the prism of a mother's. With each line that Kerry read, Lydia MacBride ceased to be the prejudiced magistrate of her own recollection or the murderous bitch of Matt's, and became the tender, loving mother of Felix's.

Rowan cried my name in a voice that summoned half the street. I maintained an outward calm while we waited for the ambulance to come. I tried to cradle Felix but could not tell from the soup of his face whether and how I should touch or hold his head so I lay on the ground and curled into his back, while he shivered. He was so brave.

At the Wellhouse I waited outside the operating theatre confident that the police, under Rowan's instruction, would find Kellaway, arrest him, charge him.

'Insufficient evidence' are the two most frustrating words in the English language. The police didn't doubt Rowan but his testimony placed Kellaway not at the scene of the crime but only in its vicinity. Kellaway's mother provided his alibi, and the onus of proof was on Felix. But when he started talking again, he could not even name his assailant's gender. He refused to talk about the attack except in the most grotesque terms. His sense of humour turned in on itself and he became defensive and sarcastic.

If I had detested Kellaway before, now he became my obsession.

Since Felix's attack, we had naturally been campaigning for closed circuit television in Cathedral Passage. There had in fact been a spate of muggings in that blind spot – half a dozen teenagers, one elderly gentleman, a small party of tourists who'd wandered off the beaten track and paid with their cameras and their wallets at knifepoint. I was becoming accustomed, though not desensitised, to the sight of police cars ringing the Green, often parking across our drive.

That night, I was alone in the house; Sophie was away at Durham, Rowan had gone to collect Tara and Felix from the cinema. I heard a shout from behind the house, hurried footsteps outside, and made it to the window just in time to see a hooded figure run between the planes, dropping something on the ground. I recognised the black sweatshirt with its neon orange piping as belonging to Ricky Jinks, a persistent offender and drug addict depressingly familiar to me from the bench. Like most addicts, he had a habit of turning up in court in his work clothes. I made for the front door to tell the police what I had seen, and as I descended the steps, a second figure emerged from between the trees.

I recognised Kellaway from a distance and on a single sighting. His face conjured Felix's, both as it had been and as it was. I had the strangest feeling at that second that I could push over one of those plane trees with my finger. By the time I was outside and down, Jon Slingsby, PC Slingsby as he was then, was talking to the boy. It was the easiest thing in the world to say that I had seen him run from the scene of the crime. The roar of revenge drowned out the voice of reason, the voice that said I ought to point them towards Jinks before he struck again. Kellaway protested and was, I think, on the verge of confessing his earlier crime, but stopped himself. He was bundled into the police car shouting nonsense about salmon, saying, with great melodrama, that his mother would die if he couldn't go home.

I returned home to wait for my family. Here is the curious thing. It did not feel like a lie at the time. I told myself that I was not wrongfully labelling him but simply doing what the police could not all those years ago when he attacked Felix. Put simply, I played God. Or I played judge. One night in the cells was if anything too scant punishment for ruining my son's face. Did I mean to let them charge him? Would I really have sworn an oath? Incriminated a child? It's hard to say, for it never came to that. I do know that that night I went to sleep surprisingly easily. I blocked Jinks from my thoughts entirely.

The scream came just after midnight. I knew it was Tara's before I was even awake, the way I did when they were babies. Lights went on all over the house, all along the terrace. We ran through the courtyard in nightclothes. In Cathedral Passage we found our daughter keening like a banshee, kneeling on the flagstones over the blood-let body of a boyfriend we had no idea she had.

For the second time that day I watched as the emergency services thronged Cathedral Passage, only this time the ambulance had no siren. Louis's body was bagged and stretchered into the floodlit interior and driven to the mortuary. It took Rowan, me and an overalled scene-of-crime officer to stop Tara lying down in the pool he had left behind.

A sergeant was bawling Slingsby out.

'Second attack in the same place in as many hours. Didn't you take someone in for it? Well, you'd better let him go because I'd bet my mortgage that this is the same guy. It's the same location, same stab wound, I'd bet anything it's the same bloody knife. Only this poor sod wasn't as lucky as the earlier one.' The sergeant held a crackling radio to his ear for a moment. 'They've just nicked someone on the other side of the Green,' he told Slingsby. 'There's still blood on the knife. You'd better let your man go.' I took a call two hours later telling me that Ricky Jinks was being held on suspicion of murder. As well as the knife, in his possession they had found Louis's cash card and another credit card belonging to the earlier victim.

The realisation of what I had done was a vice around my heart. Had I not lashed out in spite, Jinks would have been arrested and Louis would never have been attacked. I may as well have wielded the knife myself. At the time, of course, I didn't know Louis was the father of my unborn grandson. If I had done, I might not have had the strength to bear it.

My darling Jake, of course, is another matter. I see him almost every day and his face, which animates photographs of his late father, is a daily reminder of my shame. I robbed my grandchild of a father. I, who value family more than anything else, tore a hole in the heart of my own.

Poor Tara, poor Jake, poor all of them. Matt had never mentioned Jake's father at all and certainly not by name. Kerry was sure he had not known about this. He discussed every detail of his obsession with the family manically, repetitively. If he had known, she would never have heard the end of it, she would be bored of it. Matt had been so sure that Tara had told him everything, that he had burrowed his way into the centre of her heart. Well, she hadn't told him *this*. Kerry experienced the first cool creeping of contempt and she was thrilled by her own daring at feeling this.

If Matt had had these pages on Friday night how different the whole weekend would have been! It would still have been awful, but that stupid plan involving Edie would never have been made. Matt would still be alive. And what would that mean for her, for her and Felix? Of course Felix would still hate her, but for himself, not his sisters, and she thought she knew him well enough to guess that he could forgive on his own behalf what he could never forgive on theirs.

Kerry took the pages over to the sofa and read on.

20ᵗʰ January 2013
How exhausting that last entry was. After setting down my pen I slept for fifteen hours, feigning a migraine. Following the initial euphoria of confession, I felt only a partial release, and it has taken me the weekend to realise that that is because it is only a partial confession. This statement is not the whole truth unless I include what happened next to Darcy Kellaway.

I had no time in the days that followed Louis's death to reflect on where the boy might have ended up. The school and the house were suddenly full of bereft Ghanaians, their quiet, dignified grief undercutting my assumptions about ululating Africans. I held a silent, shaking Tara throughout the memorial service in the school chapel before his body was flown home for burial. The head boy delivered Louis's eulogy, making much of his prowess on the sports field, his gift for cricket, and his determination to live a full life despite the limitations of his illness, what an inspiration he was, what a hard worker, what a good boy. Caring for Tara in the days that followed was like looking after a newborn; consuming, exhausting, relentless. (At the time I thought that grief had made her ill, that the nausea and the exhaustion were her body's interpretation of her violent bereavement.) Everything else, including Kellaway, was relegated to the periphery of my consciousness. Of course there were flashes of nervous curiosity, and I half-expected him to engineer another of his doorstep confrontations. When I found out where he had really been and why, I almost wished he had.

Jon Slingsby was at our door again the day that the Owusu-Josephs flew back to Accra.

'I've got some bad news, Lydia,' he said. 'Darcy Kellaway's been making some threats, serious ones, against you and your family. We've had to formally charge him.'

I felt sick and dizzy: I ought to have known I wouldn't be able to get away with it for that long. I had to brazen it out, to stick by my original claim.

'Obviously it was a mistake,' said Slingsby, pre-empting the denial on my lips. He was so deadpan that for a second I wondered if he was trying to trip me up. 'It was dark, it was an easy mistake to make. Unfortunately Kellaway doesn't think that way.' There wasn't a flicker of suspicion in him. He was an old-fashioned sort of bobby even then, with a belief in good and evil, something that teeters between naiveté and prejudice, that years on the force had yet to quite erode.

'He's got it into his head that you killed his mother.'

That threw me. 'He's what?' I said.

'His mother died on the night of his arrest and he's decided somehow that you're responsible. I know, I know, it's ridiculous. Hence the threats.'

I had visions of him storming home and killing her in one of his tempers.

'How did she die?' I said.

'Heart attack. Hardly something you could have engineered, even up close.' Slingsby laughed but my blood ran cold. I felt a strange, secondary guilt about Heather Kellaway; the end of a middle-aged life felt like less of a tragedy than the violent murder of a schoolboy, but still it was impossible to escape the notion that had her son not been arrested, her heart might yet be beating. By abusing my own power I had tipped the balance of it in his favour. Jon Slingsby was still talking. It was hard to concentrate on what he was saying.

'Look. The point is, we're going to charge him with threatening behaviour and get a protection order out so you can rest easy. He's pretty far gone, from what I gather. You've got a while yet before you need to worry. And I'll personally tell you when he's out, and protect your property.'

True to his word, Slingsby kept watch over our house on the day of Kellaway's discharge from the Wellhouse, but as far as we know he left Saxby, never apparently to return. Wherever he is now, I hope he has forgotten all about us, for his own sake as much as ours.

Keeping Lydia's secret would be Kerry's undisclosed atonement, the last and best thing she would ever do for Felix. But she could and must reassure him that the family's shared secret was safe. A letter, she now saw, was all wrong; the written word could survive and be intercepted.

She went back into the study; Felix's mobile number was in the file Matt kept on the MacBrides, the one she wasn't supposed to know about. Withholding her own number, she dialled his. She was relieved and disappointed when it went straight to voicemail.

'It's me,' she said. 'Oh, shit, I don't know what to say. I thought you'd got me over that, being lost for words. This is the last time I'll talk to you. I want to make it perfect but I don't know how.'

She took a deep breath. 'I'm just ringing to tell you, it's going to be all right. I mean, you know . . . just that you don't need to worry about me making trouble for you. I know you won't have anything to do with me anyway. And I don't blame you. It was bad enough lying to you, but I saw your face, the way you were angry with me for what we did to your sisters . . .'

It wasn't going well. She held the phone away from her mouth and tried to swallow the rock in her throat.

'What I'm ringing for, what you need to understand, right, is that I wasn't taking Edie from Sophie. I was keeping her away from Matt. It's really important that you know the difference. I planned all along to hide her from Matt and bring her back to the rest of you. It was like . . .' She scanned the office for the right words, saw some leaflets from the building society and was inspired. '. . . an insurance policy. I know I should've just come and told you but I didn't know, I couldn't've known what he . . .' She gathered herself. 'I had no reason not to believe him at first, and by the time I realised what he was really like, it was too late. I don't want you to be worried. You won't hear from me again. You have to tell your dad and your sisters that I won't ever tell on you.' She had gone from not knowing what to say to not being able to stop. 'They won't believe me, but you will, and you can talk them round. I *know* you know me, Felix, you know me better than anyone. It started off as a lie but it got true, I promise it did.' She couldn't go on without losing it. 'I really do love you, Felix, and I'm so, so, sorry.'

Kerry hung up the phone then ran from the study, slamming the door behind her. The only noises inside the flat were her ragged breath and the relentless churn of the washing machine. She opened the window for the company of city sounds. A light breeze sifted the torn pages and sent them floating to the floor. She knelt to retrieve them, then impulsively clawed the paper to fragments which she gathered in her hands and carried in a loose nest to the toilet. There she let them fall. Tatters floated in the bowl, ink leaching into water and leaving trails like slow, sad smoke. She pressed the lever. The words blurred, bled blue, and were gone.

Thank you

Suzie Dooré, Francine Toon, Eleni Lawrence,
Imogen Olsen

Sarah Ballard, Jessica Craig, Lara Hughes-Young,
Zoe Ross and Jane Willis

Mike and Marnie, Dad and Sue, Mum and Jude, Helen
Treacy and Jennifer Whitehead Chadwick

I'm grateful to Phyllis and Derek at the Ottery St Mary
tourist office for the warm welcome and the coffee. I hope
they and their neighbours will forgive the various liberties
I have taken with their beautiful town and their beloved
festival, in particular breaking with hundreds of years
of tradition and holding it on a Sunday to fit within the
claustrophobic confines of my notional weekend.

Above all, heartfelt thanks to all the readers who took the
time to write to me while I was working on this novel.
You are the reason I finished it.

Also by Erin Kelly

The Poison Tree

'Dark, poetic, gripping, totally brilliant' *The Times*

*I have given up so much and done so many terrible things
already for the sake of my family that I can only keep going.
I do not know what is going to happen to us. I am frightened,
but I feel strong. I have the strength of a woman who has
everything to lose.*

In the sweltering summer of 1997, strait-laced,
straight-A student Karen met Biba – a bohemian and
impossibly glamorous aspiring actress.

She was quickly drawn into Biba's world, and for a while
life was one long summer of love.

But every summer must end. By the end of theirs, two
people were dead – and now Karen's past has come back
to haunt her . . .

Out now in paperback and ebook.

HODDER